WALK INTO SILENCE

OTHER TITLES BY SUSAN McBRIDE

The Debutante Dropout Mysteries

Say Yes to the Death

Too Pretty to Die

Night of the Living Deb

The Lone Star Lonely Hearts Club

The Good Girl's Guide to Murder

Blue Blood

The River Road Mysteries

Come Helen High Water

Not a Chance in Helen

Mad as Helen

To Helen Back

Women's Fiction

The Truth About Love & Lightning

Little Black Dress

The Cougar Club

Young Adult Mystery

Very Bad Things

WALK INTO SILENCE

SUSAN McBRIDE

THOMAS & MERCER

This is a work of fiction. Names, characters, organizations, places, events, and incidents are either products of the author's imagination or are used fictitiously.

Published by Thomas & Mercer, Seattle

www.apub.com

ISBN-13: 9781503937628
ISBN-10: 1503937623

Cover design by Faceout Studio

Printed in the United States of America

MONDAY

The night boxed her in like a pitch-black room with no light beneath the door.

Her head spun as she tried to process what had happened since she'd driven out of the parking lot sometime after five o'clock, when the sky had blushed a dusky pink, the clouds a faded orange.

She knew it was almost over.

Her eyes darted around, seeing only shades of dark. Maybe she was already dead and didn't know it. She clasped her hands so fiercely that her fingers numbed, and still they trembled at the voice that hissed impatiently: *C'mon, we haven't got all night. Let's do this.*

She stumbled away from the car, the hem of her jeans catching on her boot heels. After a few unsteady steps, she slipped, slamming down hard, banging her chin against the gravel. Tasting blood on her tongue, she rose to her knees and lifted her head, disoriented. Which way was forward? Which was back?

What's wrong with you? The voice grew angrier. *Move, for Christ's sake. Get up.*

She struggled to rise, fought to keep her legs from wobbling so she wouldn't go down again.

As her eyes adjusted to the lack of light, she made out the fringe of trees surrounding her. Gravel crunched beneath her shoes, creating unsure footing as she plodded forward, down an invisible path. Goose bumps prickled her flesh beneath the fleece pullover and turtleneck that had felt much too warm beneath her coat.

Now I lay me down to sleep. I pray the Lord my soul to keep. If I should die before I wake, I pray the Lord my soul to take.

She told herself that when this was over, she would feel no pain. The hole in her heart would disappear, the lies along with it. There would be only silence.

Wasn't that what she'd wanted?

Despite the cold, the air smelled dank and chalky. Raw. It was the perfect place to die, an already-dug tomb. She kept going down and down into the pit, until she reached the muddied bottom and fell to her knees again.

She squeezed her eyes shut, no longer fighting the tears, instead drowning in them and praying hard that when they found her, they would understand.

Dear God, she begged, *forgive me.*

Though no one could hear.

◆ ◆ ◆

The first knock on the door was so tentative, Jo wasn't sure she'd heard it. When it became more insistent, her initial response was annoyance. It was late, and she was tired. She was tempted to ignore it, hoping whoever it was would go away.

Her curiosity got the better of her.

She pushed back the living room drape and peered outside to see a man, ill lit by her feeble porch light, and yet she knew right away who he was. She took a deep breath before unfastening the dead bolt and opening the door a sliver.

"Hey," Adam said, huddled in his coat against the cold. "Can I come in?"

She drew the door wide and stepped aside.

He must have driven straight from work; he still wore scrubs beneath his beat-up bomber jacket. He was freshly showered, his dark hair slick against his skull, but Jo imagined she could smell the stink of the autopsy suite on his skin. The first time they had met, he'd reeked of eau de postmortem, that and the Vicks he sometimes smeared beneath his nose.

Ah, so romantic.

She bolted the door, then followed him into the living room.

He paused, glancing around the space. "The place looks good," he said, though she wondered how he could see much of anything in the dark. "It's very you."

"Why are you here?" she asked, because he wasn't supposed to do this. They'd agreed they wouldn't see each other again, not while he was still married. That was why she'd left the city and moved to Plainfield, to get away from what she couldn't have.

"I thought you'd want to know that it's over." He rubbed a hand over his whiskered face. The shadows deepened the grooves at his eyes and mouth. "The papers are signed. She's moving to LA. I'm a free man."

If it was true, if that was what he really wanted, why did he look so miserable?

"You could have called . . ."

"No." He shook his head, coming toward her. "I had to see you, Jo. I had to know that you're real, that this is real. Tell me I'm not wrong."

She could hardly breathe. She for damned sure couldn't speak.

"Say something, please," he begged.

Jo felt dizzy, like she'd been turned upside down, or maybe inside out. "You're not wrong," she said and took his hand, leading him into her bedroom.

She slipped his coat from his shoulders and reached for his face. The stubble of his jaw tickled the palms of her hands. Then she kissed him hard, and he moaned low in his throat, his arms coming around her, tugging her close.

They undressed in silence, too anxious to speak. The quiet rustled with motion as discarded clothes were kicked aside. Jo heard her quickened heartbeat, so loud in her ears, and she wondered if he heard it, too.

Adam lowered her to the bed, and she found herself pinned beneath him, beneath his hands, his thighs, his mouth.

She let out a cry, then bit her lip to silence herself, suddenly awkward, embarrassed by her emotions and how fiercely they rose to the surface, making her tremble, awakening her every sense.

He whispered her name, his breath warm on her skin. His lips touched her neck, teeth nipping, and she squeezed her eyes more tightly closed, reveling in the darkness, in not seeing, only feeling.

He pressed down into her, so hard she felt herself disappear into him, a mingling of flesh and sweat and hunger, their movements impatient, clumsy as adolescents. His hands caught in her hair, drawing back her head as she arched against him. She gasped for air, greedily drinking it in, crying out.

God, help me, she begged before all rational thought passed from her head. She didn't want to live in fear of her past and all the things she hadn't told him. *Please, don't let me lose him again.*

Then his mouth covered hers, sweet and bruising, and she tasted the sweat on his skin and the salt of her tears.

PART ONE
LOST

CHAPTER ONE
TUESDAY

The man sat so close, their knees nearly knocked.

He'd pulled the chair around her desk, so there was nothing between them but a little air and the fists he held clenched in his lap.

"Tell me, Detective, where could my wife be?" he said, less a question than a demand. "What could possibly have happened to her?"

"Take it easy, Mr. Dielman. I can see you're upset. Why don't you fill me in?" Jo Larsen had no choice but to listen. The guy wasn't going to leave.

According to the desk sergeant, he'd planted himself in the lobby good and early, asking to speak to her. Jo had found him there when she'd returned to the station house, after she and her partner had spent the better part of the morning investigating a theft at a local yarn shop. But once Jo had settled him at her desk, all he'd done was throw questions at her, like Jo was somehow responsible for his problem.

Despite his attitude, he had panic in his eyes. Jo felt sorry for him. She wondered if she had *sucker* stamped on her forehead.

And Hank thought she was such a hard-ass.

Ha.

She had nothing more pressing on her desk at the moment. Thanksgiving was little more than a week away, and a recent cold snap had effectively dropped Plainfield's low crime rate to a barely perceptible blip that pleased the city council and police brass to no end. That left Jo and her partner, Hank Phelps, with such urgent cases as band instruments stolen from the high school and the theft of a carton of cashmere yarn from The Knitting Needle.

Serving and protecting tiny Plainfield, Texas, these past two years was a far cry from her days in the Dallas PD, despite being almost within shouting distance of the city limits. Jo couldn't say that she missed the routine of daily urban violence. At this point in her life, she'd rather deal with tuba theft than murder any day of the week.

"So she'd have no reason to take off. Don't you see?"

See what? Jo realized she'd missed part of Patrick Dielman's monologue. "You might want to contact members of her family in the area, sir. Maybe she's with them."

"She doesn't have family in town." His red-rimmed eyes welled all over again. "Her only sister lives in Des Moines. She didn't even come to our wedding. They drifted apart when Jenny was married to Harrison."

"Who?"

Dielman's soft drawl hardened. "Kevin Harrison. He's a surgeon at Presbyterian Hospital, and not someone Jenny would run to see. He's remarried, too, and they hardly kept in touch."

"What about her parents?"

"Her folks are dead."

"Did you call the sister, anyway?"

"Yeah, I did." He chewed on the inside of his cheek. "I'd never spoken to the woman before, so it was awkward as hell. She offered to fly down, but I told her to stay put in case my wife tries to reach her."

"What's the sister's name?"

"Kimberly Parker."

Jo scribbled that down and then tapped her pen against her jaw. "What about friends or coworkers?"

He shook his head. "I phoned the library where she volunteers mornings. She isn't there. They wondered if she was sick. I was ashamed to tell them she was missing, like I'd lost her." The rush of words halted for an instant as he swallowed hard. "Our next-door neighbor saw Jenny in passing yesterday around five o'clock. She was coming home from work when Jenny left to go shopping." He swept a hand across his close-cut hair. "I can't imagine where she'd be unless something bad happened. Y'all need to put out some kind of bulletin—"

"Look, Mr. Dielman," Jo said, cutting him off, hardly ready to issue a BOLO on his wife. "Maybe she's blowing off steam. I'll bet she comes home, apologizing like crazy for making you worry. If she doesn't, we'll take it from there."

"Listen to me!" Dielman hissed, his brown eyes flashing. "Jenny's never done anything rash. She's never stayed away overnight. She's never missed a morning at the library, not for any reason. Don't you get it?"

Jo pressed the tip of her pen to the pad of paper in front of her, creating a smudge of ink on a page that had little else on it. "I get that you're worried."

"Worried? What if the worst has happened? What if someone's hurt her?" He reached out to grip her forearm. "You have *got* to do something."

"Okay," Jo said. "Okay." He released her, and she settled back, shifting away. "Let's go over this again, and see what we've got to work with."

"Like I told you, she wasn't there when I got home from work around seven last evening, and she should have been. She always is."

As he spoke, Jo took notes. The story was easy enough to follow. A thirty-five-year-old woman named Jenny Dielman wasn't where she was supposed to be. The last her husband had heard from her was the previous day in the late afternoon, maybe a few minutes before five o'clock.

She'd called him at work to tell him she was heading out to shop at the new Warehouse Club because she'd gotten a free guest pass in the mail and wanted to use it. He'd thought nothing of it, had finished updating some files at his job as an administrator for a large medical practice in North Dallas, and had left work shortly before seven.

But Jenny hadn't been home when he'd arrived.

She had never come home at all.

"Did you try her cell phone?"

"Half a dozen times," he replied, staring daggers. "She didn't answer."

"How about her Facebook page?"

"She doesn't have one."

"Did you try the Warehouse Club?" Jo asked next.

Patrick Dielman exhaled impatiently. "I drove over just before they closed at ten and scoured the parking lot for her car, but it wasn't there. I talked to the manager, a guy named Owen Ross. He asked if she had a regular membership card, said he could check the computer to see if she used it." He pulled a pressed handkerchief from the pocket of his Burberry trench coat and wiped his forehead. "But she had that damned guest pass, just a worthless piece of paper."

"Still, if she made a purchase with a credit or debit card, we'd know that she got to the store."

"Mr. Ross didn't offer that kind of help, Detective. Not to me," Dielman added and twisted his handkerchief into a pretzel.

"You have a plate number?" Jo jotted down his description of Jenny's vehicle—a red Nissan—and the manager's name, Owen Ross.

"How about area hospitals?" she suggested. "Maybe Mrs. Dielman was involved in an accident?"

He shook his head. "I phoned Plainfield Memorial last night and again this morning. I spoke with a nurse in the emergency room and someone in admitting. They assured me no Jennifer Dielman had been seen in the past twenty-four hours."

"Anything else?" she asked him, because he'd apparently covered plenty of territory before he'd set foot in the station.

"I know she didn't withdraw any cash from the bank because she has access only to our joint checking account, which never has more than a couple hundred dollars in it. I'm in charge of the savings and money market accounts. The credit cards are jointly held, and I already checked them to see if she'd bought a plane ticket to Iowa." He shook his head. "If she didn't go to her sister's, I can't imagine where she'd be. We keep to ourselves."

It still amazed Jo to hear about housewives who didn't have control over money. It sounded so 1950s, so subservient. A little like being kept in a cage, not something she would ever do willingly. She cocked her head. "You've been very busy, Mr. Dielman."

"I couldn't just sit around, could I?"

Or maybe he didn't trust his wife as much as he professed.

She chewed on the pen cap, trying to consider other avenues, if there were any left that Patrick Dielman hadn't covered. "Could she have run into someone at the store? Took off for a drink and got too tipsy to drive home?"

He stared at her like she was crazy. "You don't know her. She would never have stayed away all night without telling me. She isn't that kind of person, and she doesn't get tipsy. She's not supposed to drink at all."

Not supposed to?

"You're right, I don't know her," Jo said, "which is why I'm asking questions."

"I'm sorry," he said and jabbed the twisted handkerchief back into the pocket of his overcoat, dislodging a leather glove in the process. He bent to retrieve it. "I don't think you understand, Detective. The fact is, Jenny doesn't have friends. She just has me."

"I know this is hard," Jo said, because she felt bad for the guy, really. At the very least, his wife had walked out on him, or maybe bolted from her cage was a more apt description. "But let's not panic yet." She glanced down at the address he'd given her. "You live on Ella Drive?"

"In Woodstream Estates, yes."

Jo knew it as a growing area with redbrick ranch houses in an expanding subdivision for hardworking middle-class folks on the fast track to upper-middle. It was nice, even exclusive, but certainly not the kind of big bucks that would inspire a kidnapping for ransom. Besides, the guy said he managed a doctor's office. He was hardly Bill Gates. "You've been Plainfield residents for how long?"

"Fourteen months." He lifted his eyes to hers. "We moved here from the city after we got married. Jenny loved the area. She said she felt comfortable here, almost at peace. She had a rocky first marriage, which fell apart after"—he swallowed hard—"after she lost her son three years ago. The boy was just six."

"How awful." Jo felt a pang.

"She never really got over it."

"What was his name?"

"Finn." He blinked rapidly. "Finnegan Harrison."

Jo scribbled on her notepad.

"She got divorced after the boy's death. I'd been alone for a while when we met at a church group in Prestonwood. We both were pretty rusty on dating." He smiled awkwardly. "I liked her from the get-go. She was reserved, not a talker like some women I'd met. I got the sense she just wanted to be taken care of, and I knew I could do that. We fit together well."

Divorced. Lost her son. Remarried. Quiet, Jo wrote.

"Still waters run deep," she said, because it was so often the case.

His hands rubbed his knees, and he seemed to be staring down at his polished black oxfords. "We look out for each other. We're each other's best friend."

He stood suddenly, reaching beneath his coat for his wallet. "Here," he said, pushing a piece of paper at her and sitting down again.

It was a photograph, soft from being handled and creased from the bend in his billfold. The ceiling light reflected off the shiny coating as Jo examined the woman in the shot.

She was slender, with dark hair to her shoulders, a guarded smile on her face. Her wide eyes gazed off somewhere else, not directly at the camera, like someone who didn't enjoy having her picture taken. She held a black cat in her arms, its head tucked beneath her chin.

Jo shifted in her chair, unsettled by the image.

There was something in Jenny Dielman's expression, a self-imposed distance that Jo had seen in her own eyes often enough, as if she were hiding a wound that wouldn't heal. Maybe Jenny didn't mind a husband who watched her so carefully, who controlled the money she spent, because he protected her. He kept her safe from the boogeyman. Jo knew a little something about the boogeyman. She'd grown up with one, and he still visited her now and then in her nightmares.

"That's Ernie," Dielman said and poked a finger at the photo. "He's her cat."

"Ernie?" Jo didn't know what he was getting at. "Like on *Sesame Street*?"

"No. Ernest Hemingway. All the cats that live at his house on Key West have six toes. So does Ernie. Jennifer got him from the pound." His hands rubbed his thighs. "She didn't even want to go on vacation because it meant leaving him. Don't you get it?"

"Yes." She had the bad vibes to prove it. "I get it."

Where are you, Jenny? Do you even want to be found? Or did you run away from being held too tightly?

Jo forced her eyes back to the photograph. "She's very pretty."

Dielman let out a dry laugh. "She never believes me when I tell her she's beautiful. Harrison did a number on her. They were together for something like seven years. She didn't talk too much about it, but from what she did say, I know it got bad after Finn died."

"You said that Dr. Harrison was her first husband?"

"Yes." He pursed his lips. "She'd been to hell and back before we met, but things were good with us. Jenny would never just take off, not like this."

To hell and back.

Unless the runaway wife had realized her second marriage wasn't turning out any better than her first.

Had Mrs. Dielman decided to take a break?

Was Patrick Dielman being less than candid about the state of their relationship? It wouldn't be the first time a husband had fed her a white lie or two. When women went missing, or worse, it was more often than not the spouse or the boyfriend behind it.

"Did you notice if any of her things were gone, like suitcases, clothing, or toiletries?"

"No, nothing's gone. I went through the house already. Her bags are in the hall closet where they've always been. Her toothbrush is still next to mine." He blew out a breath. "Her pills are there, too."

"Her pills?"

"Zoloft," he told her. "That's why I know she wasn't out drinking. She can't mix the drug and alcohol, and she wouldn't."

Jo's antennae went up. "Is she clinically depressed?"

"She doesn't see a shrink, if that's what you mean." Dielman sounded defensive. He seemed to weigh his words carefully. "Our internist, Dr. Patil, wrote the prescription. He said she had symptoms of post-traumatic stress disorder. Jenny wasn't nuts."

His opinion, Jo wondered, or the doctor's?

"I can tell what you're thinking, but that doesn't have anything to do with this."

Jo thought it might. "She's never tried to kill herself?"

"Not since I've known her."

"Had she ever talked about it?"

"Not to me." He fidgeted. "Jenny had problems dealing with Finn's death. It was hard for her to accept, especially since she couldn't have any more children."

"Why's that?"

"They did a hysterectomy after Finn was born because of bleeding. She said it didn't matter because no child could replace her son." He squirmed. "Sometimes she acted like she'd lost—" He stopped himself.

"Lost what?"

"Everything," he said and shook his head. "I don't know. She'd been acting upset and confused lately. She complained that things weren't where she'd left them, that stuff was missing."

"Like what?"

"Her keys, a photograph, even the scarf I gave her for her birthday. Sometimes she'd swear she'd locked the door, but it was left open." He pinched the bridge of his nose. "I told her she was being paranoid."

"Did you tell her doctor?"

"No." Dielman frowned. "Do you think it's important?"

Jo fought the urge to shake him. "Why don't you tell me what you remember her wearing when you last saw her?"

He perked up. "When I left for work yesterday, she had on a turtleneck under a gray fleece top and blue jeans. She probably wore her boots 'cause it's cold out. When I saw her, she was still in her socks. She must've worn her black coat. It wasn't in the hall closet."

"Does she have any identifiable marks?"

"Like scars?"

"Scars," Jo told him, "or moles, tattoos."

He blushed and fiddled with the crease in his pants. "She has a tiny butterfly on her left hip." His Adam's apple rippled. "She got it after her divorce from Harrison."

"Anything else?"

"She has a locket she wears all the time. It's silver with the initial *F*, for *Finn*. She keeps his picture in it. She rarely takes it off."

Jo made a note.

"What else do you need from me?" He buttoned his coat, like he was ready to go.

"Just one more thing." She hesitated, hating to ask. "Could your wife have been seeing someone?"

He snorted. "If I suspected she was cheating on me, I would've told you from the start."

"What about you?" she asked. Just because Dielman wore a wedding band didn't mean squat.

"Why would you ask such a thing? Just find her, for God's sake," he snapped. "That is your job, isn't it? Now, are we done?"

Jo glanced down at the photo on her desk, then up at him. "Yes, we're done, Mr. Dielman," she told him, thinking if she were his wife, she might have run away, too.

This is my second stab at starting this journal. I tried yesterday, sitting in the car in the library parking lot. I had the notebook in my lap, and I began scribbling down my feelings, thinking of Finn, how much I missed him. But I hit the steering wheel with my hand as I tried to sip some coffee, and I spilled onto the page.

Is that a bad omen?

This time, I'll think instead of what Dr. P told me at my last appointment.

"Use the notebook to sort out your emotions and make sense of things. You don't have to forget what happened," he said in that kind way of his that always makes me want to cry. "But you have to figure out how to start moving forward instead of looking back."

It's a lovely thought. It sounds really practical and a lot less trouble than gardening. I don't know how it will help. It won't make me stop thinking about Finn and missing him. It won't change the fact that I can never have another child. I had one, and I lost him.

All I know for sure is that I can't move forward until I understand what happened, and I've promised Finn—I've crossed my heart and sworn to God—that I will do exactly that. The day after Thanksgiving will be three years since his accident. Three years of living in a fog of grief when I should have been asking questions.

Now it's time to do something about it. I need to know the God's honest truth. Even if the only one I convince in the end is me.

CHAPTER TWO

Before Dielman left the station, Jo proffered her card, assuring him she'd contact him after she did a bit of poking around. She urged him to go about his business and to get in touch if he heard from his wife, which she hoped would be the case.

Jenny Dielman could very well be a straight arrow who never deviated from the norm, but even the most predictable of creatures had to blow off steam. Maybe Jenny had things to take care of that she couldn't talk about with her husband. Maybe she wanted to stretch her leash. Once she'd done that, she'd turn up as suddenly as she disappeared.

It sounded good in theory. A part of Jo almost believed it.

She called the Plainfield Public Library, where Jenny volunteered, and talked to the director, a woman named Sally Nesbo, who echoed Dielman's sentiments about Jenny being highly responsible. She noted Jenny was often the first to arrive each morning, waiting outside until a staffer appeared with a key. Nesbo denied noticing any odd behavior in the past few weeks. "Jenny's a quiet girl. She does her job and keeps to herself," the library director had remarked, which sounded right in line with Dielman's description of his wife. Nesbo promised to phone Jo should Jenny get in touch.

Next, Jo tried Dr. Naveen Patil's office and then the next-door neighbor, Lisa Barton, leaving messages for each. She looked up the number for Kevin Harrison, MD, at Presbyterian Hospital and dialed his office, figuring she'd have a better shot at catching him there than at home. His secretary said he had surgeries booked until midafternoon, but Jo could use the voice mail on his private line.

The typical hurry up and wait.

Something she wasn't particularly good at.

Mama had always said she had ants in her pants, couldn't sit still for longer than five minutes to save her life. Maybe she'd been afraid to stay put for fear of who'd catch her.

"Go outside and play in the yard, Jo Anna, please." She could hear Mama's slurred drawl, the ice rattling in her glass as a slim, white hand banished her outdoors. *"You make me nervous with your restlessness."*

When Jo was at her desk for too long, she got twitchy, like a flea-bitten dog. She was particularly twitchy at the moment, her head filled with suppositions about Jenny Dielman—who she was, her state of mind—thinking that, if she were depressed and without her medication, that couldn't be anything but bad news.

Post-traumatic stress.

She stared at the photograph of Mrs. Dielman and focused on the faraway look in her eyes, knowing how it must have hurt to bury a son who'd never had the chance to grow up. She thought of her own mother and of the problems they'd had even before the dementia had ravaged Verna Larsen Kaufman's brain.

Jo had plenty of experience with post-traumatic stress herself, and she had the trust issues to prove it. Making a clean break from the past was a whole lot harder than it sounded.

"Hey, Larsen."

She glanced up at the firm touch on her shoulder to see Hank Phelps hovering above her like a big damn shadow.

"Y'all ready for lunch?" he asked, his sun-worn features squinting as if the fluorescent light hurt his eyes. "My treat."

"From the vending machine?" she said. Hardly an appetizing thought.

"I figure we'd go out." He hooked his fingers in his belt so that the buckle, shaped like the state of Texas, half disappeared beneath the soft belly that strained the buttons on his shirt. "You up for a little ride?"

She knew what "going out" meant to him and started to shake her head. "I'm not doing McDonald's again, Hank."

"No fast food, I promise." His grin was lopsided, like a slightly deranged Ward Cleaver. "How about we get pasta? There's the place you like at that strip mall with the Mister Donut."

"Ah, Mister Donut," she said, and carefully slipped her notes, the unfinished report, and the photograph of Jennifer Dielman into a manila folder, then retrieved her shoulder bag from her bottom desk drawer. "He and Mr. Coffee are VIPs around here."

"And rightly so."

"Pasta sounds great." She would call those numbers again after lunch, before her afternoon appointment with Terry Fitzhugh in Dallas.

Dallas.

She looked around the tiny room that served as their version of the detectives' bay, tucked into the back of the hardly grand Plainfield PD station house. The city council kept promising something bigger and newer, but until that day came, they were stuck in a shoe box with skinny hallways, bad lighting, and a holding pen with twelve beds that emitted the vague and constant smell of urine.

Man, what a difference a few miles makes, she mused as she followed Hank out the back door after tugging on her wool peacoat.

Gray skies hovered above the parking lot, the clouds thick and menacing. If she didn't know better, she might've thought they were in for snow. But it was probably closer to forty degrees than freezing.

She actually liked this kind of weather—changeable. The never-ending flat, blue sky and endless sunshine bored her with their monotony. She loved a good thunderstorm, even a little white stuff in the winter, though she was more likely to get the former than the latter.

"Hey, Jo, this way." Hank jerked his chin to the right, toward the four-door Ford three spots down from the station's rear exit.

Jo wondered how many times he'd circled the building before he'd found the space he wanted. Probably waited until the blue-and-whites had departed after roll call so he could snag it.

Her partner had an allergy to walking. "Bad knees" was his excuse. Old high school football injuries had accelerated his degenerative arthritis. "The cartilage is nearly gone," he'd told her. "My docs say I'm a candidate for bilateral knee-replacement surgery one of these days. I might have to consider it next summer, if I can take the time off."

He wasn't even fifty. Jo had a hard time believing the warranty on his parts had already expired.

She popped open the door and caught a whiff of stale french fries. "Home, sweet home," she murmured, too low for him to hear.

She belted herself in and leaned her head against the seat, listening to the ignition cough as Hank coaxed the car to life. When it caught, the police band crackled, and Jo heard a dispatcher talking to one of the patrols.

Turning down the radio and humming tunelessly, Hank flipped on the heat, which she knew would take eons to muster up a breath beyond lukewarm. One of these days, she figured, the old boat would need a tow to the scrap yard. Until then, it was their primary mode of transportation when they were on duty.

"So who was the guy bawling at your desk?" Hank asked as he steered toward the south side of town. "Did he lose his puppy?"

"His name's Patrick Dielman," she told him, glancing at his profile, noting the way his eyes crinkled even when he wasn't grinning. "And it's not a dog that's missing. It's his wife."

A tangled eyebrow peaked. "How long's she been gone?"

"Since last evening," she said. "He's pretty convinced something's up. They're the type that sticks to routine, and she's on medication she didn't take with her."

"Is she sick?"

"Not physically."

"Ah." He took a hand off the wheel to twirl a finger round his ear.

Jo felt like they were playing charades. "Her husband said she suffers from post-traumatic stress."

"Was she in the service?"

"She lost her only child three years ago, and her first marriage blew up after that."

"That's rough."

"She never came home after a trip to the Warehouse Club, and he's freaking out. He swears they were solid, that she wasn't having an affair—"

Hank grunted.

"And he's convinced she's met with foul play."

Her partner pursed his lips, and Jo waited for his comment, which could be anything from the sublime to the ridiculous.

"Maybe he's got a hoochie mama on the side, so he got rid of the old ball and chain. You know, like in that Hitchcock movie with Jimmy Stewart . . ."

"Hitchcock?"

"Yeah, Perry Mason's the bad guy, and he cuts up his wife and puts her in a steamer trunk, while ol' Jimmy's watching from his apartment across the way with binoculars."

"*Rear Window*," Jo said, playing along. "You think Patrick Dielman cut up his wife and put her in a steamer trunk? Cynical bastard," she teased, eliciting a chuckle from Hank.

Look at the husband was always the first rule of thumb, but Jo figured Patrick Dielman would have to be a Class-A dumb shit if he murdered his wife and then made such a production of showing up at the Plainfield Police Department and not leaving until Jo heard him out.

"Plenty of idiots out there," her partner remarked. "You know that better than anyone."

Jo didn't disagree, but she was thinking about Dielman's upscale trench coat, the handkerchief, and the polished shoes. "The guy's too anal."

"Maybe she's taking a break from wedded bliss. It's the thing to do," Hank said, dripping sarcasm. "Shrinks are even writing books about taking vacations from marriage." He stole a look at her. "You ever hear of anything so stupid?"

She wondered which late-night talk show had inspired this topic of conversation. No wonder Hank was so grumpy in the mornings. He caught midnight showings of Maury Povich and Jerry Springer on cable and got himself too worked up to sleep.

He tapped his finger on the wheel. "One talking head said it's okay for a wife to leave her husband and kids to go climb Mount Everest or hole up in a kibbutz, you know, to find herself."

Before Jo could comment, Hank added, "It's bullshit, that's what it is." He slapped the visor down, though the sky was a tight stretch of gray without a wink of sun between. "Climbing Mount Everest?" He snorted. "What in God's name is Disney World for? That's what a real escape's all about, am I right?"

"Puking on Space Mountain?" Jo offered.

He laughed. "Having the kids puke on *me* on Space Mountain."

"Yeah, who'd ever want to bypass that for a trip to Tibet," she said, fighting a smile.

Her partner was a real-life character from a Frank Capra movie, reconfigured for the twenty-first century—Henry Fonda with a badge, paunch, and a penchant for four-letter words. High school football jock goes to college and then to the academy, works his way up to detective on the Fort Worth PD, waits until forty to marry a woman just shy of sainthood—as far as Jo was concerned—and settles down to raise his kids in good ol' Plainfield. In her book, that qualified as normal with a capital *N*.

Something she didn't know much about.

Jo's growing up had been more Kafka than Capra. She wondered if Hank had an inkling of how much of her life she kept bottled up. If he did have questions, he didn't ask them, not often, anyway.

"Nothing comes easy," Hank said, so that Jo feared for a moment that he'd read her mind. "Marriage isn't a cakewalk. It sure as shooting isn't for cowards who need to take sabbaticals from reality."

"You should get on the talk shows yourself, you know so much," she said. "You could set the world straight."

"Hell, they wouldn't put me on *Springer*."

"Why not?"

"You've gotta sleep with your sister and live in a trailer park to even sit in the audience. If you want to get on stage, you'd better be screwing your neighbor's goat."

"Stop." She cuffed his shoulder, and he smirked.

Some piece of work, she decided with a shake of her head. He was hardly an enlightened male, if such a thing existed. But he was honest to a fault, and she trusted him. She was glad to have him watching her back. Eight years with the Dallas PD before her two years in Plainfield had taught her how rare a real partnership was. She and Hank had that in spades.

She knew Hank had left the Fort Worth PD for some of the same reasons she'd put the city in her rearview mirror. She wondered how long it would take before this bucolic molehill, for want of a better description, turned as toxic as anywhere else. Pastureland, scrubby trees, and precious creeks were being sacrificed for more houses, apartments, shopping centers, and parking lots as people fled the metroplex and encroached on this "Slice of Heaven on Earth"—which was what the billboard near the highway exit promised those entering the suburban enclave. As the population grew, so would the crime.

She hated to think about that.

Right now, being here was a balm, the fresh start she'd needed. She only had to think of her mom on rare Sundays when she made it into the city. She could focus on her job, on healing herself. And she could work on her relationship with Adam McCaffrey, now that she could actually call it that.

She and Adam had first crossed paths in the autopsy suite at Parkland Hospital. Jo remembered turning green and having to duck out before it was over. Adam found her outside, gave her a stick of gum, and told her, "It gets easier." What got easier was seeing him. Through the years, they'd developed a rapport that turned into a flirtation that led to drinks and, ultimately, her bed. She'd known he was married and kicked herself for being so stupid. But she'd fallen hard, and she didn't see a way out.

"I can't do this," she'd told him, ignoring Adam's protests that his marriage was in name only, that he and his wife didn't even sleep together, that they were nothing more than roommates.

"Then let her go," Jo had said bluntly.

"It's not that easy," he'd replied, and Jo had wondered if he was waiting for his wife to leave first, so he wouldn't have to be the bad guy.

Instead, Jo had left him, moving to Plainfield so he could sort things out.

And he must have, because he wasn't married anymore.

The brakes squealed as Hank slowed at a stop sign.

"You look tired," he said, and she felt his eyes on her even as he mashed on the accelerator. "Late night?"

"No later than usual." Her face warmed, but she didn't rise to the bait.

"Fess up." He grinned. "You had a date."

"What are you, my mother?"

"You have a mother? And I thought you were hatched." He laughed as he pulled the car into a strip mall, humming "Strangers in the Night" all the while.

As he parked and cut the engine, Jo bent to retrieve her bag from between her feet.

"Christ, is that a hickey?"

She bumped her head on the dash. "What?" She pulled down the mirrored visor.

Damn.

"It's just a bruise," she mumbled, swatting at the smudge on her neck. "I slipped in the shower. I must've banged something."

"I'll bet you banged something all right."

She yanked up the neck on her sweater, snatched open the car door, and got out, turning her back on him. She tucked her bag against her rib cage, walking a little faster than necessary toward the restaurant.

"Hey, Jo, wait up!"

Bells jangled overhead as she entered the place and kept a step ahead of him, praying he'd change the subject by the time they reached their table.

A no-nonsense waitress with a pencil at her ear and a green apron round her middle sat them quickly at an empty booth near the kitchen. She slapped down plastic-coated menus in front of them and reeled off a list of specials. Jo nearly interrupted to tell her she was wasting her breath. They never looked at menus. Every time they came, they both had spaghetti with meat sauce and Coke—regular for her, diet for Hank. Didn't matter the season.

When their drinks arrived in crackled red glasses, Jo picked the paper off the top of the straw and sipped. She hadn't removed her coat and did her best to shrink into the collar.

Hank swirled his straw against crushed ice, his gaze settling on her. "So is it that ME you used to see? McCaffrey, right?"

"He's a good friend." She forced herself not to squirm.

"I'm a good friend, and you don't let me suck on your neck."

Oh, boy. Was she the only person in the world who didn't like to talk about her sex life, especially when she had one to talk about?

"Hey, I'm glad it worked out. I like happy endings."

Only she and Adam weren't so much a happy ending as a do-over.

Five minutes later, the waitress brought a tray with their twin plates of spaghetti, and Jo relaxed, breathing easier.

Hank wrapped a healthy amount of pasta around his fork and stuffed it in his mouth, slurping up a long strand and leaving a fleck of red sauce on his chin.

She didn't tell him it was there.

"So what're your plans for Thanksgiving?"

Jo groaned and put her hands over her face. If it wasn't one thing, it was another.

"Please, don't start."

"Hey, I'm just asking. We'd love to have you. Kids haven't seen you in a while."

Thanksgiving?

She couldn't even think about that yet.

I have to finish helping Ronnie pack up Mama's things so we can sell the damned house, get rid of it forever so I never have to set foot in the place again. And then I'm going to stack everything that's left into a huge pile and burn it all to ashes.

She said only, "I'm good, Hank. Don't worry about me."

"I always worry about you."

She stared at him, finding herself at a rare loss for a quick comeback and feeling a little embarrassed.

Her cell went off, preventing further discussion. She slid the phone from her belt and squinted at the display. The number wasn't familiar.

"Who is it?"

She hesitated too long, and the call went to voice mail. Instead of waiting to hear if a message had been left, she went ahead and hit the call-back button. She held the cell to one ear, sticking her finger into the other so she could better hear.

"Dr. Patil's office," a pleasant voice answered.

"I'm Detective Jo Larsen from the Plainfield PD. I phoned earlier to speak with the doctor about a patient of his, Jennifer Dielman," she explained. "He was returning my call . . ."

"Yes, just a minute, Detective."

She found herself on hold, listening to a Muzak version of "Beast of Burden." Thankfully, it was a short wait.

"This is Dr. Patil," said a softly accented voice. Before Jo could get a word out, he said, "Can you drop by my office? It's about Mrs. Dielman. Her husband phoned sounding frantic, and frankly, I'm afraid for her, too."

To understand where I am, I have to start at the beginning: back when I was a girl, not a wife or a mom. I lived in my father's house, which is where I got a crash course in survival. I learned how to stuff my feelings where no one could find them. I couldn't have gotten up every day and gone to school otherwise, pretending everything was okay.

And I got really good at pretending.

My dad was a doctor just like K. He took care of people all day, then came home and scared the crap out of his family. I grew up thinking that nothing I ever did was right. "You're sloppy, Jennifer. Can't you move any faster? Get the hell out of my face! Give me that look again, and I'll whip your ass."

When I got out of there, I never wanted to go back. I wanted to create a new life for myself, somewhere far away where I'd be safe and happy.

I screwed up the nerve to move to Dallas, seven hundred miles away, a distance Daddy would never travel just to haul my butt home. I didn't have much, so I did a stint at Tom Thumb as a cashier. At night, I went to school to learn how to work in a medical office. A year later, I was a floor secretary in the surgery wing at Presbyterian Hospital. That was when I met K.

He was so sweet to all the girls—the nurses, the secretaries, the file clerks. He had a reputation for playing the field, so I avoided him, tried hard never to look him in the eye. Only he took my disinterest as a challenge. I'd find flowers on my desk, a little vase of violets or lily of the valley, nothing big. Then he started asking me out, to dinner and to movies. I guess I wasn't as immune to his charms as I thought because, within a few weeks, I caved. He looked good and smelled good. He spoke quietly and held my hand. He seemed to be everything Daddy wasn't.

A couple months in, after too many margaritas, I let him stay the night.

The romance lasted all of about six months. Then he stopped coming over. He stopped calling.

I think he liked the chase. But once he had me . . .

He went out of his way to avoid me at the hospital. I know he was behind my getting transferred to labor and delivery. I tried not to let it bother me, but I felt so weepy all the time. Something had changed in me. My whole body felt different. My periods stopped. I thought I was depressed. Until I realized I was pregnant.

I told him the baby was his, and when I said I meant to keep it, he wanted to get married in a hurry at the courthouse. I guess it wouldn't have looked good for the rising star on the surgical staff to father a baby with a floor secretary.

The name-calling didn't start until after I quit work and moved into the house he bought for us in Northwood Hills.

He started saying things like: "You're such a pig. You're getting so fat. You're not eating for two—you're eating for a football team!" "How much stuff does a baby need? You think I'm made of money?" "Do you have to wear those god-awful sweatpants all the time? You look like a cleaning lady, not a doctor's wife. It's embarrassing."

He began to work late more often, and he went alone to all of his hospital functions. I thought things would change after Finn was born, but they only got worse. Maybe seeing our son made him feel permanently trapped. Mostly, he just beat me down with words, but once, he shook me until I thought my neck would snap. He wanted to drive me out, I was sure of it.

I knew he was cheating on me.

But he didn't realize my daddy had trained me for a man like him. I was tougher than that, or maybe too stupid. I wanted a home for my son, and I wasn't about to lose it.

I got the feeling K hoped both of us would disappear. The night Finn died, he got half his wish.

CHAPTER THREE

Jo and Hank were quickly ushered in from a mint-colored anteroom, where patients flipped the pages of magazines, waiting to be summoned.

An assistant in floral scrubs led them to an exam room with a table covered in white paper and a metal desk with a stool and a chair.

Hank settled into the chair and looked around him.

Jo pulled herself up onto the exam table, the paper crackling beneath her. She clasped her hands between her legs.

There was a shuffle of footsteps outside the door before it opened and a smallish gentleman with jet-black hair entered. He wore a white lab coat with NAVEEN PATIL, MD embroidered in navy blue over the breast pocket. He held a fairly thick file folder in his left hand. He extended his right.

"Detective Larsen?" he said, and Jo slid down from the padded table to clasp his hand. "I'm sorry we can't use my office, but there was a leak in the ceiling. They're working on it now."

"It's okay," Jo said and nodded at Hank. "My partner, Detective Phelps."

Patil greeted him with a handshake as well, then drew the stool away from the desk with his foot and perched upon it. He set the chart in his lap and looked at Jo. "Patrick Dielman phoned earlier. He said his wife didn't come home last evening, and he's very concerned about her. He urged me to be frank with you, and I told him I would help as much as I could without compromising doctor-patient confidentiality."

Jo glanced at Hank.

"You know about her diagnosis?" Patil asked them.

She leaned against the exam table. "Mr. Dielman said she's on Zoloft for post-traumatic stress. I'm assuming that's related to losing her son."

The doctor gave a slow nod. "It was a blow to her when Finn died. From what Jenny told me, things in her first marriage had not ended well. Kevin was very work-oriented and spent little time with his family. That was hard on Jenny. She needed to feel safe."

"Who's Kevin?" Hank asked point-blank.

Patil turned toward him. "Dr. Kevin Harrison. They divorced not long after Finn's accident. I don't know much about their relationship before Finn died. Jenny didn't talk about it."

"How exactly did Finn die?" Jo asked.

"She told me he fell from a tree house and broke his neck. The trauma was fatal."

"Christ," Hank muttered.

Jo felt a pain behind her ribs.

"It happened three years ago, just after Thanksgiving. Jenny was devastated. She saw me regularly after moving to Plainfield. She was having heart palpitations, trouble sleeping, and anxiety attacks. I examined her thoroughly, did all the lab tests, but nothing was physically out of whack."

"Is that a technical term, out of whack?" Hank said, and Patil smiled tightly.

"I had Mrs. Dielman come in so we could go over her labs. We talked at length about problems in her personal life that might be causing her symptoms. That's when she opened up about the loss of Finn. She hadn't come to terms with her son's death, or the way her marriage had dissolved afterward, and I don't think she knew how to handle the powerful emotions she was feeling. Children aren't supposed to go before their parents."

Life is rarely ever fair, Jo wanted to say, but held back. If anyone knew that, it was a doctor. He probably saw as much pain as she did: people who were sick and broken, bruised and battered, confused and grieving.

"Did you start her on the Zoloft?" she asked.

"Yes." He uncrossed his arms and spread the file open in his lap. "We had to adjust the dose a few times until she was stable."

"Were there any side effects that might explain her taking off?" Jo wanted to know.

"The medication can cause or exacerbate anxiety, insomnia, decreased libido, sweating, tremors, that sort of thing." The doctor thumbed through page after page, seeming to study one here and there before he looked up. "The most serious potential adverse effect from a drug like Zoloft is hepatic dysfunction."

"Hepatic?" Hank repeated. "That's the liver?"

"Yes, it can cause liver problems, which is why we run LFTs on a regular basis."

Hank cleared his throat.

"Liver-function tests," Patil clarified. He ran a finger down a sheet stapled to the front of the chart. "In fact, Jenny's due to have blood drawn on Thursday." His gaze met Jo's. "Maybe she'll be home by then."

"Maybe," she said, but she didn't believe it. The worried look in Patil's eyes told her that he wasn't so sure either. "Might she be suicidal?" Jo asked.

The doctor closed the chart deliberately and held it tight against his chest. "Jenny is an emotionally fragile woman who suffered a severe trauma. She's doing what she could to move on. She appeared content in her second marriage and told me more than once that her library work is satisfying. But nothing fills the void left by Finn. She still misses her son. Some days, it's harder than others."

Jo felt like she was hearing Patrick Dielman's version all over again. It was the same story she'd gotten from Sally Nesbo at the library: a decent woman, good wife, and grieving mother goes AWOL without warning.

There had to be a trigger.

"You didn't answer my question, Doctor," Jo pressed him. "Are you aware of Mrs. Dielman ever attempting suicide?"

"I can assure you," he said, looking her straight in the eye, "that Jenny has not attempted to take her own life since I assumed her care."

"And before that?"

"Those records aren't mine to share."

Jo was getting impatient. "Which means?"

"You do realize HIPAA prevents me from releasing copies of records generated by another doctor or hospital without the patient's signed consent?"

"I do," Jo assured him. "But Mrs. Dielman might be in harm's way. I need to know as much as I can, or I can't help."

Patil frowned. "If I tell you I don't believe she'd do it again, would that be enough?"

"Thank you, yes." Because it meant that Jenny Dielman's old medical records likely contained reports of a suicide attempt, or at least an accidental OD.

"You must understand"—Patil's gaze darted back and forth between her and Hank—"she wasn't over Finn's death by a long shot, and the upcoming anniversary had her reliving that night all over again. She felt responsible, even though she wasn't home when it happened, or perhaps because of that. She said Finn spoke to her, that he came to her in her dreams, that something wasn't right. She wanted to figure things out for herself and make sense of it." He paused before continuing. "She believed that, if she'd been there, the accident would never have happened and her son would be alive. I asked her to forgive herself and stop asking why, but she was still seeking an answer."

"Shouldn't she have seen a psychiatrist?" Jo asked pointedly.

"I gave her some names, of course, urged her to seek treatment from a specialist." Patil didn't sound defensive. "But Jenny didn't want to go. She felt comfortable with me, and I didn't want to push her. It would have been worse for her to withdraw from any kind of treatment at all."

There was that word again.

Comfortable.

Patrick Dielman had used it to describe his relationship with his wife. And it made Jo wonder if Jenny Dielman had been biding her time. But for what? Another suicide attempt?

"If I'd felt she were a danger to herself, I would have recommended hospitalization. I encouraged her to start a journal. In fact, I gave her a notebook about a month ago to help her gather her thoughts and put them in order."

"What did it look like?"

"Just a simple composition book from the drugstore," he said.

"Did her husband know about it?"

The doctor paused. "That would have been up to Jenny."

Since Dielman had said nothing about a journal, she had a feeling his wife hadn't clued him in. She thought of something Patrick Dielman *had* mentioned that morning. "Did Jenny tell you that she was misplacing or forgetting things?"

Patil looked at her, long and hard. "I wouldn't be surprised to hear she was being forgetful. She had so much to deal with."

"You don't think she was seriously losing it?"

Patil rose from the stool, tucked the chart underneath his arm, and smoothed his lab coat with the other hand. "I don't believe she had a full-blown psychosis."

"You sure about that?"

The grooves around his mouth deepened. "The human mind is a tricky piece of machinery. It's hard to anticipate what anyone might do from one day to the next, even the most rational human being, but especially those under severe psychological stress. I didn't sense that Jenny was ready to give up, not . . ." He stopped himself, and Jo wondered if his next word would have been *yet.*

"I hope you find her," he said.

"We'll do our best," Jo told him.

"Jenny is very vulnerable. I'd hate to think someone took advantage of that."

"So would I." Jo passed off her card and asked him to get in touch if he heard from Jenny or if he thought of something else that might help.

Hank didn't say anything until they were alone in the elevator and the doors had slipped closed.

"What if this woman goes home tonight?" he asked. "What if there's no funny business involved, and Mrs. Dielman just chucked her real life for a while?"

"I'd be happy to hear it."

"You'd just walk away?"

"Why wouldn't I?"

The buttons pinged as they steadily descended past the fifth floor, then the fourth and third.

He lowered his head and shook it. "Aw, Jo," he said.

Okay, now he was pissing her off. "What?"

"You're like a dog with a bone. Once you get your teeth into something, you damned sure don't let go."

"I like to see things through," she shot back. "There's nothing wrong with that."

"Maybe I should've had the doc warn you about brain damage from banging your head against the wall."

Jo wanted to tell him he was wrong. That someone had to listen when others wouldn't, because not all victims could speak for themselves.

But she waited for the elevator doors to open and said nothing at all.

I have to know how it happened.

I was too numb that night at the hospital, too overcome by tears and disbelief to ask anything beyond, "Can I hold him? Can I kiss him one last time?"

K said that he'd been on the phone when Finn had gone out in the dark alone. Finn must have been climbing up to the tree house when it happened. He hit his head and broke his neck. It was an accident, K said. It was no one's fault. Not his. Not God's.

Why don't I believe him?

I used the library computer to look up articles on cervical spine injuries, and I searched in books on anatomy and neurology, anything that would help paint a clearer picture.

The hospital had given me Finn's things in a plastic bag: the shirt he'd been wearing along with his jeans and shoes. There was so little blood on his yellow shirt. I had thought there would be more.

It may be all in my head, but I feel like Finn is guiding me, desperate for me to recognize the clues. I just have to look harder to see them.

Back when it was all so fresh, I did something I regret. I ended up in the hospital. K told me I was losing it, that I needed help he couldn't give me. He said I was mired in grief and acting irrationally.

Maybe I was then. But am I irrational now?

Am I crazy to wonder?

Finn slept with a night-light. He cried if the bulb burned out. He would not have gone out in the dark by himself.

If I know anything for sure, it's that.

CHAPTER FOUR

Hank had arranged to talk with a couple of students from McKinney High regarding the missing tubas, following a tip that the theft was tied to next week's Turkey Day game between Plainfield and McKinney. The case appeared to be little more than a prank based on a budding football rivalry, a call to break into the opposing team's band room and grab the biggest instruments they could get their hands on, which sounded a lot like the plot for a porn flick.

Jo figured her partner could handle the interview without her help, so she had him drive her back to the station. She had a little time to kill before heading into Dallas to get her head shrunk. After the appointment, she'd make a side trip to the Warehouse Club and walk around a bit, talk to the manager and feel things out. There were too many questions about Jenny Dielman running through her brain, and she wanted to silence a few of them if she could. She wasn't sure they had a case, but Hank was right: she couldn't let it go.

She sat at her desk and checked her voice mail for messages. There was a returned call from Lisa Barton, the Dielmans' neighbor, saying that yes, she'd be willing to talk. Jo tried to phone her back, but ended up playing phone tag.

There was another message, too, a quickie from Adam. "Hey, babe, I'm just sitting here, signing postmortem reports and thinking about you," which made her smile. She was about to dial his number and thank him for the hickey—and the grief over it that Hank had doled out at lunch—but her desk phone started ringing.

"Detective Jo Larsen," she answered.

"It's Ronnie," said the familiar voice, slow and smooth as molasses.

Jo winced. "Hey, what's up?"

"Nothing much if you don't meet me at your mother's house on Saturday," Ronnie told her. "You know the place is going on the market after Thanksgiving, and we've got to finish cleaning it out—"

"All right, all right," Jo cut her off. She promised she'd be there unless something came up. She hoped like hell something would.

"I had my nephew move the boxes with the kitchen things into the garage," Ronnie went on. "You still don't want any of it?"

"Positive."

"I'll have him bring his truck and haul those things to Goodwill tomorrow, but you've got to promise to go through your mama's personal belongings, honey, and the stuff from your old room. That I can't do."

I don't want anything from Mama's house. Do whatever you want. Toss it, burn it, let it rot. But she couldn't flake out on Ronnie. The woman had already done more than enough for Mama, for the both of them. Jo didn't need that guilt on top of everything else.

"I've put her papers in a box and left them on the kitchen counter in case you get a chance to drop by before the weekend. You've got her power of attorney. There are things you ought to know about."

"I guess you're right."

Ronnie laughed. "I always am."

She held the phone for a moment after hanging up, long enough to take several deep breaths and block Mama from her head. Then she got busy typing up an initial report on Jenny Dielman. She left a paper copy on her captain's desk before picking up her coat, waving to the dispatcher, and taking off.

The afternoon air still swirled frantically, tearing leaves from trees and snatching at her clothes and hair. Once snug in the driver's seat of her Mustang, she exhaled deeply, pushing brown waves from her face and catching sight of her dark eyes in the rearview mirror.

In the shadows, it was hard to differentiate between pupil and iris. A nearly black gaze stared back at her, serious and unblinking. Perpetual smudges of gray beneath attested to sleeping badly as a matter of routine.

Hank was right. She looked so intense. No one would ever call her perky.

A dog with a bone.

She strapped on her seat belt, deciding she'd been called a lot worse.

Jo started the car and maneuvered out of the lot, fixing her attention on the road ahead. She knew her pulse wouldn't ease until she'd put the station far behind her, after she'd merged onto the highway that would take her south into Dallas.

She had a slight problem with separation anxiety, like leaving her desk when she had work to finish, but it was part of the process of "fixing Jo" that Terry was hell-bent on instigating. *No biggie,* she told herself, because a little distance could benefit a case, right? Sometimes when things were too close, they weren't as easy to see. Not until you took a step back, far enough to make the blurred edges crisp.

Maybe she shouldn't be so concerned about a woman who hadn't even been missing a day. Hank liked to say, "Don't get your heart involved," and she tried hard not to. It worked sometimes, and other times she was swept away on a raging current—a doggedness that Mama would have labeled "obstinance." And when that happened, there was no backing off. She didn't know how to work any other way.

"How can you help others when you treat yourself so badly? I don't want to see you burn out until there's nothing left of you, Jo."

She hadn't even reached Terry's office, and she could already hear her reprimand. No matter how badly she wanted to turn the car around every time, she couldn't do it. She'd promised Terry she'd stick to this twice-a-month meeting, and she would if it killed her. It just might, seeing as how their sessions meant picking at old wounds that hadn't healed. She'd rather have hot pokers shoved in her eyes.

Lord, but she was trying.

It was the best she could do.

The police band she'd installed in the old Mustang crackled to life, and Jo switched it off, turning on the radio, set to the classical music station. She tuned into von Suppé's "Light Cavalry," a piece she loved. She hummed, swayed her head.

This was about as close to being at peace as she ever got.

She always had so much on her mind that she couldn't fall asleep at night, afraid she'd missed something, hadn't done what needed doing. Then her heart would beat so fast, she feared it might stop altogether.

Terry had suggested she was having panic attacks. *"There are some good medications for that."*

Medications?

Wasn't she allowed to feel anxious every now and then without requiring a prescription? Would medicating herself really fix anything? Or just numb what ailed her? If drugs could heal what was broken inside her, she'd be an addict. Who wouldn't?

Sometimes life hurt, and you just had to suck it up.

It was unnerving at times to have a therapist who'd become her friend and understood her all too well. Terry had long been an advocate for abused and neglected children. They'd become acquainted when Jo had been with the Dallas PD and Terry had handled cases for family services. Jo had always admired Terry's directness, her ability to see past rose-colored bullshit.

She respected Terry for so much else, too: for having a settled life, a happy home, and a loving mate; for raising a child in a world that grew more frightening every day. Terry and her husband had a boy named Samuel, a little prince if ever there was one.

Jo envied the kid, knowing he would grow up in the kind of environment every child deserved. He was loved and nurtured in a way that so many were not. Seeing Samuel made her crave normalcy, a family of her own. Someday, perhaps, when facing up to her past wasn't so damned difficult.

Terry knew what had happened to Jo in Mama's house, what had gone on until her stepfather had died, when Jo was fourteen. But even she didn't have the answers to the questions Jo kept asking. Had Mama swallowed her suspicions with her bourbon and Coke because she'd just loved him more? Was it punishment because Jo's birth father had abandoned them?

She would never know, not with Mama so far gone she was more a creature of pity than the fragile and complicated woman Jo had loved and hated all at once.

"Sooner or later, you have to forgive yourself, even if you can't forgive her."

Forgiveness was tricky.

Maybe she'd soak in the tub tonight. A bath could cure almost anything for as long as the water stayed warm.

She turned the radio up as one of Vivaldi's *Four Seasons* played. The music distracted her, carried her off to somewhere distant.

Before she knew it, she was well inside the Dallas city limits. She cruised I-635 south to the Preston Road exit. Then she hung a right on Harvest Hill. Terry's office was in a three-story building not far from where the tollway rushed by, mixed in with residential neighborhoods. It was a couple of blocks south and across a busy overpass from a shopping mall.

The minute she stepped into the waiting room, the glass reception window rolled back, and Cathy beamed at her through the hole in the wall. Her spiky red hair accentuated the roundness of her face. "Hi, Jo."

"Hey."

"Let me tell Terry you're here. Just a sec, okay?"

"Sure."

The window slid shut.

Jo slipped into a chair but didn't bother picking up a magazine. Except for her, the room was empty. Cathy arranged Terry's schedule to avoid clients running into one another. There was a rear exit so no one had to walk back through this anteroom. Terry always said that people with troubles on their minds didn't need other folks eyeing them or striking up stilted conversation.

She'd barely had a chance to check her ragged cuticles before the inner door clicked open and Terry appeared, one hand on the knob, the other beckoning. "Hi, kiddo, come inside."

Jo gathered up her bag and went.

Terry hooked her arm through Jo's, chattering about how Samuel had uttered his first sentence as she ushered her up the hallway to her office, settling her on the plump, burgundy sofa. Colorful pillows surrounded her, and Jo plucked one from behind to create more space to back into. She set her purse by her feet and shrugged out of her coat.

"You want some tea? It's Earl Grey."

"Sure." She could use a belly warming.

A teapot and two mismatched cups and saucers had been set out on the coffee table. Shortbread cookies had been hastily arranged on a plate.

"So how've you been?"

"I'm fine." Jo warmed her hands on the cup, breathing in the steam that rose from the brew.

Terry had poured herself a cup but didn't touch it. She had one arm on the back of the sofa and the other on her knee, leaning toward Jo. Her brown hair was pulled away from her face with a headband. She wore an expression of unadulterated interest. No wonder she was so good at what she did. Talk about intensity.

"How fine is fine?" Terry asked without blinking.

Jo shrugged. "I'm okay."

"That's what you always say."

"Yet you never believe me."

"I wonder why. Because you'd tell me you were swell even if you had a knife wedged between your shoulder blades?" Terry nudged her before reaching for a cookie. "You have any trouble getting away?"

Jo swallowed some Earl Grey, careful not to burn her tongue. "Things have been pretty light until this morning."

"Oh?"

"Guy came in and reported his wife missing." She blew into her cup to cool it.

Terry chewed the cookie. "I'll bet you don't get many missing persons in Plainfield."

"We don't get much of anything in Plainfield," Jo agreed.

"Who's the woman? Is she senile? Did she wander away?"

"She's our age."

"Does she have kids?"

"Her only son died after Thanksgiving three years ago."

"That's a hard anniversary to stomach. Losing a child is like no other pain," Terry said, her face clouding. "I can't imagine what I'd do if anything happened to Sam." She shook her head.

"She could still turn up."

"But you don't think she will?" Terry's eyes narrowed on her.

Did it show that much?

She'd never win at poker if she was that easy to read.

Jo exhaled slowly. "Maybe it's bad vibes, I don't know." She met Terry's gaze and said exactly what worried her most: "There's the possibility she might have hurt herself."

"Is that what the husband thinks?"

"No. At least, he doesn't want to believe it." Jo blew on her tea, trying to ignore the tightening in her belly.

"But you do?"

"I don't know." She'd already said more than she should, despite how much she trusted Terry. Then she realized why her friend was pushing that particular button, and she felt her throat close up.

Terry had her head cocked, and the look in her eyes made Jo uncomfortable, as if Terry could see through skin and skull into Jo's brain and pluck out thoughts that had been long since swept aside. Ideas born on days too dark to dwell on, when the anger and guilt had been almost too much to bear.

She broke away from Terry's stare, watching the cup of tea shake in her hand.

Please, don't spill it. Please, don't spill.

Terry brushed crumbs off her hands. "Maybe it'll happen. This story could have a happy ending, you know."

Like in fairy tales and romance novels?

Jo didn't buy either.

She shifted in her seat, holding her cup in both hands, the only way to keep it steady.

"Can we talk about something else?"

"You're right. We should." Terry didn't hesitate. "How's your mother doing at the nursing home?"

Now this one she could handle.

Jo had her response down pat. "She's doing as well as expected for someone with end-stage Alzheimer's. They take good care of her, but she's pretty much a zombie."

"I'm sorry."

Jo shrugged, because it wasn't anyone's fault, wasn't anything but the hand life had dealt to Verna Larsen Kaufman. Maybe one she deserved.

"You see her often?"

"I try to go on Sundays." She didn't admit that she'd missed more than a few of them. It wasn't easy, and she didn't see how that mattered when Mama didn't know who she was.

Terry watched her carefully. "Have you given any thought to what I said before?"

She sighed. "About forgiveness?"

"Yes."

Crap.

Jo suddenly wished she'd rehearsed a better answer for this one, too.

She took a slow sip of Earl Gray, fighting the urge to flee, refusing to let the subject get her worked up the way it usually did. As informal as these sessions were, they made her want to curl up like a roly-poly. She squashed the instinct to retreat.

"If you don't find a way to make peace with your mother, Jo, you'll get stuck in this place your whole life. You'll bury the blame, but you'll never get rid of it."

"I'm working on it."

"How?"

She laughed nervously. "God, you're persistent."

Terry gave her a look that said, *I'm waiting.*

Jo let fly the first thing that came to mind. "I'm helping Ronnie go through Mama's things before we sell the house. I'm dealing with the stuff she left behind, some of his things, too." She wet her lips. "Isn't just being there where it all happened sort of like facing my enemy?"

"It can be, if you let it."

Jo nodded, thinking she'd said something right, at least. "My heart nearly stops, just seeing the door at the end of the hallway, breathing in the same air. I can still smell him, you know, like he's in the room with me." Her hands started to shake, and she was careful with her cup and saucer. "It gives me the willies. Ronnie doesn't understand what's wrong. She doesn't know the truth. She thinks I'm upset about the Alzheimer's."

"Why don't you tell her what's really going on? She's practically family, Jo, as close as she was to your mother. Maybe it would help for her to learn what your stepfather did to you."

"C'mon, Terry."

"It's possible she already suspects something . . . something that'll help you get a clearer picture of how things were. Maybe your mother even told her more about why your birth father left, why she drank so much and didn't pay attention to what was happening to her daughter."

Jo knew Mama would never have told Ronnie any such thing. Ronnie might have been Mama's best friend—her only friend—but she was hardly Verna Larson Kaufman's confidant. Mama had always been so good at pretending life was good when it was anything but.

"Ronnie doesn't need to hear that Mama—" Jo choked up. "If I try to talk to her about the abuse, what good would it do?"

"It would help her understand your behavior and why it's so hard for you to visit your mom and deal with cleaning up what's left behind."

Jo shook her head.

"All right." Terry seemed to back off but then leaned forward and asked, "Have you heard from Adam?"

"Adam?" Jo's hand went to the neck of her sweater, making sure it stood up, so that Terry couldn't see the mark on her skin. "Can we leave him out of this?" Tea slopped from her cup onto the saucer as she shoved it down on the table, china rattling. She rubbed her hands on her jeans.

Terry's eyebrows arched. "So you *have* heard from him."

Jo exhaled. "He left his wife."

"I see."

"I don't want to push things after what happened before."

"When he was married, you mean?"

That was another reason why she hated that word *comfortable* so much. Adam had used it as an excuse to stay with his wife.

"We're not in love anymore," he'd told her, "and she's away half the time, helping her firm open an office in Los Angeles. It's a comfortable arrangement, but there's nothing romantic about it."

Jo had bought it at first, thought it would make her life easier not to have him around too much. It kept some distance between them. Though, in the end, she'd wanted more of him than she could have. Instead of delivering an ultimatum, she'd moved to Plainfield, leaving it up to him whether to come after her or not.

Finally, last night, he had.

"Did you ever tell him about your past?"

"No." She swallowed and glanced toward the window, trying to ease her rapid heartbeat. She focused on the scudding pewter-colored clouds beyond the frame of glass not obscured by the shade. "Trust is hard for me."

"I know it is."

"I don't want to blow this."

"You won't." Terry took her hand and held it.

"I don't want to run anymore."

"Then stop."

"Did I tell you that I left home when I was fifteen?" Jo focused on the fine blue veins beneath Terry's skin. "Mama drank more than ever after he died, because she had no man around, and that just about killed her."

She lifted her gaze and met her friend's eyes.

"Something happened in those months, the worst possible thing." She hesitated, blood rushing like wind in her ears, and she wondered if she should shut up now before she couldn't take it back. "Mama couldn't handle me. God knows I didn't know what to do. So I went away, until it was okay to return. Until we could pretend like nothing was wrong."

"It's okay, you can tell me."

Jo closed her eyes for a minute, shook her head.

The pale fingers squeezed hers. "When you're ready."

Jo figured that might be forever.

She switched the subject again. "It's not like Adam thinks I'm the girl next door."

Terry cocked her head, looking as serious as before. "He's stronger than you give him credit for. He came after you, didn't he? He didn't let you go."

"It's different now, Terry. It's real to me."

"And that scares you?"

Jo withdrew her hand from Terry's grasp, got up, and walked toward the window. She crossed her arms to quell the flutter in her chest. "Running naked across LBJ in rush-hour traffic would be less frightening."

"You won't always feel that way."

She set her palm flush against the glass. It was cold and rattled from the wind, vibrating against her skin. "You really believe that?"

"I do."

Jo pressed her lips together, nodding.

Maybe someday she'd believe it, too.

I had the dream again last night.

It was much the same as before. I was running to the house, tearing through the front door, calling Finn's name and searching frantically for him. I felt so panicked, I couldn't breathe. Everything moved too slowly. The air rippled like water, and my legs pushed through sludge.

"Finn!" I kept yelling. "Where are you? It's Mommy."

Then I saw him out back, sitting up in the tree, his legs dangling.

I went to the sliding door and pushed, but it wouldn't budge.

"Finn, no!" I shouted at him through the glass as he stood up on a branch. The limb began to sway, ready to snap.

I watched him teeter and screamed. The ground was so far below, stark-white stones circling the pink petunia bed at the foot of the tree.

He looked up. His eyes were big and blue. I can picture them so clearly. He wasn't wearing his glasses, and I know his world must have been frighteningly blurry. Could he even see me from so far away? With a crack, the branch snapped, and he toppled forward, headfirst to the ground.

I woke up screaming and sweating, my heart pounding.

"You're all right, Jen," Patrick kept saying over and over.

But I wasn't all right, and I won't be until I understand what Finn keeps trying to tell me.

CHAPTER FIVE

By the time Jo had finished her session of soul-baring with Terry, she felt unsettled and drained. So when her cell rang as she was belting herself into the Mustang, she answered less than delicately. "Yeah?"

"Detective Larsen?"

"Yes. Who is this?" She didn't recognize the number.

"Kevin Harrison," the man said, clearly affronted. "You left a voice mail earlier, something about my ex-wife. Is she in trouble?"

"She could be." Jo looked up as a car pulled into the space opposite her. "She didn't go home last night, and her husband's frantic. Perhaps she contacted you?"

"Look, Detective, I haven't seen Jenny since our divorce, so I'm afraid I can't help you."

Whoa, not so fast, buddy. "Maybe you can. You and Jenny lost your son three years ago next week. I'm wondering if the anniversary might have something to do with her disappearance. Do you have a clue where she might have gone? You probably know her better than anyone."

He made a noise, a surprised sort of laugh. "You really do have it wrong. I hardly knew Jenny at all, except to say that, whatever Jenny's done, I'm sure she brought it on herself."

"But, Dr. Harrison—"

He cut her off. "I hope you find her."

And that was that.

Jo glared at the phone before tossing it on the passenger seat.

Thanks for nothing, asshole.

Maybe she was rushing to judgment, but she instantly pegged Harrison as an arrogant son of a bitch who wore expensive suits and handmade shirts with French cuffs and thought the world revolved around him. How had Jenny ever ended up with someone like that? And then she'd paired up with another winner: Patrick Dielman, the control freak.

Wow, Jenny, but you sure knew how to pick 'em.

Jo shook her head and started the car.

By the time she'd extricated herself from the Dallas traffic, dusk had fallen.

It was close to the time Jenny had gone to the Warehouse Club the previous night, and Jo found herself wondering if the woman had been playing her radio, going over her shopping list, contemplating what to fix for dinner. Or had she been preoccupied with darker thoughts, a need to run away, to disappear?

"I don't think you understand, Detective. Jenny doesn't have friends. She just has me."

What Jo did understand was that everyone had secrets, ones they kept even from those who were closest. Patrick Dielman could have believed his marriage was solid as a rock, but Jenny might have felt differently.

She guided the Mustang toward the southwest corner of town, where the Warehouse Club was located in a retailing mecca of restaurants and shops called Town and Country Center.

Until recently, Plainfield had still retained a rural feel, with acres of pasture, cows, and horses grazing behind fences that extended to the shoulder of roads and highways. Scrubby trees and bristled pines had dotted the landscape. An occasional office building or new subdivision had popped up, but those were few and far between the blue sky and green spaces.

In the past few years, the floodgates had opened. Folks had sold their homes in Richardson, Plano, Arlington, Fort Worth, and Dallas, packing up and moving to Plainfield until the population grew at the pace of rabbits on Viagra. The green was slowly swallowed up by concrete, the trees replaced by walls and roofs, glass and steel.

Ta-da.

Suburban sprawl.

Jo figured they'd outgrown the *rural* label once the cars had outnumbered the livestock.

She pulled into the Warehouse Club lot behind a line of vehicles with blinkers flashing and inched forward. As she scoped out the width and breadth of the enormous parking lot, she wondered if anyone would have noticed a lone woman in trouble.

Someone laid on the horn behind her, and she glanced in the rearview mirror to see an impatient teenager in a Camaro give her the finger.

Nice.

She waited until a mother pushed a stroller safely across the zebr striped path before she resumed her creep forward.

The Camaro took a hard left up a wrong-way lane, tires squea

Jo sighed.

Talk about an accident waiting to happen. The iPhone gen thought everything and everyone should move at warp speed. A help you if you got in their way. Respect didn't come easy, nor not even with a badge.

But maybe her own age had something to do with he

The only free space she could find was so far back, she was almost out of the lot altogether. As she exited the car and locked the door, she figured it was a good thing Hank wasn't with her. He wouldn't walk that stretch of asphalt, especially in this wind.

Jo wasn't too thrilled about it herself, but she tugged up her collar and shoved her hands deep in her coat pockets, trying to stay warm as she trudged past car after car, each of a decidedly upscale make and model. She strode by people with bags and boxes loaded on dollies, finally giving a nod to a Warehouse Club employee in red trousers and jacket trying to direct a serpentine line of shopping carts toward the building.

She assessed the light poles standing guard over the football-field-size area and spotted surveillance cameras directed down. She felt a flutter of hope, figuring the store had surely saved video from yesterday. If so, they should be able to find Jenny Dielman, see when she and her Nissan had shown up and when they'd departed.

There wasn't a security guard in sight, just the occasional employee in red helping a customer out or retrieving the ever-amassing carts from the gated corrals.

She looked up as she stepped through a pair of doors that automatically slid apart and noted two black boxes pointing at her from different angles.

They had the doors covered, too.

If Jenny had made it inside, she would be recorded.

Lord, let me get lucky.

"Can I see your card, ma'am?"

An elderly man with thick black glasses and bushy eyebrows in need f detangling stopped her from getting more than three feet inside the ore. He had on a red vest with a big button exclaiming We Love Our ioppers! Looking over his shoulder, Jo glanced at the enormous space, gray concrete walls and endless shelves packed with merchandise. murmur of voices seemed magnified, a constant hum in her ears.

"Your card?" he said again.

She smiled and retrieved her leather wallet from her bag, showing him her ID and shield.

"You're the police?" the man said, caterpillar brows bristling. "You here on a bust?"

A bust? It was all she could do not to laugh.

"No, nothing like that," she assured him. "I'd like to speak with Owen Ross if I could. Can you tell me where I might find him?"

"Owen? Sure." A shaky finger pointed her toward a big counter where a line had gathered. "He's at customer service. Ya need me to take you over?"

"Thanks, but I'll manage." She kept out her wallet but slipped her hand back inside her bag to retrieve the photograph of Jenny. "By any chance, were you here last night between five and five thirty?"

He nodded. "Five days a week from two to ten."

"Do you remember seeing this woman come in sometime after five o'clock? She would have used a guest pass."

He took the photo and studied it, wrinkled brow further creasing. "Pretty girl," he remarked. Then he shook his head and handed it back. "I wish I could tell ya I'd seen her, but we get so many new ones in with those paper passes that they all sort of blur together."

"Thanks, anyway."

Farther over, near the rows of cash registers, Jo spied a security guard in a blue uniform, walkie-talkie clipped to his belt and no weapon in sight. He was beyond middle age, with a paunch that beat Hank's hands down and a bored expression on his bloated face. She figured he'd easily lose to a shoplifter in a footrace.

The rent-a-cop caught her staring, and she turned away, heading to the customer service counter. She walked straight to the front despite the lines, prompting displeased murmurs and a lone cry of "Would y'all take a number like everyone else?"

She held up her shield toward the red-vested pair behind the desk and said, "I'm looking for Owen Ross."

A Hispanic woman nodded toward a twentysomething white guy with thinning hair and pale eyes who stammered, "I'm Owen." He reached for her ID with nail-bitten fingers and peered at it closely.

"Can we talk?" She put her badge away and stuck her hands in her pockets.

"Sure." He turned to the woman, told her he'd be back in a few, and motioned Jo to follow him around the counter and through a back door into a small room with a messy desk, a couple of chairs, and a bulletin board covered in promotional flyers touting vacuums on sale and specials in the butcher shop.

"I'm hoping you can help me pinpoint the time this woman shopped in your store yesterday," Jo said once Ross had settled behind his desk, and she'd perched on a metal folding chair. She passed the photograph over. "Her name is Jennifer Dielman. She was likely here between five o'clock and five thirty."

"Oh, yeah, Dielman." He sighed. "The husband came by last night, and he's already called, like, three times today. So his wife hasn't turned up?"

"No." Jo tapped the photograph. "Do you recognize her?"

"Is she dead?"

She kept her voice level. "We hope not."

His bug eyes took in the photo for another moment before he pushed it back. "I don't remember seeing her personally. We've got some regulars who come weekly, so I know them by sight. But we can get a hundred customers an hour on most days. I can't recall everyone who comes in, not by a long shot."

Jo was tempted to remark that bigger wasn't always better, but instead she leaned forward on the metal seat. "You've got surveillance cameras at the doors and in the parking lot, right? And a picture's worth a thousand words, as they say."

"Yeah, I've heard that once or twice." Ross smirked. "Except only the cameras at the doors actually work."

Jo winced. "Your surveillance cameras in the parking lot are broken?"

"Nope, not broken," he said and scratched his nose. "They just don't work. They're more for show."

Terrific.

"We've got a guard in a golf cart that patrols the lot, but it's been pretty cold out there," Ross explained when Jo shook her head. "Besides, this is Plainfield. Nothing big ever happens here."

"You must keep records of purchases, right? So you'd have a receipt with a time stamp if Mrs. Dielman bought anything."

"Let me get this straight." He squinted like his brain hurt. "You want a copy of the front-door security footage from yesterday, and I'm supposed to go through all of the receipts, too?"

"That would be very helpful."

His scowl said he wasn't enthusiastic at the prospect. "The guest pass is gonna make it harder to track. If she had a customer card, I could access her account. But with a paper pass, I dunno." He thumbed his chin where he'd sprouted a tiny soul patch. "Give me until tomorrow morning. I'll pull receipts that don't have Warehouse Club customer numbers attached. You said she was here after five?"

"Yes."

He picked up a pencil with visible bite marks and scribbled on a sheet of paper. "All right, I'll do my best."

"Any chance I could get the surveillance video now?"

Ross put the pencil down. "It could take a few minutes. You want to wait?"

Jo tried to rein in her irritation. "Whatever you can do would be appreciated, Mr. Ross, both by the police department and by Patrick Dielman. If something did happen to his wife while in your parking lot, if she was carjacked, for instance"—he blinked double time at the suggestion—"it would be best for us to have all the information we can as soon as possible."

Ross nodded. "Okay, yeah, sure, since you put it that way. If you hang around, I can burn a DVD with the footage, but it'll take until tomorrow morning to put together those receipts."

"Great." Jo twiddled her thumbs for another fifteen minutes before Ross delivered the shiny DVD in a clear box marked with yesterday's date.

"If you want the original, I'll need a warrant," he told her. "Company policy."

"Let me know when you have the receipts," she said and gave him her card.

Jo walked outside and stood in the wind, taking in the row after row of cars and the faces of the people who passed without even glancing at her. They hung on to their carts, their hoods drawn against the cold. She could've been invisible for all the attention they paid.

If Patrick Dielman was right, if his wife had come here after she'd phoned him, dusk would have settled by the time she'd left the store. The light would have faded, shadows lurking. There were plenty of places for a person to lie in wait, unnoticed.

Had someone approached Jenny as she walked to her car? Someone who asked for help with an armload of groceries, perhaps? Would Jenny have let her guard down, enough to give her assailant time to shove her inside her car, take the wheel, and drive away?

It could've happened in seconds, quickly enough to have gone unobserved.

Jo turned around again.

There were so many cars—so much space—and everyone scurrying like ants at a picnic as they prepared for the Thanksgiving holiday next week.

Would anyone have even realized it if Jenny had been taken?

"Jennifer is very vulnerable. I'd hate to think someone took advantage of that."

Maybe no one had.

What if she'd driven off by herself?

What if Jenny Dielman was right where she wanted to be?

Jo headed back to the Mustang, her cell tweeting as she settled behind the wheel. "Larsen," she said, hoping for good news.

"I think it's her." A woman's voice. "It has to be."

"Her? Who? Is this Lisa Barton?" Jo ventured to guess, putting the throaty drawl together with the earlier message on her voice mail. "Are you home?"

"Yes, it's Lisa. One of my windows has been broken, and I . . ."

Jo heard a gulp of indrawn air.

"I think it was Jenny."

◆ ◆ ◆

Ten minutes later, Jo turned onto Ella Drive within the Woodstream Estates subdivision.

Hank's tank of a Ford was there already, parked behind a squad car with its light bar throwing flashes of blue and red through the evening air. Across the street, Jo spotted a uniformed officer speaking to a man in a down coat and hat who hung on to a leash with a jumpy dog.

She pulled against the curb, glancing at the numbers on the mailboxes. The Dielmans' place was dark except for a single porch light. Patrick Dielman must have taken her advice and gone to work. She wondered if he'd been able to concentrate on anything but Jenny.

Jo got out of her car and waved at her partner, who was planted in the next driveway over, talking to a tall woman in a long beige coat.

The front door of the whitewashed-brick residence was partially open, a sliver of light spilling onto the welcome mat. Jo took a direct path across the grass to where a uniformed officer was photographing a shattered pane of glass. He turned his head as she approached, and she motioned for him to resume what he was doing.

Jo watched for a moment, taking a long look at the area outside the window, tiny holly bushes below, the leaves glinting with moisture and flecks of glass. The affected pane, a rectangle about eight inches high and six wide, had slivers protruding from the metal frame, like a set of broken teeth.

She glanced back at the driveway and the street beyond.

"Larsen, this way," her partner called, gesturing her around the corner. Jo followed, crossing the cobbled drive to where a woman with spiral blonde curls stood near the front door. "This here's Mrs. Barton," he said by way of introduction.

"It's Ms., and you can call me Lisa," the woman corrected. "Sorry for pushing the panic button, but I freaked." She attempted a smile, but it never reached her eyes.

Jo noted the creases etched around her mouth, the lines of a smoker or reformed smoker. There were no signs of Botox or a face-lift, only a pinched expression that betrayed her frayed nerves.

"What happened?" Jo asked.

"I got home from work, had just gone in with the mail, when I heard a crash in the kitchen." Lisa wrung her hands, and Jo saw pale scars below the knuckles. From an old accident or burns? "That's when I noticed the brick. It smashed through the glass and landed in the sink."

Jo thought of the window with the gash in it, the glitter on the bushes below. "You said you thought Jenny had been here. You think she's responsible?"

"I know it sounds weird, what with her being missing and all." The words tumbled out in a nervous drawl. "I wouldn't have made the connection except that I found something of hers after, when I got the nerve to look around. It was caught in the holly."

"What was caught?"

"Jenny's scarf," the woman enunciated, like Jo was hard of hearing.

Hank lifted his arm and showed off an evidence bag that contained a crumpled square of bright blue silk. "Kinda loud for my taste," he remarked.

Jo looked at Lisa. "That belongs to Jenny Dielman?"

"Yes." Face set sternly, sure as all get-out.

Jo remembered something Patrick Dielman had said when he'd plunked himself down at her desk: *"She complained that things weren't where she'd left them . . . that stuff was missing . . . her keys, a photograph . . . the scarf I gave her for her birthday."*

"You're certain it's Jenny's?" she asked again.

"One hundred percent, Detective." Lisa Barton raised her pointed chin. "Patrick should be home soon. Ask him. He'll tell you. I helped him pick that scarf out for Jenny's birthday. It's Hermes, hand-rolled silk tweed. Cost three hundred twenty bucks."

Hank whistled.

Jo chewed the inside of her cheek.

She was supposed to just buy that the slender, brown-haired woman in the photo with the cat, described by all who knew her as quiet and grieving, would pound a brick through her neighbor's window and drop her scarf as she took off?

If Lisa Barton hadn't been so damned serious, Jo would have laughed.

She gestured at the evidence bag. "Mr. Dielman said his wife lost that scarf a while back. Someone else might have found it," she suggested, "like, a neighborhood troublemaker."

"Bored teenagers." Hank snorted. "They like causing a stink, then get boners when the squad car shows up." Jo gave him a look, and he ducked his chin, murmuring, "If you'll pardon the expression, ma'am."

Lisa Barton seemed unfazed by his remarks. She glanced over at the Dielmans' house. "I wonder what's keeping Patrick. He's usually home by now." Her voice cracked. "Do y'all think you could have a patrol car keep an eye on things tonight?"

"If that'll make you feel safer, we'll arrange it, ma'am," Jo said, squinting into the gloom at the shrubs that ran around the house, feeling the itch to move, to look around. "Will you excuse me a minute?"

She edged away from her partner, crossing the pebbled drive to the grass and the clipped bushes, following their sharp angles around the side of Lisa Barton's house, hearing her own rushed breaths.

A motion-activated spotlight flashed on, nearly blinding her with its beam, and she blinked away the dots that danced against her eyelids before she entered the Dielmans' yard.

Her gut kept pushing at her, because nothing about this felt right.

Through the shadows, she saw the rustle in the deep red of a burning bush set at the corner of the house.

"Larsen!"

She ignored her partner's summons.

"Jenny?" She approached slowly, palms damp enough to wipe on her pants. "Mrs. Dielman, are you there?"

As she leaned forward and touched a trembling branch of crimson, a dark shape flung itself straight at her chest.

A feral cry rang out as it hit her in the shoulder, and she fell back onto her butt. Her eyes barely made out the black shadow that darted off and disappeared into the night.

She sat on the damp grass and caught her breath. Her heart sprinted against her ribs, the rush of adrenaline making her light-headed.

"Jesus, Jo, what the hell's up with you?"

Hank's hand came down and caught hold of her arm, hauling her to her feet. He still had the bagged scarf clutched in one hand.

She brushed off the seat of her jeans, willing her pulse to slow. "I thought I saw something," she got out.

He shook his head. "You're chasing ghosts, partner. Ain't nobody here but us chickens."

"And a cat," she said softly.

"Boys already walked the perimeter of both houses and beat the bushes before you even got here. I knocked on a few doors myself. None of the neighbors saw squat."

She walked beside him, back to the driveway where Lisa Barton stood. The woman turned up her coat collar, tucking hands in her pockets. She looked a bit like an actress from one of those Hitchcock movies Hank liked to talk about with her blonde hair, calf-length coat, and high heels. Though she was a little rough around the edges to be Grace Kelly.

"Did you find her?" she asked as they approached.

"Naw," Hank said, "just a cat."

He gave Jo a glance that made her cheeks warm. She touched her shoulder where the animal had hit her, feeling stupid.

"Poor Jenny. She should've gotten help," Lisa murmured, brow cinched. "If she'd done what was best for her, this wouldn't be happening."

"Back to the scarf," Jo said. "Mrs. Dielman told her husband she'd lost it."

Lisa sighed. "Jenny seemed to have problems remembering a lot of things lately. The other day, she locked herself out. Thank goodness, I had a spare key."

"So maybe she was flaky," Jo replied. "But that doesn't explain why she'd disappear for twenty-four hours without calling her husband, then show up here and vandalize your property, Ms. Barton."

"Who else could it be?" Lisa crossed her arms tightly. "Who else would want to send me a message?"

"What message?" Jo felt like she was missing something. "You think Jenny had a grudge against you?"

"I'd say so, yeah." The woman shook tousled bangs from her eyes and looked dead-on at Jo. "I'm pretty sure she imagined I was having an affair with Patrick."

Jo and Hank exchanged glances.

"Were you?" Jo asked. "Having an affair with Mr. Dielman?"

"No, Detective Larsen, I wasn't." Her mouth pinched. "Patrick wouldn't break his vows, not so long as Jenny was around. He's a decent man. He believes in that whole till-death-do-us-part thing." The way she said it made Jo think she wasn't exactly a true believer herself.

"You ever been married, ma'am?" Hank inquired.

She shook her head.

He grunted.

"Did Jenny accuse you of sleeping with her husband?" Jo asked, wondering why the woman would assume to know what Jenny thought about anything. "Why would she think the two of you were involved if you weren't?"

Lisa Barton glanced down at the buffed black leather of her boots. "Jenny had a lot going on in her head. Some of it was real, and some was pure fiction. Maybe that's what happens when you hurt as much as she did."

"Losing her son," Jo said.

"Losing him and having her first marriage fall to pieces."

"Did she talk about her ex-husband?"

Slim shoulders shrugged. "One time when I went over for coffee, she saw the newspaper, and Kevin Harrison's photo was there, on the society pages with his wife at some swanky function. Her eyes got really wide, and she made a snarky comment."

"Do you recall what she said?"

Lisa smiled a vague smile. "If I remember correctly, it had something to do with seeing him rot in hell."

"As so many men should," Hank remarked. "That's the punch line, right? I can tell there's girl talk coming, so excuse me." He ducked out, ambling toward the Ford.

The woman gnawed on her cheek, looking over to the street as Hank popped the trunk and set the evidence bag inside. "Jennifer always seemed on edge, like she was ready to crack. I told her to sign up for yoga or somethin', but she hated to leave the house any more than she had to. It couldn't have been much of a life for her or for Patrick."

"Where do you figure she is?" Jo asked. "You think she ran out on her husband because she thought he was cheating, then came back to hurl a brick through your kitchen window?"

Lisa Barton stared at the house next door. "I really don't have a clue what Jenny would do. But maybe it's a positive sign."

Jo didn't see it. "Positive?"

"If Jenny was here, if she did drop the scarf, it would mean she's okay, right? That she's out there alive, just not wanting to be found."

Jo didn't respond, having wondered the same thing herself.

Only her gut said something different.

I saw a picture of K in the society pages of the Dallas Morning News. I must have made a face because Patrick asked if I had the flu. I shook my head, folding the page so I didn't have to look a minute longer. I didn't want to talk to Patrick about K. But I had a game I played in my head. It was called "Liar."

Do you promise to love, honor, and cherish?

I do.

Liar.

Will you be a good daddy to this baby?

I will.

Liar.

Will you watch Finn while I go hit a couple of Black Friday sales? Will you make sure he gets his bath and takes his meds? Can you get him into bed on time?

For God's sake, Jenny, I will!

Liar.

I was on the phone with the hospital. I didn't realize he'd gone outside.

Liar.

I saw her name and number on your phone. Were you talking to her the whole time? Did she hear what really happened? I touched Finn's feet, held his hands. They were clean. Where was the dirt? Was he really outside? Did he even fall?

It was an accident, Jenny, just one of those things.

Liar.

Liar.

Liar.

CHAPTER SIX

A splatter of raindrops on the windshield became torrential as Jo turned in to her condo complex. The leaden sky had finally opened up after threatening all day. She was glad that it had waited.

Headlamps sliced through the gray as the Mustang crept forward, wipers frantically skidding back and forth. She could hardly see far enough in front of her to distinguish the road from the grass on her dead-end street. The pounding drops drowned out the dying purr of the engine as she parked in the first open spot, nearest her door.

For a few minutes, Jo sat and watched the storm outside the windshield, waiting for the rain to lighten up. She felt drained, like she was operating on half a battery. She'd gone back to the station after leaving Lisa Barton's house, made sure the department got out a bulletin on Jenny Dielman's car, and ran background checks on Barton and on Patrick Dielman.

Now all she wanted was something to eat and a hot bath. When the downpour continued without pause, she said, "To hell with it," and got out of the car, scrambling onto the sidewalk toward her steps.

Water sluiced from above like an enormous pail turned upside down, drenching her as she climbed to the safety of her tiny portico.

Her porch light glowed feebly as her numb fingers grabbed the mail from the box that hung on the railing. Once inside, she shut the door hard behind her and paused to catch her breath. The storm seemed so distant from here. Warm air hissed through the vents and enveloped her. She shivered.

Jo turned the dead bolt, then stamped her feet on the mat. She deposited her mail and keys on the hall table, extracting the Warehouse Club security DVD from her bag and adding that to the pile.

Shrugging off her coat, she breathed in the stuffy air and wished it wasn't cold and damp so she could crack a window. The scent of lavender emanated from a potpourri bowl on the sofa table. Terry had given it to her along with some candles. Jo had first stuck them away in a drawer but had started to use them, little by little. They did make the place smell good, even girlish, which wasn't a bad thing, considering most of her belongings were practical, not frilly.

She hadn't owned much before she moved to Plainfield and bought this place just over two years ago. She'd wanted to begin anew, and she'd pretty much done it from scratch, though she had brought with her the framed Impressionist prints from the Dallas Museum of Art gift shop. She'd worked everything else around them: the colors, the furniture, and knickknacks. The deep-green walls were straight from the hue of the trees and leaves in the blur of brushstrokes that depicted *Camille Monet in the Garden at Argenteuil* and the lush pads in a panel from *Water Lilies*. The cherry bookshelves nearly matched the touches of red in Manet's *In the Garden of La Villa Bellevue*, which showed a woman reading in a garden, a rake and watering can nearby. She had always assumed the model for that was Madame Manet herself, enjoying a bit of Balzac, perhaps?

I believe in the incomprehensibility of God.

What was that from?

It would probably come to her when she'd forgotten why she'd wanted to know.

She pulled the Warehouse Club disk from the plastic case and pressed the power button on the DVD player. She inserted it but hit "Pause." She was hungry and cold. She wanted food and a bath before anything else.

She went into the bathroom and got the water running hot enough for steam to rise from the spewing faucet. She shook in some vanilla-scented bath salts to soften the water and fill her head with their sweetness.

Undressing down to her bra and panties, Jo pulled on her robe and padded into the kitchen to slap together a peanut butter and jelly sandwich. She poured a glass of milk and carried both back to the bathroom. Perched on the toilet seat, she consumed her dinner well before the tub had filled.

After shutting off the faucet, she put a hand to the water, testing it before she got in. Hot but not too hot. Like Baby Bear's porridge.

Just right.

She braced herself as liquid warmth enveloped her body. Her skin prickled as gooseflesh melted into heat, and she slipped all the way beneath the surface, holding her breath as she wet her hair and face. With a gasp, she emerged, heavy curls stuck in clumps to her head. Sighing, she closed her eyes and leaned against the curve of porcelain, resting her neck so her chin skimmed the water.

Now *this* was therapy.

She breathed deeply, in and out, focusing on that and nothing else. It worked to slow the frantic pace of her heartbeat, but her thoughts still swirled like hummingbird wings. However hard she tried, she couldn't seem to quiet her brain. Even with sleep came vivid dreams, though her nightmares were less frequent. She'd begun to embrace the sense of being safe, locked in by dead bolts and storm windows.

It wasn't so much the idea of holding the world at bay but more of being the gatekeeper. She could decide who came and went. Maybe she was trying to regain the power she'd lost—had never had—when she'd lived in Mama's house.

That was the past. This was the present.

Everything was different now.

She pushed her hands against the water, creating tiny waves, the current pulling gently at her beneath the surface, gliding over her skin. Her whole body ached with fatigue, and her head felt heavy with so many bits and pieces that didn't seem to connect in any way that made sense.

It had been one of those days that felt like a week.

She rubbed at her eyes, willing herself to forget everything that had happened: Patrick Dielman sitting at her desk, stolen yarn, high school pranks, picking at scabs with Terry, Lisa Barton's broken window.

Let it go, she told herself. *Let it go.*

She inhaled, putting a hand on her belly until she felt it swell; then she exhaled. She lay motionless, willing her tendons to loosen, her head to empty. When she closed her eyes, she saw Adam's face, his head on her pillow, her hair brushing his skin as she lowered her mouth to his, his hands drawing her against him. Her fingers touched the place on her neck where he had bruised her with his rough kisses, then traced the line around her jaw to settle on her lips.

She sighed, shivering.

She stirred the water again so it washed gently over her exposed knees, eliciting a whiff of vanilla bean. She swallowed down a taste that wasn't near as inviting.

Uncertainty.

She made herself stop. *Don't.*

Don't ask too many questions. She'd only make herself crazy.

She lay back in the water, blowing out slow, deep breaths, shutting her eyes.

She felt a touch on her head, fingers ruffling her hair.

A sweet, low voice called her name. "JoJo? You ready, sweet pea? Time for us to go."

"Go where?" She looked up into his face, but he stood so tall. His features blurred no matter how hard she tried to see them.

"Away." His hand swooped down to catch her tiny fingers, holding them firmly in his grip, like he would never release her.

They walked somewhere she didn't recognize, a road that led away from home, away from Mama. They cut through a copse of trees so thick, she couldn't pick out the blue sky. Quickly, it turned dark, the forest around them denser, but she didn't feel afraid so long as his fingers were wrapped around her own.

"Wait here. I'll be right back, sugar," he said, but his voice sounded far away already, and then he let her go, her hand reaching out in the air, finding nothing there.

Nothing but fear.

Noises enveloped her: creaking boughs, breaking twigs, cries of animals. But she didn't know where to go, and the trees closed around her.

"Daddy!" she cried, over and over.

But he didn't come back. The air grew thick and filled her nose until she couldn't breathe. She couldn't breathe!

Jo jerked awake, pawing at the water, finally gripping the rim of the tub. How real the dream had seemed, enough to make her pulse race.

She rubbed her eyes with a wet hand, water dripping down her cheeks.

JoJo.

That voice, so sweet and low: it was the only thing about her daddy that still existed in her mind. She couldn't even picture him.

She wasn't yet five when he'd taken off. Mama had told her he was gone for good, that he'd left them because he didn't love them like he should. Jo hadn't understood except to think she must've done something wrong. Then the photographs had disappeared from the walls, from the vinyl-sleeved albums, and her mother had never spoken of him again.

After a while, Jo had stopped asking.

She didn't know where her birth father was, or if he was even still living.

What am I doing, playing a lone hand of This Is Your Sorry Life?

The water had turned cool around her. She shivered and rubbed her arms.

Then she pulled the plug and listened to the gurgle as her bath—and her bad dream—disappeared down the drain. With a grunt, she hauled herself up from the tepid pool, dried off, and drew her terry cloth robe around her. She wiped the heel of her hand on the mirror to clear the condensation, squinting at the face that peered back. Her dark hair tangled against her narrow brow; slim shoulders sagged with fatigue.

She tipped her chin to expose the curve of her neck. The frown on her mouth softened as she studied the spot where Adam had kissed her so aggressively.

She was almost sorry it would fade.

In the living room, she snatched up the remote. Sitting back on the sofa, she curled her legs beneath her and pressed "Play" on the Warehouse Club security footage.

She fast-forwarded through yesterday morning and early afternoon, slowing down when she neared 5:00:00 on the time stamp in the lower right corner. If Jenny Dielman had spoken with her husband by telephone around that time, it likely would have taken her another ten minutes to get to the store from their residence. She fast-forwarded again, stopping when the numbers read 5:10:00.

Her finger poised above the "Pause" button.

She watched people pushing through the doors, entering with empty arms and exiting with bags in hand or a dolly crowded with boxes. Then the woman appeared, brown hair to her shoulders, wearing a dark coat and blue jeans. Her purse swung from her arm by a strap.

Jo hit "Pause."

She came off the couch and crept closer, kneeling before the screen.

She resumed play and watched the woman pass through the second set of double doors into the store. Squinting hard, she scrutinized those who came after: a pair of older women wearing headscarves; a large man in a parka holding a cane in his right hand; a pregnant lady pushing a child in a stroller.

She stopped and started over, not sure what she was looking for but feeling triumphant nonetheless. Jenny Dielman had made it to the store. Whatever had kept her from returning home had happened afterward.

Jo settled back onto her heels and let the DVD roll through more customers coming and going, half an hour's worth, before she saw Jenny Dielman again.

There she was, pushing out the glass doors. She carried a large plastic bag in one hand, the glint of keys in the other, her purse slung over her shoulder.

She exited alone.

Jo watched intently, checking those who emerged after her—an elderly woman, a mother tugging a child's hand—but no one appeared to be stalking Jenny.

After replaying Jenny's entrance and exit half a dozen times more, she shut off the TV, the sudden quiet enveloping her.

She sat on the floor, chewing on her cheek.

If only the store had working cameras in the parking lot, maybe she'd understand what came next. Could Jenny have been jacked, forced into her car and driven somewhere? What if she'd been abducted by a rapist, a killer?

But Jo did have something now, more than she'd had this morning. She knew that Jenny had done exactly what she'd told her husband she was going to do: she'd gone shopping at the Warehouse Club shortly after 5:00 p.m. She had left a half hour later.

"You don't know her. She never would have stayed out all night without telling me."

"Jennifer is very vulnerable. I'd hate to think that someone took advantage of that."

"She had a lot going on in her head. Some of it was real, and some was pure fiction. Maybe that's what happens when you hurt as much as she did."

"I hardly knew Jenny at all, except to say that, whatever Jenny's done, I'm sure she brought it on herself."

Jo drew her knees up to her chin. She wanted to get inside Jenny's head, to feel as she'd felt. She'd tragically lost her only son. She'd found Patrick Dielman while on the rebound from a fractured first marriage. She was on medication for PTSD with a possible history of a suicide attempt or OD. Her current husband had controlled their money and their relationship.

Had Jenny decided she'd made another mistake? That her second marriage wasn't any better than the first?

"I hardly knew Jenny at all."

Was she suicidal or a victim of circumstance?

"Patrick wouldn't break his vows . . . he's a decent man."

Jo had run Patrick Dielman through the system, and Lisa Barton, too, coming up with zilch. Neither of them had a criminal record. There was nothing to make Jo doubt they were anything but what they appeared to be.

She let out a slow breath.

She'd done enough for one day. She needed sleep.

Getting to her feet, she switched off the lamps. Then she went into the bedroom and took off her robe. Adam had left a white T-shirt behind, tossed over the back of a chair. Impulsively, she pulled it over her head. Before she crawled into bed, she ran a brush through her mess of nearly dry curls; then she shut off the lights.

The rain tapped on the roof and the windows as she sat in bed and tackled phone messages. The first was from Terry, checking up on her and inviting her for Thanksgiving. She thought of Hank's invitation and groaned. Was she on everyone's pity list?

The second voice mail was from Adam.

"Man, but you're a hard woman to get ahold of," he said in that rumbly voice. "I feel like I dreamed you last night. When you get a chance, call, okay? Tell me that I didn't make you up."

Despite how tired she was, Jo dialed Adam's number. He picked up on the first ring.

"I'm real," she said, not even bothering with hello.

"You sure?"

"Do dreams have hickeys?" she asked, and he laughed. "Can you come over?"

"I wish I could." He sounded beat. "I'm working late. You'd think the bad weather would slow things down, but I haven't seen it. How about tomorrow night?"

Jo bit her lip. "Yes, please."

"You still like music without words?" he asked, his voice graveled.

"You still like sauce so hot it turns your ears purple?"

He laughed again. "Damn, but I've missed you."

"I've missed you, too," Jo whispered.

Then she switched off the table lamp and closed her eyes.

I was shelving at the library yesterday when I smelled it: the baby powder and little-boy scent that was Finn. I stepped around the stacks to see a woman leading a child toward the picture books, and the rush of hope I'd felt vanished as I realized my mistake.

I came home to a quiet house. Patrick would be at work for hours. I dug a pair of Finn's pajamas from a box in the closet and drew them to my face. His scent was still buried in the fabric. I held them and rocked back and forth, just as I'd rocked him so many times as an infant. I let myself cry until I couldn't cry anymore.

Patrick wants me to give away Finn's things, but I can't do it.

I took Finn's teddy bear to bed with me last night, despite Patrick's protests. I had another of my unsettling dreams and awoke in the dark, reaching for Pat, but he wasn't there. I heard his voice, as faint as a whisper, and I wandered up the hallway, looking for him.

He was in the kitchen, standing in the dark.

"She's so broken," he was saying. "I'm not sure I can do this. Can you help me?"

Was he talking about me? Who was he on the phone with?

I must have made a noise, because Patrick suddenly got quiet.

"Jenny?" he said, and he switched on the light above the kitchen sink.

"Who was that?" I asked as he palmed his phone.

"Wrong number," he said, but I knew that wasn't true.

Dear God, did I marry another liar?

CHAPTER SEVEN
WEDNESDAY

The local news with its perky morning anchors babbled from the television as Jo perched on the sofa and tugged on her boots. In between the right foot and the left, she glanced up, catching the blonde on Channel 8 mention a Plainfield woman gone missing.

She'd hardly blinked, and a photo of Jenny Dielman appeared to the right of the talking head. It was the picture that Patrick Dielman had given her, only cropped to zero in on Jenny's face and the cat tucked beneath her chin.

Jo let her boot fall to the floor and reached for the remote to turn up the sound.

"According to Plainfield resident Patrick Dielman, who contacted our 'On Your Side' reporter, his wife, Jennifer, never returned home from a shopping trip to the Warehouse Club in Town and Country Center on Monday evening shortly after five p.m. Jenny is five feet five inches tall and weighs approximately a hundred twenty pounds. She has shoulder-length brown hair and brown eyes. She was wearing a black coat, a gray fleece pullover, and blue jeans at the time of her disappearance. She was driving a dark red Nissan 240SX. If you've seen Jenny Dielman or know of her whereabouts, please contact the Plainfield Police Department at—"

Jo quickly flipped channels and found similar reports airing on several other stations. She wasn't usually a big fan of the media—she didn't know many cops who were—but in this case, getting the story on the air and into every house in the metro area at this juncture might make a difference in tracking down Jenny sooner rather than later. The more awareness there was about the missing woman, the better chance there was at finding her alive.

If Patrick Dielman hadn't gone to the media, Jo was sure the department would have. Jenny had been missing for more than thirty-six hours at this point. Where was she?

Had she been the one who'd bashed in Lisa Barton's window last night? If so, where had she gone? And why would she hide?

Jo was big on gut feelings, and something about this whole mess didn't jibe.

She shut off the TV and finished dressing. She clipped her cell to her jeans and slipped on the leather harness for her .38. The revolver was hers—all officers on the Plainfield force owned the weapons they carried—and this one barely met the criteria for allowable firearms. But it fit her hand like a glove. Besides, in her two years here, she hadn't been forced to use it, so it seemed more a symbol than anything else.

She zipped up an insulated nylon jacket, drawing on the hood to protect herself against the chill. Then she scooped up her bag with the DVD from the Warehouse Club stashed inside and was on her way to the station house. About a block away, her cell went off.

She dialed back Dispatch.

"What's up, Susie?"

"Where are you?"

"Around the corner." She could see the flag fluttering from the pole above the station's roofline.

"A couple morning hikers found an abandoned vehicle at the quarry, off the old farm route."

"What vehicle are we talking about?"

"A red Nissan 240SX with plates that match those of Jennifer Dielman. We've already got a couple cars on location and a crime scene van from the county on the way."

Jo's mouth went dry.

They'd found Jenny's car.

"Detective Phelps is waiting on you at the station."

"I'm pulling into the parking lot now."

Jo hung up and covered the last block quickly, driving around the back of the building to find an open space.

Abandoned.

The old limestone quarry stretched over a hundred acres. That was a lot of territory to cover, a lot of places for someone to hide, or for someone to hide a body.

If Jenny wasn't in her car, where was she?

◆ ◆ ◆

Hank's Ford bumped over the gravel road, jostling the car so roughly that Jo was afraid she'd smack her head on the roof. She braced her hands against the dash and still her teeth clacked together every time they bounced through a pothole.

Last night's rain hadn't helped matters any. The unpaved path would have been bad enough without the water to soften up the sloppy mix of dirt and gravel. It also was narrow, pretty much impossible for another car to pass without one vehicle having to drive onto the sloping shoulder.

The Ford hit a crater, sending a spray of brown into the air, splattering the windshield, shaking Jo's innards.

"Hey!"

"I'm doing the best I can," Hank muttered in his defense.

No wonder the quarry was abandoned—it was literally a pain in the ass to reach.

She gazed out the window around them.

There were scrubby pines far taller than those in the well-trafficked areas of town, thickly mixed with underbrush on either side of the rutted road that had once been used to haul tons of limestone to the now-defunct railroad depot. They'd already bypassed what seemed like the last vestiges of civilization: oversized realty signs at turnoffs that advertised lots for sale or touted developments set to go up in the next year or two, **Priced in the Low 400,000s!** Like that was a bargain for living out in the middle of nowhere.

"The city bought the property a while back but hasn't done much except parcel off pieces to developers," Hank said out of the blue. "Give it a few years, and this'll be as busy as Main Street."

She glanced at her watch and groaned at the amount of time that had passed since they'd left the station. "Are we almost there?" she asked.

Hank grinned. "You sound like my kids."

"It feels like we're nearly to Sherman." They hit another hole and took a jolt that banged her shoulder into the door. "C'mon, watch it, would you?"

"How about I push the little lever that makes the wings pop out? Then we can fly the rest of the way there."

"Smart ass," Jo said and turned back to the window.

Land ahoy.

She made out a chain-link fence farther up the road. As they neared, she could read a weather-beaten sign fastened to the metal railing: **Private Property of Rose Stone Company. Trespassers Keep Out.**

Maybe the warning had seemed fierce once, but the paint-peeled letters and cockeyed angle of the sign hardly intimidated now. The gates stood wide open, one side so badly bent it looked ready to fall off the hinges. A battered realty sign dangled. Someone had taken potshots at it with a paint gun, and it bore more than a fleeting resemblance to a Jackson Pollock painting.

Discarded trash had accumulated at the base of the fence. Soda cans, beer bottles, fast-food bags, and wrappers littered the ground and clung to the wire mesh, evidence of years of neglect, of how long the place had been forgotten by anyone who'd given a rat's ass.

Visible furrows in the soggy gravel road made her glance ahead. She spotted the cars parked farther in.

Hank slowed to a near crawl as they entered the grounds. "Hail, hail, the gang's all here," he said, and Jo squinted, trying to see who'd made it already.

There were two blue-and-whites, the colors faded against the gray. She didn't see the van from the county crime lab, but she could pick out a mud-splotched Jeep Cherokee on the other side of the squad cars. Beyond that appeared to be a rocky hillside, unnatural in the middle of nowhere: massive tons of residue dug from the quarry below.

"So it's a hundred acres, right?" she said, straining against the straps of the seat belt to look around her.

"A hundred twenty," Hank corrected.

"Swell."

How would they ever find Jenny if she—or what remained of her—was somewhere on the property? They'd have to call in the K-9 units, maybe even volunteers.

Immediately on the other side of the fence, she saw decrepit sheds and trailers with windows boarded up or missing altogether. Truck parts were scattered, bringing to mind dinosaur bones partially submerged in the earth after millions of years. Even without the post-storm gloom, it would have looked spooky, like a ghost town.

Jo wondered if Jenny had felt the same prickle of apprehension as she'd driven through the gates, the same sense of dread. Then again, she'd probably been in no position to see anything at all. Mostly likely, she'd been tied up, knocked out, or already dead.

As Hank coaxed the Ford over the ruts toward the other vehicles, Jo stared out the window at the mess the rain had made of the ground. Potholes had become puddles, and gravel had turned to slop.

Would they be able to find any sort of physical trail? A set of tread marks? Footprints? Or had it all been obliterated in Mother Nature's spit bath?

She gently bumped her head against the glass.

Damn, damn, damn.

As soon as Hank stopped the car, she got out.

The cold quickly seeped through her lined nylon jacket. She tugged the zipper up beneath her chin and locked her bag with the copy of the Warehouse Club security footage in the trunk. Then she started toward the blue-and-whites, toward the officers in dark jackets and caps and a young couple huddled together, wearing what looked like standard REI gear and backpacks.

With every step, her boots sank into mush. It felt like slogging through oatmeal. The ground sucked on her shoe, then released it, returning to its gooey consistency without leaving an impression. She shoved her hands into her pockets, raking her eyes over the mess beneath her feet and cursing.

Hank caught up with her, passing her a pair of latex gloves. She reluctantly pulled them on, wishing they were warm and fuzzy, not thin and slick. They stuck to her skin and sealed in the chill despite the powdery residue that coated her fingers, increasing her discomfort.

Hank frowned as he rolled a pair onto his big hands.

Jo cut between the squad cars and approached a familiar face that peered out from beneath a ball cap. She nodded at Officer Charlotte Ramsey.

"What'd you see when you arrived?" she asked.

"We were careful, Detectives," Ramsey assured them. "We didn't want to screw up any potential tracks, so we parked outside the gate and came on foot and recorded the scene before we brought the cars in. But the pair in the Jeep had been here awhile. They saw the Nissan when they arrived and thought it didn't feel right, but went about their hike first. The Nissan was still there when they got back, so they poked around and found a woman's purse and a shopping bag on the backseat. The keys were in the ignition. They popped the trunk, and it was empty. Then they called 911."

Keys in the ignition.

Purse and shopping bag.

Empty trunk.

Jo flashed on something Dr. Patil had said: *"The human mind is a tricky piece of machinery. It's hard to anticipate what anyone might do from one day to the next, even the most rational human being, but especially those under severe psychological stress. I didn't sense that Jenny was ready to give up, not . . ."*

Not what? Today? Not tomorrow?

"We've got no tire tracks we can use, no impressions of footwear because the ground's too wet, and a pair of kids whose fingerprints are probably all over the vehicle?" Hank glared at Officer Ramsey, like it was her fault.

She shrugged in apology.

"Never happens like this on TV," he grumbled. "They examine crime scenes without turning on the lights, and they still always find more than we do."

Jo tuned out his complaints and looked around, spotting Ramsey's partner, Jorge Rameriz, carefully walking the perimeter around the Nissan. Every so often, he'd stop and take a photograph or squat to check something on the ground with a gloved hand. She recognized the two uniforms, Duncan and Arguiles, talking to the nervous-looking couple, taking notes.

"Their names?" Jo asked.

"The hikers?" Ramsey checked the small notebook in her jacket pocket. "Tim Burke and Cindy Chow. They're students at UTD."

"They come here often?"

"Ms. Chow said they'd heard about the quarry from some friends and wanted to check it out this morning since they didn't have classes."

"They didn't see anyone while they were walking?" Jo glanced around at the thicket of brush and pines that surrounded them, at the huge wall of rock and mud that sloped up from the enormous hole in the ground barely fifty yards away. From where they stood, she could just make out the rim.

"Nothing but deer," Ramsey replied.

Where was Jenny? She could be anywhere.

Jo sighed impatiently, wishing the evidence techs would show. She wanted to get going, to start searching for Jenny.

"You okay, Detective?"

"I'm dandy," she told Ramsey, wishing her voice didn't so openly betray her anxiety, her mounting frustration at finding the car but no victim. She headed toward where Rameriz slowly circled the Nissan with the camera. "You take a look inside?" she asked him.

He stopped and faced her, his dark eyes sober. "We didn't want to disturb the scene more than we had to, considering those two had already been in the car with their muddy boots." He winced. "I did a quick visual to make sure they were correct about no one being inside the vehicle or the trunk."

"You see any blood? Any sign of a struggle?"

He shook his head. "No, ma'am, nothing overt."

Jo pressed her lips together, hands on hips, looking over the Nissan, its deep-red hue dimmed by splotches of dust the rain had left behind.

The soft, yellow earth of the quarry grounds stuck in the tire grooves. Handprints smudged the windows, though she could make out the white Warehouse Club bag in the back along with a brown purse.

Her stomach clenched, and she exhaled slowly, hoping the techs would find something—blood, semen, hairs, clothing fibers—anything that would give them an idea of what had happened and who they were dealing with.

"We'll print the two hikers to rule them out, of course."

"Of course," she repeated.

She stared past the car to the spot where the wall of the quarry rose skyward like a giant anthill, and she wondered how to get to the bottom of the pit.

The atmosphere smelled raw, chalky. She breathed it in, tasted it on her tongue. It made her want to spit. She couldn't imagine coming here day in and day out, digging and bringing up rocks to haul away so that someone could build their house out of limestone. How did it feel to be down there? It had to be like standing in a grave.

She heard the crunch of tires on gravel, and she turned to see the white van from the crime lab pulling in through the gates.

Brown stained its sides, filth kicked up from the muddy, unpaved path they'd had to take. All the cars looked that way.

Well, all the cars but the Nissan.

There was less brown and more yellow within the tire wells and near the base of the car between the wheels, which told her it had been parked before the rain. Had the vehicle been driven directly to the quarry from the Warehouse Club, or had Jenny stopped somewhere else first? Maybe she'd picked someone up. Would she have given a ride to a hitchhiker?

The slam of doors broke through her thoughts as two people exited the van, carrying large black cases. She recognized the woman but not the man, and she managed a smile as the former strode briskly toward her.

"Hey, Emma," she said, and Emma Slater nodded. "Why do I feel better at the sight of you?"

"Nice to see you again, Detective Larsen." Sharp eyes blinked from within the soft folds of skin that pleated deeply at the corners. The gray cap of Emma's hair didn't even budge with a gust of wind.

Emma worked in the same place as Adam, since both the county ME's office and the crime lab were located in one squat building on the south campus of Parkland Hospital in Dallas. If Emma Slater knew anything about Jo's involvement with Adam, nothing in her face gave it away.

"That the vehicle? The red two-door?"

"Yes."

"No sign of the driver?" Emma had set down her case and was pulling on a smock and thick, blue latex gloves. Her cohort did the same before retrieving a camera of his own, a fancy-looking digital with a zoom lens.

"The missing woman's keys, purse, and shopping bag are inside the car," Jo told her. "I'm thinking there could be blood evidence or fluids that would indicate she was assaulted inside the vehicle."

Emma gave a nod. "We'll do what we can here. Then we'll tow the car to the impound lot and finish up there. We're pretty backed up, but I'll try to call you with the preliminary report in a day or two."

"Any chance you've looked at that silk scarf yet?" Jo asked. Hank had done the incident report last night and made sure the evidence got to the lab. She hoped for something that would tell her whether Jenny had anything to do with Lisa Barton's broken window.

Emma gave a curt shake of her head. "Sorry, no."

Jo hadn't expected it but felt disappointed nonetheless. "Hey, don't let me hold you up," she said, and left them to their business.

Hank was talking to the hikers, who were pointing across the way, toward the trees where they'd doubtless been walking.

Jo had something else on her mind.

She took a stroll toward the quarry, looking for the path leading down. She approached the edge and stopped.

Her breath lodged in her throat as she surveyed the basin at least fifty feet below. The water glowed an iridescent green. Detritus floated on its surface. If there was anything down there, she couldn't tell from where she stood.

She followed the rim for about half a dozen yards until she saw where the pit began to slope. She finally picked out a rather sloppy-looking trail descending into the enormous hole and started toward it.

"Larsen!"

She heard Hank call out, but she kept going, moving carefully as she went. Her boots found meager traction in the muck, and she skidded suddenly, grabbing hold of a hank of brush growing from the muddy wall. She stopped and steadied herself. No damage done.

Roots protruded from the sides of the pit, sticking out between rocks, weeds, and dirt, and she clutched at them with latex-gloved fingers whenever she could, winding her way deeper into the earth.

She descended slowly, sensing an eternity had passed before she'd even gone ten yards, and she already felt warm with perspiration. She brushed at her face with the sleeve of her jacket, the nylon sliding across her skin.

She tried to peer down into the cavity, though her vantage point was less than perfect. A haze thickened the air, made the quarry look even more foreign, like the surface of an alien moon. She searched for colored clothing against the drab backdrop, hoping to spot something out of place. Then she reminded herself that Jenny had been wearing a dark coat and denim, dull tones that matched the landscape.

Was Jenny even here? Or was she somewhere in the thick of pines? Could she still be alive? Could she hear them?

Jo suddenly had such a strong sense Jenny Dielman was near that her heart slapped against her ribs. She was breathing hard, her breath loud in her ears.

She resumed her descent, her boots ankle-deep in sludge, the bottoms of her jeans already caked with the stuff.

"Christ, Jo, wait up!"

She ignored him.

"You never got the hang of the buddy system, did you?" Her partner's voice strained through his huffs and puffs.

She stopped, holding on to rock as she turned to glance back. "I'm waiting already."

Hank picked his way toward her, still quite a ways back. He was all awkward movements and curses.

Not a bright idea, she thought as she watched him. He wasn't in any shape to be hiking, not under these abysmal conditions, with the rain-soaked ground so treacherous.

"Hank, don't," she nearly protested, but clamped her mouth shut. What was the point? He wouldn't listen. Hey, it was his neck. It was his business if he wanted to break it.

Despite how eager she was to get to the bottom, she waited for her partner. The humidity hung thick, a wet blanket on her skin.

When he finally made it, he was panting, his face an ugly shade of purple that worried her. He had a walkie-talkie clipped to his coat, and she figured they might need to use it if he had a heart attack.

"What the hell possessed you?" she asked him, watching as he caught hold of a jutting root in the earthen wall and put his other hand on his knee, gulping in air. "And going down's the easy part. Just think how you'll feel when you have to climb up. We'll need a rope and a backboard to haul you to the top."

He muttered something between breaths. She couldn't decipher what it was, though she had a fair idea.

"Slow and steady, all right? Follow me," she told him and faced the path again, knowing she couldn't watch out for him and for herself, too.

She'd only taken a few steps when she heard Hank grunt behind her and felt the weight of him against her back. She lost her footing, the sole of her boot skidding across a slick patch. Her legs came up from beneath her. Arms flailing, she tried to grab hold of something—anything—to keep from falling.

She clutched air.

She went down hard, slapping onto her butt and twisting sideways, shoulder hitting the ground and knocking the wind from her lungs before she began to slide. The mud and gravel were like a moveable beast, propelling her downward over rocks and twigs that scratched and snatched at her clothing and hair.

For a few breathless minutes, she simply flew, unable to stop. Her vision blurred. She heard Hank yelling and another cry as well that could've been her own. Then she hit a rock and pitched forward.

She threw up her arms to protect herself and landed face-first in a low pool of freezing-cold murky green.

Jo quickly pulled her head up, sputtering for breath. Dazed and unsteady, she spat the foul taste from her mouth and blinked open her eyes. Debris swam on the water's surface, a tangle of sticks and leaves. Moisture dripped from her hair, cutting rings into the cloudy pool of green.

Her mind scrambled to focus and filter out the voices she heard from above, drawing closer. She shook her head like a dog, a chill rushing through her body. Then her vision cleared.

She saw the hair first, dark wings undulating on the surface like nut-colored seaweed, then a flash of white.

No.

Something clicked in her brain, twisted in her gut.

She made out a gray pullover, nearly disguised by the tangle of weeds. Brown strands floated away from pale skin, and she could see a wide-open eye, staring at her glassily.

Jenny?

She wanted to shout the name, but couldn't.

Anger closed up her throat, choking her into silence.

"Jo! Can you stand? Are you hurt?"

Arms reached for her and pulled her up, mud and water sucking at her as Hank drew her hard onto her feet. A fissure of pain shot through her left shoulder, down her leg on the same side, but she was unable to take her eyes off the body.

She knew it was Jenny, without a doubt.

Hank's voice filled her ears, asking over and over if she was okay.

"It's her," she said.

"Christ," he hissed, realizing what she meant.

He sloshed through the water, trying to find what she saw. He parted floating twigs and leaves with his shins, cursing before ripping the walkie-talkie from his collar and yelling into it, "We've got a DB down here in shin-deep water. It looks like our girl."

Hearing him say it aloud made Jo's head spin, helplessness and rage coursing through her. She felt furious at the world for its unfairness and at herself for what she couldn't fix.

She stumbled to drier ground and sank down, arms around her knees, shivering so hard, she thought she'd be sick. She didn't stop shaking until much later: after the medical examiner had arrived on the scene with more officers and klieg lights that filled the quarry with ultrabright beams; after the crime scene techs had done all they could with the Nissan and waded through the weeds and brush and pool of water on the floor of the crater with the impossible task of finding any trace material in the area where the body had been dumped; after the squawk of walkie-talkies and sirens and shouts had stopped ringing in her ears.

She couldn't even remember who had put a blanket around her shoulders and removed the shredded gloves from her fingers, cleaning up the cuts and scrapes on her hands and face, plucking twigs and leaves from her hair, and testing her left shoulder to see if she'd dislocated it. Her ribs hurt where her holster had dug into her side. The nylon shell of her jacket had torn at the right-hand pocket, though her mud-caked jeans had survived.

Survived.

Damn.

She knew she'd be fine despite her bumps and bruises. Sore ligaments and aching bones had never killed anyone. Jenny Dielman had not been as lucky. She'd been shot through the right temple at point-blank range with a small-caliber weapon.

They'd found a waterlogged Jennings .22 semiautomatic near where she lay. The serial number had been filed off.

Jo had been taught early on that the evidence told the story and, until it was processed, any theories were just that. But she was sure of this much: a woman was dead. Jenny Dielman was no longer a missing person. She was a statistic, a body headed to the morgue to be toe-tagged. The loose ends of her life would be filed away in a three-ring binder.

Her effects had been bagged and tagged by the crime scene unit, each item carefully logged and destined for the lab. A bracelet-type watch had been present on her left wrist, and a wedding band and diamond solitaire on her ring finger, which tossed out any theories of a robbery.

Did the gun belong to Jenny? Why the filed-off serial number, something they saw mostly with stolen weapons?

It made absolutely zero sense.

From the Nissan, they'd retrieved a brown leather Coach purse complete with matching wallet, a few credit cards, a state license issued to Jennifer Jane Dielman, and twenty dollars cash. Her cell phone was there, too, the battery dead. They had a white Warehouse Club shopping bag filled with several purchases, including an enormous jar of peanut butter, a case of Fancy Feast cat food, and a twelve-pack of Kleenex.

There didn't appear to be bloodstains anywhere on the gray fabric seats or in the trunk on the carpeting. There was nothing to suggest Jenny Dielman had been shot and killed in her car. Jo had to wonder if Jenny had been forced to drive here. But then how did the perpetrator get away? If he'd hoofed it, he'd had a long, long walk ahead of him. Did an accomplice follow them? Or had Jenny come alone?

And where did that blue scarf fit into this?

Jo had her doubts that Jenny had been anywhere near Lisa Barton's last night. Something about this whole thing stank to high heaven.

"Hey."

She looked up at Hank. He watched her with an unblinking squint.

"You okay to go see Patrick Dielman?"

"Sure." Her voice sounded rough, liked she'd swallowed some of the gravel that she'd ridden on her way down into the pit. "I'm good," she told him, though she could barely smother her grimace as she pushed off the Ford's hood.

He eyed her skeptically.

She beat down his stare with a flinty one of her own. "If I said I'm fine, then I'm fine."

God, he was just like Terry. He never believed her. What did they want from her, a signed note from her doctor?

"I've got her watch and wedding ring bagged." He patted his coat pocket. "The ME found that butterfly tattoo on her hip that you mentioned. Dielman can visit the morgue if he needs more convincing."

Jo nodded.

According to the medical examiner, the body had been well preserved by temps in the forties, which acted like a refrigerant. The water had done little damage, mostly wrinkling the skin, the same prunelike effect from taking a very long bath. Except for a cut on her tongue and the split skin around the entrance wound at her right temple, Jennifer Dielman didn't have a visible blemish. There were no indications she'd been beaten or forcibly subdued. There were no ligature marks at her wrists, no handprints from bruising, and no signs of blunt-force trauma.

"I have a feeling he's going to want to see to believe," she said.

Hank grunted. "I'd need that, too." He ran a hand over his thinning hair. "But a gunshot to the head isn't pretty, no matter how it's inflicted."

No matter how it's inflicted.

Jo had headed toward the passenger door and paused to eye him over the car's roof. "You're thinking suicide?"

He jiggled the keys. "Aren't you?"

She struggled to put into words the niggling sense of doubt, the visceral reaction somewhere deep inside that fought the idea that Jenny had killed herself. But she couldn't tell him that she just didn't want it to be. "How things look on the surface isn't always reality."

"And sometimes a cigar is just a cigar."

She hugged her arms around herself. "It goes against everything we've been taught."

It was an unwritten rule that women didn't take their own lives by shooting themselves in the head, and Hank knew it. Though times were changing and methods of violence were evolving, which could be what had him thinking the rules didn't apply anymore.

"I don't have the answer any more than you do, Jo."

Something else came to mind, something that made her question the notion of suicide. "Where's the locket she supposedly wore every waking hour?" Jo asked. "And where's her coat? I saw her wearing it in the Warehouse Club video. Techs didn't find either one."

"She wasn't robbed," Hank said deliberately. "She's still wearing her rings and her watch, and the rest is in the car—her keys, her purse, even her purchases. Maybe she lost the necklace somewhere. Could still be in that pit, and we just didn't find it."

"And her coat?"

Hank sighed. "Looks to me like this was personal. Maybe so personal, it didn't involve anyone else but the victim."

No, Jo wanted to argue. *That's not how it went down.*

But she didn't have the evidence to back it up.

She took a deep breath and held it as she turned away to see movement against the mist of gray. A drizzle had begun to fall. Red taillights flickered as vehicles headed out. She heard the slam of doors, the call of voices, and the grind of the lift drawing the Nissan onto the tow.

She got into the Ford and tugged on her seat belt.

Hank started the engine and put the car in gear, though the wheels spun in the muck before they found traction. This time, they were part of a small caravan, an exodus as solemn as a funeral procession.

Suicide.

Is that what happened, Jenny? With the anniversary of Finn's death so close, did you decide you had nothing left to live for? Did you come out to this godforsaken place to find your peace?

She turned to Hank and started to open her mouth, to insist that it was insane to assume Jenny Dielman would have driven out to oblivion, walked down into a rain-swollen pit, put a gun to her head, and pulled the trigger.

But how could Jo explain that her sense of unease came from a place inside her that he'd never seen, the part of her that had thought more than once about what it would be like to stop living and find the same kind of peace that Jenny had craved?

So instead she clammed up and faced the window.

The haunted eyes in the photograph flashed in her head.

What if Hank were right?

She realized she was gritting her teeth and forced her jaw to relax, though the rest of her was tighter than a tick.

She stared at the landscape, finding it a lonely place. The sky was dim. It was hard to tell what time it was. If she hadn't known better, she would have sworn it was dusk and not just a bleak fall day, one that was about to get bleaker.

I tell Sally I need a break, and I step outside, cell phone in hand. My legs wobble as I walk to the concrete bench around the side of the library. No one is there that I can see. It's private enough for what I need.

I take a few deep breaths before I dial the number and hear the first ring. But then I chicken out. Before the second ring, I hang up, my heart pounding.

You can't be afraid, I tell myself. Finn's counting on you. If you don't do this, who will?

I take a few more deep breaths until I settle down and go back inside.

"Are you all right?" Sally asks.

I wonder if my nerves show in my face. I try hard to smile.

"I'm fine," I say. "I just had to call the vet about Ernie. He needs to have his teeth cleaned. He's not going to like it."

Sally laughs. "Good luck with that."

I'm still shaking when I sit down at my desk and put my phone back in my purse. How long can I wait until I work up the courage to let the phone ring until the voice says, "Hello?" For me to find the words that I must say?

"Tell me again," I will ask. "Tell me what happened that night when you let our son die."

I will listen, and he will lie all over again.

But this time, I won't believe him.

CHAPTER EIGHT

The Dielmans' house on Ella Drive looked pretty much the same as it had the night before, although this time, there were lights in the windows.

The one-story ranch with its yellow trim and neat yard gave a hopeful appearance, despite the drizzle. A shiny BMW sedan was parked on the semicircular drive. Its white surface glowed like polished bone against the gray backdrop.

That was Patrick's car, Jo knew. It was much newer and fancier than the Nissan that had belonged to Jenny.

"Are you ready?" Hank asked, palming his keys as he looked at her.

"Give me a minute, okay?"

She had a chill she couldn't shake. Despite the heat from the floor vents, she still hadn't dried out completely. Her jeans felt clammy against her thighs. She'd done her best to comb her hair and scrape the yellow mud from her shoes and clothes, but it didn't take more than a cursory glance into the rearview mirror to see she'd been on the losing end of a fight.

Part of her wanted to go home, take a shower, and bury herself beneath the blankets on her bed, forgetting what she'd seen. Her body didn't hurt near as much as her psyche. She had so hoped to find Jenny Dielman alive.

She huddled inside her insulated jacket and peered through the rain-spattered window at the house, at its stillness.

"Did I ever tell you the wife and I checked out a place in this neighborhood?" Hank remarked, slinging an arm over the back of the seat. He let out a low whistle. "You wouldn't believe how much some of these babies go for. I mean, what would you expect to pay for fifteen hundred square feet?"

"Two hundred grand."

"Try three."

Jo rubbed her arms, sensing stiffness in her left shoulder. "Sounds like a lot of debt to me."

"It's called upward mobility."

"I've got a fear of heights."

He said something about trailer parks and Jerry Springer, but she wasn't listening. She stared at a Japanese maple no higher than six or seven feet that had lost nearly all of its bright red leaves. Then she looked over at a large bay window in the front of the house. She saw movement at the curtains and a pale face, watching.

A charge went up her spine. "We've been made," she said through chattering teeth.

He leaned forward, looking past her, before the curtains dropped. "Damn, I hate this," he said and opened his door.

Jo smelled the damp before he slammed the door shut. The car swayed beneath her.

Slowly, she unbuckled her seat belt and let the straps slip away. She took another quick peek at herself in the rearview, hoping she didn't freak out Dielman with her less-than-pristine appearance. Deciding there wasn't much she could do about it, she followed her partner toward the front door.

As Hank reached out to ring the bell, the door swung inward, and Patrick Dielman stood before them. His yellow button-down shirt hung over a pair of wrinkled gray trousers. He wore dark socks but no shoes. His eyes were red-rimmed, his cheeks unshaven.

He looked a shell of the polished man who'd insisted Jo listen to him yesterday morning. She imagined he'd stayed up all night, pacing, calling Jenny's cell phone, hoping to hear her voice, lying down on Jenny's side of the bed, holding her pillow, and breathing in the smell of her.

"We need to speak to you, sir," Hank finally said, and Jo was glad he broke the silence.

"You found her," the man stated simply, and she realized he'd sensed on some level that this was coming.

"Can we talk in private, Mr. Dielman?" she said.

Dielman stared past them, his chest rising and falling so quickly, a tiny twitch at his jaw. Was he thinking that if he kept them out, he could change what they would tell him?

God, how Jo wished she were anywhere but here.

"May we come in, sir?" Hank tried again.

"I'm sorry. I'm not myself." Dielman stepped back to let them enter.

Jo walked into the well-lit foyer, her boots clicking on the marble tiles.

The dining room was to her left, the living room dead ahead. A hallway led off to the right, doubtless to the bedrooms.

"Can I get you anything?" Dielman asked as he closed the door. "Something to drink?"

Jo's heart sank at the question, at his instinct to play the good host when they were here to give him the worst news of his life.

"No," Hank answered for them. "We're fine. Is there somewhere we can sit down?"

Dielman nodded. "This way."

Jo followed the two men, noting the beige paint and wall-to-wall carpeting that gave no sense of the personality of the couple who'd lived there. She took the steps down into a sunken living room. The oak furniture appeared to be a suite put together by the manufacturer; no crazy, old upholstered pieces or anything resembling antiques. The framed prints hung too high were ones she'd seen so often in retail stores they seemed generic.

Where was Jenny? Where was her footprint? Or was she plain vanilla like the house?

What Jo could see told her nothing except the Dielmans' decorating sense was unimaginative, though she had a feeling this was more a reflection of the husband than his wife.

She paid careful attention as well to the state of the rooms. Nothing disturbed or out of place. No tracks of yellow mud on the carpet.

"Can we call anyone for you, sir?" Hank was asking as he sat in a club chair close to the one Dielman had taken.

"Call someone?"

"A friend or neighbor? You might want someone with you."

Dielman ignored the question, turning to Jo. She shifted on her feet, too anxious to sit. "So she's dead?" he asked. "That's why you're here, isn't it?"

"Yes, sir, I'm sorry." Jo didn't know what else to say, how else to tell him when he obviously felt it in his bones.

"How?" he said next, a catch in his voice.

She glanced at Hank. He had slipped the evidence bag with Jenny Dielman's wristwatch and rings from his coat pocket and set it on the coffee table between himself and Patrick Dielman.

"The apparent cause of death is a gunshot wound to the head," Jo told him, swift and clean, wanting to make this go faster. "But we're awaiting the autopsy to get all the facts."

Dielman picked up the plastic bag and held it in his lap, fingering the contents. He sucked in a quick breath. "These are hers," he said.

"She had a butterfly tattoo on her hip," Jo informed him quietly, "and she was wearing the clothing you described."

"My God," he murmured, shaking his head. "My God, it's real. You see it on news and in the movies, and you never imagine it will touch your own life. But it has, hasn't it?"

Jo resented how helpless she felt. She watched Dielman's face as he handled the baggie, pushing the wedding band into the corner. A strangled noise escaped his throat, and he pressed the bag against his wrinkled shirt.

"No, Jenny, no," he choked out her name. "This can't be real. How can it be true? I thought finding her scarf . . . that it meant she might be . . . somewhere."

He shoved the baggie at Hank as he looked up. "This can't be happening. I want her back," he barked. "I want her safe and sound. I should have protected her."

"Sir, please, can we call someone, a friend who might stay with you?" Hank suggested. He scooted forward in the chair and drew his cell phone from his coat.

Dielman rubbed his eyes. "Jenny isn't coming home, is she?" he asked, as if it might be a bad dream and he'd wake up to find them gone and his wife beside him. "She's really dead?"

"Yes," Hank said, putting his phone away. "She's not coming home, sir. I'm sorry."

Dielman nodded jerkily.

Jo couldn't keep still another moment. She walked away from Hank's chair, pausing behind the sofa table with its display of silver-framed photographs. She fingered the largest one, a wedding picture with a grinning groom in tux and tails and a pretty bride in a calf-length ivory dress with a ring of flowers in her hair.

They never knew, did they? They never thought for a moment as they celebrated with champagne and cake that things could go so wrong, so fast.

"Where was she?" Dielman asked in a scratchy whisper. "Was she alone?"

"Her car was discovered by two hikers in an abandoned quarry north of town," Hank said. "We found her"—he hesitated, and Jo knew that he was avoiding saying *her body*—"alone in the quarry pit. There was no one else."

"Why?" Dielman asked. "Why Jenny?"

"We'll try to sort that out, sir," Hank assured him, without making any false promises.

Jo's stomach pitched.

She distracted herself by studying the photographs, reaching for a smaller picture. Jenny had a young boy caught in her embrace: her slim arms wrapped around his skinny chest as if to keep him from squirming. Towheaded and freckled, the child grinned gleefully, showing two missing front teeth and round blue eyes behind a pair of gold-rimmed glasses. His mother's expression was ethereal, her love for her son all too evident.

Jo set the frame down and saw her hand shake.

"You said she was shot?" Dielman asked them.

"Yes," Hank said.

Dielman sat up straight. "Did you find her gun?"

"Her gun?" Hank turned to Jo, questioning. She shook her head, as clueless as he. "Your wife owned a handgun?"

"I gave it to her for protection." Dielman got out of his chair and began to pace.

"Protection from what?" Jo asked.

He hesitated. "She was scared, okay? She flinched at things I couldn't see, would jump when the phone rang." He wiped his palms on his shirtfront. "So I got her a firearm."

"Can you tell us the make and model of the weapon?"

"I don't know. Let me think." He tapped his forehead, tugged his hair. "It was a twenty-two caliber, small and easy to grip. There was nothing special about it."

"Pistol or semiautomatic?"

"It was a semiautomatic. She kept it in her glove compartment." He dropped his arms to his sides, plunked into the chair again, breathless. "Was it there? Did you find it? Did she try to defend herself?"

Jo cut a glance at Hank.

So Jenny Dielman had a .22-caliber handgun.

"Was the weapon registered to your wife?" Hank asked Dielman, keeping his voice remarkably even. "Was the serial number filed off? Did you consider that you might well have bought a stolen gun?"

"Stolen gun?" Dielman's face went blank. "No, I don't remember even looking for a serial number. That would've meant nothing to me. That's not my area of expertise. Look, I got it at a gun show in Garland. Nobody even asked for an ID so long as I paid in cash. Something like a hundred bucks. They just dropped it into a shopping bag, threw in a box of cartridges for free. She kept it loaded."

Jo groaned inwardly.

Hank didn't hesitate. "Did she have a license to carry?" Jo could tell he was trying to keep his cool, but still, her partner's voice edged up a bit.

"No." Dielman stared at his lap. "I was told she didn't need one. That if she left it in her car, it was like keeping in the house. At least, that's what the guy said."

And that was no lie. A license to carry wasn't required in Texas when the gun was purportedly stored "on one's own premises or under his control," even while traveling.

"I didn't do something wrong, did I?" Dielman blinked tear-damp lashes.

"You did nothing illegal, no," she told him. *Just completely asinine,* she left unsaid. "We need to know more about the gun. Was it a Jennings six-shot?"

That was the make of the waterlogged weapon they'd identified at the scene. It wasn't a type that turned up very often.

She waited for his answer, hardly believing this turn of events.

Did the gun belong to Jenny? Might the bullet that ricocheted merrily around her brain be a gift her dear hubby had purchased at the Garland gun show?

Dielman's face crumpled further. "A Jennings what? I don't know. I don't know. It was just a gun."

Just a gun.

"What about the guy you bought it from?" Hank suggested. "Do you remember his name? Did he give you a business card, a receipt?"

"I don't think so. I'm sorry."

Jo clenched her jaw tight, not wanting to say anything she'd regret. What good would it do to get on the man's case now? His wife was dead. Besides, as she'd assured him, he hadn't done anything illegal in buying the .22 at a gun show. Texas was one of a number of states where the Brady Bill did not apply to private dealers, making guns available to gun show customers with no questions asked.

Sort of like a big ol' garage sale.

The fact that Dielman had bought his emotionally troubled wife an unregistered handgun—one stored in the glove box of her Nissan—threw a good-size wrench into the case, for sure. Even if she didn't want to believe it, Jo realized if Jennifer Dielman's own gun was involved, it made the possibility of suicide more likely.

Hank rubbed a hand over his face, which had turned a shade of pink teetering on magenta. He muttered something that she couldn't make out. She hoped Dielman couldn't either, because she knew for sure it wasn't a compliment.

"Was she right-handed?" Jo asked, hoping to God his answer was no, despite the watch on Jenny's left wrist that implied otherwise.

He blurted out, "Yes, yes, she was."

Right-handed. Right temple.

Jo couldn't look at Hank.

"You think she shot herself?" Dielman said, catching on. "You think she drove to the quarry and used the gun I bought her to kill herself?" When neither she nor Hank responded, he choked out, "No, you're wrong. You have to be wrong. Jenny was trying to get better. She couldn't have wanted to die."

"The medical examiner will determine cause of death, Mr. Dielman, not us." Jo hoped that would suffice, that he wouldn't ask any more questions that they couldn't answer.

"We need to look for a note," Hank said. "It may be on a computer—"

"A suicide note?" Dielman cut him off.

"Yes," Jo said simply.

"She didn't—she wouldn't," Dielman stuttered, his breaths becoming more rapid. His shoulders started shaking, and a sob rushed from his throat. "I screwed up, didn't I?" he cried. "It's my fault, isn't it?"

"Please, don't do this, Mr. Dielman," Jo said, sharper than she should have. "It doesn't solve anything."

"Can I call someone for you?" Hank asked again.

"No," Dielman sobbed. "No, I don't want anyone but Jenny."

Hank looked the other way.

But Jo couldn't ignore the man. She pushed aside her frustration and went to his side, crouched beside the chair, and patted his arm.

"I'm sorry," Dielman cried. "I didn't think that she might . . . I never imagined, even though I worried about her . . . Lisa told me she didn't seem right."

"It's okay," Jo said, when it wasn't okay in the least. "Take it easy." She reminded herself to stay calm when all the while, inside, she screamed.

"We'll call her sister for you, if you'd like," she offered, but he shook his head.

"Just leave. I need to be alone."

Jo looked at Hank.

He seemed to know what she was thinking. "If it's all right with you, sir," he said, "we'd like to take a look around—"

"No." Patrick Dielman lifted his face from his hands. "No, it's not all right. My wife is dead, Detectives, and I want you to go."

Jo didn't push it.

Hank shrugged, giving up. Her partner pocketed the evidence baggie and told Dielman they'd let themselves out, but he didn't seem to hear. Patrick Dielman sat in the chair, head down, saying his wife's name again and again, completely beside himself.

Jo couldn't move, not at first, wanting to stay, knowing they should search for a note, go through Jenny's things. It was pro forma with a homicide. But what if this wasn't that? Shouldn't they let Dielman grieve in peace?

"C'mon," Hank said and nudged her from the living room into the foyer, though she dragged her heels just the same.

Despite Dielman's insistence that he didn't want them to call anyone, when they were out of earshot, Jo borrowed Hank's cell—hers was out of commission after her water landing in the quarry—and phoned Naveen Patil, asking if the doctor could drop by the house at his earliest convenience. Not only did she believe Patrick Dielman needed someone with him who'd known his wife, she figured he could use a little something from the doctor's black bag as well: a sedative to calm him, numb him, and help him rest.

Gutting it out didn't seem like an option. For a guy whose normal demeanor seemed guarded, if not prickly, he was a freaking mess.

She handed back her partner's cell, which he stuck inside his coat pocket. He drew open the front door, the gray of light rain beyond the threshold perfectly reflecting her mood.

Rotten.

She started to take a step toward him when she caught a sudden motion in her peripheral vision, a splotch of dark against the light of the tile.

A cat.

Was it the one from the bushes?

It darted toward the door, and Jo lunged to grab the animal before it slipped outside. Though her aching bones and muscles protested, she got him. With a grunt, she scooped him up from the floor and into her arms.

"What are you doing?" Hank said, watching her as if she'd gone mad. "Put that thing down, and let's scram."

"He doesn't even have a collar," she told him. "He shouldn't go outside. He could be roadkill in ten seconds flat."

She held the cat against her chest and peered down at him. He didn't seem to mind her precarious embrace. In return, he gave her a thorough once-over with a pair of amber eyes. Then he sighed and tucked his head beneath her chin, just as he'd done with Jenny in the photograph.

"Hey, Ernie," she whispered. "How are you, baby? You okay?"

She stroked the short black fur, and the cat vibrated against her. He kneaded his six-toed paws against her jacket, catching tiny claws in the nylon. She nearly peeled him off and then thought, *Oh, well.* It was torn already. And she wasn't about to put him down yet. She held him tighter, rubbed her nose between his ears. He smelled like dust and felt like down.

"What's up with you?" Hank asked.

She barely lifted her head. "He misses his mother."

His brows arched. "I never took you for an animal person."

"It's the two-legged ones I'm not so crazy about. I like the kind with four legs just fine."

She smiled sadly as Ernie head-butted her, purring with abandon, lids rolling over half-closed eyes. *Love-starved thing,* she mused and found herself wondering if Patrick Dielman would keep Ernie when he got over the shock of losing his wife. He struck her as the type who groused about cat hairs on his suits or kitty litter on the carpet. What if Ernie got dumped at a shelter before the week was done?

Not your problem, she told herself.

It was something she didn't like to think about, all the things that victims left behind. Not only the people in their lives, not only the furniture and once-treasured belongings that usually ended up tagged with bright stickers in yard sales or dropped off at the nearest Goodwill, but the pets they loved who loved them back and who grieved when the person who'd fed them, who'd held them, was no longer there.

"Larsen?"

She set Ernie down, realizing how maudlin her thoughts had turned. But then it was hardly surprising considering the way she'd spent the better part of the day.

The cat twined itself around her ankles.

"You be good, baby." She gently shooed him away from her and stood up straight.

Pressing her lips hard together, she watched the blur of black fur disappear around the corner of the foyer.

Was he looking for Jenny?

"She got him from the pound . . . didn't even want to go on trips because it meant leaving the cat. Don't you get it?"

Jo got it. At least, she thought she did.

Would Jenny have left Ernie behind?

Would it have mattered to her? Would something like a cat have been a consideration?

Or had her grief blinded her to everything else in her life, even Ernie?

"Did you find her gun? I gave it to her for protection . . . a twenty-two caliber. She kept it in her glove compartment. Did she try to defend herself?"

Defend herself?

How about: Did she drive out to the boonies and off herself?

That was the $64,000 question.

"Hey, Jo?"

She looked at Phelps, still holding the door, letting in the damp air.

"Let's go." He motioned her out.

She nodded, glanced behind her in the direction of the living room, where they'd left Patrick Dielman sobbing into his hands.

She pulled up her hood and headed into the mist.

She took a slight detour, pausing beside the BMW, squatting first to check the tires. They looked brand new, with deep, zigzag grooves. She searched for the telltale yellow mud from the quarry but didn't find any in the tires or the wheel wells. The rain beaded on slick, white paint.

"You see something?" Hank asked.

"Nope," she said, making a pass around the sedan, alternately crouching and standing. The car looked as spotless as the house.

She wasn't sure what she'd expected.

"You think he was involved?"

"Beyond providing Jenny with the handgun that killed her?" she said, coming out of a squat and wiping off her hands.

"You know what I mean." He walked to the car, head down.

Neither of them spoke as Jo belted herself in and faced the window. Hank started the engine and veered around the white Beemer to exit the driveway.

Nosing the Ford into the street, he hit the brakes suddenly, cursing as a beige Acura sedan sailed in front of them and took a hard turn at the Dielmans' driveway, pulling in with a squeal of tires on wet pavement.

"Idiot," he let loose.

Jo peeled her palms from the dashboard and swiveled against the straps of the seat belt to watch as a tan door popped open.

"Maybe it's the doctor," she said and rubbed the back of her neck, already stiff from tension and her tumble into the pit. All she needed was whiplash.

Two long legs clad in charcoal pants emerged, attached to a woman in a beige coat that matched the car.

"Not unless he's had a sex change."

Lisa Barton held a clutch purse above her head to keep the drizzle off her short, tousled hair. She didn't look behind her once, didn't seem to notice they were watching as she dashed toward the front door. Without bothering to knock, she let herself in.

"Guess who," Jo said.

"So Dielman phoned a friend after all."

"Maybe she can help him."

"I'm sure she can," Hank remarked, giving her a look, and she shook her head.

"The doc should be here soon, so Dielman will get what he needs."

"Knocked out?"

"Let's hope so, for his sake."

Hank put a foot on the gas, and Jo stopped him with a quick, "Hold on, okay?"

The car jerked to a halt. "Christ, what now?"

"Give me a minute." She jerked her hood up again, grabbed the door handle and let herself out. She cut across the damp grass, heading straight for the beige sedan.

She bent beside it, as she had the BMW, blinking rain from her lashes as she gave the tires a thorough once-over. She touched fingers to treads, like reading Braille.

But there was no yellow mud.

If either Dielman or the blonde next door were involved, they'd done a great job cleaning up after themselves.

She retraced her steps back to the Ford through the drizzle, a vague cloud of heat enveloping her as she buckled herself in. She pushed her hood back and shook her head.

"Like it'd ever be that easy," Hank grumbled as he took the car out of park and lurched into the street.

Something felt wrong when I got home from the library at lunchtime.

I heard laughter coming from the bedroom. But I know Patrick wasn't home. His car was gone. I pulled my phone from my purse and held on to it, ready to dial 911, as I walked toward the noise, only to sigh with relief when I found the TV on.

But I hadn't left it on when I'd gone to the library this morning.

Had I?

I kept my coat on as I began to walk through the house. There was a faint smell that ran through the place, and I wouldn't have noticed except that it wasn't the lily of the valley that Patrick liked to buy me. It wasn't even his Irish Spring soap. It was more like ash or a stale cigarette. I didn't smoke, and neither did Patrick.

I opened closet doors and looked beneath the beds, but no one was hiding. I told myself I was imagining things, getting myself worked up over nothing. Until I noticed something missing: the silver-framed photo of Finn and me that I keep on the sofa table.

If someone broke into the house, why would they take that?

I got on hands and knees to peer under the couch, wondering if Patrick had knocked it down or moved it. But I couldn't find it on any other tables or shelves.

Pretty soon, I was beside myself and spent the next few hours scouring the house—digging in drawers, poking through cupboards—until I felt clammy with worry. My heart beat so fast, I thought I would pass out.

If I didn't calm down, I would make myself sick.

I phoned Patrick and babbled like an idiot.

"You're so tired, Jenny," he said. "You're probably worked up over nothing. Can you take a sleeping pill and lie down? I'll help you look when I get home."

So that's what I did.

I awoke to find him gently shaking my shoulder. The sky outside the window was dark. I wasn't sure what time it was.

Still groggy, I sat up and swung my feet over the edge of the bed. I hadn't forgotten about Finn's photo. I knew how Patrick felt about my son and all the things I kept. So when I found my voice, the first thing I asked was, "Did you take Finn's picture?"

"No, Jenny," he said, holding my arm as I stumbled. I wanted to show him it was gone.

"Then someone was here," I murmured.

"Are you sure about that?"

When I got to the living room, when I stood at the sofa table, I couldn't breathe.

"See?" Patrick said and gave my shoulder a pat. "It's right where it always is."

And it was true.

There was the photograph of me with my arms around Finn, him smiling with that gap-toothed grin. I shook my head, wondering how I could have missed it.

Wondering if something really is wrong with me.

CHAPTER NINE

The station house looked like a party was in progress.

Jo wasn't surprised that the Dallas media had begun to gather. If she didn't know that most of them relied on police scanners, she'd figure it was the scent of blood that drew them, rather like the black crows that clung to power lines above the road, waiting for a possum to meet its fate beneath the tires of an eighteen-wheeler. Several white vans decorated with the call letters of the major networks anchored themselves in the spaces in front of the building.

Though it was past time for change of shifts, Jo recognized night-shift officers at their lockers or hitting the coffee machine, looking bleary-eyed and less than clean-shaven. The phones beeped and blinked like raw nerve endings, each potentially bearing the one tip that might answer the question of why. Why had Jenny Dielman disappeared? Why was she dead?

Jo dumped her coat on the back of her chair and checked her message slips, ignoring all but one from Owen Ross, the Warehouse Club manager. He'd printed out copies of receipts from Monday night that coincided with Jenny Dielman's trip to the store, according to the time stamp on the security video. Jo would have wanted to see them, too, if they hadn't found Jenny's receipt in her car.

She crumpled up the pink slip and tossed it in the trash.

She'd just started to wade through her voice mail when their boss summoned them into his office. She grabbed her file on Jenny Dielman and followed Hank inside, taking a seat beside him across from Waylon Morris's desk.

The captain's marine buzz cut only made squarer an already angular face. His broad shoulders and thick torso—and the rigid way he carried himself—had earned him the labels of "fireplug" and "bulldog." But most everyone just called him "Cap."

She spied a tweed jacket and tie on a hanger that dangled from a wall sconce. Jo knew he didn't gussy up unless he had a date with the mayor or the press.

"We have work to do, people," Cap said, rubbing big hands together. "Chief's been up my ass already, and he's being dogged by the mayor and the city council. Brief me on what we've got so far." He jerked a chin at the jacket. "Mayor wants me to work a press conference as soon as I have all the facts."

Jo was relieved he didn't mention her or Hank participating. With the blooming bruises on her face and the dried mud on her clothes, she knew she wasn't fit for television.

She cleared her throat. "They're processing the victim's car at the crime lab impound as we speak, and we're pushing for an autopsy in the next twenty-four hours. We're looking to the postmortem for a definitive cause of death."

Hank jumped in. "We've got the Jennings twenty-two found at the scene, and we're awaiting confirmation of a match from ballistics. We've got the list of personal effects of Mrs. Dielman and statements from the couple who found the victim's car."

"We need to trace that weapon, Detectives," Cap said bluntly.

Hank glanced at Jo. "Actually, sir, there's a strong possibility that the Jennings twenty-two belonged to the dead woman."

Cap leaned his elbows on his desk. "Explain."

Jo sat up straighter. "The husband said he bought a small-caliber semiautomatic, a twenty-two by his recollection, at a gun show in Garland not long ago. He said it was for his wife's protection, and she kept it in the glove compartment of her car."

"Did she have a license to carry?"

"No, sir."

"And it wasn't registered?"

"No, sir," Jo said, feeling angry all over again. "The serial number's been filed off. Maybe the crime lab can work their magic and get something we can use."

"Let me get this straight." Cap's squint cut creases into his forehead. "We have a missing woman who turns up dead at the bottom of a quarry with a bullet in her head, and the gun used in that shooting may well have been her own?"

"It wouldn't be the first time a victim's been killed with her own gun," Jo said.

"She was being treated for depression," Hank added.

Jo gave her partner a look. "Not depression exactly. Post-traumatic stress disorder. Her only son died tragically three years ago, and her first marriage broke up because of it. That anniversary's next week, just after Thanksgiving."

"So you're thinking it's a suicide?" Cap put up his hands. "If that's the case, why aren't y'all closing the book on this one ASAP?"

Hank inclined his head toward Jo: *This one's on you.*

"It's complicated, sir," she said and drew in a deep breath.

"How's that, Detective?"

She'd been waiting on this moment, trying to figure out how she'd explain. She wasn't sure where to start. She understood that it looked cut-and-dry on the surface. But she wasn't as convinced by the suicide scenario as Hank. Something about it didn't feel right, and she wasn't going to settle on suicide as the cause of death without all the evidence.

"I realize it muddies the waters, knowing the handgun might be Jenny Dielman's," she said, "especially with what we've learned about her state of mind."

"Which is what?"

"According to her doctor, she was taking a prescription antidepressant. He intimated that she may have attempted suicide in the past, but we can't be sure. We'd have to subpoena her old medical records."

Cap shook his head. "That hardly sounds like muddy water to me."

Jo wasn't finished. "Dr. Patil doesn't believe she wanted to kill herself. She was having trouble adjusting to the loss of her son, yes, but she was working through it. Why would she have gone shopping if she planned to kill herself?" she asked. "She bought enough cat food for a month and a twelve-pack of Kleenex. If I aimed to shoot myself, I sure as hell wouldn't waste time in a Warehouse Club stocking up."

"So there wasn't a note?" Cap studied the pages in his hands. "I don't see anything listed."

"No, sir." Jo squirmed. "Nothing's turned up yet."

"Is that it?" Captain Morris didn't sound convinced.

"No. Something's missing," Jo murmured, getting that nagging feeling again that she'd overlooked a piece of evidence. She opened the folder in her lap, skimming through her report and her notes. She glanced through the list of items found at the quarry: the contents of Jenny's purse, the purchases from the Warehouse Club, the cell phone, the wristwatch, and the wedding rings.

Where was the locket? The one with Finn's photo that Patrick Dielman said Jenny never took off?

Jo's heart thumped. "Her husband said she always wore a locket in her son's memory. It's silver and engraved with an *F* for *Finn*. If she was so grief-stricken that she'd take her own life, why wasn't it with her?"

Cap raised an eyebrow. "Go on."

"It wasn't on the body or in her car," Jo said. "It should have been there, like her rings and her watch. Her coat's missing, too. I saw her wearing it in the security footage from the Warehouse Club that I viewed last night. I think there's more to this case than the obvious."

"What about you, Phelps?" Cap asked, turning to her partner. "What's your gut tell you?"

Jo wanted to know that, too.

"The point of entry was the right temple," Hank said, touching a finger to his own temple. "According to the vic's husband, she was right-handed. The placement of the watch on her left wrist backs that up."

"You believe it's suicide?"

Hank slid Jo a sideways glance. He grunted. "That's the ME's call, not mine."

Jo's chest felt tight.

The captain rubbed his jaw. "So there's the possibility our victim might not have been abducted. She might not even *be* the victim of a crime?" He shook his head. "Any chance we can run a GSR and get it over with?"

Jo started to open her mouth, but Hank beat her to it.

"There's no primer on the casing of a twenty-two, so there's no residue to look for," he said. "She'd been in the water for a while, and we all know it's not recommended to test for gunshot residue after someone's washed their hands, much less soaked in a crater full of water overnight."

Captain Morris sat quietly, brow wrinkled, digesting the information. Then he pushed his chair back and stood, reaching for his jacket and tie.

"What we've got is a suspicious death," he said. "As far as this department is concerned, it's still an open investigation."

"I want to talk to her husband again, Cap, and the ex," Jo said.

"Get on it," Cap said, then gestured at the door. "Dismissed." He was pulling up his collar to put on his tie when Jo and Hank walked out the door.

Jo stayed at the station for a long while after, talking to the uniforms who had canvassed the Dielmans' neighbors, making calls to get the Dielmans' phone records, staring at the security footage on her computer screen, enduring the twitter of ringing phones, running reports, putting up a timeline, and sucking down bad coffee until she'd had it. Hank was already long gone by the time she finally took off.

She drove home through the dark, a misty-moist haze in the beams of her headlights. She turned on the radio even though it did little to banish the noise in her head.

Once locked inside her condo, she closed the shutters, drapes, and blinds, turning on the lights inside her cocoon of bricks and mortar. After she'd peeled off her dirty clothes and put away her holster and the .38 she'd cleaned and oiled, Jo had taken as long and hot a shower as humanly possible. Every inch of her ached.

Despite the best attempts of the EMTs to clean her up at the scene, brown water swirled around her feet and gurgled down the drain. She gently scrubbed the parts of her that were abraded and bruised, wincing as the soap stung her cuts. Though steam fogged the air around her, she felt cold beneath her skin. Her mind kept jumping from one thought to the next, and no amount of deep breathing could still it.

She made the water even hotter, until it turned her flesh red, and she gritted her teeth. Still, the chill lingered, even after the shower, when she'd dried off and donned her robe. She'd only just dragged a comb through her damp hair when she heard someone at the door.

Adam stood on the welcome mat, wearing his old bomber jacket, his boyish features grimly set. Blue eyes relayed worry behind wire rims.

"I saw the news about the woman in the quarry," he said. "Is that your case?"

Jo nodded.

He shifted a brown paper sack from his right hand to his left. He reached up and cupped her chin. "How's the other guy look?"

"The other guy's the quarry."

He grimaced. "Ouch."

She tugged him in and locked the door.

He took off his jacket as he made his way into the living room, then tossed it over a chair. He set the bag on the coffee table and drew her toward him.

"You all right?" He peered at her closely, and she knew he was taking in each nick on her face, each red scratch and purple mark. The pain in her eyes. "You want to talk about it?"

He spoke with such tenderness that she wanted to weep.

What the hell was wrong with her? There wasn't much holding her together tonight, just the barest thread of control. Should the thread snap, she'd come apart at the seams.

"Tell me what happened," he coaxed, drawing her down on the couch beside him.

She trembled as his hand slid over her back, fingers moving lightly down the curve of her spine. "I saw her, Adam." She swallowed hard, worked to get it out. "I saw her face. I felt her fear." She told him all of it before she could stop. "I wanted to help her, but I was too late."

"You couldn't have saved her," he said. His slim brow creased. "You're pretty damn amazing, but you're not Superman."

Jo sighed. "I'm not even Underdog."

"I don't know about that," Adam said. "I watched you jump into White Rock Lake once to save a drowning bunny."

"You also saw me lose it when a mouse ran up the leg of my pants," she reminded him, and he laughed softly.

"So mice are your Kryptonite." He stopped rubbing her back, and she leaned into him. "Everybody's got something. Mine's Jell-O. Food should not move."

Jo smiled, but it was short-lived. "There's just so much that doesn't make sense," she said.

"About Jell-O?"

"About Jenny, the woman in the quarry." She blinked hard, the bits and pieces of the case shuffling inside her head.

"It's a crazy world."

Crazy.

She winced at his choice of words, thought of Jenny's diagnosis, the post-traumatic stress. If the medical examiner ruled her death a suicide, that would be all anyone remembered, and Jo didn't want it to go down that way.

Adam stroked her damp hair. "I wish I could help."

"Me, too."

He drew away, peering into her eyes so intently she wished she could shrivel up and disappear, like a wisp of smoke. He was so comfortable with intimacy, both in and out of bed, had always been that way, since the first time they'd been together.

While Jo didn't feel so exposed in the dark, she felt completely vulnerable when the lights were on, every time their eyes met.

He cocked his head. "Have you eaten anything since breakfast?"

"Does dirt count?"

"No."

Paper crinkled as he retrieved the brown bag from the table and removed a Styrofoam container. He spread a napkin on her lap and gave her a plastic spoon. Then he popped the lid off the cup. Steam floated up to her nose as he pressed it into her hands. "Careful, it's hot."

The heat warmed her palms, and she inhaled the rising steam. "Smells great," she said. "What is it?"

"Cream of potato from Jason's."

Sweet nectar of the gods.

He reached into the sack and removed a wax-wrapped bundle as well. "And a muffaletta," he added.

"Just put an apple in my mouth and get the spit ready," she murmured, and he grinned.

"Back in a sec."

He disappeared into the kitchen, and Jo started on the food, tearing off pieces of the muffaletta to stuff in her mouth between slurps of thick soup. By the time he brought her a Coke and a plate, she'd made a good dent.

She wasn't sure, at first, that she'd have much of an appetite. But once she got rolling, she didn't stop until she was scraping the inside of the Styrofoam cup with her finger. She finished the can of Coke and set it down on the table with a rattle.

She leaned back into the cushions, and Adam settled beside her.

"I don't think you have to worry about the hickey anymore," he said. "You've got a whole new set of bruises to keep it company."

Jo groaned.

"Are you all right?" He picked up her hands, her palms crisscrossed with scratches and scrapes. He held them so gently. "Tell me where it hurts."

"Everywhere."

Mind. Body. Soul.

He traced the line of her jaw with his fingertip, touched her neck where the vague purple bruise he'd made now blended with her new ones.

She willed herself to relax, to give in.

He slipped the bathrobe low on her shoulders, his hands soft as balm on her skin. "How's that feel?"

"Good." She squeezed her eyes shut, breathing in the smell of him, the lime of his aftershave, the maleness. He knew so well how to touch her, which buttons to push.

His hand probed her left shoulder, and she stiffened, detecting the change in his touch. It suddenly felt clinical, like an examination.

"You dislocate anything?" he asked her.

"No."

"Did you let them take you to the hospital for X-rays?"

She blinked. "That wasn't necessary."

"How do you know that, Jo? You could have hairline fractures . . ."

Breathe.

"You could have suffered a concussion. Damn it," he said softly, "you should've let them bring you in."

Jo felt a pounding start at her temples.

"You need to be checked out thoroughly. None of this macho stuff, okay?"

"Please, stop," she cut him off, felt the thread break. "Don't treat me like some rookie who doesn't know any better."

"That's not what I'm doing."

"I don't need X-rays or MRIs. I'm alive. I'm okay. I'm not dead like Jenny."

Not like Jenny. Not like Jenny.

"Hey," Adam said and drew his hands away. "Now it's my turn to say stop." He looked at her long and hard, then quietly added, "I didn't mean to tell you what to do. I never have. I'm just concerned. I love you, and I don't like to see you hurting."

"I'm fine," she said, the same lie she'd told Terry.

"You're not fine." He waited, but when she didn't speak, he said, "C'mon, talk to me, Goose."

But Jo drew her knees up, hugged her arms around them, playing the roly-poly.

"I get it." His sigh was filled with frustration.

She felt his weight shift beside her.

He caught his fingers beneath her chin, made her look at him. "You can shut me out all you want, but I'm not leaving. It won't work, not this time."

He let her go and got up, began clearing the litter off her coffee table. Without another word, he headed toward the galley kitchen with the remnants of her dinner.

The furnace kicked on, humming, breathing warmth into the room like it was any other chilly night and all was right with the world.

She thought of Patrick Dielman and wondered what kind of nightmares he'd be having tonight, if he could close his eyes at all.

When she finally went to bed, Adam was already there, glasses on the nightstand, head on the pillow. She took off her robe and crawled in beside him, slid close, pressed her bare thigh against his, settled her cheek against his shoulder. Gently, so as not to awaken him, she set her hand on his chest and felt the beat of his heart beneath her palm.

She wanted to clear her mind, to forget what had happened, to think of nothing.

Instead, she thought of Jenny and the son she'd tried so hard to protect. Had she died thinking she had failed him? Like Mama had failed her?

Her mind twisted it all into a nightmare.

She walked slowly down a long hallway. Everything painted white, doors on either side of her. So many of them she couldn't count. She touched the walls with her palms, moving carefully, floating.

She was supposed to be at Mama's helping Ronnie pack things up, but the house wasn't right. As soon as she'd stepped inside, she'd realized nothing was as she'd remembered. There was no wallpaper peeling at the seams, no faded photographs, no plaid sofa or dust-covered lampshades. The walls were too tall, the space too large. She tried to get her bearings, but there was nothing familiar.

She didn't know where she was.

She started walking, but the hallway had no end in sight.

Her room should have been the last one, the final door. She thought she could see it in the distance, but she never got closer, no matter how many steps she took.

Panic seized her, and she grabbed at brass knobs, throwing doors open to find the rooms bare. Some weren't rooms at all, just dark spaces from which voices called. Some whispered her name. "Help us, Jo," they said. "Help us." But she could see no one. She could hear only the loud tattoo of her pulse.

She moved faster, frantic.

Where was Ronnie? Where were the boxes? Where was her room?

She pushed another door wide and stared through the portal, catching sight of something, of someone. A little boy sat with his back to her, shaking as he sobbed.

She went toward him, heart broken by the sound.

"Are you all right?" she asked. "Where's your mommy? Why are you all alone?"

She was nearly upon him when he turned his head.

His face was white as paper. Wide eyes bulged, terrified. Blood trickled from his head.

His pale hair was slick with it.

"Save me," he whispered, tongue swollen and blue.

She backed away, tried to turn but couldn't move.

She opened her mouth but made no sound.

Jo sobbed in her sleep, the nightmare so intense. But when she woke in the morning, the dream was forgotten.

PART TWO

FOUND

CHAPTER TEN
THURSDAY

Jo jerked awake and reached across the bed for Adam, but he wasn't there.

Slumping back into the pillow, she squeezed her eyes shut, wishing like hell she didn't have to get up. A slim stripe of gray glowed between the drapes. She dared to peek at the red numbers on the alarm clock. It was barely six, too early still for the sun.

A few more minutes, she told herself, but her mind was already thinking about the day ahead, about Jenny.

She had a million questions running through her brain. She needed to get back to the Dielmans' house, see if Patrick had found a suicide note, go through Jenny's belongings, and try to locate the journal Dr. Patil had mentioned giving Jenny.

Jo wanted another shot at Jenny's husband, too. What specifically, if anything, had prompted him to buy her the gun? If Jenny had been afraid, as he'd said, was it because she felt threatened? By whom? Her ex-husband? Kevin Harrison had insisted he'd had nothing to do with Jenny since their divorce.

Hank had set up an appointment to meet with Dr. Harrison at his home that evening, around seven. Her partner figured that Mr. Big-Shot Surgeon might be more helpful if he were dealing with a man, and Jo didn't disagree. Harrison had agreed to see them, anyway. That was further than Jo had gotten.

Jo had arranged for them to talk to Lisa Barton again. There was that strange incident with the brick and Barton suggesting the culprit was Jenny—highly doubtful, considering Jenny was probably already dead. Had Jenny truly been suspicious of an affair between Lisa and Patrick? Dielman had denied cheating on his wife. But from what Jo had seen so far, Barton and Dielman sure seemed chummy.

Okay, okay. Enough thinking. She needed to get moving.

Gingerly, she shifted beneath the covers, disentangling herself and easing into a seated position, keenly aware that every fiber in her body ached to varying degrees. She tested her left shoulder, tried to raise her arm as high as she could; even with gritted teeth, she got no higher than her jaw.

So she couldn't do cartwheels. If she could walk and talk, she'd be all right.

Planting her feet on the floor, she slid off the mattress, placing her full weight on her knees and ankles. Nothing collapsed, so she pressed on. Although when she reached the bathroom, flipped on the light, and took a hard look at herself in the mirror, she had second thoughts about the kind of shape she was in. She turned right and then left, assessing the damage.

The bruises had ripened overnight. Her skin was as colorful as an Amish quilt with patches of yellows and greens speckling her arms and legs, and darker shades of black and purple on the backs of her thighs, her buttocks, and her left shoulder. The small scratches on her face and hands were a dull red, starting to scab.

She looked like she'd gone a few rounds in the ring and lost big-time.

Her battered appearance had worried Adam. She'd seen it in his eyes when he'd gotten a good look at her last night. Had he imagined what it would be like to find her in the autopsy suite, toes-up on the table? Jo could hear his postmortem dictation. *"The body is that of a thirty-five-year-old female measuring sixty-seven inches tall and weighing approximately one hundred twenty-five pounds with multiple superficial lacerations to the extremities and contusions to the upper and lower limbs. If only she'd stopped playing Superman long enough to go to the hospital for an MRI, perhaps it wouldn't have come to this . . ."*

Jo would have smiled at her own dark humor under different circumstances, but not now.

She struggled with her bra, clenching her teeth as she tried to use her left arm to help hook it. She finally gave up when she realized it wasn't going to work. Instead, she found a stretchy camisole and tugged it up using her right hand alone. How could something so basic be so hard? She was sweating when she finished, but she'd done it.

She was struggling into a navy cotton turtleneck when the phone rang. She batted at the material, pushing her head through the opening and finally emerging, though the trilling had stopped by then.

A muffled voice drifted toward her through the parted bedroom door.

She pushed it wide and stepped out to find Adam with a phone at his ear, his back to her. The television was on, the sound muted so that the talking heads moved their lips in silence.

She picked up the remote and switched the set off. Then she stepped in front of Adam and listened to him murmur consent.

He smiled a weary smile.

She pantomimed, "Is it for me?"

He shook his head.

She shuffled into the kitchen to take a few more aspirin and down a Coke. Adam hadn't made coffee, and she needed caffeine in the worst way.

When she returned with soda in hand, he was off the phone and pulling on his coat.

Her chest tightened. "You're leaving already?"

"Duty calls." He glanced up but kept zipping. "It's not even rush hour, and we've got a four-car pileup on Central with fatalities."

She set down her Coke and went over to him. "Probably inappropriate for me to tell you to have a nice day?"

"Depends on what your definition of *nice* is."

His hair was mussed, and he wore the same clothes he'd had on last night. There was still the hint of sleep in his eyes and shadows of fatigue below. He didn't look like he'd gotten any more rest than she.

"I asked about your girl," he said. "The post is scheduled for later this afternoon."

Jenny's autopsy is today.

Jo found her voice to tell him, "Thanks."

"You feeling better?"

"Better than I look." She rubbed her left shoulder. "I'm just sore."

He hesitated. "Maybe I'll see you at the morgue?"

"Ah, that'll be like déjà vu all over again," she teased, trying to lighten things up.

He took her hand and drew it to his mouth, kissing her palm. Then he leaned toward her and took her lips in his gently. When he pulled away, he whispered, "Be good."

"I'll try."

"Like hell." He grinned.

Jo couldn't help but smile, too.

He was half out the door before she thought of something else. She called his name, and he paused on her welcome mat, letting the chilly morning air inside. It probably wasn't the best time to request a favor, but she had no choice.

"Could you track down a file for me?" she said.

"On who?"

"A boy named Finnegan Harrison. He was six when he died three years ago, the day after Thanksgiving. He reportedly fell from a tree. If I hunt it down myself, it'll take ages. All that paperwork and red tape."

Adam cocked his head, waiting.

Jo sighed. "He was Jenny Dielman's son."

"You think there's something in the boy's records that'll help you understand Jenny's death?"

"I don't know," she admitted. How could she explain it to him when even she wasn't sure what she was looking for? "I need to find out who she was, and it might help."

"I'll see what I can do."

"Thank you."

He closed the door behind him.

Jo stood there for a moment, the cold he'd let in dissipating around her. She closed her eyes and weighed whether or not she would attend the postmortem examination. A part of her sorely wanted to be on hand to watch the ME's every move, to see what he saw as he saw it, and hear his comments as he made them. The rest of her didn't want to go anywhere near the autopsy suite. She'd never liked viewing cadavers being sliced up, less like humans than meat.

Jo picked up her can of Coke and went into the bedroom to finish dressing, adding her pancake holster because of the sore shoulder. Coat on, bag in hand, she took off.

The sun was rising as she drove to the station. Not a cloud in sight, which meant no rain.

Jo took that as an omen.

She was already at her desk when Hank appeared a little past seven. He grunted when she showed him the front page of the *Dallas Morning News*, which featured a one-column story headlined: "Missing Plainfield Woman Found Dead in Quarry."

"Where the hell were the reporters when all that yarn got boosted from The Knitting Needle?" he said dryly, picking up the paper and tossing it in the trash.

Jo didn't bother to retrieve it.

The only report they'd gotten from the county crime lab so far concerned ballistics. Tests proved the Jennings .22 was the lethal weapon. They had a verbal report from Emma Slater on fingerprints found inside and outside the Nissan. Not surprisingly, the victim's latents were everywhere: on the steering wheel, the dash, the doors, the windows. The only footprints found around the parked vehicle belonged to the two hikers who'd stumbled upon the abandoned car.

There were impressions from leather gloves on the steering wheel, dash, and glove compartment. Though they hadn't found a pair in the car or at the scene, they couldn't rule out that those glove prints belonged to Jenny.

Jo and Hank checked in with the captain for their morning briefing.

"This is an ongoing investigation until we've got the ME's conclusions and the evidence to close it up tight, you understand?" The gray beneath Cap's eyes reminded Jo that he was under as much pressure as they were to wrap up this one. "Until then, I'll liaison with the media. We've set up a separate 800 number for tips."

Good. Someone might've seen something and not even realized it.

"Be safe," he said when they'd wrapped up their powwow, words Jo had heard every day at the end of roll call when she was a beat cop. For some reason, it always made her uneasy, like she should throw some salt over her shoulder.

She got back to her phone, putting in a call to Emma at the lab and to Ronnie about postponing her plans to help at Mama's house on Saturday, though she had to leave messages both times.

Then she called the front desk at Dallas Metro Doctors, the multispecialty practice that Patrick Dielman managed, and she was put through to Dielman's secretary, Carolann Brady. The woman noted that Patrick hadn't come into work that morning and wouldn't likely be back for a few days because of the horrible tragedy. Jo explained she actually needed to talk to Carolann, not Patrick, as part of their investigation.

"It's routine," Jo assured her before proceeding to ask a few questions. After initially hemming and hawing, Carolann confirmed that Jennifer Dielman had indeed called and spoken to her husband sometime before five o'clock on Monday night. Carolann had stayed at the office until six fifteen, which her time card would verify. She noted that Mr. Dielman was still at his desk when she took off, but because the lot was attended, perhaps building security could help pin down the precise time he left.

"If you're thinking Mr. Dielman had anything to do with what happened to his wife, you're wrong," Carolann insisted before rattling off the extension for Security.

Jo took down the number and dialed but got a busy signal. She made a note to try again.

She watched the clock as she worked on reports and reread the statements of the two hikers who'd found Jenny's car until she had the words burned into her brain. They had seen no one else, no other car. They might have contaminated the scene by looking inside the Nissan and popping the trunk, but Jo couldn't fault their intentions. Besides, they were clean. Their prints had been run through the system, yielding zip. They were just a couple of unlucky college kids who'd stumbled onto a crime scene.

"Hey, Larsen?" her partner said. Jo glanced up to see him hanging up his phone. "Let's hit the road. I just talked to Dielman, and he's waiting on us."

Hank grabbed his coat, and she did the same, though a little more slowly than usual. Just shoving her left arm through the sleeve made her grimace.

"He's gonna let us do a voluntary search. He's agreed to sign a consent form. CYA," he added with a grin.

"CYA," she repeated. Cover Your Ass: the cardinal rule of cops and corporate execs.

Jo felt a rush as they left, anxious to go through Jenny's effects. Maybe they'd find something, anything, to help explain what—or who—had driven Jenny to her death.

I'm still shaking after what just happened. I nearly called Patrick to tell him, but I was afraid that he wouldn't believe me.

The phone rang just after I'd gotten home from the library. It was the landline, which rings rarely. We don't even have caller ID. Patrick says it isn't worth it. He's always using his cell, and no one much calls besides telemarketers.

"Hello?" I said, expecting it to be someone conducting a survey or a charity that had a truck in the area next week. I tried again. "Talk, or I'll hang up."

I heard a soft breath, a hesitation.

"Mommy, are you there?"

My knees turned to gravy, and I sank down to the carpet. "Baby?" I said, even though I knew it wasn't possible. "I miss you so much."

"Mommy," said the voice once more, sounding so distant.

I lowered the receiver, cradling it in my arms like it was a child; then I closed my eyes and cried and cried.

At my core, I knew it was someone playing a very cruel trick—but I wanted so badly for the voice to be Finn's that, for a second, I almost believed it.

CHAPTER ELEVEN

"Good morning, sir," Hank said as Patrick Dielman opened the door. "We appreciate your cooperating with our investigation, and we apologize for the intrusion. We understand what a difficult time this is."

Her partner sounded so sincere that Jo didn't even say, "Howdy." She kept her mouth shut.

Patrick Dielman let them in.

It was barely nine o'clock.

Dielman's eyes were bloodshot but dry. His skin looked paler than milk, but his cheeks were clean-shaven, and he'd changed into a clean shirt. Jo wondered if they'd interrupted him dressing. He still hadn't put on socks or shoes.

He seemed subdued, and neither Jo nor Hank attempted to chitchat. He didn't offer them anything to drink this time and made no apologies for the breakfast dishes and newspaper that littered the coffee table.

"How're you holding up?" Jo ventured to ask as Dielman led them up the hallway. "Did you get any sleep last night?"

"Dr. Patil gave me something," he said over his shoulder. "It put me out pretty good. Lisa told me I didn't even move until the sun came up."

"Lisa Barton?" she repeated for clarity's sake as Dielman took them past a closed door to a room at the end of the hall.

He paused at the threshold and turned, meeting Jo's gaze. "She slept on the couch." He didn't explain further. He just looked sad as hell. "Lisa's strong. I can lean on her, and I need that. I'm sorry if that doesn't sound right." He had his hands on the doorjamb, blocking their way. "She said you wanted to talk to her more about Jenny?"

"Yes," Jo confirmed. "I'm hoping we can go over there today, once we're done here."

"I'll give her a call, and tell her to stay put. She's taking off work." He shifted on his bare feet. "She wants to help with the funeral arrangements." He moved a hand from the jamb to touch his trembling chin. "I need someone to help. I can't imagine doing it alone. I thought I could handle anything life threw at me, but I was wrong."

"I get it," Jo said for lack of anything better.

Dielman turned and led them through the door.

"This is our room," he told them, though Jo could have guessed that from the king-size bed alone. The walls were neutral like the rest of the house, but a shade darker than beige. Everything was in its place. There were no clothes hanging from chairs or doorknobs. The dresser was as neat as a pin with only a smattering of perfume and cologne bottles, a silver-backed brush and comb, a crystal dish holding coins, and a smartphone.

"I looked around for a suicide note," Dielman said. "I even checked in her special room."

Jo raised an eyebrow.

Special room? Was that like a secret garden?

"I'll take you there next. I couldn't find anything besides her date book. All that was penciled in for this week were her blood tests at Dr. Patil's office and a vet exam for Ernie."

Jo had a hard time believing a woman with suicidal thoughts would schedule a doctor's visit and a trip to the vet. That—on top of the Warehouse Club purchases—cast doubt in her mind that Jenny Dielman had planned her own death.

"Did Jenny have a computer?"

"No," Dielman said. "My work laptop was always off-limits to her. I offered many times to buy her one, but she didn't want one. She wasn't very tech savvy. She said that if she needed to get online, she could use the public-access computers at the library."

No wonder Dr. Patil had given Jenny an old-school composition book to journal in. "Did you ever see a notebook," she asked, "one Jenny might have used as a journal?"

Dielman shook his head. "No, nothing like that."

Jo felt like she was striking out all over the place.

"Have you seen your wife's black coat?" she asked.

He looked puzzled. "But she must have been wearing it . . ."

"She wasn't wearing it when she was found, and it wasn't in her car or anywhere near the quarry."

"I don't know where it is." Dielman ran a hand through his hair. "It isn't here. I told you it was gone, Detective, when I saw you on Tuesday morning and reported her missing."

"What about the locket?" she asked.

"What do you mean?"

"We didn't find that either."

Dielman's brow furrowed. "But how's that possible? She never took it off."

Jo glanced at Hank.

"Are you sure she didn't put it in a jewelry box," her partner asked, "or take it somewhere to be repaired?"

"No," Dielman insisted. "She always wears the locket. I'm sure she had it on Monday morning when I left for work." He reached for a porcelain box on the dresser and dumped out the contents, frantically looking through them. "It's not here. If it was being fixed, she would have mentioned it. You don't understand. The necklace was too important."

"I'm sure it'll turn up," Hank said, putting a hand on Dielman's shoulder to calm him down.

Jo pointed at the cell phone. "Is that yours, sir?"

"What? Yes, it's mine." Dielman acted like he'd forgotten its existence. He snatched it up and slipped it into his back pocket. "It's part of my job to stay in close touch with the office and the physicians."

Jo cocked her head. "But you keep a landline, too?"

"Yes, mostly for Jenny's sake. She despised cell phones. She complained about people using phones while driving, and she hated hearing phones ring in restaurants or the library. Sudden noises made her jumpy." He frowned. "Don't tell me you couldn't find her phone."

"No, sir, we've got it," Hank replied. "It was in her car. The techs will go through it, and we'll run down recent numbers."

Dielman nodded.

Jo wasn't done with the questions. "When you reported Jenny missing, you mentioned her antidepressant medication. You said she didn't take it with her. Is it here?"

"Yes, of course." He paused at the bedside table and reached for a brown bottle. "It's her Zoloft. She recently had it filled, so there are twenty-eight pills. Just two missing that she'd taken already. I counted." He shook it. "Don't you see? She would have taken the bottle if she meant to leave. She wasn't running away," he insisted. "And she didn't kill herself."

"You're very thorough," Jo said and glanced at her partner.

"If you wouldn't mind, Mr. Dielman"—Hank walked the guy toward the door—"we'd like to get started."

Dielman turned. "You said that I needed to sign something?"

"Oh, yeah." Hank grumbled to himself, digging out the consent form from his inside coat pocket. "It's just a formality so there aren't questions about us poking around."

Dielman took the pen Hank offered and made quick business of his signature.

"Whatever it takes," he said, stony-faced. "You need anything from me, you just ask."

"Will do." Hank put away the papers, and Dielman left them alone.

Jo pulled a pair of disposable gloves from her coat pocket and snapped them on. Hank did likewise.

She approached the dresser, sliding open drawers to find socks arranged in rows by color and underwear folded. She ran her hands beneath everything, checking for anything hidden, while Hank worked on the bureau across the room.

Jo peered under the bed, expecting to find discarded shoes, but she didn't spy even a single dust bunny. The place was pristine. Either Patrick Dielman had OCD, or he'd done a fine job of covering any tracks.

The closet was no more revealing. Clothes hung carefully on the racks, arranged according to color. Shoes were displayed on wooden shelving beneath.

Jo slipped her hands into pocket after pocket but unearthed little of value: old laundry tags, a few pennies, and a stub from a two-year-old movie ticket. She went through shoe boxes and purses but turned up zilch. She took her time scrutinizing Dielman's footwear, turning each shoe over to check the treads for any sign of the yellow mud from the quarry. But everything looked clean.

Heading into the master bath, she homed in on the wicker hamper. It was half-full, and she carefully removed each rumpled piece of clothing for inspection. She didn't find so much as a spot of blood or a smudge of yellow mud on anything.

Likewise, the wastebasket held nothing more exciting than discarded tissues and cotton swabs, used strands of dental floss, and a soap wrapper.

She tackled the medicine cabinet, but uncovered nothing beyond the usual array of cold medicines, tweezers, Band-Aids, aspirin, and foot powders. There were no contraceptive pills, which made sense if Jenny couldn't have children. But there was a bottle of prescription sleeping pills.

Jo removed the bottle, unscrewed the cap and checked the contents.

There couldn't have been more than a few pills missing.

The label bore Jennifer Dielman's name, not her husband's. So it wasn't the sleeping aid that Dr. Patil had prescribed for Patrick. Jo stared at the bottle, thinking that if Jenny was hell-bent on suicide, she could have swallowed the whole damned lot and died at home atop her neatly made bed.

Why drive out to the quarry to do the deed?

Hank came up behind her. "Got something?"

She showed him the bottle, and he took it, squinting at the label. "Makes you think, doesn't it?" she said.

"Yeah," he replied. "Why do it the hard way when you can go easy?"

Jo nodded, drawing in a deep breath. She detected it then, hadn't realized what it was before: a floral scent, soft and sweet.

Squatting down, she opened the under-sink cabinet and saw a plethora of lotions and gels from Crabtree & Evelyn, all lily of the valley. She touched a gloved finger to the top of the talc, drew it back, and rubbed the powder into the latex. So maybe Jenny wasn't completely plain vanilla after all.

"Are you done?" Hank said from behind her, and she got up.

Patrick Dielman was standing in the doorway to the bedroom when they emerged from the bathroom. "Any luck?" he asked.

"Could we see Jenny's special room?" Jo said. They had yet to find Jenny's journal. It had to be somewhere.

"Follow me. It's just up the hall."

He led them to the closed door they'd passed earlier. He paused before he pushed it wide and switched the light on. "This was her sanctuary." He gestured at shelves of books above a built-in desk, at the rainbow-colored finger paintings on the walls. "It was the one spot in the world where she could be with him."

"Him?" Jo repeated.

"She'd put on music and thumb through those," Dielman replied and gestured toward the leather albums lying on a wicker table. "They're full of Finn's photos. She would stare at them for hours, like she was—" He stopped himself. "I don't know, looking for something."

"The anniversary of his death," Jo suggested. "It's next week, right?"

Dielman nodded. "You'll tell me if you remove anything?"

"Yes, sir," Hank assured him.

"Excuse me, will you? I have some calls to make. I've been trying to reach Jenny's sister. I keep getting her voice mail. Could be she's avoiding me." He glanced around the room before he shuffled out, though Jo noticed he didn't close the door.

"Let's get started," Hank said.

Jo sighed.

For a moment, she simply stood in the center of the room, taking it all in. Unlike the blandness of the rest of the house, the walls were a rich yellow, the color of butter. Bursts of sunlight filled the windows, further brightening the space. The mismatched pillows in primary colors and the purple futon reminded Jo of a box of crayons. No wonder Jenny had escaped here.

"I'll check for the date book," Hank said and headed toward the desk. "Maybe I'll get lucky and find the journal, too."

"Maybe," Jo said, but if the journal were in an obvious spot, wouldn't Dielman have already found it? Unless he had and he wasn't telling them, which Jo figured was all kinds of bad news.

She nosed around the futon, checking beneath the mattress. She didn't see anything but tufts of black cat fur, although there was a spot on the carpet nearby that had the imprint of a rectangular object. More fuzz framed whatever had been there. Was it some kind of box for

Ernie? Jo figured it would have kept him close enough that Jenny could have touched him with her fingertips. But whatever it was, it was gone.

She picked up one of the photo albums from the table and sat down with it. The cover made a sucking sound as she pried it open. Inside the sleeves were countless pictures of a child she knew was Finn.

The first was a blurry shot of the baby cradled in Jenny's arms, the child's head ringed with dark hair, eyes squeezed shut, and tiny fists tucked under his chin.

As she flipped through the pages, she realized that every stage of the boy's life had been carefully chronicled. She followed his growth from infant to towheaded toddler to boyhood. There was Finn learning to crawl and then to walk, blowing out candles on various birthday cakes, opening Christmas gifts, on the swings at a park, goofing off at the swimming pool, and clutching an Elmo backpack. More than a few later shots showed him climbing a ladder nailed against a tree trunk that led up to a tree house with guardrails and a handmade sign that read: **FORT FINNEGAN.**

The kid had led a charmed life, or so it would seem.

Jenny appeared in a few photos, her eyes always on Finn, often with one hand touching his hair or shoulder.

Jo found no shots of the boy with his father, though a handful appeared to have sections cropped off. Not a bad way to get rid of an ex, short of tossing the photos altogether, which was what Jo's mother had done after Daddy had left them. Jo had nothing but blurry recollections of the man who'd helped create her. Mama had professed she'd wanted no reminders of him and had followed through, wiping out any evidence of his existence: his clothes, his music, his tools, even his smell. All had vanished before Jo could firmly stamp his image in her brain.

Had Jenny wanted to cut Kevin out of her memories, too? Did she resent him so much? Was she afraid of him, or just angry? Dr. Patil had said Jenny hadn't been home when Finn had his fatal accident. If Jenny had blamed Kevin Harrison, could that bitterness between them have led him to a deadly confrontation three years later?

Jo had seen hate destroy a lot of lives, so she couldn't discount its power as a motivator. People had killed for far less.

Hank was pulling out books one by one from the shelves above the desk, opening the pages and shaking them.

Jo left the photo albums on the futon and went toward the room's only closet. She pushed the folding door to one side and tugged a dangling cord to shed light on the small walk-in. For a long moment, she stared in and said nothing.

The space was crammed with stuff. The clothes racks were jammed so tightly, Jo couldn't fit a hand between the hangers. Labeled boxes sat in tight rows below. Stuffed animals lined the shelves above, sitting side by side, all staring at her with their blank button eyes.

Dear God.

She tugged out the first piece of clothing—an extravagant christening gown—before she tucked it back in beside baby onesies with snaps. Farther along were toddler-size shirts and pants, little OshKosh overalls, even a lone snowsuit, everything in perfect condition, pressed and preserved, draped over padded hangers.

Jo reached for a hanger at the tail end of the rack. It held a pint-size Dallas Stars jersey stashed between colorful T-shirts and jeans that were all sized for a six-year-old. That was as big as Finn had gotten.

She felt a tweak in her chest, knowing the boy had never had a chance to grow up.

Kneeling on the carpet, she looked at the boxes beneath the clothes. She drew one toward her marked *Baby Shoes.*

She set aside the lid and reached in to find a cocoon of white tissue. She peeled it apart to reveal a pair of tiny saddle shoes, small enough to hold each in a palm.

Jo exhaled a soft, "Whoa."

Dr. Patil, Patrick Dielman, and Lisa Barton had not lied about one thing: Jenny had never gotten past losing Finn, not by a long shot.

Jo rewrapped the shoes, put them back in the box, and tucked it away. She rose to her feet and glanced up at the stuffed toys that watched her from the closet shelves.

She reached for a teddy bear, its fur pilled from many handlings. The button nose was missing, bits of thread in its place. She drew it to her face, closed her eyes and breathed in. She imagined she would smell a little boy's scent, something soft like baby powder.

But she didn't.

What she smelled was lily of the valley. She thought it might be from the talc on the latex, from handling the toiletries beneath Jenny's sink. But it wasn't. It was the bear. She leaned into the racks of Finn's clothes and realized the scent was on them, too.

"What'd you find?" Hank asked, coming up behind her. "You've been in there forever."

She put the bear back on the shelf. "It's all Finn's things. She kept everything from the time he was a baby. The albums are full of his photos. The whole lot reeks of Crabtree & Evelyn, like she couldn't leave his things alone." Jo felt sad just talking about it.

Hank peered into the closet, and she could see his mind clicking behind the squint. "I can't help but wonder if she couldn't go on living without him. Maybe it was too much."

"She was obsessed with him, yes," Jo said, only agreeing with Hank in part. "He was her only child, and she lost him. She was still hurting. That doesn't make her suicidal."

"Are you sure about that?"

She brushed past him, exiting the closet. She went straight to the desk, not wanting to argue. The only thing that was going to solve the question of how Jenny died was evidence, not emotions.

"The date book's there," Hank said from behind her. "It shows the appointments Dielman mentioned."

Jo picked up the leather-bound book and thumbed through the months until she came upon the current week, spotting circled dates, including one marked *Ernie—Vet*; another, *Patil—Labs*; and the Friday after Thanksgiving. She'd drawn a heart around that date, had written one word inside the square: *Finn*.

The anniversary of his death.

Jo frowned.

There were scribbled notes in the margins. Some looked like grocery and to-do lists, which seemed far removed from diary entries. She flipped back several weeks, stopping at a spot where Jenny had jotted down a phone number and followed it with large, loopy question marks.

She asked Hank if she could borrow his cell, and he handed it over. She punched in the number, let it ring and ring endlessly, until she hung up and gave the phone back to her partner.

"Anything?" he asked.

"Nope."

She'd do a reverse-directory check on it later.

Nothing else popped out at her. This definitely wasn't the diary of a mad housewife as much as the calendar of a very private woman. There were no lunches with friends that Jo could find, no date nights with her husband. What a lonely life to have lived.

Hank pressed an evidence bag on her, one he'd plucked from his inside coat pocket. She dutifully filled out the chain-of-custody tag with her badge number, item, location, and condition before she picked up the date book and slipped it in, sealing the adhesive flap. Then she wrote up a receipt for Dielman and left it on the blotter. "Anything else?"

"I found an empty glasses case in the top drawer."

Jo spotted the black oblong box set to the side of the blotter. "Did Jenny wear glasses?" she asked to his shrug.

"Does it matter?"

"I don't know what matters," she told him. She felt like, where Jenny's life was concerned, she had only photos with parts cropped away. She was still trying to put the whole picture together.

Hank led the way out of the room, and Jo switched off the ceiling light.

She went through the hall closet, finding several women's coats—a tan raincoat and windbreakers, but not the black wool. There was Patrick Dielman's plaid-lined Burberry that he'd worn when he'd come to the station on Tuesday morning. She recalled him dropping a leather glove from his pocket during their initial conversation.

On impulse, she reached into the pockets and withdrew one.

Would the leather grain match the impressions left inside Jenny's car? It would make sense, wouldn't it, for a husband to occasionally drive his wife's vehicle? Except that Jenny's old Nissan seemed a poor cousin to Dielman's BMW. She doubted Patrick Dielman would have wanted to drive his wife's car just for fun.

She placed the glove in an evidence bag and kept looking.

They worked their way through the dining and living rooms, examining chair and sofa cushions, getting on hands and knees to peer beneath furniture, opening drawers and rifling through magazines, until there was nowhere else to search.

She peeled off the latex gloves and shoved them in her pocket, hanging on to the pair of evidence bags. She could hear Dielman's voice on the telephone in the kitchen, speaking in a ragged cadence, and she figured he'd gotten hold of Jenny's sister and was giving her the bad news. He kept talking, turning his back to them as they entered.

Jo glanced toward an opened door beyond the kitchen. She could see a washing machine and dryer. She hooked a thumb in that direction, and Hank nodded as she detoured into the utility room.

There was nothing in the cabinets above the machines but detergents, cleansers, and glass vases that came with FTD flower deliveries.

Jo raised the washing machine lid and peeked inside. She checked the dryer as well, but both were empty.

A litter box sat in the corner, but it looked clean. Either Patrick Dielman was as fastidious about the cat box as keeping dust bunnies from under his bed, or he let the cat out to do his business.

"Jo?" Hank called, and she went back into the kitchen. Dielman was off the phone, but he still ignored them. He faced the sink, his palms braced on the edge of the countertop as he stared out the window.

Hank cleared his throat. "You have a minute, sir?"

He didn't move. "Did you get what you needed?" he asked quietly.

"We took her appointment book and a glove from your coat pocket," Jo said, indicating the evidence bags in hand.

"My glove?" Dielman asked, turning around. "Why?"

Jo kept her voice cool. "It's for comparison, nothing more."

His jaw clenched, but he didn't argue. "Did you find a suicide note?"

"No," she said, but she did have a question. "Did your wife wear glasses?"

"Why does that matter?"

"We found an empty case in her desk."

Dielman shook his head. "They weren't hers."

"Could the case belong to Finn?" Jo asked, because that would make sense. The room was practically a shrine to Jenny's son.

He grimaced. "As you must have noticed, she kept a lot of Finn's belongings. I tried to get her to donate them to charity, but she wouldn't do it. She couldn't let go of him. No matter what I said or did, she wouldn't let him go."

No, she couldn't.

Jo felt an ache deep down, and it had nothing to do with her strained muscles.

"Maybe it comforted her," she suggested, "like she still had a part of him."

"Maybe," he murmured.

He turned around again, and Jo stared at the back of his head, at a spot on his crown where his hair had thinned.

"Mr. Dielman, was Jenny afraid of anything in particular?" she asked. "Was there something that happened that made you think she needed a weapon?"

"I worked in the city, so she was alone a lot, Detective. I couldn't be with her day and night to protect her. If you haven't noticed, the world's a pretty scary place."

Yeah, Jo had noticed.

"Thanks for your time, sir," Hank said from beside her. "I think we'll head next door to Ms. Barton's. You did tell us she was home?"

"She's expecting you."

"Appreciate it," Hank drawled.

"Wait, Detective Larsen, this is for you." Dielman picked up something from the counter and twisted, flipping it at Jo.

A plastic rectangle landed at her feet. She bent to retrieve it.

"My parking card," he said brusquely. "I know you called my secretary this morning, checking up on me. Why don't you have the parking service run it for you? Then you'll know I've been telling the truth. I didn't hurt my wife."

Jo pocketed the card. She met his eyes. "I'll do that."

"We'll be off then, sir," Hank said, touching Jo's arm. "If you think of anything . . ."

"There is something." Dielman faced Hank. "I have to make plans . . . for the funeral. Do you know when they'll be done . . . when they'll release her?"

Her body, Jo thought, which was in the morgue, awaiting postmortem.

"Her autopsy's scheduled for later today," she said. "So it's possible they'll release her as early as tomorrow."

Dielman ran a hand over his hair, nodding. "Tomorrow? Okay. Do I need to call someone? How do I do this?"

"Whatever funeral parlor you choose can contact the morgue, sir," Hank told him. "They'll take it from there."

"I have to bury her by her son. It's what she wanted."

Jo didn't disagree.

Hank tapped her arm again. "Let's go."

Dielman didn't bother to walk them out, but they knew their way. They stepped out into patchy sunlight, and Hank went over to the Ford just long enough to lock the evidence bags in the trunk. Then they headed to Lisa Barton's.

I'm so tired these days. I hardly sleep. When the phone rings, I jump. I never know when the calls will come, but they're always when I'm home alone.

I answer, "Hello?" Then the voice, soft and breathless as a child's, will say, "Mommy, are you there?"

Only today, I was ready.

Today, instead of making me weep, it made me angry.

When it was over, when the soft voice was gone, I pressed *69.

I waited for someone to pick up. Instead, it rang and rang and rang. I nearly gave up, but finally I heard a tentative, "Hello?"

I asked what number I'd called, and a befuddled man rattled it off. I wrote it down but didn't recognize it. "Who are you?" I asked. "Why are you doing this?"

"Lady, I don't know what in the Sam Hill you're yappin' about. This here's a pay phone in the Presbyterian Hospital lobby. I didn't call you, and I sure as hell don't know who did."

Presbyterian Hospital?

The hospital where Finn died?

The same hospital where K has his surgery practice?

Is he trying to torture me?
Who else would do such a thing?
I've racked my brains but only came up with this: no one.

CHAPTER TWELVE

Lisa Barton was waiting for them at her front door and threw it wide as they approached.

"Come on in, y'all. I've got some coffee brewing." She gestured for them to hurry. "Lord, but it's colder than a witch's tits out there."

Tugging on a hip-length tan cardigan, she herded them into the warmth of the foyer and shut the door.

Though Jo had briefly been inside the house the night before, she was struck by the way the interior mirrored the Dielmans'. All the rooms were the same, just flipped. Such uninspired architecture was commonplace in North Texas. Builders slapped up entire neighborhoods where each home looked like a clone, or at least a near-clone, of the one beside it.

"How I hate this weather," Lisa moaned, pulling her cardigan tighter around her. "It's so bitter. Sinks into your bones, doesn't it? Good thing it doesn't last, or I'd pack up and move."

Maybe to spite her, the November wind had scattered brown leaves onto the tiled floor. Jo stepped on one, eliciting a brittle crackle.

"I hate every shade of gray," Lisa went on, looking gloomy.

She'd pinned up her blonde curls, which emphasized her downturned mouth and the unrest in her eyes. Like the temperature outside, her expression showed no warmth. She looked wrung out and on edge.

"Thanks for agreeing to see us again, ma'am," Hank said and smoothed the windblown hair across his crown.

"Any word on my brick thrower?" she asked. "I've got a piece of cardboard in the window till it's fixed, which I hope will be this afternoon. I feel so vulnerable."

"Nothing yet, no," Jo told her, looking straight at her.

Lisa turned away. "I should've figured as much. In real life, the wheels of justice turn slowly. Nothing like on TV, huh?" She glanced at her wristwatch. "Can we make this quick? Patrick needs help with the, um, arrangements."

"We'll do our best," Hank said. "Can we sit?"

"Pardon my bad manners," Lisa drawled. "Follow me."

She led them into the step-down living room, where deep-red walls, jewel-toned upholstery, and bright-spattered canvases of modern art assured Jo that the floor plan of this house was the only thing it had in common with its next-door neighbor.

"Nice digs," Hank murmured as he settled on a sofa with rolled arms.

Jo took a seat on a cane-back chair, the glass coffee table between them. She adjusted her coat beneath her, squirming until the holster didn't bite into her hip.

"You can take off your coats, if you'd like," Lisa said, observing Jo's machinations.

"I'm good." Jo decided leaving it on was a lot easier than trying to remove it with her sore left shoulder. Besides, she had a chill she couldn't shake.

Hank removed his overcoat, folding it in half and depositing it over the sofa's camelback. He tugged at his tweed blazer, adjusting it so he could unbutton it yet keep his holstered weapon covered as he sat.

Jo knew what he was doing. Despite the number of Texans who carried, some folks didn't like guns in their homes, and the sight of one upset them. Lisa Barton didn't seem any too relaxed around them to start with, so maybe that was a good idea.

"Would you like cookies with your coffee?" the woman asked, rubbing her hands together. "I've got some of those peanut butter ones left over from the last Girl Scout crusade. Little girl up the street sold me a boatload."

"Not a fan of the Scouts?" Jo said.

"It's that green uniform," she said. "Gives me nightmares. I never much liked having to dress like everybody else." She glanced at Jo. "You ever a cookie pusher?"

"No, ma'am."

The woman cocked her head, like she was sizing Jo up. "Yeah, you don't seem the type. I'll get the coffee then."

She walked away, the hard soles of her boots clicking on the floor.

"Gal's got taste," Hank said, glancing around them.

Jo figured that anyplace not littered with Legos probably qualified as tasteful to him.

But he was right. Lisa Barton might wear beige and drive a beige car, but her home's interior was bursting with color and texture. Woven rugs covered polished Pergo tiles. A clay pot with a shiny, green patina overflowed with tall stalks of dried wheat. Low-rimmed bowls with a bright red glaze had been set out on the end tables. Jo vaguely smelled ash, but the bowls looked clean. Cut-glass vases filled with Asian lilies had been artfully arranged on various tables.

She reached over to touch a yellow petal, wondering if they were real. Her fingertip came away stained. Nope, definitely not silk.

Hank ran a hand across the gold upholstery that covered the sofa. Then he craned his neck to view the enormous canvas that hung on the wall behind him. Bright slashes of blue, red, and gold crisscrossed the piece, which was signed by the artist.

He let out a whistle. "What do you imagine a thing like this costs?"

Jo squinted. "Way more than our ride."

"A pack of gum's worth more than the Ford."

She smiled, though her amusement faded fast as Lisa Barton reappeared, clutching a silver tray cluttered with coffee mugs, creamer, and sugar.

"Sorry I took so long," she said as she set it down on the table with a rattle. "It's just hard to focus, as you can imagine." She passed a steaming mug to Hank and then one to Jo before sitting down in the second cane-back chair. She slipped her hands between her knees, shaking her head. "I still can't believe that Jenny's dead."

Jo cradled the hot mug and tried to take a sip, but the brew was scalding and too bitter besides. She put it down, noting her partner did likewise. "So how long have you known the Dielmans? They moved here a year and a half ago, right?"

Lisa nodded. "I bought my house about six months before they bought theirs. I was sort of their Welcome Wagon," she said. "I went over as soon as the moving van pulled up. I gave 'em a list of phone numbers for repairmen, that kind of thing."

"How neighborly," Hank remarked.

Lisa Barton smiled tightly. "We hit it off right away."

"Did you hit it off with Jenny, or just with her husband?" Jo asked, since the woman had admitted she and Jenny hadn't exactly been bosom buddies.

"Patrick and I have a lot in common." She crossed her arms and settled back. "He's in the medical field, and so am I. He manages a group practice, and I manage a small medical supply company in the city. We got to chatting straightaway about dealing with physicians,

Medicare, HMOs, contracts, that kind of thing." She shrugged. "I think Pat liked having someone who understood what he did."

"Jenny didn't understand him?"

Lisa shrugged. "I think she had other things on her mind besides Pat's work."

"So it wasn't a good marriage?" Jo asked.

Lisa uncrossed her arms and tugged at the cuffs of her cardigan. "Like I told you already, Jenny was different. I could tell from the start that she was brokenhearted. I don't think I ever saw her laugh." She threw up her hands. "Honestly, I don't know what Pat saw in her except he has this nurturing streak. He thought he could fix her, you know, make her whole again. Well, it didn't work so well, did it?"

Jo didn't detect much sympathy, just matter-of-factness.

"Tell me about your relationship with Patrick Dielman," she said, because it was clear there was something there despite Dielman's denial. No wonder Jenny had been suspicious of an affair.

"Me and Patrick?" Lisa sighed. "Look, Pat came by when he needed a shoulder. I poured the coffee and listened." She shrugged. "Really, that's all there was to it. The guy was in agony. He loved his wife, but she took him for granted. She always had that boy on her mind."

That boy? Jo winced.

Hank leaned forward. "You didn't have much in common with Mrs. Dielman, did you, ma'am?"

Lisa stared at the ceiling for a moment. "Strangely enough, we did have something in common, but it wasn't anything either of us talked about, except once . . ."

"What was that?" Jo asked.

"Late in October, I saw her planting bulbs out front, so I went over. I asked about Thanksgiving and whether she and Pat would be spending time with family. I was curious 'cause I never saw anyone visit." Her brow wrinkled. "Jenny said she had a sister in Iowa, so I asked if that's where she grew up and if her folks were still alive, that kind of thing. I didn't expect her to say much, but she told me her parents were dead. She didn't seem any too sad about it." Lisa's laugh sounded harsh. "I told her I didn't even know my daddy. My mama was a junkie."

"I'm sorry," Jo said, understanding. Rotten childhoods were her specialty.

Lisa's chin jerked up. "Oh, no, don't feel sorry for me, Detective. I ended up with an aunt who worked her butt off scrubbing rich people's toilets. She kept me clean and fed and taught me early on that life wasn't fair."

Her bluntness took Jo aback; Hank, too, if his silence was any indication.

"It's funny," Lisa went on, "how my crappy start made me tougher, while Jenny's seemed to chew her up. You grow a backbone when you're the kid eating free lunches, stuck in after-school programs. I learned that fear can be a great motivator." She sat up straighter. "I might have screwed up a time or two, but I made it to college on scholarships. I even survived sorority rush. I never gave in. I don't think anyone ever taught Jenny that. It's too bad, too, 'cause it might've made a difference."

Jo shifted in her seat. She wasn't sure what to make of Lisa Barton's revelation. Was she playing the sympathy card for a reason? Or was she just being brutally honest? It was hard to gauge.

Lisa grasped her knees and the cuffs of her sweater rode up.

Jo found herself staring at the white scars below the knuckles. She was about to ask if the woman had been in an accident. But Lisa caught her staring and quickly crossed her arms, tucking her hands away.

"Is there anything else you'd like to know?" she said, pointedly adding, "About Jenny."

Yeah, Jo had a million questions.

"Were you aware that she kept a journal?"

Lisa's eyes widened. She was genuinely surprised. "No, I had no idea. Has Pat seen it?"

Hank glanced at Jo. "We're still lookin' for it, ma'am," he said.

"Ah, so maybe it doesn't exist," Lisa remarked with a toss of her head. "I told ya, Detectives, she lived in a world all her own. I wasn't ever sure what to believe."

"Can you be more specific?" Jo said, wanting an example, not just an opinion.

The woman screwed her mouth into a moue of disapproval. "She kept herself tucked away from reality as much as she could, doing her library work and staying home. She didn't venture out much except to grocery shop. Patrick said the past month she started hanging out a lot in that room she keeps with her son's stuff. I got the feeling she liked to wallow in self-pity. When she lost her house key and I handed over the spare Pat had given me, she made a strange comment."

"Strange?" Jo repeated.

"She said she wasn't crazy, that it was all a plan so no one would believe her, something like that." Lisa sighed. "When I tried to get her to explain, she just turned tail and ran."

"You think Jenny was paranoid?"

"Hell, yes, she was paranoid."

"Was Jenny afraid of her husband?" Jo asked, point-blank.

"No." The pale fingers curled into fists. "Patrick would never have hurt her. He's the one who bought her that little gun. If anyone scared that poor woman, it was her ex-husband, the one she wanted to see rot in hell."

That little gun.

"Did she show you the handgun?" Jo asked.

"Patrick told me he'd bought it," Lisa sighed. "Who on earth would've thought she'd go and use it on herself?"

Jo stiffened. The remark was so close to what Kevin Harrison had said: that whatever had happened to Jenny, she'd brought on herself.

At Jo's silence, Lisa turned to Hank. "Well, y'all must be thinking it was suicide, right?"

Hank stayed mum, which gave Jo the chance to ask, "Why would you say that? I don't recall suggesting Mrs. Dielman's gunshot wound was self-inflicted."

Lisa blushed. "Patrick said you were looking for a suicide note, so I just assumed . . ."

Patrick apparently couldn't keep his trap shut.

"Do *you* believe Jenny Dielman killed herself?" Jo asked.

"Are you serious? Didn't Pat show you the room?"

She said *the room* like someone would say *the Loch Ness Monster* or *Bigfoot*, as though it were some living, breathing, horrifying thing.

"Yes," Jo said, "we saw it."

"Well, then, you got a pretty clear picture of Jenny's mental state. When Patrick showed it to me, he begged me to convince Jenny to give away the boy's things. I tried, of course, but she wouldn't do it." Lisa shook her head. "She told me to go to hell."

Jo wasn't surprised.

"Could we wrap this up?" Lisa asked, pushing up a sweater cuff to check her watch. "Patrick's probably wondering where I am."

"Just a few more questions, ma'am." Even if Hank thought Jo was beating a dead horse, she didn't believe it. "You saw Jenny pulling her Nissan out of her driveway as you were entering yours, a little after five on Monday night, is that correct?"

"That's right."

"Did you stop your cars? Roll down the windows to chitchat?"

"Chitchat with Jenny?" Lisa Barton laughed. "For Pete's sake, Detective, it wasn't even forty degrees. I had the heat blasting."

"Did she wave?" Jo asked. "Could you tell if she wore gloves?"

Plucked eyebrows arched. "Gloves?" Her mouth tightened. "Is that important?"

"Everything's important," Jo said. Jenny hadn't been wearing gloves in the security footage from the Warehouse Club, but maybe she'd worn them to drive and had taken them off before she'd gone into the store. If not, the fresh imprints of grain leather from the steering wheel belonged to someone else.

"I can't remember those kind of details," Lisa said. "I saw her so briefly. I'm sorry."

"Did you go anywhere afterward?"

"After what?"

"After you came home," Jo clarified.

"No, I pulled my car into the garage and didn't leave again until I went to work in the morning."

"Was anyone with you? Did you take any phone calls? We can check your phone records if you're not sure . . ."

"Oh, wait." Lisa perked up. "I did hear from Patrick around seven thirty. He was wondering if I'd seen Jenny. He was worried because she should've been home by then. He called a bit later to ask if I'd stay at his house while he went over to the Warehouse Club to look for her. So yes, I did leave for a while. I was over there for about an hour, sitting by the phone."

"And when he returned?"

"He was pretty upset that he couldn't find her. I told him to call the police if he thought something had happened. He was checking with Plainfield Memorial Hospital when I left." She looked at her watch again. "I really need to go over . . ."

"Okay, we'll stop for now." Jo stood to button her coat. Hank gathered up his trench from the arm of the sofa, shrugging it on. "But I might have more questions for you."

Lisa Barton hustled them toward the foyer. "Please, holler when y'all have news about my broken window, although I guess it wasn't Jenny, was it?"

Jo thought that was a pretty good guess.

Hank nudged her, and they walked out to the car.

They'd barely pulled out of the driveway and into the street when Jo saw Lisa Barton scurrying across the yard to Patrick Dielman's front door. She wasn't wearing a coat but kept her long sweater wrapped snugly around her until she rang the bell and disappeared indoors.

"Stop the car."

Hank hit the brakes. The idling engine sounded like a bad cough. "What's wrong?" he asked with an exasperated edge to his voice.

Jo tried to put a finger on it. "She's not telling the truth, Hank, at least not all of it. Something's off with her."

"What?"

"The thing about passing Jenny's car, for one thing."

"How so?"

Jo peered out at the landscape between the two houses. "If Lisa's Acura passed Jenny's Nissan, it would mean Lisa headed into the left side of her circular drive as Jenny emerged from the right side of the Dielmans' drive."

"Okay." He shifted in his seat to look out the windshield and take in what she was describing. "That sounds about right."

"Pull the car around back, would you?" she told him, earning her a confused look. But he did as she asked, moving the Ford slowly down the street and then cutting the corner. She pointed toward the mouth of the alley.

"You want to go there?"

"Yeah."

The homes in Woodstream Estates all had garages at the rear, facing the alleys that ran behind. They were out of sight from the main street, which was why Lisa Barton's statement didn't make sense.

When they reached the rear of the Dielman and Barton houses, Jo asked him to park, and he did. He cut the engine and slung an arm over the wheel, squinting at the brick pens situated at the bottom of each drive that held trash cans with lids.

Jo stared, too. "Lisa said she pulled into her garage and didn't take the car out again until the next morning. But if she'd driven into the garage, she would've had to enter the alley, like we just did. She wouldn't have been on Ella Drive. She would never have seen Jenny at all."

"Maybe she parked in front initially and then moved the car around back later."

"Maybe," Jo agreed. Or maybe Lisa Barton was a liar.

She hesitated, shifting position enough to shove her fingers into her pocket and retrieve the balled-up latex gloves.

Hank stared at her as she fussed with them, using her teeth to pull them back on. "You plan on going dumpster diving?"

"Yep."

He clicked tongue against teeth.

She got out of the car and went over to Lisa Barton's bins first, removing the lids and peering down into ten gallons of plastic that held nothing but gooey residue at the bottom, a few leaves, and sticky scraps of paper.

She checked Dielman's cans next, the first one as empty as Lisa Barton's. But the second was a different story.

Jo reached into its less-than-sweet-smelling depths to pluck out a white kitchen bag, its yellow handles loosely tied. She set it on the ground and worked on the clumsy knot, opening up the bag to see what was inside.

It took her a moment to realize what the tan fabric-covered pillow was, until she saw the name stitched in the corner. She noted a brown stain across one side, and her first thought was blood.

She got up and replaced the lid on the trash can, taking the white plastic bag with her. Hank popped the trunk so Jo could toss the bag in.

"What the hell is that?" he asked, as she climbed into the passenger seat, shoving the gloves back in her pocket. "Is it evidence? Or you just into stealing other people's junk?"

"It's not stealing," she reminded him as she went around to the passenger door. "When your trash hits the curb, it's as good as public property, right?"

He started the car, giving her a sideways look. "You gonna make me play twenty questions?"

"No." She started to pull on her seat belt but then paused, glancing up the alley, at the fences and tool sheds, even a silver RV. There were plenty of spots for a feline to hide. She felt a pang behind her ribs, hoping her gut was way off this time and Jenny's cat was all right.

"You were saying?"

"It's a cat bed," she told him, "personalized for Ernie."

Hank scrunched up his brow. "Dielman threw it out?"

"It looks like there's blood on it."

"Whose?"

Jo shrugged. But she meant to find out.

"You think he threw the cat out, too?"

"Or Ernie got away," she said. "Maybe he went looking for Jenny."

Her partner snorted. "Well, if he ends up roadkill, he'll meet her fast enough, won't he?"

But Jo hardly heard him. She stared at the back of the house where a woman who'd survived an unbearable loss had lived and breathed and hoped for something better, a way out of the darkness that had gripped her heart and filled her head.

So much for answered prayers.

I started writing down everything I could remember, all the things K said had happened that night. I wrote down what they told me at the hospital, about how Finn must have fallen, breaking his neck, scraping his arms and legs.

No one explained why the scrapes on his arms and knees looked like the same ones that I'd kissed and sprayed with Bactine just days before. Finn was always flying about like a daredevil, always falling and crashing into something. When I cradled him, rocking his lifeless body beneath the hospital lights, I didn't see any new cuts or bruises. I would have remembered that. Shouldn't there have been some new marks, something more?

What happened to his socks? Why wasn't he wearing underwear? It was like he'd been redressed quickly, missing things only a mother would notice.

Like his glasses.

I thought I'd find them in the hospital bag or beneath the tree, crushed, the lenses broken. When I finally made it home that night, I found them on the sink, neatly folded.

I held on to them, believing they were a sign. I wasn't sure, at first, what they were trying to tell me. But I've begun to put the pieces together.

CHAPTER THIRTEEN

Jo called Emma Slater at the crime lab and told her she had some evidence pertaining to the Jenny Dielman case to drop off. Emma begged for half an hour's leeway. "I'm just leaving a scene on the north side of town," she said. "I've got results to share with you, so I'd like to be there when you come."

Hank suggested they stop for lunch at Wendy's on Harry Hines, not far from Parkland Hospital. He ordered like a starving man. Jo wasn't the least bit hungry.

"You were pretty quiet this morning," Jo said, once Hank had devoured a large order of fries and a double cheeseburger.

"I thought I'd let you handle the questions," he replied, wiping the grease from his fingers. "You seem to have more of them than I do."

"So humor me for a minute and play devil's advocate." She leaned forearms on the table.

He tossed a ball of napkins on his tray. "Lay it on me."

Jo cleared her throat. "For starters, let's say Jenny was abducted from the Warehouse Club lot, a random attack."

"Okay." He sat back in his chair, and the plastic creaked.

"She's alone and carrying bags, an easy mark. He gets her from behind and overpowers her, pushes her into her car, and takes off. There aren't working surveillance cameras in the lot, and nobody sees anything."

"So she's driving?"

"Yeah," Jo said.

"Is he armed?"

"Maybe he's got his own gun, but he finds hers in the glove compartment. He makes her drive to the quarry and has some fun with her before he takes her out."

Hank grunted. "We've got no obvious evidence of assault. She had her clothes on. You think he attacked her and then re-dressed her before he walked her down to the pit?"

Damn. He had her there.

Jo pondered that scenario for another few minutes. "The guy's a neatnik. He watches The Discovery Channel. He knows he has to clean up after himself. He wears leather gloves to keep us from getting his prints, and he doesn't penetrate her, so there's no chance of leaving DNA."

"You said he made her drive out to the quarry," Hank said, scratching his jaw. "So how did he get home? You figure he walked all the way back to town?"

Jo pinched the bridge of her nose. This was giving her a headache. "He had an accomplice."

"Okay, an accomplice."

She shifted in her seat. "No, nix that. Let's say it wasn't random at all. She wasn't robbed. Her cash and credit cards, her wedding ring, her shopping bag, her cell phone, everything was there, except the silver locket and her coat—"

"She could have left both somewhere else," he interrupted, "if she made a pit stop after shopping."

But where would she have stopped? There wasn't much between the strip mall and the quarry except for construction sites and mobile realty offices.

Jo went with her gut. "What if this was personal? What if her abductor was someone she knew? Maybe it was even planned. What if somebody wanted Jenny Dielman out of the way for good and had been waiting for an opportunity to grab her?"

"Who?" Hank settled his hands on his belly. "Her husband? Didn't his secretary vouch for him about working late that night?"

She nodded. Dielman had given up his parking card, too, so Jo would know soon enough if he—and his secretary—had fudged the truth.

"You think he's playing us?" Hank asked. "That he and Blondie next door are really having an affair and wanted Jenny out of the picture?"

Jo rested her chin on her fist. "They could have cooked it up together."

"But why make such a big production? Think about it. Both Dielman and Barton work in the medical field. They knew Jenny was taking an antidepressant. She had a prescription for sleeping pills, too. Wouldn't it be easier if they'd doped her up and then claimed she OD'd? Especially if she'd tried it before, which I'm guessing she did."

Crap. She hated how good he was at this game.

Jo rubbed her forehead, trying to think her way out of this paper bag he'd put her in. "There has to be a motive, right? A reason she ended up with a slug in her head. What if she stopped to help somebody whose car was broken down on the side of the road?"

He frowned. "So we're back to thinking it's random?"

Jo wanted to bang her head on the table.

She was going in circles like a carnival wheel of fortune, or maybe wheel of misfortune in this case.

Round and round and round it goes. Where it stops, nobody knows.

◆ ◆ ◆

It took about five minutes to get from Wendy's to the south campus of Parkland Hospital, where the Institute of Forensic Sciences was located. Jo planned to drop off the evidence bags from the Dielmans' house at the crime lab while her partner attended Jenny's autopsy, scheduled for two o'clock.

She decided against being there herself, preferring to meet with Emma and see what forensics had turned up so far.

There was another reason why she was skipping the postmortem, though she would never admit it to anyone else. She couldn't bear to gaze into the dead woman's eyes again. She already felt like she was failing Jenny somehow. This case was giving her an itch beneath her skin that wouldn't stop.

As Hank drove the Ford into the cavelike darkness of the hospital's parking garage, she blinked at the fluorescent-tube lighting that illuminated rows of cars against the gray.

A shadow darted in their path, a slim figure slipping from behind an SUV, and Hank hit the brakes, sending Jo's heart into overdrive. The woman wasn't even looking at them, so absorbed was she in tugging a child along behind her.

Hank cursed under his breath and waved impatiently for them to pass.

Jo had braced her hands against the dash and held on, watching as the pair hurried toward a nearby stairwell. The child turned to stare back at them until his mother jerked his arm, and he slid his gaze from the car to his feet as she dragged him forward.

"Good thing I wasn't playing Angry Birds on my phone," Hank said sarcastically.

Jo willed her pulse to slow down.

"God watches over invalids and little children," Mama had said to her when she was a child herself, and she'd known even then it was a lie.

I believe in the incomprehensibility of God.

The Balzac quote popped into her head again, and this time, she knew where it was from: one of the letters he'd penned to Madame Hanska, the second of his wives, perhaps his greatest love, who'd held his hand as he'd died. That was exactly how Jo felt. If there were a God, He was most certainly incomprehensible.

"Well, shit on a stick," Hank grumbled, drawing her attention from her own thoughts. "All the good spots are taken."

"It won't kill you to walk."

He muttered something unintelligible, and she pointed to an empty space ahead. It wasn't as close to the stairwell as he would've liked, but too damn bad.

Bum knees and all, Hank still managed to exit the car before she did. He slapped the driver's-side door closed while she was still working to unfasten her seat belt, hating how much her strained left shoulder restricted her motion.

While she extricated herself, Hank went around to the trunk. By the time she got out, he held the evidence bag with Dielman's glove and the trash bag with the cat bed.

Jo clenched her teeth as she stretched aching ligaments, glad at least that he couldn't walk fast enough to get much ahead of her. Between his worn-out joints and her battered ones, she figured they looked like a pretty pathetic pair as they slowly shuffled down the stairwell.

"You ready for this?" Jo asked.

He grunted. "I'm not gonna start getting queasy now."

"Even after a double cheeseburger?"

"Been here too many times, Larsen," he said. "Piece of cake."

"Uh-huh."

She wondered if the ME could give him a barf bag, just in case.

They picked up visitors' badges, and Jo relieved him of the bags before they separated. Hank headed for the subterranean floor that housed the morgue, and she toward the Trace Evidence Analysis Lab, where she would meet Emma.

After a quick trip on the elevator, bypassing white-coated personnel who moved through the hallways like ants, Jo found Emma in the hallway outside her office.

The petite, gray-haired lab tech quickly whisked her into the room.

Adam had once told her that Emma had been earmarked on several occasions for an administrative position running the lab, and she'd turned down the offers flat. "She loves going out in the field," he said. "She'd wilt behind a desk, working on budgets and filling out employee evaluations. She likes to get her hands dirty. That's the fun of it for her."

Jo understood one hundred percent.

She turned over the cat bed taken from the Dielmans' trash along with Patrick's leather glove. Then Emma flipped open a manila folder, exposing a sheaf of notes, computer printouts, and photographs clipped together between the covers. She thumbed through them, found what she wanted, settled her arms on the desk, and fixed her gaze on Jo.

"Let's start with your victim's car," she said in her no-nonsense voice. "The Nissan 240SX found at the quarry."

Jo set her small notebook on her thigh, her pen ready to scribble down the information. "Shoot."

"Wish I could tell you differently, but there wasn't much we could do with the fibers we pulled from the seats." Emma frowned. "We've got a few synthetic fibers that don't match anything Jennifer Dielman was wearing. But unless you've got a standard for comparison, it doesn't mean much right now."

A standard, Jo knew, meant a suspect, or suspects.

"Did you find gloves that matched the imprint on the steering wheel?"

"Nope," Emma said, "we didn't find gloves in the car or with the body." She tapped the evidence bag Jo had delivered moments earlier. "Though I'll give this a going-over today, see if it's a match." The crinkles around her eyes deepened. "We did find a few other things that should interest you."

Jo sat up straighter.

Emma removed two photographs from the folder and passed them across the desk to her. "Look at the position of the driver's seat. Jennifer Dielman was approximately five feet five inches tall, correct?"

"Yes." That's what was on her Texas DL.

"The driver's seat was adjusted to accommodate someone with longer legs than that, perhaps a person at least five foot eight to six feet."

Jo studied the photograph of the interior of the Nissan as Emma spoke, reading the numbers on a tape measure that ran from the pedals to the cushion. All too evident was that the driver's seat had been moved back farther than the passenger's seat beside it.

"So someone besides Jenny was driving?"

Emma nodded. "That'd be my guess. But the mirrors weren't moved. Rearview and side were still angled for someone your victim's height. So whoever took the wheel must not have had far to go, or at least wasn't worried much about traffic."

Jo realized what that meant. Someone else *had* driven Jenny's car to the quarry, from a nearby location. A pit stop, like Hank had suggested during their "what if" session.

"There were no bloodstains in the trunk, no trace to suggest your victim was in there," Emma continued. "The Nissan 240SX has a very small carrying capacity besides. You could transport a child in the trunk, no problem, but you'd be hard-pressed to fit an adult female, even one as petite as Mrs. Dielman, unless she was incapacitated and manipulated into the space."

"Okay."

So Jenny was likely killed at the quarry. If she had been killed elsewhere and moved, there'd be a trail of blood.

But that still didn't answer the question of how their suspect had gotten away from the quarry, unless another vehicle was involved, one whose tracks had been obliterated by the rain.

The goddamned rain.

She handed the photographs back, making a few notes in her book. "What about the weapon?" she asked. "Any prints on the twenty-two?"

Emma paused a beat. "No, not a one. Though the water could have degraded the surface, I don't think it was submerged long enough to polish it this clean. It was buffed shinier than the mayor's Bruno Maglis."

"You think it was wiped down deliberately before it hit the water?" That was pretty calculating.

"Inside and out."

Jo could hardly sit still.

No prints on the gun, not even Jenny's. Nothing.

"She didn't kill herself," she said.

Emma smiled dryly. "Be kind of tricky to pull that off without touching the weapon."

An ugly realization took up residence in Jo's mind: someone had deliberately left the gun for them to find, hoping they'd misread the evidence and believe the death to be suicide.

No stranger would do that.

But someone who knew Jenny would.

"Was there any skin tissue beneath her fingernails?" Jo asked. Had Jenny put up a struggle, or had she given up?

"Just the yellow dirt from the quarry."

"No defense wounds?"

"None."

Jo pinched her eyes shut.

Did you want to die, Jenny? Did you just let him take you and kill you without a fight?

"There's something else that might be significant," Emma remarked, and Jo forced her attention toward another photograph, this one of Jenny Dielman's fleece pullover, or at least a small portion of it. "See there?" Emma's pinkie fixed on a smudge on the sleeve.

"Is that blood?" Jo asked, though it was too dark, more an inky black than rust.

"It's lubricant."

"From the car?"

"No, like WD-40," Emma said.

"Could she have brushed up against door hinges?"

"That's a possibility."

Jo figured the grease could have come from anywhere. Maybe the pullover had been worn another day without a washing in between, and the stain was old. Although she kind of doubted that was the case after seeing the spotless state of the Dielmans' house.

"What about human hair? Any that weren't Jenny's?"

"I have to tell you, Detective, that was one extremely clean vehicle." Emma clasped her hands, settling them in front of her, atop the papers and charts. "We didn't find much, except the synthetic fabric fibers that I mentioned and a few strands of hair on the driver's seat and the passenger's side that matched the decedent. But there were a number of black animal hairs."

Jo had a pretty good idea about those. "Were they feline?"

Emma gave her a long look. "They were."

"Jenny has a black cat."

Had a cat.

"That would explain it. She transferred what the animal shed from her clothing onto the cloth seats in her car."

"Did you find a silver locket in the car anywhere?"

Emma scanned the papers in front of her, although Jo was sure the woman had each report memorized, stored in her brain neat as computer files. "No, no locket."

Maybe Patrick Dielman had been wrong about Jenny always wearing it. She could have taken it off, packed it away, or buried it in the backyard. Hell, it could be in the pocket of her missing coat.

"Her watch did prove helpful," Emma continued. "It's stainless steel with a chronograph. No watches are entirely waterproof, and this one had a relatively low threshold for water resistance. So it leaked."

She had Jo's full attention.

"The watch died in the water," the evidence tech said. "It was stuck on Monday's date, and the hands stopped at eight forty-five, though that's not necessarily time of death. It probably took a while for the case to fill and the movement to stop. The autopsy should confirm it, but Jennifer Dielman was dead in the quarry the night she disappeared. There's no way she could've tossed a brick through her neighbor's window."

"Are you sure?"

"The car was driven out to the quarry before the rains came. Your vic wasn't going anywhere."

Jo could hardly breathe.

There was no suicide.

Jenny was killed on Monday night.

The .22 had no prints.

It wasn't so much that she felt in the right; but she felt justified, sure that Jenny's death hadn't been by her own hand. There was something more to this case, a *reason* for everything that they didn't understand, not yet. But they would.

"I still need to look at that blue scarf, so I'll get back to you on that soon." Emma paused before sifting through the file to grab a page.

"I did get the vic's phone running, but there wasn't much there." She handed the paper to Jo. "She mostly used it to call Des Moines, Iowa, a number listed as Kimberly Parker, as well as a local veterinary clinic, and"—Emma arched her brows—"a recent call to a pay phone at Presbyterian Hospital."

"A pay phone?" Jo stared at the number on the sheet. It seemed familiar. Was it the one Jenny Dielman had jotted down with a question mark in her appointment book?

"Any texts or e-mails?"

"No. It's like the vic hardly used it."

"I can't thank you enough," Jo said, heart skidding so fast behind her ribs that she felt a little light-headed. "What about the final reports?"

"It might take a while to get them transcribed. We're a little backed up these days."

Jo shoved her notebook and pen inside her coat pocket and started to rise, but Emma gestured with a small hand.

"Sit, sit. I'm not done with you yet. I've got one more thing to share."

There's more? Jo arched her brows but did as asked.

"It's interesting what you don't notice until you take your time," Emma started. "Once the vehicle's impounded and we have better lighting and a more controlled environment, it's amazing what turns up."

Jo tried not to fidget.

"We recovered a piece of paper, crumpled up pretty thoroughly and wedged beneath the driver's seat. It was stained with coffee, which is probably why it ended up trashed." Emma withdrew a sealed plastic bag from the opened folder. She extended it to Jo, who took it with trembling fingers. "Still, I think you'll find it very interesting."

Oh, God.

Her mouth went dry.

It couldn't be.

The paper was thoroughly rumpled and most of it a dingy, tea color. The ink was blurred but legible, the edge ragged, as if hastily torn from a notebook so the damp wouldn't soak through the other pages.

"We got a print off a corner, and it matches your vic," Emma went on, but Jo barely heard her. "Figured you'd want to take a look, and we're done with it here. So there you are."

"Oh, God," she breathed, fingers shaking as she ran them over the words encased in the plastic, making certain it was real.

It was a page from Jenny's missing journal.

It's happened again.

I can smell it in the house. That stale scent that isn't Pat's or mine.

Has someone been here while I was at the library? Do they know my schedule and break in while I'm gone?

But how? The doors were locked. I checked. Yet there were crumbles of mud just inside the back door, like they'd been tracked in on shoes. The floor was clean when I left for work. Pat doesn't like messes. And I know he wouldn't have worn muddy shoes inside. He's phobic about germs.

This time, I didn't call him. I didn't get so hysterical I had to take a pill and lie down. What I did was carefully look around, making notes of what seemed off. First, the dirt, then my bureau drawers, not quite closed, the things I folded so carefully mussed like someone had riffled through them. Someone searching for something? What did they want?

I was sitting at the kitchen table when Pat got home. I was calm as could be. When I told him I was sure this time someone had been here, he sighed. "It's easy to forget little things," he told me, like I was imagining things or maybe responsible for them.

"Can we change the locks?" I asked, because it made me nervous to think anyone could get in and walk around while we weren't home.

Patrick sat down beside me and took my hand. "It's the anniversary coming up, Jen. I'm sure it's got you in knots again. No one's wandering through the house just to mess up your underwear. Everything's fine. You're just stressed out."

Did my blue scarf disappear because I was stressed out? It was gone from my dresser drawer. Patrick had given it to me for my birthday last month. It was the prettiest color, bright blue like a peacock.

I told Patrick the scarf was missing. I thought he'd believe me, that he'd suggest we call the police right away and report an intruder. Instead, he said I'd probably misplaced it, and it would likely turn up soon.

But I hadn't misplaced it. I'd been so careful with it. Lisa had made a point to tell me how much it cost.

"I'm not making this up," I said for all the good it did.

Unless Patrick didn't want to call the police because he knew who'd come into our house.

Or even worse, had let her in.

CHAPTER FOURTEEN

Jo knocked on the door to Adam's office. When no one answered, she tried the knob. It turned easily. She let herself in and paused, sighing as she looked around.

The room was in its usual state of chaos, with books filling every available nook and cranny. There weren't enough shelves to hold them all, so Adam had stacked them on the floor between the simple furnishings.

Holding the bag with the page from Jenny's journal against her hip, she went over to his desk, noting the number of files piled in the in-box. There were so many papers, mail, and photographs scattered about, she wondered how he ever knew where anything was. He'd told her he had his own filing system and never had a problem finding what he needed.

Jo resisted the urge to straighten up.

She did a quick scan of the desk for Finn Harrison's file, wondering if he'd had a chance to pull it for her yet. Then she gave up the futile task. Only a psychic could locate it amid the clutter.

But her digging did unearth something else.

Caught in the leather corner of the partially buried blotter was a photograph, and Jo pushed aside a fistful of mail in order to remove it.

Her heart leapt.

The ill-focused shot showed a woman with inky curls tossed wildly around her face, head thrown back, and grin wide with delight. Her skin browned by the sun, she wore cutoff shorts and a red bikini top. Her lean arms were extended, her hands busy with the reel of a fishing rod. In the bottom-right corner was the silver glimmer of a striped bass caught on the hook, flipping out of the water.

Jo could still feel the heat of the day on her back and shoulders, could hear the water lapping at the boat and Adam laughing as she'd reeled in the fish. "Hold it a minute," she remembered him crying. "Where the heck's my phone so I can get a picture of this?"

That was four years ago.

She couldn't believe he'd kept the picture.

They hadn't been involved for long, maybe a few months, when he'd taken her camping on Lake Granbury for a weekend. They'd spent the second night at a bed-and-breakfast, a beautiful old Victorian that sat right on the water. She'd lost herself in him, had let her guard down, and he'd whispered in her ear after making love how good he felt when he was with her, how she made his heart race. He'd even put her hand against his chest to feel it, murmuring as he did: "See what you do to me?"

And she had given in to her emotions, forgetting until they packed up the next morning to go home that he wasn't hers.

For the next few years, Jo had accepted his married state because it gave her what she needed: an excuse to be with him without the commitment. Avoiding intimacy was a pattern. Vulnerability only brought pain. Until she'd realized she wanted more of him—all of him—and he belonged to someone else.

Jo had pulled up her emotional drawbridge, but it was too late. People who knew them—in the Dallas PD and at the ME's office—had started to talk, and it got too uncomfortable. Jo had left Dallas not long after.

Adam had accused her of running, of being afraid of her emotions, and she let him believe he was right. If he left his wife, she wanted it to be his choice, not because she pressured him or because they got caught. Jo had figured that after she moved to Plainfield, Adam would forget about her. Only he hadn't, had he? Adam and his wife had split, and he had ultimately chosen to be with her. The only thing hanging between them now was *her* past, and Jo would deal with that, too.

She tucked the photograph back into the corner of the blotter and smothered it with papers, wishing her pulse would slow down.

Letting out a held breath, she sank into his worn leather chair, its contours molded to the shape of his body. It even held his scent, a musky maleness mixed with subtle lime-tinged aftershave. She ran a hand over the crackles in the armrest as she settled in, feeling uncharacteristically dainty in its overstuffed confines. Her feet barely touched the floor. She wasn't a shrimp by any means, but Adam was half a foot taller.

She thought of the driver's seat in Jenny's Nissan, how Emma had suggested it had been adjusted to accommodate a taller person, and adrenaline rushed through her.

A taller person.

There had been someone else in the car. They would find whoever it was. Jenny deserved that.

Jo set the baggie with the stained and wrinkled page in front of her and simply stared at it for a good long while, studying the slightly smeared handwriting and imagining Jenny scribbling down her deepest emotions, sipping coffee as she paused between thoughts.

She felt almost guilty for looking.

I see Finn in my dreams.

In the best ones, his laughter fills my head, and I am whole again. In the worst, he's afraid and calling for me, but I can't reach him in time.

She swallowed hard, feeling horribly intrusive. Even in those first spare sentences, Jenny's pain washed through her, sharp as a knife.

He feels so close to me that my heart bangs with hope that I'll open my eyes, and he'll be there. But he isn't and won't ever be.

She was more certain now than ever that this woman, whom everyone had found to be unobtrusive and quiet, had harbored so much more inside than they would ever know.

I wake up aching for him. And I can't stop crying.

Tears slid down Jo's cheeks, and she used the cuff of her coat to wipe at her face, the wool rough against her skin.

I know I'll never see him again, not as long as I'm here.

She thought of Jenny's eyes in the photograph, how haunted they'd seemed, like she had seen things she'd never forget but wished she could. Jo understood the truth all too clearly then, so that she felt sick to her stomach at what that meant.

Jenny Dielman hadn't killed herself.

She just hadn't wanted to live.

Had whoever helped her cross that line realized the difference? Had it made it easier to pull the trigger? Like her killer was doing her a favor in the end, releasing her to someplace sweeter than the bleakness that had tormented her on Earth?

Jo's pager went off—she was still short a cell phone—and she started at the sound, swiping sleeve to runny nose before grabbing the thing from her belt, fingers trembling.

She used Adam's phone to dial Dispatch. "Yeah, Susie, what's up?"

"Sorry to bother you, Detective, but I've got a lady on hold. She's called several times already this morning. She really wants to talk to you."

"Who?"

"Her name's Kimberly Parker. Said she's the sister of the woman you found in the quarry."

Jo's pulse picked up a notch. "Patch her through, okay?"

"Give me a sec."

She heard a series of clicks before Susie said, "Go ahead," and then a hesitant voice came on the line.

"Detective Larsen?"

"Yes, I'm here." She settled on the very edge of the chair, leaning against Adam's desk. "You've been trying to reach me?"

"I need to talk to you, about my sister."

"First, let me say how sorry I am."

"Thank you." It was softly uttered, almost dismissive, like that was all the sympathy she could handle. "I'm flying down for her funeral on Friday, but I had to tell you something. I don't know if it'll mean anything to you or not."

"Go on." Jo held the handset to her ear and waited.

"Jenny had been calling me lately, in the morning when she was on break at the library. She said she couldn't talk freely when Patrick was around, that there were things she didn't want him to hear. He treated her like a child. It would've driven me crazy, but I think she liked having her husband pay attention. Kevin was the opposite. He didn't give a damn what she did."

"Kevin Harrison," Jo said.

"Yes, the good doctor," Kimberly remarked sourly. "He mostly ignored Jenny, which I don't think was bad, all things considered."

Jo gave her room to continue.

"The past few weeks, I don't know . . ." Jenny's sister sighed, sounding agitated. "Something was up, and she wouldn't tell me what exactly. I do know it had to do with Finn and trying to make sense of why he died. She wouldn't let it go."

Jo knew that much already.

"Last week, she sent me a shoe box that she wanted me to hold on to, just in case. It's like she knew something was going to happen. I wish she would've told me what had her so nervous."

Jo took a stab. "Was her journal in the box?"

"It wasn't a journal. It's a yellow T-shirt and a pair of eyeglasses. The shirt's a size six, and the glasses are smallish. I'm pretty sure they were Finn's."

A T-shirt and glasses?

"Was there a note?" Jo asked.

"Just the letter that told me to take the box to the police if anything went wrong," Kimberly said and sighed again. "I thought she was being melodramatic, you know, to get my attention. Jenny was pretty overloaded on emotion."

"Will you bring the box with you when you come?"

"I will."

"Did you tell anyone else about it?"

"No," Kimberly said, her voice turning edgy. "I didn't tell Patrick anything. I figure that's who you mean."

Yes, Jo thought, but didn't say.

"Look, I'll fly down as soon as I can work things out with my babysitter. You can have the box. If it has anything to do with Jenny's death, then I sure don't want it. I'll call when I get a flight to Dallas. I've got to take care of a few things with my family here first."

"You're married?"

"Divorced with two kids," she said with a sad laugh. "It's a wonder Jenny or I could stand to be married at all, what with our folks as an example."

"Oh?"

"If Patrick didn't fill you in, then maybe Jenny didn't clue him in either." Kimberly sniffed. "Our father was the only GP in the Iowa town where we grew up."

"He was a general practitioner?" Jo tried to clarify.

"Jenny used to say it stood for *gutless prick*. He wasn't a nice man, Detective. When he had a bad day, which was pretty near every day, he picked on my mother. And when she wasn't around or he got tired of her, he'd pick on Jen." Jo heard the slow intake of her breath. "He knew how to hit in all the places that wouldn't show, so no one at school would ask questions. But mostly, he yelled and put us down, just to keep us in our places."

Jo understood it now, that faraway look in Jenny's eyes in the photograph. She knew it all too well. "Did he sexually abuse her?"

"I don't think so." Kimberly paused. "I was six years younger. She kept him away from me, took the brunt of it herself. God"—she hesitated, drawing in a breath—"I don't know how she survived as long as she did, but I owe her for it."

Jo swallowed hard. It was no surprise to learn that Jenny had been victimized as a child. That explained her failed marriage, clinging to her dead son, letting Patrick hold all the cards in their relationship. It all fit.

"It's kind of ironic, isn't it?" Jenny's sister continued. "That she went to work at a hospital and married a doctor. You would've figured she'd stay away from men who thought they were God, after our daddy. Jen never said it outright, but I think Kevin pushed her around. She did tell me once that she caught him screaming at Finn, and it freaked her out enough to threaten to take Finn and leave."

Kevin Harrison pushed her around?

"He cheated on her, for sure, with that rich bitch he married. Jenny knew it was going on, but she let it slide because she loved Finn more, if that makes sense. People don't learn, do they? My therapist says it's a cycle, and those of us who've been burned keep sticking our fingers in the fire, over and over again."

Over and over and over.

Jo rubbed her eyes.

"You'll get him, won't you?" The voice that asked sounded so small, the hopeful tone of a little sister.

"We'll get him," Jo said, wondering if the thought had crossed Kimberly's mind that *him* might be someone Jenny had known very well, had perhaps even loved.

Gently, she put the handset back into the cradle. Then she returned her focus to the slip of paper captured in the evidence bag. She read the words Jenny had written until they felt burned into her brain.

And I can't stop crying. I know I'll never see him again, not as long as I'm here.

"Must be some letter."

Jo jerked her head up at the voice, something melting inside her.

Adam stood across the room, watching her. She hadn't even heard him enter.

He approached the desk, coming around behind her, trying to get a peek at what she was reading. "I've never seen anyone so thoroughly engrossed. What've you got there?"

"Just a page from the diary of a lost soul," she said quietly. She felt as though she'd lost her equilibrium and needed to find it again.

"The woman from the quarry?"

"Jenny, yes."

"Wow." He removed his glasses and rubbed the lenses on his scrub shirt, squinting at her until he replaced them. "Where'd it turn up?"

"Emma found it after they'd impounded the car. It was shoved under the driver's seat. We still haven't tracked down the journal."

"You'll find it, Jo."

She dropped her head.

He nudged her with the toe of his Puma. "You okay, Rocky?"

She self-consciously fingered the scratch at her jawline as she lifted her chin. "I'm scabbing up rather nicely, don't you think?"

"How's the clipped wing?"

She bent her left arm and gingerly raised it, grimacing when she approached shoulder level. "Better every minute."

"Don't push it," he warned.

"I won't if you won't."

"Funny." He leaned a hip against the desk and folded his arms across his chest. His green scrubs looked fresh, and no booties obscured the black shoes. He must've cleaned up after a postmortem. She wondered if he'd seen the victims from the multicar pileup, but didn't ask.

She shifted in the chair, which emitted mournful creaks. "You wouldn't know what's happening—"

"With your vic on Baldwin's table?" He watched her closely, thick eyebrows cinched, adding, as if to show he'd paid attention, "Jenny."

"You didn't poke your head in, perchance?"

"Perchance?" he echoed and smiled his crooked smile, eyes crinkling. "Matter of fact, I bumped into your partner in the hallway outside the autopsy suite. It seems he needed a breath of fresh air."

Mr. Been-Here-Too-Many-Times-It's-A-Piece-Of-Cake? Ha!

"Hank needed air?"

Adam rubbed his jaw. "He said he had a bug."

More like a Wendy's double cheeseburger and acid reflux. She kept a straight face, but it was tough. "Did he say how much longer it'd take?"

"He mentioned sticking around to see the skull cracked."

"Any idea when that'll be?"

"From the sounds of it, Baldwin had the bone saw running." Adam glanced at the clock on the wall, drawing Jo's eyes there as well. "Give him another hour, more or less."

God, she hated waiting.

She blew out a slow breath, already impatient to get back to the station, to tell Captain Morris what she'd learned from Emma Slater, to type up her notes before their interview with Dr. Kevin Harrison at seven.

"It really sucks, you know," she said.

"What? Phelps getting sick?"

"No." She met Adam's eyes. He was still keeping a distance, leaning against the corner of his desk, barely near enough to touch. "All the ways people hurt each other."

"You can't fix the world, Jo," he said.

"Of course I can't."

"But you want to, which is why you're so good at what you do. I love that about you. You're so passionate, so intense."

There was no guile in his face, nothing but affection. He was so well meaning. He made her feel like a liar sometimes, even when she hadn't lied except by omission.

"Thanks for that."

His brown hair stuck out in unruly tufts, and she wanted to smooth them over, to touch the grooves at the sides of his mouth, the lines on his brow, creased with concern. He worried so much about her.

She wished she could pour out her heart. Tell him everything.

But she couldn't. She wasn't ready.

Instead, she stuck to what was foremost on her mind.

"I'm sitting here, reading her thoughts, and I want to weep for her. I can't imagine how painful her days were. She was racked with guilt about Finn's death, taking meds to cope, but never getting over him. You should see the closet she kept with all of his—"

Adam snapped his fingers, and she stopped in midsentence.

"Finnegan Harrison," he said, and his eyes went wide behind his preppy glasses. "You just reminded me."

"I did?"

"Yeah." He pushed away from the desk and turned to shuffle through the mess that buried the blotter. "I found that file you asked me to track down. Here we go." He shuffled papers and photos and charts so that it appeared he was only making things worse. Then he magically extracted a manila envelope from amid the chaos and handed it to her.

She set the bag with the journal page behind her back and fumbled with the clasp to open the envelope. Carefully, she emptied its contents into her lap.

Inside were several pages of records from Presbyterian Hospital. "Did you look already?" Jo asked him.

Adam crossed his arms, nodding. "Yes."

"And?"

"Apparently, the kid's neck snapped when he fell from a tree."

"Nothing suspicious?"

"Not on paper."

Jo flipped to the copy of Finn's death certificate. Then she read the emergency room record, which basically reiterated what Adam had just told her: the child had suffered broken vertebrae after he'd toppled from his tree house, dropping fifteen feet onto his head. Minor abrasions and bruises were noted on palms, knees, and elbows. There was a note listing the clothing he'd worn: a yellow T-shirt and blue jeans. He had on shoes but no socks.

Was that the T-shirt Jenny had mailed to her sister with Finn's glasses? Jo wasn't surprised that Jenny had saved it, not after seeing the closet filled with Finn's clothes. But why would Jenny send those items to her sister and tell Kimberly to take them to the police "if anything went wrong"?

Jo blew out a breath and read on.

The certificate of death showed the TOD as 8:11 p.m., precisely three years ago next Friday. The certifying physician's name was Howard Shue.

"Who's Shue?" she asked.

"He was an attending ER physician when the boy was brought in." Adam scratched the side of his nose. "He may still be at Presbyterian. You want to talk to him?"

"I don't know." She shuffled through the few remaining papers. There were notes from the paramedics who'd transported Finn to the hospital. He was unresponsive and not breathing on his own. They'd intubated him, working on him all the way to the ER. Skin was blue-gray, limbs were flaccid, pupils dilated, no pulse. Continued attempts to resuscitate in the ER were futile, and he was pronounced dead a half hour later.

There were some additional notes saying that Dr. Harrison had done CPR on his son after he'd called 911, because he'd claimed he'd felt a shallow pulse. There was Harrison's description of finding the boy at the base of the tree in the backyard. Six-year-old Finn had purportedly climbed a ladder made of two-by-fours nailed into the trunk that led to a wooden platform in the tree's crotch.

Finn had been unsupervised. Dr. Harrison admitted to being on the telephone and had not seen his son go outside. The boy had reportedly fallen from the platform onto the ground below. He had never regained consciousness.

Jo could find no reports of X-rays or CT scans of any body parts, but she knew why they hadn't been done. The boy was a goner. What was the point? Finn's father was a surgeon at the hospital to which he'd been transported. The staff likely knew him, respected him, and the ER doc who'd examined and pronounced had seen nothing funky, at least not enough to warrant an autopsy.

There was a notation in the chart that Finn had been taking the prescription drug Ritalin.

"He had ADHD," she murmured.

"Which probably explains a lot," Adam said. "The fall, I mean. If Harrison was alone with the boy, and he ignored him, even for a little while, maybe an accident was bound to happen."

Jo closed the chart. "He should've known better. He should've been watching his son, not talking on the phone."

Adam had the gall to laugh. "If you want statistics, accidents are the leading cause of death in children under twenty-one."

"I just wish they'd done X-rays," she said.

"To look for what?"

She shrugged. "Other fractures."

"They wouldn't do a CT if the boy had no pulse, much less take films. It's unnecessary."

"But it doesn't give me . . ." *Much to go on,* she almost said, but she stopped herself.

"Give you what?" Adam narrowed his eyes at her.

She slipped the thin file back into the envelope. "You said these were copies? Can I hold on to them?"

"They're yours."

"Thanks." She seemed to be thanking him a lot these days.

He sighed, running a hand over his ruffled hair, and she knew he was trying to play it cool, not tell her what to do, no matter how hard he had to bite his tongue to keep from giving her advice.

"Stop looking at me that way," she said softly.

"You just seem really hungry to nail someone to the wall."

"And that's a bad thing?"

He touched her shoulder, and she leaned against his arm. "Maybe what you're looking for isn't in that file. Maybe it's somewhere else."

"I'm not sure I even know what I'm looking for."

"If you want to talk about it, Jo, it won't go past here. I promise," he said.

She shifted her eyes back to his, not certain of what she had to tell him. It was early still. She didn't even have the autopsy results yet, though Hank would know the preliminary findings soon enough.

It was just this uneasiness that crept through her, a chilly uncertainty, like a touch from the grave. Almost as if Jenny Dielman were looking over her shoulder, making sure she followed through, that she didn't let anything slip between the cracks.

"I don't know what it is." She shook her head. "I've just got this hunch that we're not seeing something."

"Like what?"

"I have questions about Jenny's first marriage to Kevin Harrison. Did it just fall apart because of Finn? Or was it not a good marriage to begin with?"

"You're not suggesting abuse?"

"Jenny's sister seems to think Harrison pushed her around."

"You have any proof?" Adam asked.

"No." Jo didn't have squat.

"Did she ever press charges?"

"No such luck," she said and drew away from his hand, sinking into the chair and hearing its gentle creak as disapproval. Hank had run a computer check on Harrison and, other than a handful of speeding tickets—uncontested and fines paid promptly—they'd found zip.

"Have you found any medical documentation of injuries?" Adam pressed.

"No."

But Jo knew that was so often the case. Wives bleeding and bruised often denied abuse when police appeared to check out a domestic disturbance. They feared even worse if they put their spouses in jail. It happened every day.

"Jenny's husband mentioned her being afraid. She was scared enough that he bought her the twenty-two used to kill her." Jo quietly added, "Or else she was just paranoid, like the neighbor keeps telling me."

Adam stared at her, his expression frighteningly sober, and she saw something click in his face. "That's why you wanted Finn Harrison's file? Why you were hoping for X-rays on the boy? You thought if they revealed old fractures, it would prove that Dr. Harrison beat his wife and his child, that he had a violent streak, maybe a murderous one."

She felt her cheeks burn and wished she'd kept her thoughts to herself.

"It's just a theory," she said. "One of many."

"I hope so, because you can't go around slandering a guy like Kevin Harrison without proof, or you'll get your balls ripped off."

"My balls?" she scoffed. "Harrison's a surgeon, that's all. He's not the mayor."

"That's all?" Adam stepped away from the desk, stood in front of the chair, and bent toward her. He trapped her with his arms on either side, close enough so that she could see the worry, wild in his eyes. "Google his name when you have a minute, if you haven't already. He's up for chief of surgery at Presbyterian, and he's married to Jacob Davis's daughter."

Jacob Davis.

Jo sucked in a breath. *Damn.*

She might not have heard of Kevin Harrison before, but she was well aware of Jacob Davis. The guy was Big D's version of Donald Trump, only more genteel and less mouthy. He'd built half the skyscrapers in downtown Dallas and had his fingerprints on countless new developments outside the city. He was also big into charities. Jo had rubbed shoulders with him once—well, more like glimpsed him across the room—at a gala for the Dallas PD's Widows and Orphans Fund.

Talk about connected.

"Kevin Harrison may have been a lousy husband to your victim, but he's got a lot of powerful friends," Adam said. "Everything's politics. Remember that."

What was she? Stupid? A rookie who needed a lecture?

"Thanks for the tip." It came out more sharply than she'd intended.

But he wasn't done yet. "Tread lightly, Jo. Harrison isn't someone you want to publicly accuse of wife-beating or murder unless you've got video of him doing it or a full confession."

"I'm not accusing him of anything," she said.

Adam pulled away. "Be careful."

"I know how to do my job."

"Yes, you do." He nudged his glasses. "But you're just so dogged when you get something stuck in your head."

A dog with a bone.

She sighed, feeling tired and sore and frustrated. "I'll be careful," she promised, not for the first time.

"That's all I'm asking."

He was right. She had nothing on Kevin Harrison. She had nothing on anyone. Only hearsay and a coffee-stained page ripped from a dead woman's notebook.

He leaned over the arm of the chair until she felt his breath on her skin. And then he kissed her. She closed her eyes, his mouth on hers, sweet and warm.

He released her with a little moan. "You drive me crazy."

"I know." She pressed her lips together, still tasting him.

"I gotta go," he said and cleared his throat.

All she could do was nod.

He headed for the door, stopped there to look back at her. "You can wait here for Phelps. Tell him I hope he feels better."

"I will."

"See you later?"

She wanted to tell him yes but hesitated, unsure how long their interview with Dr. Harrison would run and if they'd head back to the station afterward. There was still so much to do. "It might be late."

"How about we play it by ear?"

"Okay."

He patted the doorjamb before he turned to go.

"Hey," she called out and felt herself blush. "I owe you one."

"Just one?"

"A million and one."

He looked at her across the room, such raw emotion on his face.

Then he took off.

Jo glanced at the clock and willed the hands to move faster. Closed her eyes and wished that Hank would show up as soon as she opened them.

But when she did, he wasn't there.

She used Adam's phone again, putting in a call to the parking office at the building where Dielman worked. She told them who she was and what she wanted. They asked her to read a ten-digit number off the back of the card Dielman had given her. She was put on hold, listening to an oldies station for a good three minutes before the voice returned to the line.

Jo took down what she was told: Patrick Dielman's card had been used to exit the parking lot at 6:50 p.m. on Monday evening. Depending on traffic, he would've arrived home in Plainfield within forty-five minutes.

Exactly what he'd told them.

So maybe Dielman would defy the statistics. Maybe the guy had nothing to do with what happened to his wife. Though a car leaving a parking lot didn't prove much, not when they knew Jenny's killer had to have an accomplice.

Maybe it was Kevin Harrison, who thought Jenny had brought on whatever happened to her, or Lisa Barton, who blamed a dead woman for a brick chucked through her window, one Jenny couldn't have thrown.

Shit.

Just plain shit.

I saw their photo again in the paper, K and his wife. What did the caption say? Something like, "Dr. Kevin Harrison has more than a few reasons to celebrate—which is probably why he and his better half broke out the champagne at Bistro 31 last night! Harrison is tagged to be Presbyterian Hospital's next chief of surgery, and he's going to be a new daddy as well! Hope you're as good with a diaper as you are with a scalpel, Doc!"

How nice for him that he moved on so smoothly. How easily he wiped his slate clean, like Finn and I never existed.

I think that's what gave me the courage to call him last night while Patrick showered. This time, I didn't hang up after the first ring. I waited until I heard his voice, and then I started in.

"Tell me the truth this time," I said. "Not that bullshit story you had everyone at your hospital believing."

He tried to get me off the phone. He said I was being irrational. Finn is gone, he said, as if I needed reminding, Stop obsessing. Move on, take a hike, and don't call again.

I dug in my heels and threatened him. If he didn't tell me what really happened, I would go to the police with the yellow shirt, Finn's glasses, and all my questions.

I would stir things up, make things look bad for him, smear his reputation.

"All right, all right, calm down," he said. "I'll tell you what I remember."

He went through his version of how Finnegan died as if it was a script he'd memorized. There was never more, never less. It never varied, never changed.

When I called him a liar, he got angry. "Stop calling me, Jennifer, or this will get ugly."

He hung up as I laughed.

How much uglier could it get?

CHAPTER FIFTEEN

Hank tracked her down in Adam's office a full hour later.

He shuffled into the room, bum knees dragging, looking tired and older than his forty-five years. She wanted to tease him about the "bug" he'd mentioned when Adam had caught him taking a breather in the hallway of the morgue.

But she didn't have the heart.

With a loud sigh, he plunked down into a chair on the other side of Adam's desk. "Can you smell the stink on me? Christ." He sniffed a sleeve and grimaced. "I should shower and change before we meet with Harrison, if there's time. If we hurry, we can get to the station and back." He half rose from the chair, then hesitated. "So you wanna talk now or in the car?"

"Sit," she instructed, and he planted his butt firmly in the seat.

His shower could wait. She had plenty to tell him but gestured for him to go first.

"I almost hate to say it, but your gut called this one." He leaned his elbows on his knees and clasped his hands together, lifting his head so his eyes met hers. "It's definitely a homicide."

She already knew but let him explain.

He cocked a finger to his temple. "Contact wound left a bruise in the shape of the muzzle. The impression of the front sight ramp was at about three o'clock." He tried to turn his arm to demonstrate but dropped his hand to his thigh when he couldn't do it. "Too awkward a position for our vic to have shot herself."

Jo nodded.

"Lividity had settled in on her left side. Doc Baldwin thinks she was probably kneeling when she was killed. She fell into the water, which was cold enough to preserve her corpse rather nicely."

Jenny had been kneeling.

Jo swallowed down the dreadful taste in her mouth. "Was there evidence of sexual assault?"

Hank shook his head. "No."

She wasn't raped.

As if being abducted and murdered weren't torture enough; Jo felt relieved nonetheless.

"Was there any indication she'd been tied up?" she asked. "Any marks on her wrists?"

"There was faint adhesive residue. Baldwin figures it was duct tape. There was negligible bruising. He doesn't think she was bound for long."

Just long enough, Jo thought.

"There wasn't duct tape found at the scene, right?" She didn't recall it being on the list of evidence recovered at the quarry.

"No."

Jo figured that explained one thing at least. "I think the duct tape's in the same location as Jenny's coat," she said. "They probably took her coat off to make it easier to bind her wrists. I mean, who cares if she was cold? They were going to kill her." She raised her eyes to his. "If they're as smart as they seem, they've already disposed of both."

Hank didn't respond. He had a funny look on his face, so she knew he wasn't done.

"There's something else?"

Her partner let out a slow breath. "Okay, listen. It might be nothing, so I don't want you to read too much into it. It might mean squat."

Read too much into what?

Between Adam advising her to "be careful" with the investigation and Hank telling her not to jump to conclusions, she wanted to pop the both of them.

"Tell me," she said.

He wrinkled his brow. "Baldwin found some old fractures on X-ray, hairlines in a couple ribs and fingers, a healed spiral fracture of the right ulna."

Jo knew a spiral fracture meant a twisting injury. It was pretty damned hard to twist your own arm.

"You said old fractures? How old?" she asked.

He shrugged. "More than a couple years and healed over pretty good."

Left over from Jenny's growing up, when her father had used her as a punching bag?

"He knew how to hit in all the places that wouldn't show."

Or were they remnants of her marriage to Dr. Harrison?

"I think Kevin pushed her around."

"What about a tox screen?" she said.

"Should be back in a week, and I'd expect we'll see the antidepressant in her system and not much else. Stomach was empty. No visible syringe marks. Nothing that would indicate she was doping it up." He jerked his chin at her. "So? I'm waiting."

"For what?"

"For you to say I was wrong, and you were right." His wiry eyebrows peaked. "What? You're not gonna gloat?"

She shifted forward in the chair and placed a hand on the piece of paper Emma had given her. It lay atop Finn Harrison's file. "I'd rather tell you what the crime lab turned up, if that's all right."

He relaxed. "Lay it on me."

She went over everything Emma had told her: the position of the driver's seat in the Nissan, the absence of prints on the .22 Jennings, the lack of skin beneath Jenny's nails or any sign of defensive wounds, the grease on the fleece pullover, the watch that had stopped on Monday night sometime after Jenny hit the water.

She shared what the parking attendant had confirmed about the time Patrick Dielman had left the lot. Then she showed him the torn page from Jenny's journal and the slim file on Finn Harrison's death.

When she finished, Hank ran his fingers over his head, smoothing the thin strands trained to cross his pink crown. "Makes me wish this one had been a suicide." He slowly rose from the chair, drawing his keys from his pocket and weighing them in his hand. "We could've closed it this afternoon."

"You don't really mean that," she said, gathering her things as she stood. She followed him out of Adam's office.

"It's an opinion, that's all."

"Well, it stinks." She sniffed the air around him. "And so do you." She waved an arm and put a few extra feet between them as they walked through the hall. It was like he had cooties, and she didn't want to catch them.

Hank held out a small tube, which he'd removed from his jacket pocket. "You want some Vicks for the car ride?"

"Can I just put the pine-tree air freshener on you?"

He shot her a drunken grin. "It depends where you want to hang it."

She managed a smile but kept her distance until they got to the parking garage, and she realized she'd be riding inside with him. He reeked of Vicks VapoRub and death, a combination Ralph Lauren definitely wouldn't want to bottle as aftershave.

Yuck.

She cracked the window in the Ford, letting in the chilly air, despite her partner's complaints, because it was the only way she could bear to sit in the same vehicle with him.

Hank groused again about wanting a shower to wash the stink of the morgue off his skin before they showed up on the doorstep of Dr. Harrison's swanky Preston Hollow mansion, and Jo knew he was right. Despite her better judgment, she gave him directions to her mother's house. He could clean up, and she could take care of some business while she was there.

After all, it stood empty, except for the boxes and the furniture that hadn't been given away or hauled to the dump. What harm would it do? Hank could use Mama's bathroom—the only one with a shower—and she could pick up some of the things Ronnie insisted she take. Kill two birds with one stone.

It seemed simple enough, as long as she ignored the tension creeping into her neck and the knot tying up her belly. Her past wasn't something she'd shared with her partner, and she'd certainly never imagined taking him inside the very place that had filled her nightmares for years.

"Isn't just being there where it all happened sort of like facing my enemy?"

"It can be, if you let it."

If she let it. Right.

Maybe having Hank there would make what had happened within those walls not seem so real anymore, just a bad dream from long ago that she needed to stop fearing. It couldn't make things any worse.

"You need to call and tell your mom we're coming?" Hank asked, tapping his cell phone, stuck in the console between them. "It'd be polite to warn her we're dropping in."

"She's not there."

"Did she move?"

"Yeah, she moved."

"Okay, so don't tell me."

She gave him directions, and he whistled as he drove, something that sounded irritatingly like "It's A Small World," which made Jo grit her teeth. In another ten minutes, they ended up on Mockingbird.

He stopped whistling. "You grow up on this street?"

"Pretty much."

"Bet things changed a lot when they built Love Field."

The airport that was home to Southwest Airlines was but a mile away. The rumble of jets in the air had been a familiar sound once. She recalled how the windows had rattled as they'd passed overhead while she lay awake in bed. Often she'd close her eyes tightly, wishing she could be on one of them, going somewhere else, anywhere.

"The traffic changed," she told him. "Mama hated the noise, cars on the road at all hours."

"It's not a bad area," Hank said, though she knew that he'd change his tune once they crossed Lemmon.

She watched the houses they passed go from expensive brick two-stories with well-tended yards and frou-frou cars to paint-peeled cracker boxes with bars on the windows and crumbling sidewalks, all in a matter of blocks.

Mama's was among the latter, a pint-size clapboard with a badly patched roof and a dejected-looking facade. Shades sagged in the front windows, and the yellow-brown lawn was overgrown and littered with dead leaves. Ronnie had promised to have her nephew rake and mow before the real estate agent began showing the house after Thanksgiving. They'd talked about having the wallpaper stripped and the interior walls painted, but Jo wasn't sure the expense was worth it. Someone would likely buy the place for the lot and tear the house down, which sounded perversely appealing.

If she could, she'd set a match to it and watch as it burned to the ground without an ounce of remorse.

"Are we close?"

"That's it, with the shin-high grass and the Realtor sign," she said and pointed. The **COMING SOON** sign sat half-obscured by weeds.

Hank slowed the car, turned on the left blinker, and waited for cars to pass before he made a U-turn and bumped the Ford against the curb.

"It's hard for older folks to keep up a house," he said as he cut the engine, and Jo wanted to laugh at his diplomacy. "Where'd she move to?" he asked, making no move to get out of the car. "Someplace like Florida, I'll bet."

Here we go, she thought, ignoring his inquisition, fumbling with her seat belt, impatient now to get this over with, to get in and get out.

"Did she leave Dallas?" he tried again, and still she didn't answer. "What? Is it a state secret?"

She forced her hands to cease their frantic motions, willed her heart to slow down and her voice not to snap. She couldn't blame him for asking about Mama. She'd never told him much about her family, or what was left of it. It was only natural that he'd be curious, since she'd met his wife and kids.

Do it, Jo. Tell him.

"She's in a nursing home near Presbyterian," she said in a rush. She drew in a deep breath, listening to the hiss of passing cars. "She's not well."

"Cancer?"

She shook her head.

"Stroke?"

She made herself say it. "Alzheimer's. She's pretty out of it, has been for a while. Sometimes she knows I'm her daughter. Mostly, she doesn't."

"That's gotta be tough," he said. "I can't believe you never told me."

Why? What good would it have done?

"It's something I have to handle on my own," she said, though she hadn't, not really. She'd tried to ignore it, had left Ronnie in charge of Mama for far too long. When she'd chucked Dallas, it had been so much simpler to pretend Mama didn't exist.

"No, Jo, you didn't have to handle it yourself," Hank said. "You chose to."

It seemed to Jo that Mama had done the choosing all her life, and she'd had to live with the consequences.

"Did you ever tell him about your past?"

No. There were pieces of her past she'd never shared with anyone. She wasn't sure she ever would.

Jo felt it starting again, the ache in her head, the throbbing at her temples.

She turned away from Hank and put her hand on the door handle, squishing her eyes closed for a long minute. "Can we not do this now?"

"What?"

"I don't want to talk about my mother, okay? And I don't want your sympathy," she said. "I don't need it."

"Hey, think you could quit playing tough guy for a minute?"

Between his lectures and Adam's, she wanted to tear her hair out. What was so wrong with looking out for herself?

"We're partners, right?" he dug in. "No, more than that, we're friends. So I don't get why you have to keep—" He looked at her and suddenly stopped. "Look, I'm sorry. I don't mean to pry. If you don't want to talk about it, it's your call."

Her call.

Uh-huh.

So why was everyone always trying to tell her what to do?

"It's a long story, Hank," she finally said, averting her gaze and staring squarely out the window. "And I don't think now's the time to tell it."

Maybe this was a bad idea. Maybe she should ask him to start the car and get the hell out of there, away from the emotional landmines.

"If you don't find a way to make peace with your mother, Jo, you'll get stuck in this place your whole life. You'll bury the blame, but you'll never get rid of it."

She didn't want that. She didn't want to be angry and ashamed forever.

Jo gazed at the sad little house, at the peeled paint, the rotting eaves, the cracked concrete. It wasn't much, was it? It was pretty pathetic. And there was no one inside who could hurt her anymore. There hadn't been for years and years except in her mind.

"Where's my little Joey? Where's my sweet, sweet girl?"

She shivered.

"Hey." Hank's big hand reached for her shoulder and patted clumsily. "Let's not sit out here in the cold. How about we go in?"

She hated how paralyzed she felt: a grown woman still scared of a boogeyman.

Get a grip, she told herself.

She could do this.

"Lock the car," she said, fighting the tremor in her voice. "It'd be a shame for someone to steal this fine machine."

Hank guffawed. "Like I'd get that lucky."

He climbed out of the Ford and went around to the trunk, where she knew he kept an extra shirt and a shaving kit, a holdover from his days on the Fort Worth PD.

Hinges squealed as she pushed the passenger door wide and stepped into grass that reached above her ankles. Then she slammed the door soundly. She crunched through the brittle stalks and fallen leaves to the front door.

Her fingers clumsy, she found the key on her ring and let them in.

The musty smell hit her as soon as she crossed the threshold. Even Ronnie's cleaning couldn't mask the staleness of a place closed up too long, a place where an old woman had declined and decayed, and the house along with her.

The heat had been kept low, only turned up when Ronnie was there putting things to rights, and the chill touched her face, crept up her spine like a closing zipper.

She heard Hank's cowboy boots as they creaked on the old floors and knew he was seeing the faded wallpaper and the patched linoleum, feeling the sense of abandonment that permeated the very air they breathed.

"So this is it?" he said.

"Afraid so."

"It's got four walls and a roof, right? Everyone comes from somewhere, and it ain't always Buckingham Palace," he said. She was glad that, at least, she heard no pity. "Are you having a yard sale?"

"No." She and Ronnie had talked about that, but neither of them had wanted to stand around on a Saturday, bartering with strangers over Mama's things. "Just giving away what isn't worth keeping."

There were boxes in every corner. Only a few pieces of furniture remained in the living area and kitchen, what Ronnie and her nephews hadn't taken, carted off to Goodwill, or resigned to the dumpster behind the liquor store up the block.

"Where's the shower?" Hank asked. He had the shaving kit in one hand, a slightly rumpled button-down shirt draped over his forearm.

Jo knew Mama's room was still fairly intact. Ronnie had been waiting for her to go through her mother's personal stuff, despite Jo's insistence that she wanted none of it.

Ronnie had packed up all of Mama's personal papers, and that was more than Jo wanted to take.

"There's gotta be something you want of hers," Ronnie kept insisting, no matter that Jo assured her she didn't want a single trinket.

"This way."

She led her partner down the hallway, toward her old bedroom, past squares on the wall darker than the rest where photographs had hung: pictures of Jo as a girl, of Mama and the man she'd married after Daddy had left them, of the three of them, pretending to be a family.

The door to Mama's room stood wide open, but she hesitated before stepping in.

She reached a hand inside and flipped on the light switch.

The timid yellow from the overhead fixture was probably a godsend, making the gaping wallpaper seams less evident, likewise the stains on the carpeting. Her eyes darted around to the heavy old bureau and bed, matching relics from a bygone era when things were built to last forever. The bed was stripped, and the tired mattress sagged over the box springs. Boxes leaned against the walls, each clearly marked with Ronnie's handwriting. The whole of Mama's life packed away, and Mama wouldn't even miss it.

Neither would Jo.

Hank plodded in behind her. She turned her head at his footstep and smiled feebly. He looked as uncomfortable as she.

"You sure this is kosher?" he asked.

"Yes, I'm sure."

"I won't screw up anything?"

"Fat chance," she said. It was too late for that.

She went to the connecting bath and switched on the light. A bulb sparked and then fizzled out over the mirror, but the other two still beamed brightly.

Towels were stacked neatly in an unsealed box, and she removed several from the top.

The cabinets and drawers were bare. What Mama hadn't taken with her to the nursing home—her prescriptions and the like—Ronnie had probably tossed.

But there was still shampoo sitting on the rim of the tub in the enclosed shower. Hank could use it as soap.

She got him set up and then left him alone, shutting the door on her way out. Then she glanced up the hall to her old room.

She debated a second before walking toward it.

When she reached the closed door, she realized she'd been holding her breath. She stood for a moment with her hand on the knob and slowly exhaled.

It's over, Jo, she told herself. *He's gone for good.*

She turned the knob, pushed the door wide, and entered.

Instinctively, she reached right for the switch plate and flicked on the ceiling lamp. The room brightened halfheartedly, like sunlight through haze.

Tiny rosebuds surrounded her from papered walls with split seams. The once-pristine white background had discolored with age. Never replaced, never changed. Mama hadn't touched anything in the house in forever. She'd left it all just as it had been when Jo was a kid.

Jo turned around slowly.

God, it looked so small to her now. Like she could stretch out her arms and touch the walls on either side. The tiny closet was empty save for abandoned wire hangers. Beside the bed stood a whitewashed chest of drawers that matched the headboard and knobby posts.

She ran a hand down the carved wood, thinking how she used to swing herself around them, bumping against the mattress, her head spinning. She could see where the paint was worn bare. How rare they'd been, those carefree moments. She'd never had many friends. She'd always been terrified they would see in her face that she wasn't like everyone else, that they'd smell him on her, and they would know. She could never have had them spend the night. She had been afraid he'd hurt them, too.

"No one can ever know." Isn't that what he used to tell her? *"If you tattle, your mama will leave you, just like your daddy."*

She let out a slow, shaky breath, telling herself, *You're okay. It's over and done.*

Like Mama's bed, hers had been stripped. She knew if she turned the mattress over, she'd find an old stain. She tried not to remember the dip of the bed as he'd settled beside her, reeking of liquor and aftershave, the stink of him filling her nose and cutting off her air.

She held fast to the bedpost, bumped her head against it.

Stop it.

She tightened her mouth into a line and turned away.

Three cardboard boxes squatted low behind the opened door, what remained of her childhood tucked inside: clothes she'd left behind when she'd moved out after high school, books and stuffed animals, dolls and records. Mama had never given anything away, though Jo had never intended to take any of it with her. She'd always imagined that, once gone from this house, it would be a clean break. She would take off and never look back.

How wrong she'd been.

The pipes groaned through the wall as Hank cut off the shower. It was the same noise that used to wake her in the mornings. She would curl up tightly beneath the sheets, hardly daring to breathe, waiting until the front door closed with a slap and the car engine started. Then she'd be safe—for a while, anyway.

Her stomach tightened so violently, she felt she would be sick. It was long ago and still so real. How was she supposed to forget when her memories were so clear?

"Hey, Jo?"

She froze in place, brushed her thumb across her cheeks, and straightened up, ignoring how her hands were shaking.

Hank appeared in the doorway. "So this used to be yours?" he asked.

"Yes." Her voice sounded so timid.

It's a room, she told herself. *Just a room.* It had nothing to do with her anymore. It had little to do with the life she led now.

"Were you an only child?"

"Yes."

Not like Kimberly, who'd had Jenny to protect her.

"It's hard to imagine you as a kid."

She wanted to say, "I never was." Instead, she said, "Let's get out of here."

"Not much on sentiment, are you?"

"No."

"I didn't think so." He watched her, looking like he had something to say. Then he turned and passed through the door.

She followed him, switching off the lights as she went, pausing in the kitchen to pick up the box of papers Ronnie had left for her on the counter in case she didn't get back on Saturday. She didn't plan to.

"You want to grab some dinner first?" Hank asked as he put the key in the ignition and jerked his chin toward the clock in the dash. "We've still got an hour."

"Sure," she said, though she wasn't the least bit hungry.

They drove north and got off the tollway, stopping at a Pizza Hut situated on the corner of a nondescript strip mall.

Hank worked on a small Meat Lover's pie.

Jo picked at a salad, speared a cherry tomato and toyed with it, checking her watch for the tenth time, and noting how dark it looked beyond the windows.

She put Mama's house and its ghosts out of her head, which was much easier to do when she had something else to think about. She thought instead of Jenny Dielman, of the despair written on that single page from her diary, and wondered who'd killed her.

"All set?" Hank asked when he'd finished and wiped a smear of sauce from the corner of his lips.

Jo wasn't sure how set she really was. She wished she'd had a chance to talk again to Kimberly Parker and better prepare herself for squaring off with Kevin Harrison.

"Jo?"

She realized he was waiting for her answer. "Yeah, I'm good."

They pushed their chairs back and left.

Is Patrick so worried about my sanity that he has the neighbor checking up on me? I've seen a beige car just like hers not far behind me driving through Starbucks on the way to the library. I've caught her looking out her window when I'm in the front yard. She hides behind the blinds, but they shimmy, and I know she's there.

Once when I felt her stare, I started waving, so she'd know I could see her. Maybe that was a mistake. She came outside, smiling and tugging a sweater around her. I'm surprised she didn't have on a hat and gloves. She's always saying how much she hates the cold.

"Isn't it late in the season for bulbs?" she remarked.

I shrugged and kept planting, hoping she'd leave.

"So you like gardening?" she asked, making chitchat. "I haven't got much of a green thumb. I kill everything."

"They're narcissus," I told her. "They're hard to kill."

"Can you believe it's November already?" she prattled on and glanced at the house, probably hoping Patrick would appear and make the trip across the lawn worthwhile. "Are y'all having family over for Turkey Day? Do they live around here?"

Was she finagling an invitation?

I said I didn't have family except for my sister in Des Moines. That my parents were dead, and I was as good as orphaned. She got all wide-eyed, told me we had something in common. She was an orphan, too.

"If anything happened to me," she said, "no one would care."

"If anything happened to me," I told her, "I wouldn't care."

I meant to shut her up, and it worked. I don't like her, and it isn't just because she flirts with my husband and sticks her nose where it doesn't belong.

I don't trust her as far as I can spit, and I want her to go away and leave me the hell alone.

CHAPTER SIXTEEN

The night pressed down hard, the sky an inky black. There wasn't a star in sight, just an icy glow around the moon and the orange blur of passing streetlamps.

Hank had the heat on, but Jo still felt chilled and unsettled after being at Mama's. She rubbed the arms of her wool peacoat, trying to warm herself and get her blood flowing. She had to focus on their interview with Kevin Harrison.

What kind of a man was he? She had Googled his name, as Adam had suggested. In fact, she'd used Adam's desktop computer to do it. Every article she'd found painted him as larger than life: a respected surgeon who lived the good life and ended up in photographs on the society pages with his trophy wife. According to Jenny's sister, he was also an adulterer and possibly an abuser.

Dr. Jekyll and Mr. Hyde.

"The guy's operated on billionaires, Olympic athletes, and CEOs." Hank had done his homework as well. "He's up for chief of surgery at Presbyterian—"

"So I heard," Jo interrupted.

"I'm figuring he's a major-league asshole."

"Me, too."

Kimberly Parker had said as much on the telephone earlier.

What if something Jenny had done or said in the past few weeks had made Kevin Harrison feel threatened? With a huge promotion hanging in the balance, what might he have done if his ex-wife had decided to air their dirty laundry?

Whatever kind of man Harrison was, he'd played a big part in Jenny's life, and Jo wanted to hear from his own lips about their relationship and about what happened to Finn.

"His wife's a big-time socialite," Hank was saying, like Jo hadn't read the same scoop he'd read. "She comes from a prominent family. Daddy's a big-shot developer."

"I know."

"If anyone scared that poor woman, it was her ex-husband, the one she wanted to see rot in hell."

Had Dielman given Jenny the .22 because she'd been afraid of Harrison? Or had she been frightened of someone else?

Was Kevin Harrison responsible for the old fractures—the broken fingers and ribs, the spiral fracture in her forearm?

Did Jenny fear that he'd come after her again, despite how much time had passed? They'd been divorced for almost as long as their son had been dead: three years.

Could Dr. Harrison have had an obsession with his first wife? Maybe he was possessive to the point that he couldn't let go, couldn't imagine her with anyone else, even if he didn't want her for himself.

"The past few weeks . . . Something was up, and she wouldn't tell me what."

Something was up.

What, Jenny? What was going on? What were you up to?

Jo didn't like the idea that seeped into her brain.

Jenny had had post-traumatic stress disorder. She'd been mourning a dead son. Her husband had given her a gun because she felt spooked. What if there hadn't been anything out there? What if it had all been in Jenny's head?

Paranoia . . . self-destroyer.

"The Kinks," she said aloud without meaning to, and Hank took his eyes off the road long enough to ask, "You got a kink?"

"A couple, yeah." She let out a slow breath and leaned back her head.

"You okay?"

"I'm just tired," she told him, refusing to share what was on her mind. She was too exhausted to think straight.

She rolled down the window, taking a shot of cold air to the face. Then she rolled it up again when Hank nagged that she was letting out the heat.

What was wrong with her?

Her left shoulder throbbed, her head ached, and she felt sucked dry, inside and out. She'd rather be heading home than toward Harrison's house. She wanted a hot bath, wanted Adam's arms around her so she could feel safe.

"You can't always get what you want," Hank said, his voice breaking into her mental meanderings, and she stared at him suspiciously.

"What?"

"I'd have to sell my soul to the devil to buy a place in this burg," he told her. "And I'd probably have to throw in my first- and second-born. But damn." He whistled. "If it could happen, I might have to think twice."

It took a second to realize what he was talking about.

They were in Preston Hollow.

She stared at the hulking shadows of the homes they passed. Not so much homes as mansions, overgrown edifices on sprawling grounds, sometimes gated, sometimes not. Jo thought they looked like hotels.

Even through the dimness, she could see the outline of the Harrison home as they crept toward it on Larkglen. Soft lighting outlined the two-storied structure, nearly hidden at first by artful, privacy-enhancing landscaping.

Hank angled the Ford along the curve of cobblestones surrounding an island of carefully positioned shrubs and red-leafed Japanese maples, with yellow mums planted as a border.

Motion lights clicked on as they got out of the car and walked toward the front door.

Jo stuck her hands in her coat pockets, her collar turned up against the cold, the bite of the air on her cheeks enough to wake her up. She felt fully alert.

Here we go, she told herself and raised her chin as Hank reached the door and rang the bell. She thought of Jenny and swallowed hard.

Will I know if he did it, just by looking at him?

Loud chimes echoed from within as Hank pressed the bell again for good measure.

A voice sighed over the intercom. "Yes?"

Hank leaned toward a speaker on the wall, squinting at the buttons before he pressed one and said, "It's Detective Phelps, ma'am, and Detective Larsen from the Plainfield police. We have an appointment with Dr. Harrison."

"You have an appointment with Kevin?"

C'mon. Jo shook her head.

"Yes, ma'am, we're here to talk to him about Jennifer Dielman."

"Jennifer?"

"Dr. Harrison's first wife."

Dead silence.

Hank hit the "Talk" button again. "He agreed to see us at seven, ma'am. And we're on the money. It's freezing out here, so we wouldn't mind coming in."

"Of course, Detectives, I'm so sorry. Give me a minute, y'all, please."

Hank murmured, "A minute, yeah, sure." Then he hit the intercom with the flat of his hand. "I get the feeling Mrs. Harrison didn't know we were coming."

"Or why." Jo shoved her hands deeper into her coat pockets, ducking her chin into the collar.

Hank did the same, braced his back against the door, and waited.

They stood there, facing each other, not speaking. Each breath they exhaled blew puffs of white into the air, evaporating as quickly as they appeared.

Within a few minutes, Jo's ears burned, and she could no longer sense the tip of her nose. She imagined this was how it felt to be leftover meatloaf.

When finally she heard the slide of a dead bolt and the click of the knob releasing, she nearly whooped with joy. She sensed the heat as it seeped past the threshold, and she stepped closer to the doorway, standing at Hank's elbow, as eager as he to get inside.

"Sorry to keep y'all waiting." The attractive woman who greeted them didn't appear any too happy to have a couple of detectives standing on her stoop. "It's been a long day, and, well"—she tugged at the hem of her white shirt with manicured fingers—"our housekeeper had to leave early, so I was workin' on dinner. Cooking's not exactly my strong suit."

"Mine either," Hank offered. "I'm Detective Phelps. This is my partner, Detective Larsen."

Jo nodded. She was otherwise occupied, trying to keep her teeth from chattering.

"Forgive my dreadful manners," the woman murmured in her soft Southern voice. "I'm Alana Harrison, Kevin's wife."

She was thin as a rail and a few inches taller than Jo, with shiny copper hair to her shoulders, drawn off her face by gold barrettes. Her features had that homegrown Texas brand of pretty that made men stare—even Hank had stopped blinking—but the tiny lines around her eyes and mouth betrayed her age as north of thirty. Her tailored white blouse and tight black jeans emphasized a toned physique. She kept her back so ramrod straight that Jo imagined she'd been taught to walk with a book on her head. Or else she'd been an athlete, a dancer maybe. She was even wearing flat shoes that looked like ballet slippers.

So this is the woman Kevin Harrison cheated on Jenny with, Jo mused, wondering if he'd considered Alana an upgrade.

"My God, but it's cold." The second Mrs. Harrison's breath fogged the air.

"Even colder if you've been standing outside for ten minutes," Hank commented.

Jo was grateful for his bluntness. Another few minutes, and she wouldn't feel her toes.

Alana Harrison blushed. "Please, Detectives, come inside," she said, opening the door to them. "Kevin's showering, but he'll be with you shortly. He had a very long day at the hospital, as y'all can imagine. I'll take you to the den." She ushered them in through the foyer. "I must say, I'm surprised the police make house calls at this hour."

"It was the only time your husband could meet us, ma'am," Hank said. "He's very busy."

So are we, Jo wanted to say, but bit her tongue and followed the woman into a spacious entranceway with a peaked cathedral ceiling. An immense fixture hung overhead, light refracting off myriad crystals, and Jo was reminded of *The Phantom of the Opera* and the crashing chandelier.

To her right, a wrought-iron banister curved up to the second floor. The tiles beneath her feet were large squares of pale yellow. The same color as the mud at the quarry. She wondered if they were limestone.

She caught a glimpse of the great room. A fire burned in a fireplace comprised of smaller squares of the same yellow stone. Huge, overstuffed leather furniture hugged an Indian-inspired rug, and enormous vases and bowls of flowers were everywhere. Floor-length windows provided a view of a lighted pool out back. Jo heard the strains of something bluesy in the background, maybe BB King, and a part of her felt like she was in the lobby of a swanky hotel.

Hank leaned in to whisper, "You could fit the whole station house in there."

More like two of them.

They trailed Alana into an adjacent room, a good-size library with shelves lined with leather-bound books, gilded titles pressed into their spines. Jo wondered if any of them had ever been read, or if they were just for show.

There were framed photographs decorating every surface. The first few she peered at showed a sun-browned couple in goggles and hats on a ski slope. There were some distant shots of a single skier blazing a trail down a white mountainside. Jo moved on to images of a man—sometimes several men—in orange jackets posing with dead deer, elk, and bear, always standing somewhere amid thickets of trees, occasionally posing by the hood of a Land Rover.

"Your husband's a hunter?" Jo asked, thankful there were no dead animals tacked up on the walls.

"Yes, and a good one." Alana came up beside her to see what she was looking at. "His father taught him to shoot when he was a boy. During deer season, Kevin's gone every weekend. I went huntin' with him a few times in the beginning, but it's not my thing. Now, he just goes off with his friends and doesn't come back until he's got something to brag about." She smiled with obvious affection, enough to warm her eyes. "Well, they're all doctors, so I figure they can patch each other up if anyone gets hurt."

Jo turned to see if Hank was listening, but his gaze was glued to another set of photographs arranged in neat columns behind a large desk. She wandered over, standing at his elbow, looking over endless pictures of Dr. Harrison and his wife posing with recognizable celebrities and politicians.

"Can I take your coats?" Alana asked from behind them. "I could hang them up for y'all, if you'd like."

If there was one thing Jo admired about Texas women, it was their innate hospitality, no matter how unwanted the company.

"Really, ma'am, that's not necessary," Jo assured her.

Hank already had his trench coat off, and it hung over his arm, baring his shoulder holster.

Jo went ahead and followed suit, unfastening the buttons on her wool coat so that her pancake holster was visible as well. This was obviously not a house inhabited by folks who feared guns. She was right. Mrs. Harrison didn't even flinch.

"Please"—Alana gestured at a pair of club chairs—"sit down wherever you're comfortable."

Hank tossed his coat over the back of one before settling in. Jo perched carefully on the other while the lady of the house remained standing, a hip braced against an oversize desk made of polished red wood that had to be cherry.

"You have a lovely place, Mrs. Harrison," Jo said.

Alana smiled vaguely and smoothed her hands over her abdomen. "Thank you. We've certainly enjoyed living here. But we have started looking around for something a bit bigger."

"Bigger?" came out without Jo meaning it to.

"My daddy's got a couple homes picked out for us to look at. His company built them. Jacob Davis? You've heard of him?"

Hank's head bobbed eagerly. "He put up those new high-rise condos in Turtle Creek, right?"

Alana looked proud as punch. "That's right. Daddy's got his fingerprints all over the city, and not only on the buildings. His scholarship foundation's put a lot of kids through school who couldn't afford it."

"I'm surprised he's not running for office," Hank said, sitting up straighter, smiling like a frat boy flirting at a mixer.

Alana laughed, a soft, silvery sound. "Believe me, he's working on it, Detective. He's made quite a few friends in the mayor's office after spearheading so many high-profile developments downtown. In fact, he's so busy on the handshake circuit these days that he's talkin' about my taking over the commercial arm of the business, too. But for now"—she shrugged—"he's got me selling the houses he's putting up all over Dallas and north to Plainfield, and I'd do anything for Daddy."

Oh, good, Jo mused, *a bona fide daddy's girl with no mind to call her own.*

"You said you're looking for something larger?" Hank glanced around at the impressive den. "These digs seem all right to me."

"It's not so much what I want as what's best for the family." Alana plucked at her starched collar. "My father's got a bee in his bonnet about us moving into a place he just finished on Brookview, a six-bedroom Georgian on a full acre. The problem is prying Kevin away from the hospital long enough to take a look."

"Six bedrooms?" Hank whistled. "You thinking of putting up the front court of the Mavericks?"

Alana tipped her head, veiling half her face in a red-gold curtain, flashing as coy a look as Jo had ever seen. "Not a bad idea, Detective. Maybe someday we'll have a front court of our own. We're working on it anyway." She touched her belly again in such an obvious manner that it didn't take a genius to figure out what was up.

She was pregnant.

Hank caught on as well. "Ah, I see . . . congratulations, ma'am."

"Thank you, Detective." Alana beamed.

"Boy or girl?"

"I know it's old-fashioned," she said, "but we're gonna wait and see. Still, my instincts say it's a boy."

A boy.

Jo couldn't seem to get any words out. She thought of Jenny losing Finn, then undergoing a hysterectomy so she'd never able to conceive while Kevin would have another chance to be a father. It hardly seemed fair.

"Dr. Harrison must be happy about getting an heir," Hank remarked.

"We're both very happy."

"When are you due?"

The Southern-belle drawl turned as gooey as syrup. "In six months, God willin'. It seems like an awfully long wait at this point."

Hank leaned forward in the chair. "Is it your first?"

"It'll be our firstborn, yes." Something tightened in her face. "But we've been tryin' since we got married almost three years back. We've had a nursery ready forever."

"The best things come to those who wait, right?"

"I hope so, Detective Phelps. I really do."

Jo wanted to laugh and not in a happy way. It was not quite three years since Finn had died, barely that since Jenny and the doctor had divorced. Guess *forever* was in the eye of the beholder.

Hank kept up his small talk about kids.

But Jo couldn't sit still another minute.

She got up from the club chair, eased around the coffee table, and headed toward yet another wall full of framed photographs. These, she realized as she neared, were not of Kevin or the couple together, but of Alana. There she was in a cheerleading outfit, raising pom-poms to the sky. In another, she was wrapped like a shiny chiffon package with a sash that read Miss Junior Texas. Others showed her in pearls and bare shoulders in a gauzy black-and-white sorority composite from the University of Texas at Austin and in white gloves and a floor-length gown curtsying at her debut. The largest photograph of them all showcased Alana in an even more extravagant white dress, one with a veil and train, standing at the altar in front of a church on Kevin Harrison's arm.

"He cheated on her, for sure, with that rich bitch he married. Jenny knew it was going on, but she let it slide because she loved Finn more."

Jo tasted something nasty in her mouth. She tried not to think of how easily Kevin Harrison had gone on with his life while his ex-wife had mourned their son so deeply, it had as good as killed her. She certainly hoped the soon-to-be chief of surgery would take greater care with the child who had yet to be born.

"Did your husband live here with Jenny Dielman when they were married?" Hank asked as Jo turned away from the wedding picture and forced her head back into the conversation. "Is this the house where their boy fell from the tree and died?"

Jo returned to the chair she'd vacated, her eyes on Alana, who still leaned against her husband's desk, hands placed protectively on her belly.

For an instant, her face shut down, and all the sweetness and light disappeared from her voice. "My word, what a question, Detective," she said tightly. "I'm not sure Kevin would want me to talk about that. It's not something we discuss much, even in private. It's very painful for him. He doesn't like to bring up the past. It's a sore spot, as you can imagine."

How sore? Jo wondered. Sore enough to want his ex-wife permanently out of the picture so she couldn't cause a stink?

"How about this?" Alana's tone softened again. "I'll leave discussing Jenny up to Kevin. But I will answer your question about this house. Jenny Dielman never lived here. Their place in Northwood Hills was sold as soon as the divorce was final. I do know Kevin tore down that old tree house before he moved out."

Jo's heart stopped. "He tore it down?"

"He razed it to the ground. Can you blame him?"

Did he tear it down because of guilt? Or to cover up evidence?

"I got this place for us," Alana went on, "and we moved in right after we married. I didn't want Kevin to wallow in the past. I wanted him to come into our relationship with a clean slate."

"Did it work?" Jo asked flat-out. "Could he forget so easily?"

"What do you mean by that?" Alana wrinkled her tiny nose.

"Did your husband keep in touch with Jenny after their divorce?"

Alana glanced at Hank as if he might stop this line of questioning. But he didn't. "Why would he stay in touch with Jenny? He didn't owe her alimony, not once she found herself a new husband. Kevin didn't owe her anything."

"Something was up, and she wouldn't tell me what."

Jo knew there had to be more to it than that.

"So they weren't in contact the last few weeks?"

Alana opened her mouth, then pinched it closed. She glanced at the door. "My husband spent a good chunk of his life with that woman. More than she deserved. But, as Kevin will tell you, they were over and done even before Finn died, whether Jenny knew it or not. So there's no earthly reason why Kevin would've contacted her. She only brought him pain."

"He didn't worry about how she was holding up?" Jo asked. "Or how she was handling Finn's death with the three-year anniversary approaching?"

"Kevin isn't stuck in the past," Alana reiterated, but she cast her eyes down.

"Did you know Jenny?" Jo asked. "Had you met her?"

Alana shook her head, red-gold hair shimmying around her pretty face. "I'm sorry, y'all, but I don't feel comfortable talking about this. Kevin should be down any minute. Though I can't imagine how he can help. He only found out about Jenny when he turned on the news last night. He was shaken up, I know, because he couldn't sleep. Sometime in the middle of the night, he left the bed. I found him right in here"—she gestured at the desk—"sitting in his chair in the dark, staring into space."

"What time did he get home on Monday evening, Mrs. Harrison?" Hank asked.

Alana looked back at the door. "You don't know my husband, or you wouldn't even ask such a thing."

Jo heard the tap of footsteps on the limestone and turned her head, like Alana, watching as a broad-shouldered man with damp hair and pressed khakis strode into the room.

"Forgive me for being late, but it's been a hell of a day," Dr. Harrison announced, the same excuse his wife had already given.

At least they had their stories straight.

He reached out to pump Jo's hand and then her partner's. "I needed a shower to feel civilized." He glanced at Alana. "Thanks for keeping them company, hon." He rubbed his hands together. "Could anyone use a drink?"

When Jo and Hank both declined, he asked, "Coffee?"

"Actually, that'd be great." Jo figured she could use the warmth and the caffeine, despite the edge she felt just being in Harrison's presence. His voice sounded much the same as it had on the phone, a smooth baritone, less angry than he'd been when he'd told her that Jenny had gotten what she deserved. His ex-wife wasn't dead then, just missing.

"Make that two," Hank said, lifting his fingers.

Dr. Harrison faced his wife. "You think you could handle that, Allie? I know Maria's left, but could you put on a pot and throw a tray together with some cheese and crackers?"

"Anything for you," Alana said with a smile. "I'll be back in a pinch." She approached her husband and offered her cheek for a kiss. He placed his palm gently on her abdomen and whispered in her ear.

When he released her, Alana headed straight for the door, like she couldn't wait to get out of there. The flat heels of her shoes clicked on the tiles until they could be heard no more.

"Your wife told us you're expecting," Hank said, kick-starting the conversation. "Congratulations."

Harrison chuckled. "Allie might as well just wear a sign, right? Yeah, we're over the moon." His eyes lit up in the same way Alana's had, and

Jo wondered if he'd felt that way when Jenny had gotten pregnant. "A baby changes everything, doesn't it?"

"Oh, it damn well does," Hank agreed and embarked on more small talk about kids, leaving Jo the opportunity to observe and to listen.

At first glance, the man certainly didn't appear to be a monster, though she well knew that people weren't always who they seemed on the surface. Not every wife beater lived in a trailer park and walked around in sleeveless undershirts. Some of them lived in mansions and had little Polo men on their sweaters and socks.

Dr. Harrison clapped his hands and rubbed them together. "Shall we get started? I know you have questions about Jenny." He shook his head. "I still can't believe what's happened. I'll help you however I can."

"We appreciate that, sir." Hank settled back into his chair, appearing far more relaxed than Jo felt. She stuck to the edge of her seat, elbows on thighs and knees bent, as if ready to leap.

Harrison slung his arm across the back of the sofa, showing off toned muscles beneath the snug cashmere. He was tall and lean, probably kept fit with all those hunting trips with his buddies, slaughtering Bambi.

Did you kill your ex-wife, Doctor? Did you do it?

He turned and caught Jo staring.

She looked away, at the wall of framed photographs above the desk, trying to imagine how Jenny had ended up with Kevin Harrison when Kimberly had mentioned their father, the doctor, who'd been so abusive. Had she been repeating the cycle?

"What can I do for you exactly?" Harrison asked. He settled his hands in his lap, entwined his long fingers, the light glinting off the gold of his watch and his wide wedding band. "I'm not sure how I'll help. I hadn't seen Jenny in several years."

"Your wife said you heard about Mrs. Dielman's death on TV last night," Hank said.

"I did." He blew out a slow breath. "It was such a shock to catch on the news that she was dead. It's horrible to imagine how she ended up in that situation." He rubbed his thumbs together, one over the other. "It felt unreal, like hearing about a movie plot, not something that happened to someone I used to know."

"Someone I used to know." Jo bristled at his choice of words. Not *someone I once loved* or *someone with whom I buried a child.*

She curled her fingers around the chair cushion, digging her nails deep into tweed.

Hank kept up the dialogue. "That's a common reaction, Dr. Harrison. You said you hadn't seen Jenny in a few years, but had you been in touch recently?"

There might have been the slightest hesitation before he said, "No."

"Are you sure?"

Harrison wrinkled his brow. "I'm fairly sure, yes."

Fairly sure? Jo sought out the lie in his face, but his expression didn't change a bit.

Hank leaned forward. "So you're saying you had no contact with Jenny before Monday evening, when she went missing?"

He pursed his lips. "I didn't contact her, no."

"Did she contact you? Think hard, Doc," Hank advised him. "Because if we find out later that you weren't up-front with us, we will have a problem with that, you understand? And I'd hate for that to happen, 'cause you've got a baby on the way and a big promotion coming. I imagine that's plenty of stress without having the police on your ass."

Harrison fixed his gaze across the room at the photos of Alana. Then he cleared his throat, looked at Hank, and quietly said, "Look, I told you I didn't contact her, Detective Phelps, and that's the God's honest truth. But I didn't say she hadn't called me."

Jenny called him? Jo's heart skipped a couple of beats.

Hank started to speak, but she jumped ahead, too impatient to wait.

"Let me get this right, Dr. Harrison. You're saying that Jenny phoned you? Not the other way around?"

"Yes."

"When exactly did this happen?"

Harrison sighed and slid his palms over his thighs. "It was a week ago, I guess. She left a message on our voice mail. She sounded strange, really wound up, and I was almost afraid to return the call. It had been so long since we'd spoken, and I didn't want to get into it—" He stopped himself.

Didn't want to get into what? Discussing Finn's death and his part in it?

"Did you return the call?" Jo pressed.

"Yes." He didn't sound too happy about it. "I waited until the next morning. Then I made myself do it. Whatever it was seemed urgent, and I knew she'd keep trying if I ignored her. Jenny could be pretty irrational when she was emotional. The call didn't last but a couple of minutes. She hung up on me in the end."

Jo stared at him, disgusted, knowing he'd wasted precious time.

Why had he not come forward? What the hell was wrong with him, keeping a secret like that? Damn, but he needed a kick in the pants.

She shoved her anger aside, only a vague tremor in her voice as she asked, "What did she want from you?"

Harrison cleared his throat, eyeing the doorway, as if willing his wife to reappear with the coffee so he wouldn't have to answer.

"Dr. Harrison, what did Jenny Dielman want to discuss with you?" Hank repeated in a stern tone. No more buddy-bonding there.

Harrison sucked in a deep breath and then exhaled slowly. "Finnegan . . ." He sighed the name. "She wanted to rehash the night he died."

"She wanted to talk about the accident?" Jo said.

"Yes. She wanted to go over every detail, moments I've tried so hard to forget." He kneaded his hands. "But she begged me, said she needed to hear it so she could make some sense out of it. So I did." He pursed his lips, jaw taut. "I relived that awful night for her, talking her through it again . . . dragging myself through it again. But Christ Almighty—" His face flushed, fingers curling against thighs. "She wasn't satisfied with my performance. She got angry at me, screamed that I was a liar, and hung up."

"Why?" Jo didn't get it. He was leaving something out, she was sure of it. A big chunk was missing. "Why would she do that?"

"I don't know why, Detective. The whole conversation was pretty crazy."

He wasn't telling them everything. He couldn't be.

"Jenny and I—we didn't understand each other, and it got worse after Finn died." He lowered his voice and continued. "She told me that she had dreams about him, that he spoke to her. He wanted her to find the truth. He couldn't see, she told me, because he wasn't wearing his glasses. She wasn't making sense."

Jo willed him to go on, and he did.

He shook his head. "She said she should never have left the house that night. That it was as much her fault as mine. Then she yelled at me for ignoring Finn, for taking a phone call when I should've been getting him ready for his bath." He rubbed his chin. "The worst part was, she was right."

"He had ADHD," Jo said.

Harrison blinked, looking at her. "Yeah, he did. He was on Ritalin. He was a sweet boy, but out of control sometimes." He wet his lips. "I wasn't good with him. I wasn't as patient with him as Jenny."

Jo didn't care about his excuses. "Do you think the anniversary of Finn's death triggered Jenny's call? Had she phoned before that?"

"No, never," he said, absolute. "I just wish she could have let it go."

Jo thought of what Dr. Patil had mentioned about Jenny's nightmares and her guilt over Finn's death. It sounded like she'd been looking for answers from Kevin and hadn't exactly found what she'd wanted.

"Did she call again, or leave any more messages on your voice mail?"

Harrison's fingers went through his hair. "No," he replied. "None that I'm aware of."

Hank cleared his throat, ducking back into his good-old-boy tone. "I hate to ask you this, Dr. Harrison, because you seem like a decent guy. But was your marriage to Jenny violent in any manner?"

Harrison's shoulders stiffened beneath the blue sweater. "Violent? What are you implying?"

What do you think? Did you push her, slap her, or twist her arm behind her back so that it left a spiral fracture?

"Was there ever physical abuse during your marriage?" Hank pressed.

The man's cheeks drained of color. "Are you asking if I hit Jenny?"

"That's what I'm asking, yes."

"Where in God's name is this coming from?" He turned on Jo, as if it were her fault. "Are you accusing me of something? What does that have to do with Jenny's death?"

Hank pushed at the air with his hands. "Whoa, simmer down, Doc. We're not accusing you of anything, just trying to get our facts straight. There's a question of some old fractures on your ex-wife's post-mortem X-rays, and we've heard tales of a troubled marriage. But I'd like to hear it from you. If I'm wrong, set me straight."

Sic him, partner.

Jo sat so still, she might as well have been invisible. She had to remind herself to breathe.

"I don't know what old fractures you saw or who you've been talking to," Harrison said, "and I sure as hell don't know who could've suggested such a thing to you."

"X-rays don't lie," Hank shot back.

"You think I hurt her? You think I broke her bones? That's not what happened. It was never that simple with me and Jenny." He pinched his nose, sat like that for the longest moment before he allowed himself to go on. "Look, you have to understand that handling Jenny and Finn—they were tricky." He leaned forward, beseeching. "I'm not claiming to be the most patient man in the world, but I would never have hurt either of them intentionally. You have no idea what it was like to live with a hyperactive son and a woman who was never happy."

And you weren't responsible for any of that unhappiness? Selfish bastard, Jo thought.

"After our son died"—he shook his head—"she was impossible. She didn't eat, wouldn't leave the bed. She was catatonic for days. Yes, I wanted to shake her hard enough to wake her up again, to force her to go on with her life, but I never beat my wife. You got that? Never."

"Got it," Hank said.

Jo heard her own heart thudding in her ears, wondering what the hell was going on. Who was lying, and who was telling the truth?

Patrick Dielman? Lisa Barton? Kevin Harrison? Jenny's sister?

"I can't do this." Harrison pushed off the couch and stood. He looked downright grim. "I'll have to ask you to leave. I don't think I should talk to you anymore without my lawyer. I've already said more than I should."

"One last question, please?"

Jo had begun to rise from her chair but hesitated as Hank spoke.

Her partner remained seated, arms resting on thighs.

"All right," Harrison said and sighed. "One more question."

"Where were you between five and nine p.m. on Monday evening of this week?"

The night Jenny vanished.

Jo heard the *tap-tap* of Alana's footsteps; she saw the glint of the silver tray coming through the door to the library as Hank repeated, more loudly, "Your whereabouts on Monday evening?"

The *tap-tap* stopped.

"You think I had something to do with Jenny's death?"

"What's going on here?" Alana set the tray down with a clatter.

Jo watched the creamer tip, the white puddle spreading across the silver tray.

Harrison didn't answer. His eyes were on Hank as he calmly replied, "If I had wanted her gone, I could have let it happen right after Finn died. She tried to kill herself, you know. Did your source tell you that? She swallowed a shitload of Valium." He wiped a hand across his mouth; his fingers shook. "I saved her life. If I hadn't found her and rushed her to the ER, she would've been gone. So why would I kill her now?"

Because you have so much more to lose, Jo thought.

"Kevin, don't do this," Alana whispered.

"It's okay." He took his wife's hand, clung to it. "Good night, Detectives. I do believe we're finished here."

Jo didn't protest. She was disgusted by Kevin Harrison's martyr act—and an act was all it was. She didn't bother to button her peacoat as she walked toward the door. But she only heard one set of footsteps: hers.

She realized Hank hadn't moved.

"Monday night, Dr. Harrison," she heard her partner ask for the third time. "Please, don't make this more difficult than it has to be. Just tell us where you were, and we'll be done with it. Easy as pie, right?"

Jo turned, watching Kevin Harrison.

"I was at Presbyterian Hospital performing an emergency cholecystectomy," he said. "That's a gallbladder removal, for you laymen. I ended up repairing an abdominal hernia before I closed, so it took nearly two hours. We started right around five o'clock. I stayed at Presby for another hour, monitoring my patient and doing some paperwork. Alana had been showing houses all afternoon, so after I got home and changed, we had dinner with her father at Bistro 31 in Highland Park Village at nine o'clock. We weren't back until midnight. Isn't that right, hon?"

"That's right," Alana said flatly. Her gaze never left her husband's face.

"I wasn't anywhere near Jenny on Monday evening, or any other evening."

His wife stood beside him, clinging on to his hand.

"Now, I've answered your questions," he said, "so please, go."

"If we need anything else, we'll be in touch, sir." Hank got up and shrugged into his coat. Then he followed Jo to the front door, and they ventured back out into air so cold that it knocked the breath from her lungs.

She saw Hank exhale, creating a cloud of fog as he muttered, "Son of a bitch."

Which she thought summed things up rather neatly.

I left the library early. I've been sleeping so badly and I had a terrible headache, so I told Sally I needed to go home. I parked in front rather than in the garage, and I found the door unlocked. I thought maybe I'd forgotten. Patrick has me convinced that I'm not thinking straight these days, what with Finn's anniversary so close. He's right. I am preoccupied.

But when I entered the house, I smelled that vague scent again, like stale cigarette smoke. I knew who it belonged to, and I was sure she was still here.

I found her sitting in my yellow room. She was on the futon, a photo album in her lap.

"What are you doing home, Jenny?" she asked, like I was the one out of place.

"What do you want?" I said.

Instead of answering, she made a sad face and glanced down at Finn's photographs.

"Don't you miss him?" she asked. "Don't you wish you could hold him again?"

"Yes," I said, because it was true. "More than anything."

"Patrick said you can't have children, and he's always wanted kids."

"That's none of your business." I stood in the doorway, so angry I shook.

"If you could have anything, Jennifer, what would it be?" She closed the photo album and held it against her chest, hugging it. "I think I know. You'd want to be with your baby."

"Get out," I told her, but she shook her head, like she was in charge, not me.

"Let's you and I have a girl-to-girl talk, sugar," she drawled softly, but her eyes looked harder than flint. "If you're gonna really live your life, you have to stop being maudlin. You're killing Patrick, you know. This room full of the boy's things—it has to go."

He must have told her. How else could she know? Had he asked her to do this?

"Go to hell," I said, and she looked like I'd slapped her.

She put the photo album down and came toward me. "Someone should shake you," she said. "Really shake you hard."

K had already tried that. He'd shaken me so hard, I thought my neck would snap. I wanted to tell her that it didn't work.

"Give me back the spare key," I said, holding out my hand. I didn't care what she told Patrick.

She frowned and fished in the pocket of her sweater, dropping it into my palm.

"Don't blame anyone but yourself for losing him," she said before she sidestepped me and walked out.

Losing him? Hadn't I already lost him?

Unless Finn wasn't the "him" she meant.

CHAPTER SEVENTEEN

An hour's drive through city traffic, and they were back at the station.

Jo barely had time to dump her coat at her desk before she and Hank were called into Captain Morris's office.

"I heard from the ME, and it looks like we've got ourselves a homicide," Cap said without preamble.

"Yes, sir," Hank replied and proceeded to dig out his notes from the postmortem. All he left out was the part about him getting sick.

Then it was Jo's turn to share everything Emma Slater had told her. Like Hank, she omitted one thing: the file on Finn Harrison that Adam had snagged for her, because she wasn't sure how—or if—it fit into the case.

"Something on your mind, Larsen?" the captain asked.

"It's about our interview with Dr. Harrison, Jenny Dielman's ex-husband." She cleared her throat, careful where she was stepping. "He's a hunter, sir, and a good one, according to his wife. He's been handling guns since he was a kid."

"You think he's familiar with the quarry?"

"I'd bet he is." She suddenly wished she'd paid more attention to the locations in the photographs plastering the walls of Harrison's den. But could they place him at the scene? "He's got an alibi for the night Jenny disappeared. He says he was doing emergency gallbladder surgery until seven on Monday evening, and he stuck around the hospital until eight or so. After that, he met his wife and her father at Bistro 31 for a late dinner. He practically dared us to check it out."

"Do it," Cap said. "What about Patrick Dielman? You check his alibi yet?"

Jo still had Dielman's parking card in her pocket. "Yes, sir, and it looks like he was at his office in Dallas until almost seven on Monday evening. The parking security card has him leaving at six fifty."

"So that's where we stand?" Cap said.

Jo nodded, and Hank grunted his assent.

They started to rise from their chairs when their boss said, "One last thing, and we'll call it a night." He shuffled papers on his desk. "We've received over a hundred calls on the tip line already, and I think we might have a live one. A woman said she saw Jennifer Dielman in the Warehouse Club parking lot on Monday at dusk. I'll send a unit to her house tomorrow morning to bring her in. All right then." He patted his desk. "Go home. Get some rest."

But Jo wasn't ready to leave the station.

She went straight to her desk and checked her messages. She had a voice mail from Patrick Dielman, telling her the morgue had released Jenny's body for burial and the memorial service would take place the next day at one o'clock at the nondenominational Grace Church, a half mile east of the Dielmans' subdivision.

Jenny's sister was next, noting she'd be flying in from Iowa in the morning and would be staying at the Hampton Inn at the highway exit into Plainfield.

Jo played the messages twice, jotting down times and locations. She wanted to be at Jenny's service and not just for professional reasons. She felt like she owed it to Jenny.

She got on her computer and Googled the number for the Hampton Inn in Plainfield. Then she phoned and left a message at the front desk for Kim to find when she checked in.

Maybe the contents of the shoe box Jenny had sent her sister would help them figure this out, though she wasn't sure how.

Before she got back to work, she called Adam to say she'd be very late getting home and suggested they get together another night.

"Call if you need me," he said. "I don't care how late it is."

"I will," she told him, even though she had a feeling she'd be out like a light as soon as she crawled into bed.

With that out of the way, she slid Jenny's appointment book from the evidence bag and found the page with the phone number and the question mark. She checked it out with the reverse directory. It was exactly as Emma had noted: a pay phone in the Presbyterian Hospital lobby.

Presbyterian Hospital.

That was where Kevin Harrison practiced surgery.

Was there a connection? Or did she just *want* there to be?

Jo stared at the calendar in the appointment book, at the date that Jenny had circled and marked *Finn*. The anniversary of his death.

Was Jenny the paranoid, irrational woman that Kevin Harrison and Lisa Barton wanted them to believe? Or just the poor soul whose broken heart Patrick Dielman had apparently failed to patch? Had Jenny gotten herself into something she couldn't get out of? Had she pushed the wrong buttons without knowing exactly what she was doing?

It was almost midnight when Jo finally left the station. She was dragging, and there was no point in pushing herself further.

Hank had brought her the box from Mama's house before he'd taken off an hour earlier. Jo hauled it out to the Mustang and shoved it in the trunk before she belted herself in and turned the ignition.

She drove home on autopilot, ignoring the throb of her aching shoulder and the knot in her neck. She focused on the road beyond her headlamps but saw something else: the fragile smile of a woman who had lost everything.

What am I missing?

The locket and Jenny's coat hadn't turned up yet. Had her killer taken them, or had Jenny left them behind at a secondary crime scene? If that was the case, Jo would bet they'd been disposed of already.

Still, she felt in her bones that she wasn't seeing something, not the way she should. Her brain was too fuzzy to think straight at this hour. The only thing she wanted to do was crawl into bed and close her eyes.

It felt like forever before she pulled into a parking spot at her condo building. She cut the lights, dragged herself from the car, and slammed the door. Not another soul was in sight as she crossed the grassy front lawn to her porch.

The quiet of midnight seemed to magnify each sound: the click of the dead bolt as she unlocked it, the clank of her keys dropping onto the hall table, the swish of her coat coming off her shoulders, and the shuffle of her footsteps to the kitchen. She needed a Coke before she hit the sack, knowing the caffeine would do little to keep her up.

She was so freaking tired.

Jo drank the soda while standing at the sink, her reflection thrown back at her in the dark of the window. She looked like a train wreck. Felt like one, too.

After she tossed the empty can, she started toward the bedroom and remembered the box from Mama's house sitting in her Mustang. She could leave it there all night, and it wouldn't bother her a bit.

Except that it was personal paperwork, Ronnie had said, probably with birth dates and Social Security numbers for Mama and maybe her, too.

She didn't bother putting her coat back on. Just headed out into the dark with her keys and popped the trunk. The box wasn't bulky—white cardboard from the office supply store with a lid that Ronnie had loosely taped down—so Jo tucked it against a hip to carry it. The thing banged against her mailbox as she stood on the welcome mat, and Jo groaned.

Another thing she'd almost forgotten.

Get the mail, she told herself, then straight to bed.

She opened the door and crossed the threshold enough to set down the box. Then she leaned back out to push open the lid of her mailbox and reach inside. Her fingertips jammed into something sticky and warm, like smashed grapes, and then her nose caught the smell.

She held her breath and drew her hand out, lifting it toward the halo of yellow from the porch light. A dark stain smeared her fingers and palm. She knew what it was, could almost taste it: blood.

Swallowing hard, she peered into the metal box, hung on the railing, seeing only the sheen of black, the glint of a glassy eye beneath the porch lamp.

Ernie, she thought instinctively, though he was too big to fit in the mailbox, if he were all in one piece.

She backed away, bumped into the door behind her, bile rising in her throat.

No, she thought. *Please, God, no.*

The night fanned around her, silent and lurking, full of shadows.

He could still be out there, whoever stuffed the tiny carcass in her mailbox, whoever wanted to scare her. And she was alone.

She stumbled past the threshold and shut the door, threw the locks, and hustled into the kitchen. She grabbed the landline, punching in numbers drunkenly, until she got it right and heard Adam's foggy-sounding voice on the other end.

"I'm sorry for waking you up," she said, running over the words. Her voice seemed to belong to a stranger, so vulnerable and distant.

"Jo? What is it?"

"Somebody's been here. They left something—" She tried to stay calm as she explained, but it was impossible to keep from shaking. "I need you, please."

"I'm on my way."

She made one more call; then she hung up, stared at her bloodied hand, and waited.

Yesterday in the middle of the afternoon, I got another call, the one that sounded like Finn's voice, and I was begging whoever it was to leave me alone when Patrick came home unexpectedly from work.

He grabbed the phone from me, barking into the receiver, "Who is this? What did you say to my wife?"

But by then, they'd hung up.

He turned to me. "What's going on, Jen?"

"I don't know," I said, because it was the truth. I had started to shiver. "Someone's messing with me. I'm not crazy. It's real."

"Okay." He pulled me near and held me tight. I think he knew I was afraid.

Patrick left the house this morning "on an errand," he said. He was gone for several hours and when he returned, he handed me a small bag. "This is for you," he said. "It'll keep you safer than new locks."

My gift was swaddled in newsprint, which I hesitantly unwrapped.

"For all the times I'm not with you," he explained as I stared at the thing in my hands. "Put it in your car when you're out, all right? Don't be afraid to use it."

My God.

It was a gun.

CHAPTER EIGHTEEN
FRIDAY

Jo awakened to the whir of a Weedwacker, an angry buzz in her ears, and she struggled to open her eyes. The high-pitched hum receded as she raised herself up from the couch, swung her legs over the edge, and touched bare feet to the floor. Sunlight slipped through slanted blinds as she gave a gentle stretch and winced. Every muscle and joint ached at once, though her psyche felt banged up the most.

"Hey, how're you feeling?"

She looked toward the voice and saw Adam seated across the coffee table in an armchair. He didn't appear to have slept at all, or much more than she had, anyway. He set his glasses on his nose, and she wished he hadn't, figuring she'd look much better blurry.

"I'm all right." She didn't feel fully conscious. Hadn't she fallen asleep just moments before? What time was it anyway? She squinted gamely at the mantel clock but couldn't get a fix on the slender black hands.

Was it seven or eight?

She had to think hard to recall the day.

Friday, she remembered. Jenny's funeral was at one. Her sister was flying in this morning.

"Jo?" Adam got up and came over, settling beside her. He stroked her hair, following the curve of her neck and sliding down her arm.

She sighed and leaned into him, resting her cheek on his shoulder. She wished she could stay like this forever, knowing how fast such moments disappeared.

"You should take it easy today after last night—" he started, but she shook her head, and he didn't finish.

It was fresh enough in her mind. Nothing needed repeating.

She'd found an eviscerated crow in her mailbox—not a cat, and thankfully not Ernie. The worst part of it was that whoever had delivered the dead bird—whoever wanted her scared—knew where she lived.

She closed her eyes, willing herself to relax as Adam rubbed her shoulders. She forced herself not to think of how shaken she'd been when Hank had shown up on her doorstep and then a squad car with sirens had appeared, until the whole damn condo complex had known something was up and that she was in the thick of it.

She wondered, too, if the bearer of her "gift" had been out there in the shadows, gloating and watching it all play out.

"Someone's trying to warn you off," her partner had said, as if she couldn't figure that out herself. "He's messing with you."

Yeah, but who? And why?

She wasn't the only one working the Dielman case.

"Maybe this freak has been keeping tabs on you," Hank went on. "Could be he thinks you've got something that'll blow this thing wide. You find anything you haven't told me about?"

Anything I haven't told you about?

She had a copy of Finn Harrison's file from the Presbyterian ER, but Hank knew about that. If she had anything that made their killer nervous, she wasn't sure what it was.

When Hank and the boys in blue had departed, they'd taken the whole mailbox off the railing, butchered bird and all, and bagged it as evidence. But Jo doubted they'd find anything besides her prints and those belonging to her mail carrier. Whoever had done this—whoever had killed Jenny—was too smart to leave a trail.

Of course, none of the neighbors had seen squat. The condos were deserted during the day, all the singletons off to work.

"I don't think you should be alone," Adam said, his breath ruffling her hair. "At least, not until this case is closed. I've got a bag in my trunk, so I'll hang here until I'm sure you're safe."

He worried so much about her. But then, she gave him good reason.

"Stay home today, please? I've got the day off, and I've cleared my weekend. I don't think you should be putting yourself out there, not after this. Your partner agreed. He said he'd talk to the captain, that he'd understand if you missed the interview this morning. Let him take care of it for you."

A noise of disbelief escaped her lips. She turned her head, met his eyes dead-on, and said, "It's not up to either of you, though, is it?"

"Jo, I'm afraid for you, and I just—"

She put her fingers over his lips to silence him. She didn't want to argue.

"I can't lay low," she said. "Please understand." She knew where his concern was coming from. She wasn't exactly feeling as cool as a cucumber, but she wasn't backing off this case. She wasn't going to abandon Jenny.

He glanced away with a sigh, and she touched his cheek, drawing his gaze back.

"If someone's dogging me, at least now I know it, and I'll watch my step. I promise. You can stay here until we get this guy, if that makes you feel better, but let me do what I have to do. And I have to do this, Adam."

He gave a hesitant nod. "I know."

He took her hand and turned it palm up, pressing his lips firmly into its curve, nose caught against her thumb, causing her heart to leap. She nearly gave in, told him she'd stay with him, that she'd forget about Jenny Dielman just for today.

But she couldn't do it.

"I want to be there for the interview with the potential witness from the Warehouse Club parking lot, and I have to be at the funeral later. Jenny's sister's coming in, and she's bringing something Jenny sent her."

"What?"

"Some things of Finn's from the night he died."

"Oh, man." He lowered her hand in his, holding it tight against his thigh, and he raised his chin, looking at her with an expression so full of concern, it made her chest ache.

She knew she wasn't easy to love, but somehow he did. It was clear in his eyes. She rubbed a thumb over his lips.

"I'm not sure what to do with you," he said, a catch in his voice that tore at her soul.

"Be patient," she asked, as if she hadn't asked a thousand times before. "Let me figure things out. I have to be who I am."

"I know who you are, Jo."

She saw his earnest expression and believed that he meant it. She wanted to believe, too, that he'd love her still when he knew everything about her. All the pieces she'd hidden.

She left his arms to take a shower with promises he'd put on some coffee. The hot spray on her face didn't quite make up for the lack of sleep, but she felt better afterward, better still when she'd dressed and pulled her holster snug against her hip and snapped in her sidearm.

She humored him by chewing on a piece of toast and swallowing a few gulps of caffeine before she donned her coat and picked up her keys, which Adam promptly took from her hand.

"I'll drive you," he said, in a way that made her not want to fight him.

"So now you're my chauffeur?"

He gave her a flicker of a smile as he pulled his coat over the rumpled T-shirt and jeans he'd slept in. "I'm off today, remember? I've got nothing to do but shuttle you around."

"You could find me another mailbox."

He cocked his head. "Anything else?"

She thought of Kimberly Parker and the package she'd be bringing, and she said, "How about meeting me at Grace Church at, say, quarter to one? I might need your help with something."

He didn't say a word, so Jo didn't complain when he walked her out to his SUV and opened the door for her, helping her in and all but fastening her seat belt.

By the time Adam dropped her off at the station house, Hank was there. And from the looks she got as she buzzed through the door and past Dispatch, word had gotten around about the dead crow found stuffed in her mailbox.

Her partner shoved a cell phone in her hand as soon as he saw her. "It's my wife's," he said. "Just take it until you're issued a new one."

Jo hadn't even had time to fill out the paperwork on the phone she'd fatally maimed in the cold quarry waters. She thanked him, and he nodded.

They said no more about it.

Jo went with Hank into their captain's office, and after reassuring Cap that she was fine, they sat and waited for the witness who reportedly saw Jenny in the Warehouse Club parking lot sometime around 5:30 p.m. on Monday night.

The woman was a sixty-five-year-old widow named Hannah Sykes who ran a day care center in Plainfield. She'd called the tip line yesterday, and Captain Morris had sent officers to pick her up and bring her in.

"She looks credible," he'd assured them, tapping broad knuckles against a file. "She's got a current license to run her business, not a single complaint against her, and no rap sheet. She taught junior high school for twenty years, God bless her, and she didn't strangle a single kid."

"She's a regular Mother Teresa," Hank quipped.

"Let's just hope she has twenty-twenty vision." Jo was too nervous to joke with them, too anxious to smile.

After a strained fifteen minutes, Mrs. Sykes appeared in the captain's office, settled into a chair, and declined an offer of coffee.

Jo couldn't sit still, so she stood, her arms crossed, watching the woman shrug out of an aqua-colored car coat with Hank's assistance.

With a broad drawl, Sykes dealt him a "thank you, darlin'," as he hung it on a rack near the door. She smiled fleetingly, patting at gray hair cropped close to her skull. She looked around, her eyes large behind red glasses that perched on a slightly beaked nose. Grooves creased her face, and skin sagged at her jawline, but she looked trim and fit in purple sweater and matching pants.

The captain had finished his "we appreciate your coming in" speech by the time Jo finished visually appraising Hannah Sykes. "We'll have you work with our FACES artist—that's a computer sketch artist, ma'am—and take a formal statement from you when you're done here, if that's all right."

"Just so long as I'm back at the center by noon," she said. "That's when we do lunch for the kiddos and sing along with *Barney* after cookies."

"We'll do our best," Cap assured her as Hank positioned a chair beside Mrs. Sykes. "Can you tell us what you saw, ma'am?"

Mrs. Sykes clasped her hands in her lap and tipped up her chin. "I'll tell you exactly what I told that nice police officer on the telephone. I went to the Warehouse Club on Monday, oh, about five thirty, leaving Earlene waiting for Bobby to get picked up from the center so I could get our supplies for the next month and be home in time for *Jeopardy*. That's on at six thirty, if it matters any."

Jo nodded encouragement as the woman glanced in her direction.

"It was getting dark by then, but the parking lot is brightly lit. I pulled into the first empty spot and looked straight through the windshield as I turned off the car." Mrs. Sykes nodded. "That's when I saw her, the woman who went missing, although I didn't know who she was at the time, not until after I saw her picture on the news and heard the description of her car. But it was her, all right." She tapped the red rim of her specs. "With these puppies, I can see things sharp as a tack."

"How far away were you parked from Mrs. Dielman?" the captain asked.

Hannah tugged an earlobe. "Well, now, the spot I pulled into was one row over from where the red car sat. I was pretty far away from the store, but it's so darned hard to find a space that I'm just relieved when I find one that's empty."

Jo toe-tapped the floor, wishing Hannah Sykes would speed things up. Sometimes it seemed folks liked to draw things out, just for the sake of feeling important. Here was a widowed ex-teacher who changed diapers and sang *Barney* songs all the livelong day, so she probably relished having the attention of three adults who weren't finger painting and didn't need a chaperone to the potty.

"Ten yards, would you say?" Hank suggested, and the woman looked at him thoughtfully.

"I was close enough to see that her coat was dark and her purse was brown. And she was carrying a big shopping bag." The woman raised her chin, making the tendons in her neck turn ropey. "My car was facing another car, and hers was in the next lane over, but I was getting out of mine and locking up. So I was standing, and there wasn't anything in my way. I saw her talking to a skinny fella. They were on the passenger side of the red car. She was about to put her bag in, only he came out of nowhere and set a hand on her arm, so she stopped what she was doing and faced him. Then they started talking."

“Talking or arguing?” Jo asked.

“No one looked mad, if that’s what y’all mean.”

Something didn’t feel right, but Jo wasn’t sure what it was. “Are you certain it was a man?”

“Fairly certain . . .” She paused and continued with less confidence. “Though it’s hard to tell sometimes these days, isn’t it? There are so many young fellas with long hair and earrings and gals with crew cuts who look like boys.” She squinted through her specs. “He was at least half a head taller than Mrs. Dielman.”

Jenny had been five-foot-five. Half a head would make their suspect closer to six feet. That would fit with the distance the driver’s seat was pushed back in the Nissan.

“What else did you notice about him?”

“Hmm.” Mrs. Sykes hesitated. “Well, he was wearin’ a long, tan coat that covered him down to his shins. He wore a hat, too, the kind with flaps over the ears, which I thought was kinda odd, but folks around these parts are so thin-skinned when it starts getting cold. He might’ve had a scarf wrapped around his neck. I couldn’t see down as far as his shoes.”

“Did you see his face?”

Mrs. Sykes deflated, chin sinking. “No, hon, and I wish I had now that I know what happened. I mostly just saw the back of him, maybe a little from the side.”

“Do you think you could recognize him again?”

The woman sighed. “If he was dressed the same as that, with the coat and hat, maybe I could. Otherwise, I’m not so sure.”

Jo glanced at her partner. She couldn’t even look at Cap.

They weren’t going to get much of a composite out of this woman, and any description they issued from her statement would sound so vague, it could be almost anyone.

Damn.

"Another question, Mrs. Sykes, if you would," Hank said, giving Jo a rest. "What happened after this man approached Mrs. Dielman?"

"They talked for maybe a minute. Then they got in the car and drove off."

"Did he force her into the vehicle?"

Owlish eyes blinked behind red rims. "Well, I can tell you this. Nobody pulled a gun, and nobody twisted any arms as far as I could make out."

"Was the man wearing gloves, Mrs. Sykes?"

"I don't rightly recall." The woman pursed her lips. "Well, now that I think about it, when he reached for her arm, I saw brown. So it must've been gloves, unless he was dark-skinned."

Jo struggled to keep from throwing up her hands. The woman seemed so eager to please, so happy to oblige that her descriptions got vaguer by the minute.

"Who was driving the car? Do you remember that?" Hank asked, and Mrs. Sykes turned to him and smiled.

"Now *that* I do remember, clear as day. It was the gal, the one who disappeared. The fella with the hat was in the passenger seat." Mrs. Sykes frowned. "He's the one who killed her, isn't he?"

"That's what we're trying to find out," Hank said and patted her hand.

Jenny was driving?

Jo wanted to shake her head and tell them, "No, that can't be right."

Because the driver's seat in the Nissan had been adjusted to accommodate someone who was nearly six feet tall, the size of the stranger Mrs. Sykes just described. So Jenny couldn't have been driving, unless the pit-stop theory was no theory. Jenny and her abductor had stopped somewhere between the Warehouse Club and the abandoned quarry.

But where? And why?

At least one thing was apparent: Jenny and this man from the parking lot had gone to an unknown location, at which point Jenny must have shed her coat and had her hands bound with duct tape.

But why had Jenny given a lift to this person in the first place?

Jo rubbed the back of her neck, her thoughts spinning.

"Do you recall exactly where the victim's vehicle was parked, ma'am?" Hank pressed. "If we took you over to the lot, could you point it out?"

"You know, Officer, I'm not sure I could. It was so crowded that day, and I remember drivin' in circles until I found the empty spot. I was parked between a pretty sports car and a shiny Mercedes, and that's all I made a point to recall so I could find my car when I left the store. It was a far piece back. That I do know."

"With the rain we've had since Monday, it might not matter a whole lot," Cap commented.

"Scene's been compromised already, what with all the vehicles that have parked there since," Hank agreed.

Jo blocked out their voices, listened only to what her head was telling her about the slender man dressed in a long coat and wearing brown gloves. That sounded a lot like a doctor she knew, one who hunted and skied and probably owned a winter hat with earflaps, and who happened to be doing emergency surgery at the time his ex-wife disappeared.

◆ ◆ ◆

Jo called Presbyterian Hospital and was put through to Inpatient Surgery.

That was the easy part.

A nurse named Jackie stuck her on hold for a good fifteen minutes while she checked Monday's schedule and talked to a member of Dr.

Harrison's surgical team who'd assisted on the emergency gallbladder removal.

When she got back on the line, the nurse not only confirmed that Harrison was in surgery for two hours beginning at five, doing the cholecystectomy with associated abdominal hernia repair, but Jackie herself recalled seeing Harrison checking on his patient while the man was in post-op, well after the surgery, sometime after seven o'clock. As if that weren't enough, the nurse noted that the good doctor had personally entered post-surgical medications for his patient into the hospital system, which had logged the time as 8:05 p.m.

Okay, so maybe Harrison had set up an airtight alibi, smart guy that he was, figuring he'd likely become a person of interest in the investigation. Maybe he had someone else intercept Jenny in the Warehouse Club lot, beg a ride from her, and lead her to some preordained spot where she'd be held until Harrison was free.

"They talked for maybe a minute. Then they got in the car and drove off. . . . Nobody pulled a gun, and nobody twisted any arms as far as I could make out."

What if Harrison's accomplice was someone Jenny knew from their married days, someone from the hospital or a hunting buddy without a conscience who owed him a favor? Thinking about it was enough to give Jo a migraine.

She called Bistro 31 and spoke to the maître d', who knew Dr. and Mrs. Harrison well. "They eat in sometimes, or they'll order ahead, and Dr. Harrison picks the food up on his way home." He confirmed that the couple had a reservation for nine o'clock on Monday evening. "I remember that Mr. Davis"—Alana's father—"arrived first, perhaps a few minutes early, but the Harrisons came in about fifteen minutes later. Is that what you wanted to hear?"

Wanted to hear?

Hell, no.

Harrison was at the hospital until 8:05 p.m. Factoring in the trip from Presbyterian to his house, a shower, and change of clothes, then the drive over to Bistro 31, it would have been a tight fit for Jenny's ex to get out to the quarry and back again before dinner.

Too tight.

Still, Jo knew Harrison was somehow connected to the case. She felt certain Jenny's disappearance and death had something to do with what had happened to Finn. Harrison was a surgeon. He was careful and precise, a perfectionist, someone who didn't screw up.

Too bad, because it would have helped if he'd shown up at the restaurant with blood on his coat, wearing an idiotic hat with earflaps and leather gloves, and yelled to the crowded room, "Sorry I'm late, but I just came from the old limestone quarry, where I put a bullet in my ex-wife's skull."

Jo chewed on the cap of her pen, wishing she could force pieces together that didn't fit. But no such luck. After a few minutes of throwing her own private pity party, she looked up a number online, then picked up the phone and dialed.

"Jacob Davis Properties," a voice chirped.

She asked for Alana Harrison's secretary.

After a "Hold, please" and a few clicks, she reached Alana's assistant, whose friendly twang didn't sound quite so solicitous once Jo explained who she was and asked where Alana Harrison was between five and nine o'clock on Monday evening.

The woman harrumphed, telling her theirs was a very busy office and that Alana Harrison's schedule was always swamped like the Everglades. So couldn't this wait?

Jo reminded her that this involved an ongoing murder investigation, not an invitation to a charity ball. But that only earned her an impatient sigh and a clipped reply: "All I can tell you is that Alana's last appointment was around five on Monday. She mentioned checking on some property before dinner with her husband. Is that what you wanted to know?"

"Could I possibly speak with Mrs. Harrison?" Jo asked.

The assistant sniffed. "I could put you on hold while I get her on her cell. But she's off today. She doesn't even have any showings scheduled, so it could take a while to track her down."

Jo had a bad feeling Alana's assistant would put her on hold indefinitely, what with the snooty attitude. She started to say, "I'll try again later, thanks," but didn't even finish before she realized she was talking to dead air. "Bitch," she said into the phone before she hung up.

"You about ready?"

Hank rested his hands on her desk and leaned over, doing his best impression of superglue. He'd barely left her side all morning and had offered her a ride when she mentioned wanting to see Patrick Dielman before the funeral. She needed a picture from Jenny's photo album, the one of Finn's tree house. Okay, and she had one other objective as well, but she hadn't told Hank. He'd think she'd gone soft, God forbid.

"I'm ready." She gathered her car keys and her wallet, stuck them in her coat pockets. She locked everything else in her desk.

"Did you call Dielman?" her partner asked.

"He didn't answer," she lied, because she hadn't. She was afraid he'd tell her no, that he couldn't deal with the police on his doorstep right before Jenny's service. And Jo didn't just want those photos. She wanted to push a few buttons while she was at it.

Hank leaned away from her desk, fiddling with his tie, which looked about to choke him, and she realized that he'd actually dressed for the funeral. He was decked out in black, from his polished Lucchese boots to his slacks and tweedy jacket. He even had a solemn purple-and-gray-striped tie over his white button-down. Jo wondered if his wife had picked it out.

"Let's go," he said, cheeks turning pink beneath her steady gaze.

Then he walked her out.

The day looked flat-out dreary. Low-hanging clouds smothered the sky beyond the spindly reaches of near-leafless trees.

Hank didn't even try to make conversation as they got into the Ford and bounced out of the lot. Jo figured he wasn't any more certain of what to say to her than Adam had been. She'd rather have silence than a fatherly warning anyway.

He turned up the heat, and she faced the window, leaned her cheek against the cool glass, gazing out into gray, looking for answers that weren't there.

She straightened up as they entered the subdivision and passed Lisa Barton's place, approaching the yellow house next door. The white BMW sat in the front, much as it had the day they'd come to tell Patrick Dielman his wife was dead. Everything looked so quiet and ordinary.

Hank parked on the street, pulling the Ford so close against the curb that he bumped it, rocking them none too gently.

"Sorry," he said.

When had he ever apologized for a bad parking job?

"Look, stop it, okay? I'm not made of glass. I'm not about to duck and run because of a dead bird in my mailbox."

"What would it take, Jo, a horse's head in your bed?"

"I didn't piss off the mob, for Pete's sake."

"But you did piss off a bad guy."

"I'm always pissing off somebody, aren't I?"

He shut off the ignition, keeping his hand on the keys for an interminable minute. "I took that damned crow down to Parkland myself," he said without looking over. He stared at the street. "I paged your friend Emma Slater, who met me in the middle of the freaking night." He finally turned his gaze on her, and it burned into her hard. "Someone had carved that thing up like a Thanksgiving turkey. You get the message?"

"Yeah, I get it," she said, her mouth dry. "But they didn't break in. They didn't put a gun to my head. Whoever sent it isn't sloppy. They won't hurt me when I'm with you or Adam or anyone else. And you've got me surrounded."

Hank stared at her without blinking, and Jo knew what he was thinking. She could see it in his face as clearly as she had in Adam's.

Would he be so concerned if she were a man?

She put a hand on his arm. "Hey, nothing's going to happen to me. I've got you watching my back, don't I?"

"Always."

The way he said it made her blush, and she busied herself unhooking her seat belt.

"C'mon, let's go." She grabbed the door handle and got out of the car. The near-freezing air hit her like a rude awakening as she crossed the sidewalk and crunched across brittle grass on her way to the door.

She rang the bell, and within seconds, the door swung wide.

Lisa Barton greeted them, looking as surprised to see them as Jo was to see her. "Ah, Detectives, what's goin' on? Did you find out something about my broken window?"

Jo thought for an instant she'd gone to the wrong house. "Is Mr. Dielman around?" she asked, figuring he must be. It was still over an hour before the funeral.

"He's getting dressed, but he should be out soon," Lisa said, not inviting them inside. Jo wondered how Jenny would feel, having the neighbor answering the door as if she lived there.

"Mind if we come in?" Jo asked.

"Oh, sure, go right ahead." Lisa took a step back, and Jo gratefully crossed the threshold into the warmth of the foyer. "Pat's having people over after the service, so I've been tidying up. He doesn't even know how to run the dishwasher, poor thing. Jenny did most of the housework." She reached up to fiddle with her hair, tucking loose strands behind her ear, and Jo again noticed the white scars on her fingers.

"Were you burned?" she said, something she'd been dying to ask since she'd first noticed.

"Burned?" The woman glanced at her hands self-consciously. "Oh, that? No, but I did something stupid when I was a teenager. Tattoos," she explained with a nervous smile. "I was tough back then, always trying to prove something. Thank God, doctors can laser 'em off when you're old enough to know better."

"I'll kill my kids if they ever do that," Hank interjected. "Pay somebody to draw on their bodies, I mean."

Jo thought of the tattoo on Jenny's hip, the butterfly that had signified her freedom from Kevin. Only maybe she hadn't been as free of him as she'd imagined.

"Look, Detectives"—Lisa crossed her arms and tucked her hands away—"I don't mean to rush you or anything, but I've still got a few things to do in the kitchen before we head to the church. The caterer's coming here after the service. They're bringing cold cuts and such, and I've been cleaning up the mess Pat's made. I just want everything to be perfect."

Everything to be perfect?

Jo wanted to laugh. The woman sounded like Martha Stewart hosting a soiree.

"What do you need Patrick for anyway?" Lisa asked. "Did you find out who killed Jennifer?"

"Not yet, but we're working on it," Jo said simply. "I actually need something from him. Could you see if he's dressed?"

Lisa's face tightened. "Just don't keep him too long, okay? We're fixin' to head over to the church soon to talk to the pastor and check on the floral arrangements." She uncrossed her arms and plucked at the fabric of her tight black dress. Black suede boots poked out below the calf-length hem. "Poor Pat. He's been on the phone all morning. Jenny's sister got into town, and he tried to talk her into riding with us to the service. But apparently, she declined."

So Kimberly Parker had arrived.

"Does she need a lift to the church?" Jo asked. "We could swing by and pick her up."

And get the shoe box that Jenny sent her, Jo thought.

"No, she's taken care of." Lisa frowned. "She rented a car at the airport. She can follow us back here afterward. We'll take her into Dallas to the cemetery for the burial later." She checked her watch, looking uneasy. "Let me get Pat, and I'll tell him you're here."

Jo watched her stride through the foyer and disappear into the hallway that led to the master bedroom, the route they'd taken yesterday.

She mulled over Lisa's remark about getting her fingers tattooed as a teenager, and she wondered if it was a rebellious act or if she had been in a gang.

"Just because she looks like Goldilocks doesn't mean she is," her partner bent to whisper. "That's what you're thinking, isn't it?"

"You figure if she had a rough childhood, she'd grow up to be a killer?" Jo said quietly. "We ran her through the system. She doesn't have a rap sheet."

"That we can *find*," he reminded her. "The tats on her hands kind of have a juvie jailhouse ring to 'em, don't you think? You still have pull with anyone in the city? Someone you know who remembers everybody's names, some retired sergeant who's never tossed his notes?"

"Maybe," she told him, wishing he'd stop reading her mind. She'd check with Terry, too, see if she could tap into any records from the Department of Family and Protective Services. If Lisa Barton had been in real trouble as a kid, her records were likely sealed.

With a tap of heels on marble tiles, Patrick Dielman emerged from the hallway, flushed and a bit wild-eyed. He greeted them with an apology. "I didn't realize y'all were coming by, and I didn't hear the doorbell."

"You have other things on your mind," she said.

"Too much." He ran a hand over neatly combed hair, patting down a cowlick that dipped over his brow. A wave of sadness swept across his face, and Jo hoped he wouldn't start to cry. "It took me all morning to decide what suit to wear," he remarked. "Jenny hated black. She said it reminded her of losing Finn." He sniffed. "So I put on gray. Do you think that's all right?"

"Yes, I do," Jo said, thinking how different Dielman seemed now compared to the man who'd sat at her desk three days prior. Had losing Jenny softened him? His grief seemed real, but any psychopath worth his salt could cry at the drop of a hat if it helped him get away with murder.

Dielman glanced down at his dark pants, belted at the waist, and smoothed his hands over the fine creases. He wore a crisp, white shirt with a gray paisley tie. His cuffs hung apart, unbuttoned, and a piece of toilet tissue clung to a spot on his jaw that had bled through a deep red. Did he even know it was there?

"I was hoping you had some news." His eyes went from Hank to Jo. "But Lisa said you needed something from me."

"It's a little of both," Jo said, just as Lisa Barton returned, wearing a black trench coat. She sidled up behind Dielman, his tan Burberry folded over her arm.

Jo continued, "We did find evidence that there are two suspects involved in your wife's death. We also believe she was taken somewhere first, before the quarry."

"Oh." Dielman's Adam's apple did a jig. "So you're closing in?"

Jo watched his face. Then she looked at Lisa Barton. "We're making progress, yes," she told him.

"That's good." Dielman nodded. "That's very good."

"Patrick, we really should go." Lisa held out his coat.

"We don't want to hold you up," Hank said. "Do we, Detective Larsen?"

"No," Jo said, "of course not. If you don't mind, sir, I'd like to take a photo from those albums in the yellow room."

"Another picture of Jenny?" Dielman asked as he shrugged into his Burberry. "But I already gave you one, and I'm not sure why you'd need it now."

"It's the shot of Finn's tree house."

"The tree house, huh?" Dielman touched his jaw, connected with the bit of toilet paper and ripped it off. A tiny spot of blood remained. Though his demeanor looked calm, his voice shook. "Take the damned photo, Detective. Take every photo from those albums, for all I care. What the hell am I going to do with them now?"

Lisa hustled him toward the door. Dielman frowned as he patted his pockets, and Jo wondered if he was looking for the leather glove that she'd bagged as evidence. Did he even remember she'd taken it?

"See y'all at the service," Hank said as they departed.

Jo stared after them.

"Did you get the response you were looking for?" Hank asked bluntly.

"I don't know," she said. "I guess we'll find out, won't we?"

"Go on." Hank nudged her. "Get what you need. Then let's get out of here."

She hurried down the hallway and opened the first door on the right.

The photo album lay on the coffee table, just where she'd left it. She thumbed through the pages until she found what she was looking for: the picture of Fort Finnegan, the tree house that no longer existed.

She plucked out a shot of the boy for good measure, one where Finn wore gold-rimmed glasses and a grin wide enough to show missing teeth. She slipped both into her coat pocket.

Hank waited for her in the foyer, thumbs hooked in his belt, gazing into space.

"Can you give me a minute?" she asked, as he started for the door.

"Larsen . . ."

"I just need to do one more thing," she told him.

He gave her a look, like she'd better not be up to anything. "I'll be outside, waiting on the blue-and-white."

The department had arranged for a squad car to sit outside the house during the service, since the case was so high profile. They'd keep an eye on the place until Dielman returned.

Hank headed out and closed the door.

Jo did a quick walk-through, eyeing plumped sofa pillows, vases filled with fresh flowers, and carpeting with vacuum tracks. There were no dishes on the coffee table, no newspapers spread about, zero evidence that anyone had slept on the couch, and no sign of a fur-shedding black cat.

"Ernie," Jo called as she walked around. "Here, kitty, kitty."

She listened for the sound of paws padding across the floor but heard nothing.

The front door flew open.

"The uniforms are here," Hank called into the house.

But Jo wasn't ready to go. She had to find Ernie.

"C'mon, partner, let's roll."

Reluctantly, she followed him out, though she hung back while he greeted the guys in the squad car, parked smack in front, where the white Beemer had once been. One of the uniforms lifted a cup of Starbucks in greeting, and she nodded back. Exhaust fumes plumed the chilly air behind the sedan.

She was about to give up and head to the Ford when she saw motion in the low-lying holly bushes. She heard the plaintive mew and stopped in her tracks.

"Ernie?" she called out. "Come here, kitty." She crouched down, opened her hand on the brittle grass. "Hey, baby, where are you?"

Trimmed green branches shimmied, and a shadow blew out, the dark shape shooting across the driveway to where she squatted. He pushed his damp nose into her palm. The black coat was matted with burrs and leaves, and he shuddered hard as she picked him up, tucking him against her coat to warm him. She felt his ribs beneath her fingers, and the icy pads of his paws.

Jo glanced back at the front door, debating what to do.

Take him inside, or take him with her?

"You have a problem, Detective?" One of the uniforms rolled down his window and stuck his head out. "You need some help with that critter?"

She spoke without thinking. "I've got it under control, thanks."

He gave her a thumbs-up. His window whirred closed.

She started walking toward Hank, who leaned against the Ford, looking none too pleased when he spied what was in her arms.

"Don't tell me you're stealing the Dielmans' cat."

"He was Jenny's," she said, because it made a difference. Ernie butted his head against her jaw, clunking skull on bone, and she felt an unexpected surge of laughter catch in her throat. "He tossed the cat bed already, Hank. I have a feeling Ernie's next."

"Well, you can't just take off with him."

"Why not?" Jo said. "He doesn't belong to anyone anymore."

Her partner squinted. "What exactly do you aim to do with him?"

"I'll bet your kids would love to have a pet."

Hank snorted. "They've got a turtle."

"Isn't that a little like having a pet rock?"

He frowned. "No cat, Jo."

Her gut wrenched. "Well, I can't leave him here. Dielman doesn't seem to give a rat's ass. Besides, it looks like he already has a new pet."

"Goldilocks?" Hank's caterpillar eyebrows rose. "Take him to your place, then."

"My place?"

"Well, I sure as shit didn't mean mine." He shrugged. "Besides, don't cats kill birds? Maybe he can keep the crows away."

"Very funny."

He pulled open the passenger door and said, "Get in, Sister Christian."

So she did, sliding into the seat, careful to keep Ernie secure in her arms while Hank shut them inside. The cat vibrated so hard against her chest, it felt like part of her own heart beating.

She gazed into the trusting yellow eyes and thought: *Dear God, what have I done?*

I dialed K's number again today. I wanted to tell him that I had put more pieces together, that I wasn't going to stop until I had it all figured out. Only it wasn't K who answered.

"What do you want?" his wife demanded, acting so high and mighty. "Can't you see that we've moved on? We have a baby on the way. Surely you understand what that means."

Oh, I understood, all right.

K would get a second chance to be a father. It was crueler than cruel.

"You should have more sympathy now," I told her. "You should understand why I can't let this go."

"I will not have this conversation with you. I'm hanging up—"

"Wait!" I thought of something then, the one thing I'd been dying to ask her. "I know you were talking to him when Finn . . . when it happened. You heard everything, didn't you? How can you cover up for a man who could hurt a little boy?"

She was silent for a moment, and I prayed she would break wide open.

"Leave us alone," she said sharply, but her voice shook, so I knew I'd struck a chord. "Kevin won't like that you called again. You need to stop before you make him angrier."

"Then tell him to stop calling me!" I screamed into the phone.

"Calling you? You're crazy."

"Tell him to stop pretending he's Finn—"

But she was gone.

CHAPTER NINETEEN

Grace Church perched on the corner of a large lot in a mostly residential area. Plainfield Elementary School sat across the street, its playground encompassed by metal fencing. The church's well-tended grounds looked brown like everything else in North Texas. The fledgling trees were bare of leaves, branches bucking with each gust of wind.

Several blue-and-whites were prominently parked on the property, but Jo saw no sign of the media or curiosity-seekers. The place looked peaceful, as it should. Jenny deserved a dignified send-off. Jo hated when memorial ceremonies turned into freak shows, crying survivors captured on camera for the evening news, as if grief were entertainment.

The lot held a number of cars but wasn't full by any means. Hank found a space he could live with and put the Ford in dry dock, with fifteen minutes to spare. He took a blanket from his trunk to make a nest for Ernie on the floor of the backseat, and they left the windows closed against the cold, figuring that if the cat had survived mostly outside since Jenny's death, it surely wouldn't freeze in the car during the funeral service.

Jo watched Hank walk toward the church while she waited out front. She had his borrowed gloves on her hands to keep them warm. She'd called Kimberly Parker and arranged to meet her there before the service. She would bring the box Jenny had sent.

Adam was due to show up any minute, so she was on the lookout for him, too.

Sitting on the ledge that sloped alongside the stone steps, she cast her gaze up the length of the spire that reached into the gray sky, wondering about Jenny's connection to this place. Had she sought solace here? Had she come for answers or prayer?

Mourners continued arriving, glancing at her as they passed, shoes shuffling across the stone walkway.

"Detective Larsen?"

A woman with a head of brown curls approached in black pumps and a black-and-red plaid skirt beneath a leather belted jacket with flowing red scarf. Jo thought of what Patrick had said about Jenny hating black, something Kimberly Parker had clearly known.

"You're Kimberly," she said, the shoe box in her arms all too telling.

"Yes."

She didn't resemble her sister much, not when compared to the photographs Jo had seen. But there was a similarity in the shape of the face, the wariness in her eyes, like she'd learned early in life never to trust anybody.

Jo rose from the ledge.

"Call me Kim, please." The woman squinted into the wind, brushing hair from her cheeks, looking at the church doors. "I'm running a little behind, so can we talk more after? I just wanted to be sure you got this right away."

The package she pushed into Jo's hands amounted to little more than a battered Keds shoe box covered with stamps, labels, and broken tape.

"Are you coming in?" Kim asked.

"In a little bit."

Jenny's sister nodded before turning away to climb the stone steps, holding her skirt against the wind.

Jo sank back down to the ledge, staring at the box in her hands, the postmark dated a week ago. It bore Jenny Dielman's return address.

She hesitated before removing the lid, and her pulse made a loud rush in her ears as she lifted it, knowing what was inside and feeling anxious just the same. Fingers clumsy in Hank's gloves, she touched the pale yellow shirt, tightly rolled around the glasses, the metal barely visible.

This had to be the yellow T-shirt noted in Finn Harrison's file from the night he died, and these had to be the boy's glasses from the empty case. As far as Jo could remember, the glasses weren't a part of the report. Had the emergency room physician who'd pronounced him dead merely missed them?

"She told me that she had dreams about him, that he spoke to her. He wanted her to find the truth. He couldn't see, she told me, because he wasn't wearing his glasses. She wasn't making sense."

Jo closed her eyes, going over Kevin Harrison's confession about Jenny's phone call, a week or so before she went missing, about the time she'd sent the package to her sister.

It wasn't coincidence, she was sure of it.

Jenny had been searching for answers, and Jo had to think she'd found something. Why else would she take such pains to protect the contents of the shoe box?

"Detective?"

Jo opened her eyes to find a woman standing beside her on the steps. She wore black slacks and a calf-length trench coat with a fur collar. Shiny, red hair fell loose on her shoulders, and large sunglasses nearly obscured her face.

It took a moment for Jo to recognize Dr. Harrison's wife, Alana.

"I didn't mean to disturb you," she said.

"No, it's all right." Jo quickly rolled the T-shirt around the glasses, setting it all back in the box the way she'd found it, and closed the lid. "You're here for the service?" she asked.

"You look surprised."

That was putting it mildly.

"Is your husband parking the car?" Jo glanced around Alana, but didn't see the good doctor lurking, couldn't imagine he'd dare show his face.

"No, I came alone. Kevin doesn't know I'm here." Alana pressed rouged lips into a tight line before declaring, "He wouldn't harm her, you know. He's a good guy at heart."

Not to mention a cheater, cheater, pumpkin-eater.

"You're looking at the wrong person," Alana insisted. "All Kevin wants is to move on with his life. You can't know what it means to lose a child." She hesitated, and a gloved hand drifted to the buttons over her belly. "Kevin knows it well. We both know, Detective. I've had two miscarriages in the past three years." Her glossy lips trembled. "It's devastating."

"You can't know what it means to lose a child."

Oh, yeah?

Jo's palms turned slick inside Hank's heavy gloves.

"I should get inside, before I'm late. I don't want to cause a disturbance." Alana looked up at the doors of the church, not seeming too sure of her decision.

Without thinking, Jo got to her feet, clutching the box to her chest. "Mrs. Harrison," she said firmly enough to force Alana to turn. "I don't think that's a good idea."

"What?"

"Jenny doesn't . . . she wouldn't want you here," Jo stated, knowing it was the truth. "Please go home."

Alana's jaw clenched, and she hissed in reply, "She was a mother who suffered the loss of a child, and I sympathize—"

"She was also a married woman who suffered a great loss when you started sleeping with her husband. Where was your sympathy for her then?" The words came out before she could stop them.

"We all make mistakes, Detective Larsen. Surely you've done things that you regret."

The woman looked at Jo like she could see through her, like she knew that Jo had worn a scarlet *A* on her forehead once, too.

But Jo didn't back down. "I'm not sure what you're doing here, Mrs. Harrison. If you're looking for forgiveness, seek it somewhere else. This isn't about you."

Alana stood stock-still, pressed a finger to the sunglasses that covered half her face, and Jo saw her gloved hand shake. "You have no idea what you're talking about."

"I think I do. Now go home, ma'am, please."

The woman opened her mouth, then snapped it shut.

She brushed past Jo and went down the steps, scurrying along the sidewalk to the parking lot. Jo followed her movement, wondering what the hell that was about, until something else caught her eye.

A black Pathfinder pulled up to the curb and put on its hazards.

She clung to the shoe box and hurried down.

Adam unrolled the window. His pale eyes looked her up and down. "So you're still in one piece?"

"So far, so good," Jo said, passing him the shoe box and the photos of Finn and the tree house that she'd shoved in her front pocket. She told him what she needed and asked him to call when he had anything for her. The sooner, the better.

"So much for taking the day off," he murmured.

"Thank you, Adam," she said, leaning down to give him a kiss.

He started to roll up the window until she caught it with her fingers, and he stopped the upward slide.

"Oh, hey, will you pick up some cat food and litter while you're out? I'm not sure I'll have a chance."

"You got a cat? Since when?"

"Twenty minutes ago."

"You're kidding, right?"

She touched his face before she left him, quickly climbing the steps to the church and pulling open the heavy doors as quietly as she could.

She found herself in the narthex, the space no larger than about eight by ten feet. There was a coatroom to one side and a table littered with programs on the other. Noise seeped through a partially opened door that led into the nave, and she heard a surge of well-meaning voices singing "Onward Christian Soldiers" to the accompaniment of an organ.

A fellow appeared from behind her, startling her with a tap on her shoulder.

"May I take your wrap, ma'am?" he said in low tones, clearly respectful of the service beyond the doors. He smiled at her benignly, blinking watery, blue eyes. He waited for her answer with hands clasped at his chest.

"Thank you," she said, fumbling out of the too-big gloves and unbuttoning the peacoat, only then realizing how filthy it looked with stray cat hairs and bits of muck that Ernie had left upon it.

He helped her out of it and took it from her, giving her that same flat smile and nod as he walked over to the coatroom to hang it up.

Jo smoothed her hands over the pockets of her blazer, feeling the pancake holster hidden at her hip. She turned her borrowed cell to vibrate before she slipped it back in her pocket.

Sure she was presentable, she went inside.

Someone reached for her arm as she entered, drawing her against the back wall. She knew by the scent of drugstore cologne that it was

Hank. Whenever he spruced up, he slapped on a little of whatever his girls had given him for his birthday or Christmas. Jo thought it was endearing of him and even tolerable, as long as they never got stuck in a broken elevator.

She stood with him at the rear of the church, noting that barely half a dozen pews were filled with people. At least they were rows away from being heard.

She felt sorry for Jenny, for the small turnout. Then she realized that, had it been her in the casket draped with red carnations, the crowd would likely be as sparse. Like Jenny, she had little left of her family and few real friends, fewer still who really knew her.

It was a sobering thought but hardly devastating.

"You're still in time for the first act," Hank whispered. "Dielman's in the front pew with Lisa Barton. There's a brown-haired woman I didn't recognize, came in after the pair of them but sat right up front."

"That's Kim," she said, keeping her voice down. "Jenny's sister from Iowa."

"You met her already?"

"She brought me something from Jenny."

"Something from Jenny?" He blinked. "Like what?"

"It's Finn's shirt from the night he died, and his glasses."

"Why?"

"I don't know," she said. She hadn't figured out how all the pieces fit together yet.

He raised his eyebrows. "And when were you gonna tell me about this?"

"Adam's taking them to the lab for testing," she said without answering him directly. "I'm working on a theory."

"Oh, a theory." He shook his head. "Jesus, Jo, you might've mentioned this before you got a crow in the mail."

But I had nothing to back it up, she wanted to say, just gut instincts telling her that Finn's accident was connected to Jenny's murder.

"I should have discussed it with you," she said softly. "I'm sorry."

He grunted and looked away.

The preacher, in solemn black robes, waited for the sound of voices and lingering organ notes to fade before he began to speak of rebirth and renewal, of death being not the end but the start of a journey into another, better life.

Jo hoped it was better for Jenny than the life she'd had in this world.

The preacher said something about "joining Jenny with her loved ones in heaven," and Jo shifted her attention to the front of the church. If there truly was justice in the universe, then Jenny would have her son back in her arms about now.

"We're still waiting on phone records for the Harrisons, but I checked in with Cap, and Dielman's records were e-mailed this morning. He told his carrier to give us whatever we needed. He told his bank to give us access to his records, too."

"Was there anything there?" she asked.

Hank reached a hand inside his coat. "We got zip on the bank records. No large cash withdrawals that seem hinky. But his cell's another story." He withdrew a folded page, smoothed it open on his thigh, then passed it over.

Jo glanced at the string of about two dozen numbers. Several had handwritten notations beside them, like *office*, *home*, and *pizza delivery*.

Her partner pointed his pinkie at one number in particular, highlighted in yellow pen. "This one's registered to an Elizabeth Ann Barton," he said, keeping his voice down. "That's Dielman's friendly neighbor, Lisa."

Jo saw the same number highlighted half a dozen times.

"Check the date and hour here." Hank tapped a finger on the last line.

Jo let her gaze trail down. She realized the time of the call was just two minutes after five on Monday. The night Jenny disappeared.

"He must've called Lisa Barton right after he talked to his wife," she said. "After Jenny told him she was going shopping at the Warehouse Club. Why didn't he tell us?"

"He could've been returning her call," Hank suggested. "Maybe Barton tried to call while he was talking to Jenny. He could've dialed her right back after he hung up with his wife."

Jo didn't like how that sounded. Something about Lisa Barton unsettled her: the scars on her fingers, her easy answers to their questions, the way she pressed the point that Jenny was in a bad state of mind.

"What if," she started slowly, "Lisa Barton was keeping tabs on Jenny through Patrick Dielman? What if she was the one Jenny was afraid of?"

"Why?"

Jo raised an eyebrow.

"You think she was after the husband?"

"Lisa told us that Jenny didn't deserve him, right? Besides, her story doesn't wash."

"The one about passing Jenny in front of the houses?" Hank whispered.

"That and the brick through her window, finding Jenny's scarf, all of it feels very—" *Wrong,* she was going to say, but Hank beat her to it.

"Convenient?"

"Yes."

Hank grunted. "She's a tall drink of water. You figure she dressed up like a man, followed Jenny to the Warehouse Club, made up some story in order to catch a ride, then forced her to drive to the quarry, and put a bullet through her head?"

"There had to be someone else involved," Jo whispered. "They had to stop somewhere in between. There had to be a second car."

"Who'd she meet up with? Patrick Dielman? Kevin Harrison?"

"I don't know." Jo gnawed on her bottom lip. "I think Harrison's involved somehow."

But he couldn't have been in two places at once, and even his surgical team at Presbyterian Hospital had confirmed that he was operating from five until seven on Monday night, the same time that Jenny disappeared with the man from the parking lot, according to their eyewitness. Harrison even had an alibi for afterward, staying at the hospital until eight and dining at Bistro 31 with Alana and her father at nine.

"We've got no physical evidence that puts Lisa Barton anywhere near the shopping center or the quarry," Hank reminded her. His voice started to rise, and she put a finger to her lips.

Patrick Dielman had stepped up to the dais.

He held a piece of paper in his hands, and Jo could see him tremble even from way in the back.

"My wife was always looking for peace," he began, and his voice was clear despite its tremor. "I don't think she ever found it, not while she was alive."

Jo glanced at her feet. Her throat closed up, and she swallowed to keep it clear.

"So how about this," Hank breathed in her ear, drowning out Patrick Dielman's eulogy. "What if there's a link between Barton and Harrison?"

"Like what?"

"He's a surgeon. She manages a medical supply company that's located not far from Presbyterian Hospital. Say they know each other, got to talking."

"And planned his ex-wife's murder?" Jo met his eyes, not sure he believed that any more than she did.

Patrick Dielman finished speaking, folded up his papers, and yielded the podium to Jenny's sister. They passed each other without so much as a glance.

Kim Parker lifted her head and looked over the church. "Jenny was my big sister, my protector. I loved her so much. I still can't believe that she's gone when she hardly had a chance to find real happiness."

Jo winced as she listened.

"Jen did what a big sister was supposed to do. She looked out for me. She tried to keep me from harm's way, to help me from making bad decisions. She put herself before me even when it brought her pain . . ."

The rawness in those words rattled Jo hard. They jabbed at what was unhealed inside her, sliced through her so that she felt like she was ripping apart.

"When Jenny loved, she loved fiercely, but she didn't always love herself."

"I'll be outside," she said to Hank and pushed away from the wall, slipping out the door into the narthex and closing it behind her. She walked straight for the vestibule and shoved open the doors, not slowing until she felt the cold wind nip her face.

She stopped at the top of the stone steps, crossing her arms and rubbing them, sucking in the crisp air so that it stung her nose and the roof of her mouth. She wanted to cry out, to release a bloodcurdling wail that set free all the blackness inside of her.

But she wouldn't, not here.

Why, Jenny, why?

If she'd found something that proved her son's death was no accident, why hadn't she gone to the police with her suspicions? Instead, she'd called her ex-husband and asked him to go through the events of that fateful night again. Had she told him that she was looking for proof to use against him, so she could ruin his fairy-tale life? Because Jenny had wanted him to suffer, too, hadn't she? To wallow in the same guilt she'd been drowning in for three years.

That's how you wanted it to go down, wasn't it?

Jenny had wanted Kevin Harrison to share in her torture. But in the end, she had sacrificed everything.

"You'll get him, won't you?"

She sucked in the cold air until it filled her lungs and quelled the restlessness she'd felt.

Yes. I promise, I will.

A gust of wind swept around the north side of the building, and its icy breath wrapped around her. Jo pushed her hands into the small pockets of her blazer, but they didn't offer much protection. Her teeth chattered.

"Jo?" She felt the weight of her wool coat settle on her shoulders, smelled the pungent scent of Old Spice. "What the hell's up with you? It's forty-two degrees, if you didn't see the temp on the bank sign coming over."

She worked her arms into the sleeves, ignoring the twinge in her left shoulder. "I had to clear my head."

Hank grunted. "Well, they're through in there, so you can relax. Dielman should be out in a minute, and the sister, too." He zipped up his own coat, pulling on the gloves she'd borrowed from him earlier. "You want a ride back to the station, or you have other plans you haven't told me about?"

They descended the steps and stood off to the side at the bottom.

"Kim wanted to talk."

"Well, then, I'll stick around." He crossed his arms. He had that Papa Bear look of concern on his face.

Jo nodded. "Thanks."

She reached in her coat pocket for the loaner phone, making a quick call to Terry Fitzhugh. She asked Terry if she could mine her old family-services connections for any dirt on Elizabeth Ann Barton. She relayed what she knew about Lisa: the junkie mom, the cleaning-lady aunt who'd raised her, the scarred knuckles.

She was pocketing the phone when the front doors of the church flew open, and mourners began trickling out.

Within a few minutes, Dielman emerged with the black-robed minister. Barton trailed a few steps behind. They hesitated, the cleric taking Dielman's hands and clasping them as they conversed.

Hank jerked his chin toward the doors as Kim Parker emerged from the church into the dull afternoon.

The preacher caught her hands and spoke to her as he had to Patrick. When she drew away, she looked around, saw Jo, and headed in her direction. Patrick Dielman and Lisa Barton followed in her footsteps.

Jo introduced Kim to Hank, then asked, "You holding up all right?"

She shrugged. "What choice do I have?"

Her eyes looked pinched as she dabbed at them with a tissue. In her other hand, she carried a red carnation, taken from the spray on the casket.

"Detective Larsen," Kim began haltingly, "if you don't mind, I have some questions about Jenny. Could we go somewhere more private than this?"

"But, Kimberly, we need you back at the house," Patrick Dielman said from over Kim's shoulder. "Aren't you following us home in your car?"

"I'll be a little late, okay?" Kim was unapologetic. "Like I told you in the church, there's something I have to do first. Somewhere I'd like to go."

"It can't wait?" Patrick asked, not sounding pleased in the least.

Kim shook her head. "No, it can't wait."

"C'mon, Pat, let's go." Lisa Barton grabbed Dielman's arm and urged him around the three on the steps, though he wrested free and paused not far below, as if hoping Kim would change her mind.

"Can we leave now, Detective?" Jenny's sister said, impatient. "We can take my rental."

"I don't know if that's a good idea, Jo." Hank didn't seem any too eager to let her out of his sight. "I could drive y'all wherever you want to go."

"I'll be okay," she told him. "I won't be alone."

"You've got the cell?"

"Check." She patted her pocket.

He gave a reluctant nod. "I'll head back to the station and see what's up. Then I'll stop by the Dielmans'." He hooked a thumb toward Patrick, who huddled in his tan coat with Lisa Barton hovering beside him, both near enough to hear every word.

"If you're still there when we're done, Kim can drop me off," Jo told him.

"Sure, no problem," Kim said, looking anxious. "Now can we go?"

"Go where?" Jo asked.

"To the quarry, please." The dark eyes stared at her, beseeching. "If it's all right with you, I want to see where my sister died."

I sat in the breakfast room after Patrick left for work, staring out the window and waiting until I saw her Acura zip through the alley. I had thirty minutes before I had to show up at the library, and I knew how I wanted to use them.

I pocketed the spare key she'd given Patrick long ago, neatly labeled in an envelope inside a kitchen drawer, and I left through the back, crossing the driveway and lawn, not bothering to glance around as I let myself in. If anyone saw me, I didn't care. I could always say I was returning something borrowed. Isn't that what neighbors did?

When I was safely inside, I listened to the house. The heat hummed through the vents. The TV was on in the living room, and morning-show voices chattered.

I didn't know where to go first. I wasn't even sure what I was looking for.

I closed my eyes and breathed in an oddly familiar smell: of someone who took a smoke now and then but tried to hide it. I had smelled it before in our house all those times I came home and knew something was wrong, that someone had been there uninvited.

My guess was Lisa. She'd had a key to our place, after all, one she hadn't been afraid to use until I'd taken it away.

Curious, I looked around. She had pretty furniture and nice artwork, yes, but where was her past? What was her story? Who was she, really?

I saw books stacked on a bedside table. They looked like mysteries with dark covers, all by the same author, Patricia Highsmith. I ran my fingers down their spines, then reached for the brass pull on the top drawer, tugging it open.

There were blue earplugs, a pair of reading glasses, and a Bible that looked brand-new and generic, less like an old family heirloom passed down through generations and more like the one you find in motels. It had a red tint to the edge of the pages, only the red was interrupted by a bookmark in one spot.

A newspaper clipping had been folded, the creases tight, like it had been there a long, long time. The date on the piece was more than fifteen years ago. It was an article about Dallas kids who'd gotten scholarships to college. There was a photograph at the bottom, depicting a handful of students surrounding a man: "Local philanthropist Jacob Davis touts the success of his KickStart Foundation with his first group of scholarship recipients."

I saw a familiar face among the girls. She was brown-haired then, but just as tall. She stood to the right of Jacob Davis, his hand resting on her shoulder. Her eyes stared dead ahead at the camera. She didn't smile.

The caption identified her as Elizabeth Barton.

Lisa.

The portable phone on the table bedside rang, and I jumped.

I refolded the article and slipped it between the Bible's pages; then I put the book back where I'd found it. Hastily, I shut the drawer and hurried to the door. I hadn't been in the house longer than ten minutes, but now I wanted out.

As I drove to the library, my heart pounding, I made a decision: tonight, I will tell Patrick everything.

I don't care if he doesn't believe me. I'm sure he thinks I've lost my mind. Even if he doesn't, it won't stop me from going to the police. I will tell them about Lisa being in our house, the phone calls from the lobby of Presbyterian Hospital, the missing scarf, and the things out of place.

I will get the shirt and glasses back from Kim and tell them about Finn. I will let them dig up my baby if that's what it takes to find out what really happened. I couldn't do it before, but now, I'm ready.

If nothing comes of it, at least I will have tried. At least I will have stood up for myself and my son instead of lying down to die as I've done the past three years.

I will rub my locket for luck.

I will get Ernie his favorite Fancy Feast to celebrate.

I will free Finn from my nightmares.

And free myself.

CHAPTER TWENTY

Kimberly's rental was a nondescript two-door coupe, white like so many cars in North Texas. The lack of color was supposed to deflect the heat, but it reminded Jo of white patent leather shoes, the kind Mama used to make her wear to church on Easter Sunday, the only time they attended, as if that would make up for sins racked up the rest of the year. She'd hated those shoes. They scuffed so easily and made her feet look two sizes too big.

Jo thought the car smelled of plastic, like crayons warming in the sun. She clicked her seat belt on and settled in as comfortably as possible, despite the holster at her hip and the borrowed cell phone in her coat pocket.

"You sure you want to do this?" she asked, turning to Jenny's sister. "We can go somewhere else to talk."

"I'm sure." Kim set the red carnation carefully on the dashboard, belted herself in, and started the car.

Jo kept her eyes on the flower, on its gentle vibrations as they drove.

Jenny's sister didn't say much at first except to ask directions, and Jo didn't press her. But once they'd gotten away from Grace Church and the surrounding neighborhoods and strip malls that populated Plainfield proper, Kim sighed heavily, and Jo waited for the words she was certain would come.

"You know that saying, Detective, that only the good die young?"

"Very well," Jo said.

"It's true in Jenny's case. She was as good a person as there ever was. Not that she was an angel or anything. God knows, she could be a pain in the ass." Kim expelled a noisy breath. "But she was the one who took on our dad because our mother wouldn't." Her voice softened. "She worked in the Des Moines food pantry after school for years, did you know that?"

"No, I didn't."

"How many teenagers do that instead of hanging out at the mall?"

"Not many."

"She used to cry when she saw roadkill. She took in stray animals, too. She'd pluck them right off the street if she could catch them. My father never let her keep anything. He made her give them away or take them to shelters."

"She had a soft heart, huh?"

"She was a marshmallow. She couldn't say no, which makes me wonder if she picked up a stranger, gave someone a ride that night." Kim took her eyes off the road to glance at Jo. "You think that's what happened? Do you think she was helping someone when she died?"

"Maybe." Jo didn't mean to mislead her, but it wasn't a lie.

"Do you have a sister, Detective Larsen?" Kim asked.

"No."

"A brother?"

Jo shook her head.

"Have you ever lost someone close?"

That one wasn't as easy. But Jo answered with the truth as she knew it.

"I have," she said.

The father she had barely known, the mother she'd never been able to please and who'd begun to slip away a long time ago. The little girl inside her who'd had to grow up far too quickly.

"She felt damaged," Kim went on. "No matter how hard she worked at living her life, Jenny never felt deserving. She always figured that happiness was fleeting, more fiction than reality. But, Lord knows"—she shook her head—"she could handle pain."

Jo said nothing, turning toward the window.

"Every morning, Jen and I woke up afraid, because we weren't sure what was coming."

Kim's tone turned cool, and Jo shifted her stare, watched the young woman wrestle with old demons. "I can remember how we used to pray for Daddy to be smiling when he walked through the door at night. He got upset over the tiniest things, like a toy left on the lawn or dishes in the sink. If he didn't take it out on Mom, he took it out on Jenny." She grimaced. "But Jenny kept him away from me. She'd shove me into the closet and lock me in or tell me to run next door until she came to get me."

"I'm sorry," Jo said, understanding all too well.

"I worshipped her." Kim's chin quivered, but she clung to her composure, kept driving as if nothing was wrong. "It near to crushed me when she left Des Moines. She'd gone to Drake on a partial scholarship, and she lived at home because our daddy didn't want her in the dorms. He thought she'd go wild, told her if she ever got pregnant, he'd kick her out and cut her off."

"What did your mother do?"

"Do?" Kim laughed. "God forbid Mom should ever stand up to Daddy. In her warped way, she loved him, maybe more than she loved us." Her right hand released the wheel to rub her nose, but Jo saw no tears. "I wish she'd taken us away, before he'd hurt Jenny as bad as he did. I can't blame her for leaving, because she had to. She stood up to him before she went, telling him if he ever laid a hand on me, she'd call the cops and turn him in. To this day, I still can't believe she had the guts to talk back to him. But he never hit me again."

Jo strained against the seat belt, not sure how to ask what she wanted to ask. Knowing no way to put it delicately, she dove right in. "Did your father ever break Jenny's bones?"

She thought of the fractured fingers, forearm, and ribs discovered in postmortem X-rays. She needed to know who caused them.

"Why? What did you find?"

"Old breaks on X-ray," Jo told her.

Kimberly gnawed her lip. "Daddy was smart, Detective. He'd never have left a paper trail, if that's what you're wondering. He never would have taken Jenny or my mom to the hospital, not for anything. He knew how far he could go, and that's what he did." She scrunched up her forehead. "I do remember him grabbing Jen's arm, twisting it so hard, she cried." She made a noise that sounded like a hiccup. "I was so young when it happened, and Jen always kept me from seeing the worst. He was good at not leaving marks. Or, if he did, he'd keep her home from school for a while." Her chin wobbled. "You think my father caused those injuries?"

"If he didn't, someone else did."

"Kevin Harrison?" Kim's stare turned to stone.

Jo felt a surge of adrenaline, wondering if Jenny's sister knew more than she suspected. "What can you tell me about Dr. Harrison? Did Jenny say much about their life together? Did she ever mention how he treated her?"

"Yeah." Kim sniffed. "He treated her like crap, and I knew he would from the first moment she described him. The guy sounded like a carbon copy of our dad. I couldn't believe she'd go through with the marriage, but she was already pregnant with Finn."

Jo waited for her to go on.

Kim's voice fell abruptly. "I told her I'd help her out. Our folks were gone by then, and I begged her to come back to Des Moines. Jenny wouldn't leave him. I was so pissed at her, and she was so angry with me for not supporting her. We didn't communicate much for years. She was so wrapped up with the baby after he was born that I don't think she cared about anything else, not for a long time. Not until Finn's accident."

Patrick had mentioned the sisters being estranged, and it appeared he was right.

"I didn't know Finn was dead until she called me, crying hysterically after his funeral." Kim swiped at her eyes with her coat sleeve. "I feel horrible that I didn't know sooner, that I wasn't there for her when she needed me most. God, I'm sorry," she murmured, pulling off the gravel road so the car came to rest on a tangle of weeds and grass in the shadow of the pines.

Sobs shook her shoulders as Kim gave in to her grief. She dropped her head to her hands, making pitiful choking sounds as she wept.

Jo felt like an intruder and looked the other way, out the window at branches ruffled by the wind. She thought of unhooking her seat belt and set her hand on the door latch, tempted to get out of the car and leave Kim alone until she got ahold of herself.

She wasn't good at this kind of thing. She chewed on the inside of her cheek until she tasted blood.

It was a few minutes before Kim stopped crying. She blew her nose and pulled herself together. Then she started the car, tires grinding on gravel until they were on the road, kicking up dust in their wake.

Jo stared at the brown trunks of trees, rolling past them like flip cards, until the clusters of pine thinned out, replaced by the flutter of plastic flags: neon-bright triangles waving toward developments not yet built. Arrows pointed to dirt paths, forking off on both sides. **JUST A HALF MILE WEST**, a sign declared in bright red letters. **STOP IN AT JACOB DAVIS PROPERTIES' MOBILE OFFICE! SEE PLANS FOR THE PINE RIDGE DEVELOPMENT! OPEN SAT AND SUN 10–5!**

Jacob Davis Properties.

Jo squinted at the name until it fell too far behind them.

"My daddy's got a couple homes picked out for us to look at. His company built them. Jacob Davis? You've heard of him?"

Alana's father had a development out here? It was so close to the quarry.

Why hadn't Mrs. Harrison mentioned it, considering where Jenny's body had been found?

Jo shifted in her seat, felt a prickle at the back of her neck.

She would have Kim make a quick stop at the mobile office on their way back, as long as they were out here.

After silently bumping along the rutted road for another few miles, they reached their destination.

Kim slowed down as they headed off the road onto the quarry grounds, though the rental hit a pothole and jolted hard enough to shake the red carnation from the dash. It fell to the floor, near Jo's feet. She picked it up and set it in her lap, fingering the petals and wishing she were somewhere else.

When they approached the chain-link fence, Kim brought the car to a dead stop. Remnants of yellow crime scene tape tied to the mesh rippled with each gust of wind. The battered sign with the faded warning to trespassers banged against the opened gate. Someone had looped a shiny new chain through the links, but it had been cut, and dangled like a broken bracelet. A few forlorn-looking grocery-store bouquets leaned against the base of the fence.

"So this is it?" Kim asked.

"Yes, this is it."

"It's kind of creepy, huh?"

Despite the ebb and flow of media and curious public in the days since the story had hit the airwaves, the site stood deserted, scattered with the skeletal remains of equipment. It looked as abandoned and neglected as the first time Jo had seen it.

"Can I drive in?"

"Sure."

Moving ahead at the pace of a snail, Kim drove forward, retracing the path Hank's old Ford had taken on Wednesday, after the rain had turned the earth to muck and the gravel to oatmeal.

Jo directed Kim to the spot where they'd found her sister's Nissan and told her to park. There was no one else in sight. No hikers, no gawkers. It was as if they'd dropped into a black hole. About to push her door open, Jo noticed Kim's hands clutching the wheel, her knuckles a painful shade of white.

"Are you sure this is what you want?" she asked, not so certain that this was the best way for Jenny's sister to find closure.

"No, I'm not sure at all," Kim said. "But it's what I need." She reached for the handle and got out.

The slam of their doors echoed around the stagger of trees that ringed the crater.

Jo carried the carnation, walking over to where Kim stood near the hood. The wind tossed brown hair across her tear-stained face, and Jo had more second thoughts about coming. They could have had this conversation at a Starbucks or the police station. What the hell was she thinking? The woman's sister hadn't just died here; she'd been led to her grave and murdered.

Kim took a step forward and hesitated. "You were the one who found her, weren't you?"

Jo flashed back on the brown strands of hair floating away from pale skin, one eye staring at her glassily.

"Yes." Jo tried not to flinch.

"Was she tied up?"

"No." *Not then.*

"Had she been raped?"

"No," Jo said, grateful it was the truth.

"Where was she exactly?"

"Down there, in the pit."

She didn't embellish, didn't talk about falling from the path into the pooled water and finding Jenny, dark hair floating about her head, debris clinging to her clothes and skin. Those were things Kim didn't need to hear. Things she wished she could forget.

"It's so quiet. I can't even hear the birds. Why is it so still? Maybe she's around," Kim said. "Maybe she's with us."

Jo didn't usually believe in such things. But since they'd arrived, she'd had a sense they weren't alone, that someone else was there, looking over their shoulders. Maybe it was Jenny, or whatever part of her she'd left behind in this place.

If it comforted Kim to believe it, Jo didn't see the harm in supposing it could be true.

Jenny's sister turned in a slow circle, taking in the evergreen of the forest around them, the way it seemed to stand sentry over the man-made hole in the middle of the earth.

Angry gusts batted at them, an invisible pugilist, tugging at Jo's hair, whistling with each chilly breath. The air smelled of dust and rock, of things rotted.

Jo shivered and pulled her wool collar high so it tickled her chin and brushed her ears. She shoved her left hand in her pocket, grasped the carnation in her right, the stalk caught between her fingers.

"I hope she's at peace. Do you think she is? Can you feel her with us?" Kim said and stretched her arms out, fingers reaching for something—for someone who wasn't there. "She's close, isn't she? Do you sense it?"

Jo didn't tell her what she really felt, or what she smelled on each breath she took. It wasn't peace but sadness, decay, and death.

She said instead what Kim wanted to hear. "She's close, yes."

"Are you holding him, Jenny?" Kim asked the wind, tilting her face to the sky. "Are you happy now?"

Jo hung back, wanting to give Kim her space. She was trying hard to stay impassive and not give in to the powerful things she was feeling, that threatened to wash over her and take her down.

Jenny's sister turned, reaching out. "Could I have the flower? Then I can say goodbye."

Jo held out the carnation, and Kim took it, slowly walking away. She headed toward the pit, and Jo let her go.

Stopping six feet from the edge, Kim bowed her head like she was praying. Then she tossed the flower to the wind. For a moment, it arced, a blot of crimson on gray.

Jo stared into the clouds, half expecting an ethereal hand to reach out and snatch the carnation from the air. But it didn't happen.

The flower dropped away, out of sight.

Ashes to ashes, dust to dust.

How quickly we could go. One last breath, and it was over. No second chance to get it right. You got a shot; then your turn was up.

Jo thought the whole thing sucked.

A screech rent the air, so like a woman's cry. She turned to see the uppermost branches on a pine tree shudder as a flutter of wings hit the sky, pitting black against the dove-gray heavens. The hair at her nape prickled again.

Kim was right about something.

Someone was here. She felt it more strongly than before.

And she wasn't so sure it was Jenny.

◆ ◆ ◆

Cords of plastic flags stretched left and right from the roof of the mobile realty office, creating a triangle of color that vibrated like a thing alive. Light danced off dusty windows. Gravel surrounded the boxy structure, as slate-gray underfoot as the sky above.

Jo had asked Kim to stay put, told her she'd only be a few minutes. She closed the door, muffling the blast of country-western music as Kim turned the radio on and Keith Urban twanged about wanting to kiss a girl.

Jo buttoned her coat and looked behind them at the road, the dust since settled and nothing in sight to stir it. Wind rattled through the boughs of the bordering pines. She flipped up her collar and turned away, walking with the gusts at her back.

She took in everything: a sign with the proposed plots laid out in neat squares; the broken twigs and fallen pinecones at her feet; the swoop of a crow as it came to land on the stump of a tree. It cocked its head at her, staring, letting out a rowdy *caw-caw* before it took off again and joined a couple of its cackling brethren on the roof of the trailer. They sat in a neat row, watching her, accusing, black heads bobbing.

A murder of crows.

Maybe they were related to the carcass left in her mailbox. As long as they didn't come after her, like they had Tippi Hedren in *The Birds*.

Jo tried to shrug off her unease, shoving her hands in her pockets. Her fingers touched the cell phone for reassurance as she made a slow circle of the single-wide structure. She approached a window and peered inside between frosted glass shutters, slanted at an angle that allowed only glimpses of a desk and chairs. She moved to a second window along the same wall and was able to discern a tiny kitchen, the counter cluttered with brochures.

She went around the front, shoes crunching on dead leaves and bits of rock. Holding the railing, she climbed the steps to a white metal door and tested it, but no dice.

It was locked tight.

The posted hours of operation indicated the place was open on weekends and by appointment only. She noticed the phone number listed was the same one she'd dialed when she'd been looking for Alana Harrison.

Who had shown up at Jenny's memorial service . . . *out of guilt?*

Who was married to Jenny's ex-husband . . . *and would do anything to protect him, his career, and their future?*

If Jo had come to seek answers, maybe she was starting to find them.

Standing on tiptoes, she cupped hands around the diamond-shaped pane, nose to the glass, the best view she could get. The top of the desk was visible now, filled with stacks of paper and files, a cup holding pens, coffee mugs—the usual office detritus.

Something hung from a coatrack just to the right. Even with her cheek pressed to the pane, she couldn't see what it was. A winter hat? The dark sleeve of a coat?

Damn.

Her breath steamed the glass, and she came off her toes, rattled the handle once more for good measure. Then she leaned her hand against the metal jamb, disappointed. She felt something sticky and held up her fingers. They were smudged with black.

WD-40?

Like the stain on Jenny's pullover?

Beeeep.

The bleat of the car horn startled her from her thoughts, and she checked her watch. She'd told Kim five minutes. A few had surely passed, but barely that. Kim was doubtless impatient to get to the reception at Patrick's.

Jo took the steps down, sighed, and looked around at the roofline of the trailer, at the mesh of chain link protecting a pair of propane tanks stored under the stairs, at the ground beneath her feet.

A fleck of black against the gravel caught her eye, and she stepped toward it, crouched low and stared. Was it blood?

She touched a finger to the spot, finding nothing more than a black button about the size of the ones on her peacoat. Was it from a black coat, like Jenny's?

She slipped it into her pocket. Then she grabbed the chain link to pull herself up. As she stood, she saw the flash of something shiny. Somehow, she'd missed it before, the silver blending into the chain link. Holding her breath, she untangled the necklace from where it had been snagged and brought it close to her face.

It was a locket on a sterling chain.

She blew at a layer of dirt on its surface, held it right to her eyes to see the *F* so delicately engraved.

"She has a locket she wears all the time. It's silver with the initial F, for Finn. *She keeps his picture in it. She rarely takes it off."*

Jo tripped the latch with her fingertip and opened it up to reveal a tiny photo, showing the puckered face of an infant.

Finn.

She pressed her palm on the ground to steady herself, dizzy with the thought that Jenny had been there. Had she dropped the button and locket, hoping someone would find them like Hansel and Gretel's breadcrumbs?

Lifting her face to the breeze, Jo glanced around, her pulse surging fast with a mix of urgency and elation. Was this the site that she'd been looking for? The place where Jenny had been forced to drive by the man she'd spoken with in the Warehouse Club parking lot? Was it where her coat had been removed and she'd been bound with duct tape before she was taken to the quarry and killed? Had her abductor kept her here until the accomplice had shown up?

Something Emma Slater had said came back to her, and it all clicked.

"The mirrors weren't moved. Rearview and side were still angled for someone your victim's height. So whoever took the wheel must not have had far to go, or at least wasn't worried much about traffic."

Why change the mirrors when you just had a couple of miles to go on a gravel road with no other cars?

Jo stared at the locket in her hands.

Jenny had been brought here because it made sense.

Jacob Davis Properties.

Was Alana a part of this?

Jo could hardly fathom that a pregnant woman would kill another woman, one who'd lost her own child.

What about Kevin Harrison? Would he mix up his wife in a murder plot when it seemed more logical that he'd have gone to his father-in-law for help in ridding the world of a troublesome ex, to save his reputation and his career?

Aw, hell.

She rose from her crouch and slipped the locket into a coat pocket, digging in the other for the borrowed cell phone. Her emotions on overdrive, she punched in Hank's number and started walking around the end of the trailer.

"Hey, pretty lady," she heard him answer, and she figured he saw his wife's number and momentarily forgot he'd loaned out the phone.

"Hank, it's me," she said, and he quickly sobered.

"Oh, yeah, Jo. You okay?"

"I found something." The words came out faster than she intended, but she couldn't hide her excitement. "I'm at the mobile realty office for Jacob Davis Properties on the farm road just about two miles from the quarry. I've got Jenny's locket. We have to get a search warrant for the trailer. There's a dumpster behind it. They might have missed something, Hank, and we have to find it before they have a chance to destroy it. This is the place," she insisted, and it was more than a gut feeling this time. "Can you get a judge to sign off and meet me out here?" She finally paused to ask, "Where are you now?"

"I'm at Dielman's, looking for Lisa. I went to the station first. Your friend Terry Fitzhugh kept trying to reach you, and Emma Slater was looking for you, too. I talked to Emma myself. She said she ran the scarf, and it's loaded with Jenny's DNA—"

"Well, it was her scarf," Jo said, interrupting.

"From her saliva," Hank went on. "Emma thinks it was used to gag her."

"Oh, God." Jo blinked, taking that one in, hating how this case kept twisting and turning just when she thought she'd figured it out. "You have to find Lisa Barton. We need to bring her in, sit on her. That scarf could tie her to the murder, and it can't be the only thing—"

"I know," he talked over her. "That's why I came back to the Dielmans' house. Hold on a sec." Jo heard the hum of voices, the scratch of static on the cell phone, then Hank's mumble before he came back on. "Dielman said she went for ice at least a half hour ago, and she hasn't come back."

A crow cried and alighted from a tree, rattling leaves, and Jo put a hand to her heart, startled. Damn, but she was jumpy.

"You there, Larsen?" Hank was saying, but a noise—tiny annoying pings—swayed her attention from the phone to the graveled parking lot.

She spied the white rental car where she'd left Kim listening to Keith Urban. The front driver's-side door stood wide open.

A brief shower of sun between clouds glinted off the beige roof of a car parked on the other side of Kim's rental.

Someone else was there.

Jo saw a flutter of red across the gravel.

Kim's scarf.

Oh, no, no, no.

"Kim!" she called out, lowering the phone from her ear.

The crackle of rushing footsteps behind her came as a warning too late.

She half turned, glimpsing the spade of a shovel swinging fast. It clipped her shoulder and knocked the phone from her hand as she fell to her knees, pain shooting through her arm like fire. The shovel came at her again, striking the back of her head, sending her facedown into dirt and rocks. For a moment, she felt only agony.

Then she felt nothing.

CHAPTER TWENTY-ONE

Smoke.

Jo smelled it even before she could get her eyes open wide enough to see.

Wincing, she lifted her head from the ground, a tsunami of pain flooding her skull so fiercely that it made her stomach roll in waves. She fought the urge to vomit and gritted her teeth till her jaw ached. It felt like the mother of all hangovers, and it took her a minute to figure out where she was, what she was doing lying on her belly in the grit.

Lifting her hand, she gingerly touched the soft spot above her nape, felt no damp, just a knot the size of a Whataburger. Her left shoulder throbbed, and she could hardly get it to move.

Hank.

Her partner's name jumped out at her, reminding her of something, of needing to talk to him, and calling him to tell him about this place.

Where had she dropped that cell phone?

A loud crack filtered through the ringing in her ears, like the pop of a firecracker, and she forced herself upright, squinting at the world around her, everything in duplicate until she squished her eyes closed for a moment, then tried again.

She saw the smoke first, puffing from the rooftop of the trailer maybe five yards away. The lick of orange flames ate at the plastic line of flags and chewed on the flimsy shoe box from the inside, lighting up the frosted windows.

Burning down the house.

Bowie? No, no, Talking Heads.

More like burning down the trailer.

Her thoughts zigzagged, making her even dizzier.

A blood-red carnation.

Kimberly's scarf.

Red, red, red.

Where was Jenny's sister?

Blurry double vision set in again, and she blinked hard, focusing to clear her disjointed thoughts. Every nerve in her body shouted for her to stay still, to put her head down. Instead, she wobbled to her knees, crawling on gray pea gravel that dug into the skin of her palms and pricked through her jeans.

Just beyond the rental car, black shoes protruded at odd angles. Then she saw bare legs beneath a checkerboard skirt.

There.

Kim sprawled on the ground within arm's reach, unmoving, trails of crimson streaking from ear to cheek.

No, don't let her be dead like Jenny.

If she could just crawl over without her head falling off.

Jo had almost reached her when she heard the pop again, like the crack of a rifle. Instinctively, she dropped down flat, hands over head, glass shattering from the trailer's windows and raining to the ground, the fire louder now, hot enough that Jo could see black ashes fluttering down upon her skin.

She dragged herself another few inches until she could touch the other woman, could reach fingertips to upturned wrist and feel a pulse.

Not dead, not dead, not dead.

Who would've done this? Left them alive, but torched the trailer to cover tracks?

Jo lowered her forehead to her hands, willing the stabbing pain in her brain to cease. She rolled on her back to catch her breath, to close her eyes for a moment, listening to the fire grow angrier behind them, knowing she had to move them away, remembering metal tanks beneath the stairs.

Propane.

Lord, she was so tired.

Another voice came to nudge her, whispered in her ear.

Get up. Get going. Don't give up. It isn't over yet.

Jenny?

The heat reached closer, hotter, harder, the trailer engulfed in a ball of flames and thick black smoke. Something pushed at her, made her get up on her knees, onto wobbly legs, long enough to grab hold of Kim's coat by the collar. She started pulling hard, dragging Jenny's sister away from the flames, toward the far side of the rental car. Jo fought the gray haze that clouded her eyes and threatened to shut down her thoughts like drawn curtains. Each step was painful, each breath ached, until she couldn't go another inch.

She dropped down beside Kim as the sky exploded into pitch, and she covered her head and her ears from the noise and the ash that rained around them.

She heard the distant cry of a siren.

It's okay. You're all right.

She took Kim's cold hand and held tight before she slipped into the dark again, far away from the fire.

Hands jostled.

Voices swirled, in and out, out and in.

Out.

◆ ◆ ◆

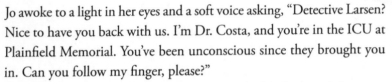

Jo awoke to a light in her eyes and a soft voice asking, "Detective Larsen? Nice to have you back with us. I'm Dr. Costa, and you're in the ICU at Plainfield Memorial. You've been unconscious since they brought you in. Can you follow my finger, please?"

She saw two digits first, slowly moving. She blinked until there was one, tried to keep her focus on it until she heard, "Not bad. Pupils are equal and reactive, just slightly dilated."

She wet her lips. "Which means?"

Was that her voice? It sounded rough as sandpaper.

"It means you're a lucky woman. Your CT was equivocal, so we just need to keep an eye on you. Can you sit up a bit? I've got some dandy pain meds that'll help."

Jo grimaced as she struggled to sit upright. Her shoulder screamed as she used her left arm to prop herself up.

Was I in a train wreck?

The dark-skinned woman in the white coat pushed a tiny cup of pills and a larger cup of water at her, but Jo raised a hand, her palm streaked with scratches. "Nothing stronger than aspirin, okay?" She couldn't do what she had to do, not if she was doped up.

"Detective, please."

"I've got to go." She swung her legs over the bed, grimaced at how much effort it took.

"Hey, not so fast, partner." Hank stepped forward and nudged Dr. Costa aside. "Take it easy, okay?" He rested his hands on her knees, and she realized how filthy her pants were, covered with dirt and stains. Turning to the doctor, he said, "Mind if we have a private powwow?"

"I'll be back with some Tylenol in five." Costa set the cups down and left them alone in the cubicle, though Jo could still see her—two of her—beyond a large window, looking in.

She squeezed her eyes closed, getting rid of the doctor's twin, and at the same time, causing a flicker of memory: red on the ground and a pale face streaked with blood. She ignored the noise in her head. "How is she?"

"Jenny's sister?"

"Yes." Jo swallowed, afraid from the sober expression on her partner's face that Kim Parker had been DOA. But she'd had a pulse, hadn't she?

"She's in surgery," he said. "Whoever took her down hit her over the ear." He tapped his own head, as if to demonstrate. "They said it was an epidural hematoma, something to do with the cerebral artery."

"Will she be all right?"

He shrugged. "They think so, yeah, but it's one of those wait-and-see things."

"Can I visit her?"

"Sounds like it's gonna take a while for them to work on her, maybe a couple hours. So I'd give it until tomorrow before you drop in."

"Damn it."

"Hey, it's not your fault."

"Isn't it?" If Jo hadn't felt like crap already, that would have done the trick, because it *was* her fault, stopping where they had, because she'd had one of her gut feelings, a sense of being drawn to the spot because of the sign.

"The trailer," she said softly, recalling that she'd peered inside, saw a coatrack, thought maybe Jenny's missing coat was in there, or even the coat of her abductor, or the hat with flaps. She winced as she flashed on orange flames and plumes of black smoke. "Is there anything left?"

"My wife's cell was DOA. Found the poor thing busted on the gravel. Looks like someone pounded it with a jackhammer. Sort of like your skull." Frowning, he crossed his arms over his chest. "I didn't stick around to see the FD hose down the trailer, but it didn't look like much more than cinder."

"Crap." She wanted to remember everything, but pieces were missing. Fallen into holes she couldn't find. There was something else, something more. "What did you see?"

"I saw you lying on the ground, Larsen, and it scared the holy hell out of me." He put his hands on his hips, parting his dark jacket, and exposing his sidearm. He shook his head, as if he didn't know what to say. And he was never short on words, not with her.

"I'm all right," she assured him. "I'm alive, anyway."

He turned on her, his eyes angry. "This time."

No more guilt. She couldn't take it.

"Did you call Adam and tell him anything?"

"Not yet."

Thank God for small favors.

"You're a mess, you know, all scratched up like an alley cat."

"An alley cat, huh?" *Jesus.* She remembered then. Jenny's cat. Where was he? "Ernie," she said, but Hank waved off the question.

"He's fine. Dropped him off with the girls in Dispatch, and they're taking care of him until you get there."

"Thanks." She'd already said that a hundred times, hadn't she?

"Forget it." Her partner sighed. "What I want to know is who was there, at the property. You didn't spot a car or see somebody coming at you? Was it Lisa Barton? She never returned to Dielman's house, not while I was there, though I got a BOLO out on her and took off as soon as I lost you on the cell."

"I didn't see anyone, Hank." She wanted to recall, tried so hard to think, put her hands to her temples and pressed, like that would fix everything. "There was another car in the parking lot," she said, recalling a smudge of tan rooftop behind Kim's rental. "It was beige."

Didn't Lisa Barton have a beige Acura sedan?

She'd been standing right below on the church steps when Kim had talked about wanting to go to the quarry. She must have overheard them.

Had she been afraid of leaving a loose end? Had she told Patrick they needed more ice for their post-funeral reception, only to hightail it to the trailer? Except when she'd gotten there, she'd found Kim in the parking lot and Jo poking around?

What about Alana Harrison? Her secretary said she was off today. What color was her car? Her husband drove a dark Mercedes, so it wasn't him. And no way would Jacob Davis have driven out to the boonies to torch the trailer himself. He'd have goons for that, wouldn't he?

But Alana was a different story. She'd shown up at the church, which didn't make sense. What if she'd stuck around and followed them? What if she'd panicked, seeing where they'd gone?

"We have to go back, Hank," she said and swallowed hard, her throat so dry. "We have to find the evidence before it's all lost."

"There's no reason to go back, Jo. I told you, there's not much left for the arson boys to sift through as it is."

Orange flames. Black smoke. Ash in the air.

"That can't be," she said, under her breath.

"You told me on the phone that you found something," Hank reminded her. "Jenny's locket."

Concentrate, Jo, concentrate.

She saw it then: a silver flash in her mind's eye.

She reached down, looking for the pocket where she'd put it. "Where's my coat?" she asked. Her sidearm was gone, too. "My thirty-eight?"

"Hey, hey, don't panic. I got your gun locked in my trunk. The docs took off your coat in the emergency room, and I picked it up. It's right here." He retrieved a folded bundle from the only chair in the cubicle, brought it over, and set it in her lap.

She slid shaky fingers over the wool, dipping down into the right front pocket until she found what she was looking for and held it out to him.

He squinted at the object in her hands.

"It's Jenny's. It has to be," she said. "It was caught in the fence below the steps at the realty office trailer."

She could see in his face that he understood.

"There was a black button, too. It could have been from her coat. I feel like she was leaving a trail for us to follow," she said, digging into her pocket again before Hank stopped her.

"Okay," he said, patting her hand. "Okay."

"She was there." Jo curled her fingers around the locket and looked her partner in the eye, thankfully seeing only one of him. "Why would Jenny be at that place, huh? It makes no sense, unless Lisa took Jenny there to wait for Alana. If that was Lisa Barton's beige Acura I saw . . . what's their connection? I thought it was Kevin Harrison, but he was in surgery. I even considered Alana's father, but I can't imagine he'd want this mess on his hands. He'd work it another way, have Jenny arrested for harassment, or get her committed. This was too personal, too emotional."

"You think it has a woman's touch?" he asked, and she didn't even fault him for being a chauvinist because that was exactly what she thought.

"Lisa and Alana don't have alibis. We need to pick up both of them, Hank, pit them against each other. Push them hard."

"We'll put the fear of God in them, how's that?"

"Fear's good." She started to slowly scoot her way out of bed just as Dr. Costa returned with yet another tiny paper cup and a tan water pitcher.

"Hold on, Detective Larsen. Where do you think you're going? You need to rest, and we need to monitor you for at least another twenty-four hours."

"No time to rest." Jo took Hank's arm and stood, not daring to show how unsteady she felt on her feet. She clung to him as he helped her into her coat, the locket still clutched in her hand. "We've gotta catch us some bad guys."

"Bad guys? More than one? Or are you still seeing double?" The brown forehead pleated.

Ah, a wiseass doctor. Perfect.

The physician's well-modulated voice went flat with disapproval. "You're leaving against medical advice. You realize that, of course?"

"It's nothing personal, Doc. She never takes my advice either," Hank offered.

Jo would have rolled her eyes if it didn't hurt so much.

"At least take these." Dr. Costa proffered the cup with the nonprescription pills, and Jo leaned heavily on Hank as she tossed them back and chased them with water. "I'll get a wheelchair and your paperwork. But I wish you'd reconsider."

"No."

That one was easy.

The doctor left the room, and Jo saw her approach the nurses' station, shaking her head and conversing with a pale woman in pink scrubs, who kept glancing over, brows cinched.

"You sure you're all right?" Hank asked, and Jo feared for a moment he'd side with Dr. Costa, make her stay.

"I'm okay," she lied.

She wanted out of this place. If she could just keep her head up, keep her eyes open, put one foot in front of the other, she'd be dandy.

After Dr. Costa delivered the discharge papers, which Jo signed in a barely legible scribble, the nurse in pink pushed in a wheelchair, fussing with the footrests and settling Jo in, as if she were a hundred-year-old invalid and not a thirty-five-year-old cop with a splitting headache.

Hank took the handles of the chair and rolled her past the nurses' station, toward the elevators, and Jo concentrated fiercely on staying alert, focusing ahead, ignoring the hacksaw cutting into her brain because she didn't have any time to waste. They were so close now, so very, very close.

When the cool air outdoors hit her smack in the face, she breathed it in, sucked it hard into her lungs, until she could feel the energy stir inside her again. It cleared some of the cobwebs from her mind.

Hank left her to sit in front of the building while he brought his car around, and Jo waited, pressing the locket between her palms, needing her connection to Jenny. She squinted into the bank of leaden clouds, hanging so low in the heavens that she feared she'd bang her head on them if she stood too quickly.

The dusty old Ford pulled curbside, and she pocketed the locket, getting out of the wheelchair and using her own two legs to walk to the passenger door alone before Hank had the chance to park and get out.

Her partner settled behind the wheel and called their captain, repeating what Jo had told him about possibly seeing Lisa Barton's car at the torched trailer and Alana Harrison's ties to the place. Jo heard the word *warrant* more than once on Hank's end.

Search warrants, she figured, hoping by day's end they'd have enough evidence for arrest warrants, which would be even better.

When Hank set his phone on the seat between them, Jo picked it up and dialed Adam's cell. She caught him on the first ring.

"It's me," she said.

"Where are you?" he fired back instead of *hello*.

"With Hank," she said simply, as opposed to telling him she was leaving the hospital ICU after getting her skull cracked.

"Can you get down to the crime lab? I need you to see something. I've got Jon Morgan looking over Finn Harrison's hospital records from the night he died, and the photos you sent."

"And the T-shirt?"

"Yeah," he said and hesitated before adding, "It's too bad no one looked a little closer three years ago."

Jo's pulse kicked up a notch. "So it wasn't an accident?"

"Just get down here, okay?" he told her. "Emma needs to see you, too."

"We'll be there as soon as we can." Jo had nearly hung up when he shot another question at her.

"You never said where you are. You're not still at the church?"

"No." She squirmed against the seat belt.

There was no way to avoid telling him, was there?

Hank started the car and let it idle, waiting as she gave Adam a CliffsNotes version of what had happened out near the quarry, hating the silence on the other end almost as much as if he'd gotten on her case about it, as Hank had.

"Oh, Jo." He sighed when she was through.

How guilty those words made her feel.

"I'm okay," she promised him, making further reassurances before he'd let her hang up.

Then she asked Hank to drive into Dallas, and she gently set her head back against the vinyl seat, pressing her palms to either temple.

She hoped she wouldn't be sick on her shoes before they got to Parkland Hospital.

◆ ◆ ◆

The trace-evidence exam room felt airless without windows, no natural light seeping in to discern night from day.

The yellow T-shirt lay atop a crisp, white sheet of paper on a stainless-steel table that smelled of the bleach used to clean it. A man in a white lab coat with blue latex gloves hovered over it all, pinching a pair of forceps to stretch the T-shirt, which had been turned inside out.

Adam stood at the opposite side of the table with his hands crossed over his chest, watching Jo, not the performance of his colleague, Jonathan Morgan, a clean-cut fellow that Jo thought looked more like a banker than a blood-spatter expert.

She could hardly bring herself to look at Adam, not the way he stared at her, surveying the damage from her latest run-in: the scratches on her face and hands, the way she squinted because the light made her head hurt more.

"See, there, below the collar," Dr. Morgan said, indicating small brown smears visible against the sunny hue of the cloth. "Most of the blood's on the front underside of the shirt, not the outside. I'm thinking the boy wasn't wearing this when he fell, that he was probably redressed. You want to see it under the glass?" He set down the left forceps and swung around the arm of a lighted magnifying lens, fixing it right above the stains.

Jo didn't need to look. It was clear enough to the naked eye—even with the vague fog at the edge of her vision—but she leaned over the circle of glass and peered through anyway.

Hank followed suit when she was done.

"Notice anything else?" Morgan asked, grasping the sleeves of the T-shirt with gloved fingers. He displayed it like a red flag before a bull, then turned it right side out and held it up again.

Jo could see only wrinkles.

Hank scratched his nose. "It looks pretty clean."

"Ay, there's the rub," the blood expert quipped, giving a half smile, like he was enjoying this. "No trace of any plant material on the shirt, not from a tree or vegetation. I couldn't even find microscopy of dirt."

"So the kid didn't fall?" Hank said, and Jo leaned a gloved hand on the table edge, holding on, waiting.

"I looked at the photos you provided, Detective Larsen, and if the child had fallen from the tree house while climbing that ladder, he would've likely landed on his back, which would have put him in the flower bed below. If he'd fallen from the tree house itself, he would have probably hit the grass. There's just one problem." He punctuated the air with a tap of his finger. "The only residue I found on the shirt, other than the blood, is mineral, not vegetable."

"As in what?" Jo said, not in the mood for playing games.

"As in talc," Morgan finished.

"Like talcum? Baby powder?"

"Exactly like that."

"Then she yelled at me for ignoring Finn, for taking a phone call when I should've been getting him ready for his bath."

"What else?" Jo asked.

"The glasses." Adam stepped in, indicating the pair of small gold frames that sat on a separate piece of white paper farther down the table. "They're not damaged, not even dinged. The boy's wearing them in the picture, and if he'd had them on during a fall, they would've been damaged. No question."

"She told me that she had dreams about him, that he spoke to her. He wanted her to find the truth. He couldn't see, she told me, because he wasn't wearing his glasses."

"They're not damaged because Finn wasn't wearing them," Jo said and rubbed her forehead, knowing that Jenny had stumbled onto evidence that she hadn't known how to deal with. "He wasn't wearing the T-shirt either."

"Maybe the boy didn't have a stitch on," Hank kicked in. "Maybe the kid was in the bathroom, not outside. That would explain the presence of talc."

"Although talc can come from a lot of places," Dr. Morgan reminded them. "Baby powder, chalk, cosmetics, even paper."

"Okay, forget the talc," Jo said. "How can we prove that Finn didn't die by a fall?" She sensed that question was at the crux of Jenny's murder. "We need more evidence than this."

Dr. Morgan gestured at Adam. "That's one for the medical examiner. Now if y'all will excuse me, I've got a couple months of backlogged cases calling my name, and they ain't sounding any too happy."

He pulled the door closed behind him as he walked out.

"So what's next, Doc?" Hank asked Adam.

But Adam was looking at Jo as he said, "You'll need to get a court order to exhume the remains."

"Exhume? Christ, this is crazy," Hank said, shaking his head. He touched Jo's arm. "You think the son of a bitch killed his ex-wife because she knew about this?"

"I'm not sure it was him." She didn't take her eyes off Adam. "But I think someone was involved who felt equally threatened."

"Harrison's wife?"

"We all make mistakes, Detective Larsen. Surely you've done things that you regret."

Like commit murder?

Alana was practically a Stepford Wife. She was a trophy wife, for sure, and a big-time daddy's girl. But was she a killer? If Alana was involved, someone else had pulled the trigger. Jo wasn't sure that Harrison's pregnant wife had the spine for it.

But Lisa Barton did.

Jo saw in her mind's eye the flash of sun glinting off a beige car, a glimpse of black boots before the shovel came down. She gripped the table edge tighter and squeezed her eyes shut until a wave of vertigo passed.

"Larsen?" Hank said.

"Hey, Jo." Adam had a firm hold of her arm by the time she opened her eyes again. "You should be in the hospital." He nodded toward Hank. "You should have made her stay."

"Me and what army?" Hank snorted.

"Stop, okay?" Jo gritted her teeth. "I need to think."

She righted herself and gingerly moved out of Adam's grasp. She went over to a board where the photos she'd given Adam had been enlarged and tacked up with pushpins.

There was Finn with his gap-toothed grin and the tiny gold rims perched on his freckled nose. There was the tree house that had been destroyed.

"I'm not claiming to be the most patient man in the world, but . . . you have no idea what it was like to live with a hyperactive son and a woman who was never happy."

What if Kevin Harrison had shaken or grabbed his son hard enough to snap Finn's neck? What if, out of anger or impatience, he'd killed his son accidentally?

What if he'd panicked and made up a story to cover his ass, never letting on to his wife what had really happened? Telling only one other person, someone he trusted and loved, the woman he'd been having an affair with?

What if, three years later, Jenny had put all the pieces together and threatened him? Maybe she'd even suggested having their son's remains dug up and examined.

A buzzing noise cut through her thoughts, and she turned slightly as Hank flipped open his phone and uttered a terse, "What have you got?" Then he went into a maddening series of "Uh-huhs" that made Jo hold her breath until he was done.

He had a grim smile on his face when he slapped the cell shut. "We got the Harrisons' phone records," he said, "landline and cell. And guess what?"

"What?" she ground out.

"There's a direct link between Harrison and Lisa Barton," Hank said. "More than a couple calls a day from the Harrisons' account in the past few weeks."

Jo swallowed down a bitter taste, knowing what he would say but asking, anyway. "Kevin Harrison called Lisa?"

"No." Hank shook his head. "But Alana Harrison did."

Alana and Lisa.

So the two women weren't strangers, though neither had mentioned knowing the other, because they couldn't. *Wouldn't.* It would have cast suspicion on them from the start.

What was it Lisa Barton had said?

"Patrick wouldn't break his vows, not so long as Jenny was around. He's a decent man. He believes in that whole till-death-do-us-part thing."

But what if Jenny were dead?

Then Patrick would be a free man.

What if Alana Harrison and Lisa Barton had plotted together to get rid of the one woman who was a thorn in both of their sides?

"Can we go to the Harrisons' house?" she asked her partner. "I want to see Alana. I think she's close to cracking."

Why else had Alana shown up at the funeral unless she was feeling guilty?

"We can break her down. I know we can." She was pregnant, and not half as tough as Lisa Barton. Jo wanted to attack the weakest link. "They can't get away with it, Hank. They couldn't have done this without making mistakes."

"We've got warrants in the works, Jo, and patrols are out looking for Lisa Barton. Be patient; we'll get 'em."

Patient? Not her strongest virtue. "Yeah?"

"Yeah."

Her partner stripped off his latex gloves and tossed them in a biohazard container. He opened the door that Jonathan Morgan had closed, leaving it wide, allowing bright fluorescent light to spill in from the hallway.

Jo got rid of her gloves, too, but didn't move. She felt Adam come up behind her.

"Don't forget Emma," he reminded her, and she faced him, not saying a word, thinking more was forthcoming. But he said only, "You should go."

"Right." She started off, her steps slower than usual, her gait still not as steady as it should be.

"Jo?"

She caught the doorframe. "I know," she said. "Be careful."

"No," he replied, adding so softly she had to strain to hear. "I don't want to lose you, but you scare me, baby."

"You won't lose me, Adam," she promised. All she could do.

He shook his head, and she left him, heading down the hallway to Emma Slater's office. She knocked on the door and pushed in when a voice called out, "Enter."

The tiny woman perched behind her big desk, its surface neatly arranged with folders, photographs, and papers. So different from the chaos that filled Adam's work space.

"So you got my message?" Emma surveyed her with narrowed eyes as Jo settled into the opposite chair, but she made no comment about the scrapes and bruises.

"Did the blood on the cat's bed belong to Jenny Dielman?" Jo asked, not wanting to beat around the bush. There wasn't time.

"No, it was animal blood. One hundred percent feline."

Jo sucked in a breath, tried again. "You said the silk scarf had been used to gag Jenny, that it was consistent with DNA from her saliva. What about the brick? Anything there?"

"I studied the photographs your boys took at the scene, and there was an awful lot of backsplash of glass outside, on the sill and on the bushes below. If that brick had hit the window with enough force to shatter the pane, it wouldn't have landed in the sink." Emma rocked forward in her chair. "I'd bet someone used a hammer, to be sure the job was good and done, then staged things to make it appear like vandalism."

Staged things?

The way Jenny's murder had been staged to look like a suicide?

Jo nodded, digesting it all.

"That glove you said belonged to the vic's husband?" Emma shook her head. "Not a match to the prints. The grain's different."

"Thanks, Emma," Jo said, getting ready to rise.

But the other woman raised a hand. "There's something else." Emma pushed up from her desk, picking up something from her desk as she came around toward Jo. "The cat bed. It unzipped so the cushion inside could be removed and the exterior cleaned in the washing machine. Only it looks like it was used as a hiding place." She held out a black-and-white-speckled composition book.

"Oh, God, it can't be." Jo reached for it, hoping it was what she thought it was.

"I do believe that we found your girl's journal."

Jo leaned back in the chair and stared at the cover of the book.

"We checked for prints but only found Jenny Dielman's. We also made copies for your department. You want a light on that?" A swing-armed desk lamp soon illuminated the notebook in Jo's lap. "I'll leave you alone for a few minutes if you want to take a peek."

Emma smiled and left the room, but Jo barely paid attention. How her fingers trembled! How fast her heart beat.

She opened the journal, flipping through the handwritten pages until Jenny's familiar script blurred in her vision, and she had to squeeze her eyes shut to clear them.

When the words finally stayed still, she began to read and didn't stop till she was done.

CHAPTER TWENTY-TWO

En route to the Harrisons' house in Dallas, Jo phoned Terry Fitzhugh, catching her between sessions.

"Did you dig up something on Lisa Barton?" she asked, her adrenaline rushing.

"I got ahold of Nell Hertel. She's retired, but she ran Child Protective Services for years, back when your Elizabeth Ann Barton had a few close encounters with social welfare. Nell confirmed that the mother was a crackhead and neglected the kid. Social workers stepped in, and they took the girl away and dumped her into foster care. She had a brief stint in juvie after beating up another foster."

"We couldn't find any record," Jo said.

"No, you wouldn't have," Terry told her matter-of-factly, "because her records were sealed tight."

"And Lisa knew it," Jo muttered. She'd known that if the police ran a background check, she'd look clean. She hadn't counted on them digging deeper.

Hank glanced over, hands on the wheel, mouthing, "What?"

Jo waved him off, not needing the distraction. The pounding in her brain was distraction enough.

"You asked about tats, and Nell remembered the girl having *FEAR* etched above her knuckles. Nell didn't mention a gang but did say she was a mean girl, a real bully. They had her tested, and she was diagnosed as having antisocial personality disorder. No empathy, a misplaced sense of entitlement, lots of anger issues, and a liar. But her IQ was sky-high."

"Anything else?"

"Just that she was bounced from foster care and moved in with an aunt who cleaned houses. One of her aunt's clients was Jacob Davis. He'd just founded a program called KickStart for troubled kids with smarts, kind of like boot camp and summer school combined. The aunt got Davis to let Lisa take part, and she did a one-eighty. She shaped up and got her GED. Davis even paved the way for her to go to UT–Austin on a scholarship he sponsored."

"Thank you so much, Terry," Jo said, because that was more than she'd needed. It was a clear link between Lisa Barton and Alana Harrison.

"You think she killed that woman from the quarry?" Terry asked.

"Yes," Jo said aloud, firmly believing it.

She believed as well that Lisa Barton had roped Alana Harrison into being her accomplice. Maybe Lisa had suggested they scare Jenny into splitting town. Maybe she hadn't mentioned killing Jenny at first. It could be that Jenny hadn't cooperated, or Lisa's rage had escalated and there was no turning back. Unless Lisa had always intended for it to end the way it had, with Jenny dead, the victim's own .22 the murder weapon, all signs pointing to suicide.

Jo felt dizzy, and not just from the concussion—from her own anger and disgust that she'd ever bought a single word that Lisa Barton had said.

"Please, be careful," Terry said, like Jo hadn't heard that a hundred times already.

She hung up and gazed out the windshield.

They'd arrived at the Harrisons' house.

Hank pulled into the long driveway, parking beside a bright-red Maserati with vanity plates that read REALST8.

That had to be Alana's.

It wasn't the vehicle Jo had glimpsed before getting her head bashed in with a shovel.

"You need a hand?" her partner asked as he shut off the ignition, but she assured him she was fine.

Jo pushed open the door and got out, steadying herself against the hood of the car before heading to the front door, her partner hovering at her elbow like she was an old lady who couldn't cross the street without assistance.

Hank knocked with a heavy hand, not bothering with the bell, doing a good impression of beating the door to death.

The frightened voice that addressed them through the intercom didn't wait long to let them in after Jo leaned on the button and said, "Police, ma'am, open up."

A housekeeper in black slacks and white blouse flung open the door and stood on the threshold, wringing her hands. "I'm glad you're here!" her voice rushed on breathlessly. "Come, please, she's upstairs, and she won't let me in. That horrible woman left a good while ago, but there was so much screaming and yelling! I stayed in the kitchen until she was gone."

Jo looked at Hank, and he seemed as confused as she was.

"What woman?" she asked. "Do you know her name?"

"I heard Mrs. Harrison call her Lizzie."

"Elizabeth . . . Lizzie," Jo said, looking at Hank. "That's Lisa."

Hank frowned. "Dropped by to threaten Alana to keep her trap shut, or risk ending up like Jenny, did she?"

She hoped Alana was all right, that Lisa hadn't hurt her.

"Where's Dr. Harrison?" Hank asked the woman as they quickly walked toward the stairs.

"He was at the hospital, but he's coming home. I called him and said, 'The missus is in trouble!'" she told them, scurrying across the tiled foyer. "She's up in the baby's room. She wouldn't let me in, even when I begged her."

Jo eyed the curving stairwell that seemed to go up endlessly and wondered if she'd be able to make it, even clutching at the banister.

Her partner must have read her face and touched her shoulder. "I'll go up, Larsen. You wait here. I'll bring her down."

The frightened housekeeper led the way, and Hank followed on her heels.

Jo walked deliberately into the den, bypassing the photographs of Kevin Harrison on his hunting trips and heading straight to the spot where Alana's mementoes hung. She ran her bleary gaze over the beauty-queen shots and the cheerleading poses, stopping when she found the thing she'd ignored on her last visit.

A sorority composite from the University of Texas.

She leaned in, squinting at the tiny names beneath the black-and-white photos, each no bigger than a thumbprint, mostly blonde girls with monikers like Bunny, Honey, and Sissy.

It wasn't long before she saw what she was looking for: stuck between Emily Delaney Barstow and Courtney Shea Beatty was a long-haired, apple-cheeked girl, deceptively innocent-looking. No one would have guessed she'd served time in juvie and beat the crap out of a fellow foster kid.

Elizabeth Ann Barton.

"I learned that fear can be a great motivator."

Was that why Lisa had tattooed *FEAR* on her knuckles? Had fear really motivated her, or had she used fear to intimidate others?

"I might have screwed up a time or two, but I made it to college on scholarships. I even survived sorority rush. I never gave in."

No, she didn't give in. She used whatever means it took to get exactly what she wanted.

Jo skipped a few rows down the faces to the *D*s, running a fingertip over the picture of a dewy-eyed Alana Davis.

The debutante and the scholarship girl.

Sisters in the bond.

Cold-blooded killers.

Jo wondered how it had all come up. Had Lisa and Alana kept in touch, or had they only reconnected when Lisa realized they each had a tie to the troubled and troublesome Jenny? Had they joked about getting rid of her before the conversation turned into actual plans to get Jenny out of the picture?

She realized suddenly that Alana showing up at the church made sense. Did Harrison's wife regret her participation in Jenny's death? Was she not a monster, like Lisa?

Jo was halfway to the foyer when she heard a loud pop and crack from upstairs.

What the hell was that?

The hairs rose on the back of her neck, and she rushed toward the foyer as fast as she was able, reaching the stairs just as the housekeeper descended, red-faced and frantic.

"The detective—he had to break the door down." The words came out in gasps. "The missus—she's bad off. She swallowed too many pills."

Jo took the woman by the arm. "Call 911 and have them send an ambulance. Then wait at the door for them, okay?"

The woman nodded, pulled away, and click-clacked toward the kitchen.

Despite the fog in her head, Jo grabbed the banister and took the steps up two by two, gritting her teeth to dull the pain. When she hit the landing, she held still, willing the dizziness away as she put one foot in front of the other and walked toward the door with the splintered frame. She heard Hank's voice saying, "C'mon, ma'am, wake up. Open your eyes . . . can you hear me?"

Jo entered the room to find her partner bending over Alana Harrison, who lay still upon a daybed, an arm's length away from a whitewashed crib. A mobile of the stars and moon hung above, equally motionless.

On the nightstand nearby was a brown vial spilling white pills, along with a half-drunk glass of water.

"She took a boatload of Valium," Hank said as Jo approached. "She's still breathing, but it's shallow. Christ Almighty, what a stupid trick."

He tried to sit Alana up, but it was like moving a rag doll. Jo thought she heard the woman groan, imagined the pale eyelids flickered.

"Mrs. Harrison, can you hear me? Please wake up," he kept saying over and over.

Jo moved toward the window, pearl-gray light slanting through the blinds. She backed up against the wall, staring at the slender, white arm hanging over the daybed. She looked above her, at stars painted on the ceiling, and her hand went to her mouth as a wave of nausea struck. She closed her eyes as her vision turned fuzzy and her ears begin to ring, buzzing like a siren, so noisy she could hardly bear it. She raised her hands to her ears to make it stop.

She wasn't sure how long it was before the room filled with people, and Hank was touching her elbow, drawing her aside as a pair of EMTs removed Alana on a stretcher and Kevin Harrison stood in the doorway, screaming, "What the hell did you do to her? What the hell have you done?"

That was when Jo lost it.

"What the hell did *you* do to Finn?" she said, the anger in her own voice shaking her to the core. "What the hell did you do that killed him, because he damned sure didn't fall out of a tree house!"

Harrison stared at her, like she'd lost her mind.

"Jo," Hank reached for her, but she couldn't stop.

"Jenny was right!" Jo pointed a finger and shook it. "You were responsible. You lied. She had the evidence to get your son's body exhumed. If you had just told the truth, she'd still be alive, and your pregnant wife wouldn't have involved herself in Jenny's murder!"

The doctor fell back against the door as if Jo had pushed him. "Alana didn't do anything—"

"Oh, yes," Jo said. "Yes, she did, and it's your fault. If she loses this baby, you can blame yourself for that, too."

"It was an accident." He shuddered and grabbed hold of the jamb to steady himself. "I didn't mean for it to happen. But he wouldn't listen. I just wanted him to settle down." Harrison sobbed. "He wouldn't settle down."

Hank saw that Jo could barely stand, and he caught her arm.

She heard his phone ringing, but he ignored it.

"You okay?"

She shook her head, pulling away.

She made it to the hallway and found a bathroom. She got to the sink before she bowed her head to vomit, retching until it was only dry heaves, and her head banged with the effort. Tears sprang to her eyes as she turned on the tap and washed the bile down the drain, took some water in a shaky hand, drank it, then spit it out.

When she finally emerged, Hank was standing there, waiting.

"Harrison?" she said.

"He went to the hospital, and I didn't stop him. We'll haul his ass down to the station once his wife's stable. He's not going anywhere. We'll get his confession on paper."

"Lisa Barton," she croaked.

"That was Cap calling," he told her, and he patted the pocket with his phone. "A patrol car caught up with her at a car wash on the edge of Plainfield. We've got her, Jo, and she's not going to worm her way out. Trust me on this. You do trust me?"

"Yes."

She really did.

He squeezed her shoulders gently. "Haven't you had enough crap knocked out of you lately? Let's go pick your cat up from the station, and I'll take you both home to Adam, okay?"

She whispered back, "Okay."

"C'mon, Sister Christian, I've got your back."

And he had her elbow, too, as he led her from the bathroom, out of the house, and into fresh air and hazy sunlight.

CHAPTER TWENTY-THREE

SUNDAY

Jo walked slowly through the still-green grass toward the plot that Adam had marked on the memorial park map, skirting the etched headstones, marble angels, and crosses bathed in rings of mums long dead or wilted flowers still wrapped in cellophane.

She looked at the yellow roses in her hands, swathed in tissue and tied with a ribbon as bright as the petals. She found herself hoping Jenny would like them. They reminded her of the walls in the room where Jenny had escaped: sunny and vibrant, far removed from the gray of the quarry.

"We're almost there," Adam said from behind her. "Up ahead, near the maple."

Jo glanced ahead to the tree, red leaves scattered over the ground like a carpet. Two granite headstones seemed to rise from the roots beneath.

One for Finn, she knew, the other, polished and new, for Jenny, her grave still fresh, the earth still turned. Jo approached warily, afraid to get too close. She hugged the roses to her breasts, grateful for the sun that warmed her face and Adam's touch on her arm.

"I'll wait somewhere else if you'd like to be alone," he said.

But she shook her head. "Please, stay."

She took a breath, drawing in air that tasted springlike, not laced with the chill of the days before. She stepped forward to the edge of Finn's plot and withdrew several roses from the bunch in her arms, placing them beneath the words Beloved Son carved into the stone.

Rest in peace, Finn, she thought, because now he could, couldn't he?

He had his mother beside him, and his broken body could remain where it was. There had been no exhumation. Kevin Harrison had given a formal confession that he'd caused his son's death. He had taken a phone call from Alana, leaving the boy undressing for his bath. Finn had "misbehaved," running about the house naked and shrieking. Harrison had caught his son and had shaken him fiercely before shoving him into the bathroom. He hadn't realized until Finn pitched backward, falling to the tiled floor, that his son wasn't breathing.

Jenny had been right. Finn hadn't fallen from a tree. Her ex-husband was to blame.

Harrison claimed that he'd loved the boy and had never meant to harm him, that it was just a horrible accident. His expensive lawyers would probably plea down the charge of negligent homicide to child endangerment, though Jo hoped a jury would have the chance to weigh a charge of manslaughter at the very least. She wanted to see the man suffer as he'd made Jenny suffer. He deserved as much and more.

Alana was recovering from her overdose, under twenty-four-hour watch at Presbyterian Hospital. She was conscious and alert, the baby okay. She was talking, blaming Lisa for everything: the eerie phone calls to Jenny, the plot to abduct her as well as murder her. Alana's daddy's slick defense attorneys were already canoodling with the DA, trying to get her a plea.

Lisa Barton would not get off so easily.

Her not-so-expensive lawyer was advising her to keep her mouth shut. So far, she had. But it didn't matter. They needed only one of them to cooperate. And they had that already.

Another bright spot: Lisa would never have Patrick. The man had avoided visiting Lisa in jail, situating himself firmly in the ICU waiting room at Plainfield Memorial Hospital, not leaving the place—so Jo had heard—until Jenny's sister had opened her eyes. Though Kim seemed confused, the doctors reported normal speech and reflexes. She didn't remember what had happened the day of the funeral, which Jo decided was probably a good thing.

Patrick Dielman had made arrangements to fly in Kim's kids and the babysitter so they could see their mom while she recovered. Though he might not have been the best husband for Jenny, he wasn't an ogre.

"Take care of your mom, Finn," Jo whispered, patting the boy's headstone.

She got up from her knees, but didn't bother to brush off her jeans before she stepped over to Jenny's grave, still a soft mound of loam. She crouched beside it, setting the rest of the roses down at the base of her marker. BELOVED WIFE, MOTHER, AND SISTER, it read, and Jo knew Jenny would like that, even if she hadn't believed in that love or believed in herself.

You were those things, Jenny, all of them.

Jo put her hand on the soil and dug her fingers in, leaving an imprint.

Tears blurred her eyes, and she lowered her head, not wanting Adam to see them. It was too late. He came behind her, wrapped his arms around her, and sighed into her hair. "Oh, baby. It's okay. It's okay."

It was time to tell Adam everything.

God, it's time.

She leaned into his chest and said softly, "Let's go home."

They didn't speak all the way back to Jo's condo. Adam didn't even try to fill the void. Jo knew he understood what she was feeling. The silence was necessary, like a pause between pain and good intentions.

As soon as she unlocked the door, Ernie appeared out of nowhere, a black flash darting toward her ankles, wending about them.

She was afraid at first that he'd try to escape through Adam's legs as he came in behind her. But he didn't. Instead, he mewed and arched against her, begging for her to pick him up. So she did, and the cat tucked his head beneath her chin as he'd done in that photo with Jenny.

Jo felt a lump in her throat.

"Looks like he was busy while we were gone," Adam said, nudging the white box with the papers from Mama's house that Jo had left in the tiny foyer.

Jo rubbed Ernie's head and surveyed the damage. He'd managed to get into the box despite the tape, tipping the lid askew so he could wiggle his way inside. He'd nearly pushed a couple of old letters out, making a nest for himself.

"What's that about anyway?" Adam asked as he took off his coat.

"Stuff from my mom's house," Jo said and put Ernie down. She shoved the letters into the box and replaced the lid as the cat bounded off toward the kitchen. "It's kind of a long story."

"Is it your story?"

She sighed heavily. "Yes."

"Then I want to hear it." Adam reached for her hand and squeezed it. "You want to tell me now or later?"

This time, Jo didn't pause.

"Now," she said.

He eased her coat from her shoulders and drew her toward the sofa.

Jo settled next to him, thinking of Jenny. She couldn't help it. She recalled the last words written in the journal:

I will get Ernie his favorite Fancy Feast to celebrate.

I will free Finn from my nightmares.

And free myself.

Jenny Dielman had grown up with abuse, had wed a man who'd treated her badly, who had killed her only son, and still she hadn't given up. She had fought for Finn to the very end . . . for Finn and for herself.

Jo drew courage from her.

"It started when Daddy left us," she began, not sure how to do this. "I was almost five. It was just me and Mama, at first, only it didn't stay that way for long." She wet her lips, not able to look at Adam. "She was drinking a lot . . . she'd stay out late and leave me all alone. And then one night she brought *him* home, and he never left." Jo's throat closed up, but she kept going, her voice raw. "Oh, God, how I prayed he would go, that she would see what kind of man he was and kick him out. But instead, she married him."

Adam laced his fingers through hers, tightly, like he would never release her.

Go on, Jo heard a voice in her head. *Free the child from your nightmares. Free yourself. Adam's not going anywhere.*

She kept talking, slowly. Quietly. Adam listened, and when she was done, she let the tears fall, overwhelmed by grief for a woman she'd never met but understood all too well.

For what she herself had lost.

For the little girl she'd never been and a child she'd never known.

ACKNOWLEDGMENTS

First and foremost, thank you to Christina Hogrebe and Jessica Errera for believing in *Walk Into Silence* and for finding it such a good home! I am so grateful to Kjersti Egerdahl and Jacque Ben-Zekry for loving this story and wanting to get it into readers' hands. And it wouldn't be the book that it is now without the amazing guidance I received from Caitlin Alexander, who cracked the editorial whip until *Walk* was in peak form. Even after seventeen years in this business, it still amazes me how a story I thought was strong to begin with can become so much more.

Last but hardly least, thank you to my husband, my daughter, and my mother for making my life more entertaining and emotional than any fiction I could write. I love you madly!